SOMETHING ABOUT STACY

BY

AMY JOHNSON

World Castle Publishing, LLC

WCP

World Castle Publishing, LLC
Pensacola, Florida

Cover: Karen Fuller
Editor: Maxine Bringenberg

DEDICATION

This book is dedicated to my very own Air Conditioner Repairman who not only fixed my air conditioner but also repaired my broken heart. I love You.

PROLOGUE

"You are so beautiful Stacy," Thad said to me as I melted into his arms. The things this man said to me during intimate moments turned me inside out and left me longing for more. Gently taking the washcloth, he lathered it up and washed my back, my neck, my arms. "Your body is absolute paradise to me. I could spend an eternity touching every inch of you, and it still wouldn't be long enough." That could get the blood pumping.

"Thad, let's get out of here," I said, no longer satisfied lying relaxed against him in the bathtub. I wanted him inside me that very second. I needed him.

Thad frowned, pulled me back down against him, and caressed my breast lightly. His touch was delicate, deliberate, and absolutely drove me wild, and he knew the effect he was having on me. "In a minute Stacy; I just want to savor you a little while longer." His hands continued their sensual assault, and it took everything I had in me not to shatter before him, which was what I thought he wanted. But two could play at that game.

Slowly, I rolled to my side and started planting sweet, gentle kisses on his temple. Moving down, I nipped at his ear, kissed his jaw, his neck, his shoulder blade. I ran my hand up and down his abdomen, feeling his breath catch as I caressed below his belly button, and then to his sex. I trailed kisses along his nipple, down his ribs, lower still. "Stop," he pled as I continued my tender torture.

I shook my finger at him to let him know I wouldn't stop. Our eyes locked, his smoldering gray and burning right through me. I loved having this effect on him. Even though he never told me he cared about me or that he loved me, I knew he did. I saw it in these moments; in his eyes, in the words he spoke.

I moved slowly to his sex, took it in my hand, and stroked gently. Very slowly, I took him in my mouth, the water in my face, his hands in my hair, his breathing ragged. "Stacy," he growled, and raised his hips so that I could take him deeper and deeper into my mouth. "Stop or I'm gonna come." I shrugged my shoulders and continued taking him closer and closer, sucking, teasing, and stroking. He tasted delicious and I didn't want to stop. I wanted him to lose control and fall apart from my touch. He tangled his hand in my hair, his body stilled, and I heard his slow deep growl. He tried to move my head, but stubbornly I refused, and before long he lost control and came violently, his salty release warm in my mouth. I smiled sweetly and sunk back into his arms, my cheek on his chest, a satisfied smile on my face. I had most definitely won that round.

"Stacy, Stacy, you're crazy. You know that right?" Thad said, his voice laced with humor.

I smiled. "Hey, all is fair in love and war, darling."

Thad raised my head to face him. "Well, you may have won the battle, Stacey Dupree, but you won't win the war!"

"Game on," I retorted, and in one fluid motion he grabbed me by my hips, positioned me on top of him, and slammed into me. I cried out in surprise, pleasure, and pain. He tilted my chin up so that our eyes locked, and again I saw the real Thad. The Thad that was loving and vulnerable, needy even. I tried to match his thrusts, but I was lost in his eyes and limited by the constraints of the bathtub. He pulled me into a kiss and nibbled his way down my neck. I was so close. I was about to lose it and it felt so good…he felt so good.

Suddenly, he pulled my head up so I could face him. "Come for me!" he breathed, and I began to lose it. "Look at me," he said, and gazing into those smoldering eyes I shattered, because I knew he loved me and I could feel him getting close to his own release. He smirked, and quickly pushed me off him, stroking himself to find his release, which he did quickly, his sweet come warm and welcome across my breasts.

"No condom," he explained as I looked at him, perplexed. He had never pulled out of me before.

"Oh my God," I exclaimed, and he nodded. "I forgot. I was so caught up in the moment and—"

"Me too, Stace, but I think we are okay." I looked at him, horrified. How stupid could I have been?

"Let's get out of here," he said, and lifted me out of the tub. I was too shocked and sated to move. He gently sat me down on the foot of my bed and wrapped my robe around me. Tears sprung to my eyes. Tying my robe, he said reassuringly, "Stacy, don't worry about it. We are fine. I pulled out in time." I nodded weakly. "No more tears then," he said, and began to get dressed.

"You know you can stay, Thad," I muttered, but what I actually meant was "please stay the night and hold me. Just once." The thought of another night alone was painful.

"No, I got work tomorrow."

I frowned because I knew he wasn't going to stay. "I have an alarm clock, Thad." He sat on the bed to put his shoes and socks on, and once again he turned into cold, collected Thad, no more feeling or emotion. I gave up. We'd been down this road before. He was gone. The Thad that cared about me and loved me was gone. He was only visible during sex. And why I couldn't let him go I just didn't know. But I did know one thing. He wouldn't stay. Tears burned my eyes and I tried to stop them. I wanted him to stay and hold me all night, but I didn't want his pity.

"Stacy, don't cry." He brought my face up to look into my eyes. "Please, don't do this. Let's not complicate this, okay?"

I nodded as more tears appeared, and I couldn't find my voice to respond.

He pulled me to my knees and hugged me.

"Please stay," I mumbled, and he shook his head.

"I can't, Stacy. I just can't."

"I don't want to be alone, Thad." I was begging him at this point. I could not stand another night alone, especially after the lovemaking we'd just done. I wanted him, but I needed him too. Why couldn't he see that?

He sat on the bed and pulled me into his lap. Gently, he caressed my face and wiped away my tears. He cradled me and rocked me back and forth.

"Please stay," I whispered again.

Frowning, he said, "I can't, Stacy. I just can't. I don't stay the night. You know this."

I looked down at my hands as the tears continued to fall. "I know," I conceded, and I knew at that moment he was leaving and I would be in bed alone. And the loneliness was killing me inside.

I looked up at Thad and his eyes had softened. He was struggling too...but I mustn't take that for granted. I thought he was in unchartered territory emotionally as well. He released me and motioned for me to move up in bed. I did so with my heart in my throat, thinking he was going to stay. I lay on my side and he came to lie behind me snuggled close, completely clothed, boots and all. His nose nuzzled my hair. He held me tight and told me not to cry another tear. I couldn't control my excitement.

"Go to sleep," he said. I reached for him, and he removed my hand and shook his head. "Just go to sleep, beautiful."

"Why?" I asked, already knowing the answer.

"So I can leave," he responded, and the tears returned and stung my cheeks.

CHAPTER 1

It was Tuesday, or Wednesday. Shit, I couldn't keep up. There was a loud knock at my door, but I ignored it and scooted further under the covers. I did not want to get up. If I ignored them, they would go away. Right?

Wrong. The knocking got harder.

I heard the lock tumble and I knew whoever was out there was coming in. I pulled my covers over my head and pretended to be asleep, saying a silent prayer that it wasn't my mother. I could NOT deal with my mother right then. Please Lord....

"Stacy," I heard, and relaxed a little bit. It was just Megan, thank God. "Stace, where are you?"

I closed my eyes and continued to fake sleep.

Megan wasn't buying it. "Stacy, it's 2:00. Get up! I know you are awake." Megan had the mom tone in her voice, hands on her hips, and I knew that she wasn't going to give up.

I opened one eye. "I don't feel good."

"You don't smell good either," Josie chimed in. Josie was standing there tapping her foot, all big boobs and ginormous blonde hair. She was holding a big water gun, and it was pointed directly at me. "Can I squirt her, Meg?" she asked, and Megan shook her head no.

Megan's eyes softened as she took in my surroundings. There were empty tubs of ice cream, boxes of Kleenex, and a stack of books on the nightstand. Clothes covered just about every surface, and the TV was permanently stuck on Lifetime. "Oh boy," Megan said. It was obviously worse than she'd thought. But not as bad as it could have been...there was no alcohol to be seen.

"Stacy, get up and let's get you in a shower."

1

I frowned. "I don't want to get up! I don't want a shower! I want to be left alone!"

Josie took aim. "Now, Meg?" she pled. "Can I squirt her now?"

Megan scowled and yanked the covers off me. "Get up!" she shouted.

Now I was pissed. "Leave! Me! Alone!" I yanked the covers back and tried to bury myself in them.

"Squirt her, Josie," Megan ordered, and Josie took aim and squirted me in the face. When I put my hands up to block the next spray of cold water, Megan yanked my duvet and sheets once again, and I was left exposed in nothing but a t-shirt and panties. "Squirt her again!" Megan shouted, and Josie let her rip, squirting my face, my ass, my feet.

"Okay!" I exclaimed. "I will get up. Stop freaking squirting me! Geez!"

Josie looked at Megan and Megan nodded for her to stop.

I threw my legs off the bed and my feet onto the floor, giving Meg and Josie the death stare as I stomped to the bathroom. Megan followed me in and started the water for the shower. "Hey," I protested, demanding a little privacy, but I was ignored. I answered the call of nature and turned to walk out of the bathroom when Megan grabbed me.

"Oh, no you don't," she said. "You! Shower! Now!"

Ignoring her, I walked thru the doorway, where Josie was ready and waiting, standing in a shooting position, both hands on the trigger. "Stop or I'll shoot!" she shouted, and before I knew it I was dodging her shots. The water was freezing cold, and Josie had the spout all the way open. It looked like I was getting that shower one way or the other.

I retreated to the bathroom and ran smack into Megan, which wasn't hard to do considering my bathroom was small and Megan was large. She grabbed my hands and sat me gently on the toilet, then knelt on the floor in front of me, our hands intertwined, her expression soft.

"Stacy, I love you. And I know it has been a rough couple of months, but it is time to deal with it and get over it. I need you. We all need you!"

Tears hit my eyes. Megan continued, "You're depressed, Stacy, and you need some help. We are all here for you. We would do anything for you. And if you don't get your ass in that shower, I will drag you outside by your hair and use the water hose on you."

"You wouldn't," I said, and Josie stepped in the doorway and said "No, but I would." At that moment, Josie catapulted over Megan and landed beside the bathtub. She sat on the edge of the tub, removed her cell phone from her bra, discarded her Christian Louboutin sandals, and before I knew what had hit me, she grabbed my hair and yanked, causing us both to fall into the bathtub. The water was ice cold and my head was wedged into Josie's cleavage.

"Josie!" I screamed, and she stuck a washcloth in my mouth to shut me up. My hands were pinned underneath me and it was a good thing, because I would have been kicking Josie's ass otherwise. Josie took the body wash and squirted it on my t-shirt. She had begun lathering me up when I got my hands back and pushed her away, spitting the washcloth out.

"Okay!" I conceded. "You freakin win! I'll take a shower! Geez!"

Josie stepped out of the tub and adjusted her boobs. Megan stood and clapped her hands. "Good girl," she said with glee, and together, she and Josie exited the bathroom, leaving the door open.

Josie, dripping wet, frowned. "Too bad we didn't get to use the water hose on her."

***

After a quick shower, I donned my robe that Megan had laid out for me, brushed my teeth, blasted my hair, and applied mascara, eyeliner, and lip-gloss. Even with the make-up, my complexion was pale and I looked gaunt. I'd lost weight, even on an ice cream diet, and my hazel eyes looked too big for my face. I looked about like I felt.

I went into my room in search of something to wear and found Josie trying on my clothes and Megan making my bed. All the empty ice cream cartons had disappeared, the TV was off, and my clothes had been sorted and neatly stacked in piles ready for the wash. Megan looked up at me, smiled, and said, "Me and Josie will be in the kitchen while you get dressed."

Bending to scoop up a load of laundry, Megan tilted backwards, lost her balance, and landed softly on her back in a pile of laundry. I couldn't help the smile that landed on my face. Here was Megan, my best friend in the whole world, eight months pregnant, looking like a turtle stuck in its shell. Josie and I both helped her up, she assured us she was okay, and Josie scooped up the laundry and they headed to the kitchen.

Fifteen minutes later I entered my kitchen wearing low-slung jeans and a pink scoop neck t-shirt with a peace sign on it, rhinestone belt, and earthy hemp wedge shoes. I felt a little more like myself. The kitchen smelled of fresh coffee and laundry soap. Megan was fussing over something at the stove, and Josie was in her bra and panties watching her clothes spin on the ceiling fan. I got a cup of coffee and cocked my head towards Josie. "I probably don't want to know, but I'm gonna ask anyways. Josie, why are your clothes on the ceiling fan?"

Josie looked at me like I was stupid. "They were wet," she explained.

Rolling my eyes, I looked at Megan, who gave me a what-do-you-expect-this-is-Josie-we-are-talking-about look, and I couldn't help the giggle that escaped my lips. I took a deep breath and realized how much had I missed these girls. Gesturing to the dryer, I pointed out the obvious. "Josie, you could have just put your clothes in the dryer."

She tilted her head up, pursed her lips, and said innocently, "I never thought of that."

***

After a late lunch prepared by Megan, she and Josie shuffled me to Megan's SUV. Josie strapped my seatbelt and climbed in the back seat.

"Josie, I'm not ill or injured. I can fasten my own safety belt," I growled.

Josie was nonplussed. "Stacy, Jon said depression is a disease." She tipped my chin up to face her. "It's—okay—that—you—are —sick—Stacy." She was talking to me like I was three years old or trying to understand a foreign language. "We—still—love—you—and—will—be—here—for—you."

4

I resisted the urge to punch to her.

"Josie, she is depressed, not retarded!" Megan hissed. Josie pouted.

I knew Josie meant well, and I loved her, but dear Lord, she could be a piece of work. I took a deep, calming breath and counted to ten.

"So where are we going?" I asked.

Megan slid on her large sunshades, adjusted the steering wheel to accommodate her belly, and checked her mirrors. Backing out of the driveway she said, "We are going to run some errands." She gave me a sideways glance. "We have to stop by the bridal shop and get you fitted for your dress, and then we are going to hit the grocery store." She frowned. "You have nothing in your house except for ice cream and breakfast items."

I smirked. "That's not true. I have Oreo cookies, too."

Megan stifled a laugh. "Stacy, you can't live on ice cream, Oreos, and cereal. You need real food."

"Hey," I protested. "Ice cream is made from milk, and milk is good for you, right? And plus, I love cereal. It's my favorite meal."

"Well, tonight you are having dinner with Jack and me," Megan insisted. "And then you are going to join us for a movie. And who knows what else?"

I groaned. I loved Megan more than life itself, but I really truly just wanted to be alone. "Megan, really...." I tried, but she wasn't hearing it. She turned the music up and Beyonce drowned me out. She wasn't going to negotiate. I gave up, slumped back into the seat, and listened to Josie belting out Beyonce completely off key and at the top of her lungs.

**

Our first stop was the bridal shop. I was less than thrilled. I had been putting this off for over a month. Don't get me wrong, I was happy for Josie, and I was so glad she had found the ONE and asked me to be in her wedding. I loved her and wanted her day to be perfect. That's why I couldn't be a bridesmaid.

I turned to Josie and saw the excitement in her eyes. I frowned and stared at my hands. This wasn't going to be easy.

"Josie," I said softly. I took her hands and the excitement in her eyes turned to alarm. "Josie, I can't be in your wedding." There, I'd said it. I winced and waited for her reaction.

Josie remained stock-still and didn't say a word, as if she was trying to absorb the information. Megan stared at me open-mouthed, absently rubbing her stomach. The sales woman brought out a hideous purple and silver dress and laid it across a chair. I looked from her to the dress, then finally to Josie.

Josie hung her head and started sobbing, big, blood curdling sobs that shook her whole body. I was dumbfounded. I had known Josie since kindergarten and I had never seen her cry. I had seen her dumped, cheated on, and fighting mad, but I had never seen her shed a tear.

I hugged her close and tried to soothe her. She cried harder. "Josie," I said, and tilted her chin up as she had done to me earlier. "Don't cry. I just...I just don't want to spoil your special day."

"You not being there will spoil it, Stacy!" Josie wailed. "We are best friends. You have to be there."

"I will be there, Josie...I just won't be in the wedding party." Josie looked lost. I continued. "I will be there; I just won't be a bridesmaid."

Megan handed Josie a tissue. She wiped her eyes, blew her nose loudly, and softly asked why.

"Two reasons," I said. "First of all, I don't want to ruin your special day by bringing you or anyone else down. In case you haven't noticed, I've been a bummer to be around lately."

"No you haven't," Josie insisted. "So don't worry about that. I love you and want you there standing beside me."

I took another deep breath. "Reason number two is Thad."

Josie looked at me, confused. "Yeah, so what about him?"

I sighed. "Josie, he broke my heart and is the reason I am depressed, and you have me paired with him at the wedding."

"First of all, he broke your heart three months ago. It's time to get over that! I've already told you that the best way to get over one guy is to get under another one." I opened my mouth to protest, but Josie wasn't done yet. "And when I 'paired' you guys, y'all were all hot and heavy. Y'all were worse than me and Jon. You couldn't keep your hands off each other."

She was right. Four months ago I was infatuated with Thad and thought we were in love.

What a mistake that had been! Sure, it was three months of mind numbing sex, but that was about it.

I'd actually known Thad for years, and was re-introduced to him through friends after my divorce. Within a week we were dating. Within two weeks we were having hot crazy monkey sex. Within three months we were done. I'd allowed myself to fall for him foolishly and he let me; all the while he never wanted anything more than sex. I was just a fling for him, a notch in his belt, a creative way to spend his time. When I got too attached and said those three stupid little words, he cut me loose.

Cowardly.

By sending me a text.

My heart had been broken.

Again.

So I'd sworn off men.

Again.

And this time I meant it.

"Josie," Megan said softly. "Why don't you go try your dress on again?"

"But I just tried it on two weeks ago," Josie said, perplexed.

"A lot can change in two weeks, Josie," Megan said. "Let's do it just to be sure everything is still perfect." Megan eyed me. "Because your wedding is going to be absolutely perfect, isn't it Stacy?"

I nodded. Josie went off to try on her dress again and Megan pulled me down to sit beside her.

"Look, Stace. I know how you feel about Thad, but this isn't about him. This is about Josie. And I know she is a handful, but she is one of our best friends. She has been in our weddings, held our hands through divorces, helped clean up our messes, and always had our backs. No matter what, she has always been there, and I won't let you ruin her day by not being there for her."

I fought back tears. "Thad hurt me deep, Meg. I don't know that I can keep it together. I don't want to cry and lose it and ruin the wedding."

Megan waved a dismissive hand. "It's a wedding, dumdum. Everyone cries!"

7

"I know, but—"

"No buts!" Megan said sternly. "You just have to suck it up and deal with it. She would do it for you."

She was right. Josie would do it for me. In fact, she would probably do just about anything for me. That was just how Josie was. And she would have never had Thad paired with me if she knew this was going to happen.

As I was having this internal struggle, Josie stepped out of the dressing room. Tears burned my eyes as I took her in. She was stunning in a beautiful Maggie Sotterro dress. It was white, fit like a glove, and was very sparkly...very Josie. It had three-dimensional flowers sewn into a backdrop of lace and tulle, with Swarovski crystals scattered delicately about, and a corset closure in the back. It was beautiful, romantic, and fit for a princess. I knew at that moment that I couldn't break her heart. My tears flowed freely as I hugged her.

"Well, what do you think?" She asked.

I was truly speechless. "You look like a fairytale princess bride," I said, and as if on cue the sales associate set a delicate tiara on top of Josie's head. Josie smiled shyly. "Jon calls me his princess," she said. "So I thought a tiara was fitting."

"I agree," I said, and I meant it. I kissed her cheek, picked up the purple dress, and made my way to the dressing room.

***

In the dressing room I remembered my wedding day. The simple white dress I wore, the spring flowers in my hair, the small but beautiful ceremony. The way Scott smiled at me, and the weakness I felt in my knees because I was so desperately in love with him. We were going to be together forever. We were going to live the fairy tale. That was the plan anyway. Until Scott decided to shag the dog walker on the living room couch. So now I had a small condo and a healthy alimony check, and Scott had the dog walker. Fair trade if you asked me. Or so I told myself.

Truth was I missed Scott. I missed the companionship. I missed his warmth at night in bed and sharing my day with him. I missed the sex. Okay, let's be honest...I missed the sex a lot. Of course, I could have gotten the sex. At 5'8, 140 pounds with an hourglass figure I'd had plenty of opportunities. But I just was not the type to have meaningless, casual sex.

Well, I wasn't until Thad.

"Don't go there," I told myself. I admired my reflection in the mirror. Not bad. The dress was retched and needed minor alterations, but *I* didn't look so bad. With my hair up, some simple jewelry, and silver high heels, I could absolutely rock this dress. I took a deep breath. This wasn't going to be too bad. I would look magnificent, do the bridesmaid thing, and make Thad drool. He was going to regret what he'd done to me, and I would enjoy watching him eat his heart out. And when he came crawling back…. This could work. Smiling, I stepped out of the dressing room and faced Josie and Megan.

Josie studied me. "I think I love it."

"Me too," I lied.

"It's settled then," Josie declared. "This is the dress! Can you believe it, Stace? I'm actually getting married!" Josie was giddy with excitement, jumping up and down in her amazing wedding dress. She looked so young and carefree and…in love.

"I am so happy for you, Josie," I said, and I genuinely meant it. I would have been a lot happier if Josie and Jon eloped, though; that way, I wouldn't have to wear this hideous dress or link arms with Thad.

Josie took both of my hands and was jumping up and down, chanting, "I'm getting marr-ied, I'm getting marr-ied!" She stopped and her smile made her eyes sparkle. "Stacy, I never thought this would happen to me." Neither did I. Josie was the last person I ever thought would get married. Josie was the self-proclaimed man-eater of our little group of friends. She was almost thirty, a platinum blonde with ginormous boobs and sky blue eyes. She was loud, obnoxious, and a little challenged in the etiquette and common sense departments. Josie was scatterbrained, clueless most of the time, and she was always dressed to the nines. And Josie exuded sex…always. It wasn't her fault…she couldn't help it. It was just part of who she was. She reminded me of a modern day Marilyn Monroe. She was fiercely loyal, and when she loved you she did it completely and unconditionally, which was why I would wear this ridiculous dress and hold hands with Thad.

The sales woman, ever attentive, was taking notes, listing the alterations that needed to be made. Megan, as usual, was handling all the details.

"You are going to be a beautiful bride, Josie," I said, and she grinned.

"And you are going to break hearts in that dress, Stacy. Thad won't know what hit him! Thank you for being my bridesmaid."

I felt a lump forming in my throat. I loved my friend so much. "It will be my pleasure Josie."

Josie bounced off to change out of her wedding dress and Megan came and gave me a hug. "You really do look gorgeous Stacy."

"Thanks, Meg," I said, and she swatted my behind and ushered me toward the dressing room.

"Go," she said. "Change. I'm hungry." We had just eaten.

I laughed. "You are always hungry," I replied.

She rubbed her belly and smiled. "You are depriving my baby here of vital nourishment that is essential to its development. Now hurry the hell up!"

***

After a mad dash to Dunkin' Donuts to quench the baby's sweet tooth, we eventually made it to the grocery store, then to my house to put the food away and finish the laundry. I unlocked my door, and was immediately hit with an unwelcome wave of heat.

Perfect...just freaking perfect. My air conditioner was broken again. I'd already had it repaired twice and shelled out over $500. This was bullshit!

"Oh Lord," Megan said. She headed to the kitchen, put her bags down, and opened the back door to get some air moving through the kitchen. "Let's just put this stuff up and leave."

Josie fanned herself. "Is it hot in here or is it just me?" she said playfully.

"I'm calling the air-conditioning company again. I want this fixed now!" Irritated, I grabbed my phone and scrolled through the call log. I knew I had their number somewhere. I found it and hit the call button. Bypassing the bullshit, I cut straight to the chase. I wanted to talk to the manager. I was immediately put on hold.

"I know a guy that can probably fix it, Stace," Josie offered. I shook my head. "Actually, we used to date. As I recall, he was really good with his hands." I rolled my eyes. "And his tongue…. Oh geez, I'm getting all hot just thinking about it. I've got to sit down. I think I'm having a heat stroke." She sat at the table, picked up the water gun, turned it backwards, and squirted her breasts. "There, that's better. My sisters were suffocating."

I was still holding and still fuming. How freaking hard was it to fix an air conditioner? The manager was finally on the line. I explained what was going on, and I couldn't help but sound a little disgruntled. I had been so depressed lately that I had spent most of my time at home, and it was not fun when it was ninety degrees in the house…not to mention the cash I'd forked over.

The manager gave me his apologies and promised to rectify the situation as soon as possible. Josie was in the background waving at me, so I asked the manager to hold on.

"What?" I asked her.

She took the phone away from me. "You are being too nice," she said. "I'll handle it from here, Stacy." She held her hand out to reassure me. I lightly banged my head on the wall.

"…and send someone that knows what he's doing this time. And is it too much for me to ask that the technician be good-looking? I mean, some eye candy on a hot day would be nice."

I jerked the phone away from Josie. "Muzzle her, will you?" I said to Megan, and I scheduled an appointment for the maybe hot, but highly skilled technician to come in the morning.

Josie was still yelling in the background. "Send a single guy if you have one. My friend here is in the market for a man." I gave Josie a stern don't-fuck-with-me look. She giggled and batted her eyelashes.

"We really have to put a leash on her," I told Megan. "She is out of control!" I finished my call.

Megan laughed and ordered me to pack an overnight bag. "It's too hot to sleep here," she said. "You can stay with me and Jack." I groaned. "It will be fun. We will make it a sleepover. Like old times."

"Yay! I love sleepovers!" Josie shouted, and I knew protesting would get me nowhere. I packed my bag and headed to Megan's.

CHAPTER 2

Cooper Carson loved women, and women loved him. Sometimes they loved him a little too much. He liked them blonde, young, and without strings attached. He lived by the "catch and release" procedure.

But of course that didn't always work. Sometimes they got attached, and then he found himself in awkward situations, like the one he was in now.

"Is the coast clear?" he said into the phone.

His secretary and wannabe dating coach, Colleen, answered, "Not yet, Hot Stuff. She's still out there."

Cooper lightly banged his head on the wall. "Geez, how long can she stay out there? Don't women need to pee often or something?"

Colleen laughed. "This one is tenacious, Cooper. I don't know where you found her, but she's got some stamina."

"Well what the hell is she doing out there? It's like a hundred degrees."

"Maybe she will get heat stroke and die," Colleen said as she stifled a laugh.

"Don't even say that!"

"You would agree if you knew what she was doing."

Cooper cringed. "Okay, do I want to know?"

"Probably not." Colleen responded, then because she couldn't help herself, she added, "But I'm going to tell you anyways."

He waited for her to continue, and when she didn't he prompted her. "Well?" He said impatiently.

"Never mind," she teased. "You really don't want to know."

"Colleen!"

She was full on laughing now. "If you weren't hiding out in the bathroom you could see for yourself."

"I'm not hiding," Cooper lied. "I'm just avoiding a situation."

"A situation you created, Cooper. I mean seriously, at some point you are going to have to grow up and quit playing with these high school girls—"

Cooper cleared his throat. "Um, she's in college."

"...and start dating girls your own age. Maybe then they wouldn't be camped out on the hood of your car...."

Cooper had a white knuckled grip on the phone. "She's what? That's a seventy thousand dollar car!"

"Oopsie," Colleen said. "That just slipped out, boss."

"You have to do something!" Cooper half shouted in the phone.

"Nope, Stud Muffin. Not happening. I just got my hair done. I'm not getting it ripped out in a catfight with one of your groupies." She lowered her voice. "Plus, this one looks tough. She might be able to whip my ass, and the health insurance you provide isn't worth a shit."

"Colleen!"

"Uh oh, got another call coming in. Please hold."

There was no other call and Cooper was well aware of that. He ended the call and called Colleen back.

She answered in her usual perky professional tone even though the office had caller ID and she knew damn well it was Cooper. Cooper kept his tone even. "Colleen, just get her off my car. I don't care how you do it. Just do it."

"You don't pay me enough for that."

Cooper sighed. "I'll give you a raise."

She laughed. "You'll do that anyways. Look Cooper, seriously, you might have to get a restraining order. I mean, this is day seven of this. This is beyond infatuation. This here is stalker status."

She was right, but he kind of felt sorry for the girl and didn't want to deal with the embarrassment that a restraining order entailed. "Will you at least go into my office and close the blinds so I can get in there and get some work done?"

"Nah. I rather enjoy watching you hide out in the bathroom." She was laughing hysterically at this point.

"Ha ha." Cooper said. "If you don't close the blinds in my office you're fired." Cooper stole a peak down the hallway and saw her gather her handbag from her desk drawer and stand to leave. She had a huge smile plastered on her face.

"Sweet, I need a vacation," she said.

From Cooper's view he saw Kayla coming to the office door. He ducked quickly and slammed the bathroom door. "Wait!" he shouted into the phone. "Don't leave!"

"Sorry boss, but I've been fired!" The bell on the front door chimed.

"I changed my mind," Cooper said in a hushed whisper.

"What's in it for me?" she asked, and then he heard her greet Kayla and knew he was running out of time.

"What do you want?" he asked, knowing it might be easier to just face Kayla.

"Well like I said, I could use a vacation."

"Done. Now get her out of here!"

Colleen wasn't done yet. "And hour and a half lunch breaks for the next month."

Cooper was losing his patience. "Two weeks."

"Okay," she said, and Cooper breathed a sigh of relief. "But I also want a gold fish named Waldo and a cappuccino machine. And those are non-negotiable."

Cooper gripped the phone harder and resisted the urge to throw it at the wall. "Fine!" He whispered through gritted teeth. "Deal!" He heard Kayla ask Colleen if she could use the restroom. "Tell her it's out of order," he hissed urgently.

"Sure, hon," he heard Colleen say. "It's your first door on the right." The last thing he heard before the call disconnected was Colleen's laughter.

***

Megan lived about four blocks from me in a charming little house that she and Jack had bought last year and completely remodeled. In the months following my bitter divorce and the Thad disaster, I had spent a lot of nights in their spare room. Megan had it decorated tastefully in neutral colors and dark wood. It felt very homey and safe, and I always felt very

15

comfortable there. After unpacking my bag and putting my toiletries in the adjoining bathroom, I went in search of Megan, who was probably in the kitchen. For some reason, I felt the sudden urge to open the door to the nursery, and I couldn't help the smile that developed.

The nursery was perfect. Muted yellows and greens made a very relaxing and soothing color scheme. The crib was polished, and neatly made up with safari themed bedding. The changing table housed everything needed to complete the task of diaper changing, and the closet contained the cutest little articles of clothing on the littlest hangers I had ever seen. I ran my hand along the crib rail. It was hard to believe that in a month's time, there would be a precious perfect baby sleeping in that crib, and Megan would be a mommy. I was so excited for her. But even so, I couldn't shake the sadness of knowing that I may never experience this for myself. Next month, I would be turning thirty. I currently had no husband, no job, and no desire to seek either. I'd been in this funk for far too long, but I didn't know how to get out of it. Burying my head in my hands, I blinked back tears. How did I end up like this? Who did I piss off in a former life to have karma drop kick my ass like this? It hadn't always been this way.

I had met Scott in college and we got married at age twenty-two. We thought we were perfect for each other. But looking back now, I realized we were doomed from the start. He was an academic genius who focused solely on school and career, while I was a party girl who barely made the grade. Scott was very well grounded and goal oriented, while I was more of a free spirit. We were like oil and water, fire and gasoline. I saw that now. I thought everything was okay until, after seven years of marriage, I caught Scott doing the dirty with the dog walker on the sofa. It absolutely broke my heart, and at times I just wanted to die. Looking back on it, I didn't blame him. I wasn't completely available to him. I was drunk most of the time. My marriage was falling apart and I didn't even know it. Or perhaps I did, and that's why I was drinking.

I had tried to shed the party girl image after college and be the sensible wife. Too much of my childhood had been unstructured and spontaneous, and I felt I needed the routine, mundane, sensible life. I lost me, and after that happened I got lost in the bottle. Sensible Stacy was nowhere to be seen. After Scott cheated I told him I was willing to forgive him, give him another chance. He gracefully declined and I plummeted into depression.

Just as I was getting back on track, Thad came along, and the whole Thad thing was a disaster from the get go. Sexually we were dynamite, but that wasn't enough for me. I needed love, and he didn't have it to give. When I pushed for commitment, he ran and never looked back. I was just a booty call for him. Hell, we could still be having heart-stopping sex if I hadn't wanted or needed more. So now I was alone, and had made up my mind that I was done with the opposite sex.

I made my way to the kitchen and found Megan washing vegetables for salad. She refused my offer to help and poured me a glass of fresh squeezed lemonade.

"The nursery looks amazing."

Megan's eyes lit up. "Thanks Stace. All that is missing is baby." She rubbed her belly. "I can't believe I'm going to be a mommy."

"You are going to be an amazing mom, Meg."

Megan smiled sweetly. "I sure hope so, Stacy. I'm actually a little scared."

I dismissed her with a wave. "You will be fine. You and Jack were made for this. Speaking of Jack, where is he?"

"He will be home shortly. He is training a new guy, so he has been getting home late."

There was a sharp knock on the front door that startled us both. Megan wiped her hands on a towel and went to the door. She looked through the peephole and said, "It's my dad. Hi, Daddy," she said after opening the door.

Behind Megan's father was her grandmother, carrying a small suitcase and wearing a flowing, colorful, summer dress and four-inch clear heels. Headphones were in her ears, and her head was bopping to the beat of the music while she sang along to the parts she knew.

Megan cocked her head at her dad. "Rap?" she asked, and her dad gave her a palms up gesture.

"That," he said, "is your friend Mickey's fault. He bought her the stupid pod thingy and put music on it for her. I thought it could keep her occupied so she couldn't get in so much trouble. It has done that, but now she thinks she is a rapper. She never shuts up! It's like this all day every day."

Megan laughed and invited her dad and grandma in. Hugging them both, she eyed her dad speculatively. Mr. Johnson was not big on visiting. "Did you stop by to visit?" she asked, and her dad got straight to the point.

"Okay, here's the deal," he said. "Your granny is driving me nuts. Bonkers! I'm either gonna have to kill her or myself if I have to spend another second with her. Your mother and I need a break."

Megan shook her head, eyes wide. "Daddy, I'm pregnant...the baby."

"She can come back before the baby gets here. She can help you prepare for the baby."

"But I'm having a dinner party tonight," Megan pleaded.

Her dad smiled. "Good, Granny can be the entertainment. She is a rapper, you know."

I cringed. This was not going to turn out well.

Megan tried again. "But Daddy, I don't have room." She pointed at me. "Stacy is staying in the guest room for a while. She's lonely and heartbroken and...well, she's just a pitiful wreck, Dad. Aren't you, Stacy?"

Gee, thanks friend. I nodded. "Yep, I sure am."

"Even better! Granny can move in with Stacy then," Megan's dad said. He clapped his hands. "It's all settled then. No more loneliness for Stacy. Granny will be fine company. I'll deliver the rest of her luggage tomorrow. Good day girls!" Before either of us had a chance to protest, he was out the door and down the sidewalk.

I was stunned and at a loss for words.

"We will figure something out," Megan whispered, trying to comfort me. "Daddy will cool off and I'll take Granny back in a couple of days."

A couple of days? With Granny? That could take years off my life! I looked to the heavens. "What did I do to deserve this?" I asked God. I got no immediate answer. No anvil fell on my head. No bus burst through the house and killed me. It looked like I was stuck with Granny. Shit!

As I helped Megan set the table, I noticed that there were seven place settings. I mentally did the math. Megan, Jack, Granny...that was three. Myself, Josie, and Dr. Ross, that made six.

"Meg, I think you gave me one setting too many."

Megan counted down on her fingers. "Nope, there is going to be seven of us since Granny is here."

"Okay, who all is coming?" I asked.

Megan was bustling around the table fussing over napkins. She enjoyed her role as host. "Well, there's me and Jack of course, you and Granny, Mickey and Josie, and Mickey is bringing a guest." Mickey? A guest? That should be interesting. Megan gave me her glowing pregnant smile. "Why don't you go freshen up? I've got everything under control here."

"I feel like I should be helping you Meg." She looked like she could pop at any minute. She should've probably been in bed with her feet up or something.

"Nonsense! I don't need help. Now off you go. Get out of here."

On my way to my room I ran into Granny, who immediately grabbed my hand and drug me to the sofa. On the coffee table she had spread out her tarot cards and crystal ball. She turned my palm face up and began tracing the lines of my hand. "Interesting," she muttered. She quickly placed both hands on the crystal ball and whispered some creepy chant. She took my palm again and then started with the tarot cards. I saw the love card come up. Oh my.

All this voodoo mumbo jumbo gave me the creeps. "Granny, I have to get ready for dinner. You can predict my future after dinner." I was just trying to stall because Granny and I both knew that after dinner and a couple of swigs of her "medicine," she would be snoring like a lumberjack.

I stood to leave, but Granny stopped me. "Stacy, I keep seeing sex and money. The cards are telling me that you are going to get lucky very soon. Make sure you keep your legs shaved and wear the naughty, naughty undergarments."

I blushed seven shades of red. I couldn't talk about this stuff with Granny. She was like eighty years old, for heaven's sake.

"Granny, I have no job and I've sworn off men. The only lucky I'm getting is when the supermarket has red velvet ice cream."

Granny was not detoured. "Tomorrow we will go shopping. We'll buy some condoms and some lottery tickets. Then we can go to that Victoria's Secret store and buy you some sexy underwear. And maybe a corset. Men love corsets!" I frowned, and Granny tried to reassure me. "Don't you worry, Stacy dear, I'm a pro at this sex stuff. I guess you could call me a sexspert. Why, before I married Grandpa I was quite the—"

I crossed my eyes and covered my ears, refusing to hear this. "Granny, I have to help Megan." Making a hasty get away and practically running to the bedroom, I mentally wiped the last twenty minutes from my brain. Besides, I didn't really buy into all that psychic jazz and didn't see any sex, love, or money in my future. Maybe I would buy a couple of lottery tickets, but that's as far as I was taking Granny's ridiculous predictions.

Back in the guest bath I ran a brush through my long brown hair, turned my head upside down and fluffed it, applied lip gloss, and gunked on some more mascara. I changed shirts, opting for one of Megan's with a low neckline. I looked in the mirror. Good enough. I didn't have anybody to get all dolled up for anyways. It just felt good to feel like I looked good.

I entered the dining room, and was snatched up immediately by Mickey. He grabbed me in a bear hug and twirled me around. I think he had missed me.

"Look at you, Ms. Dupree." He took a long look. "Love the fuck me hair, and your ass looks fan-tab-ulous!"

I smiled. Man, I had missed my friend. "Why, thank you, Mr. Long. You look amazing as well."

Mickey was the only guy in our group. His real name was Michael, but we all called him Mickey. He was 6'5, skinny as a string bean, and hairy all over. Mickey worked at a bank by day and was a drag queen named Michaela at night. He frequently wore size thirteen stilettos, and was a big fan of rhinestones and sequins. His grandmother was a seamstress, and made most of his costumes. The rest of his apparel was a mix of suits and ties, daisy dukes, and halter-tops. Mickey was unpredictable and over the top. He was openly bi-sexual, and to my knowledge had never had a serious relationship, but had big shoulders and gave great bear hugs. I just considered him one of us girls.

Tonight he was wearing a tight denim mini skirt and hot pink halter top with plenty of hairy midriff showing. He had accessorized with large pink hoop earrings, a bolo tie, and zebra print pumps. His frizzy blond hair stood on end, his eye shadow was smoky, and his lips were bright pink. For some reason he reminded me of the Pink Panther in drag. I couldn't help but giggle.

"Where's your guest?" I asked him, excited that he had a date. Mickey never had a date, so this was big.

Mickey gave me a mischievous wink. "He should be here any minute." He...so his date was a boy. How exciting. He must be special, because we'd never met any of Mickey's "boy" friends.

I wiggled my eyebrows and winked at Mickey.

"Honey Buns! Is that you?" Granny made her way to the dining room to greet Mickey. Granny stood five feet tall. Mickey was over a foot and half taller in his heels. He bent down, scooped Granny up, planted a huge kiss on her lips, threw her over his shoulder, and spun her around. Granny hooted and hollered, and when Mickey sat her down she slapped his butt and sashayed away, pointing two fingers at him. They shared their own little private joke. Mickey and Granny had that kind of relationship. I didn't ask questions, because I really didn't want to know the answers.

Megan ushered everyone to the table just as Josie showed up. Her shirt was on inside out and her cheeks were flushed. "Sorry I'm late guys. I had a...well, I was um...." She waved her hand. "Well, I was at the emergency room." Josie's fiancé was an ER doctor.

"Did you have an emergency?" Granny wanted to know.

Josie hugged Granny, "Um no...well, kind of...but I'm all good now."

"Did you get an injection while you were there?" Mickey asked teasingly.

Josie looked confused. "Why would I? I didn't go there because I'm sick."

Mickey tickled Josie in the ribs. "Sure you didn't get some penis-cillian?"

"No, Mickey, I didn't need any medicine. I'm not sick. I was just horny. We did it on the x-ray table. We had to hurry. Some dumb kid broke his arm or something and they needed the room." She studied her nails. "Next time we are doing it in the elevator. At least in there we can hit the emergency stop button."

I rolled my eyes. "Josie, you can't have sex in the hospital elevator."

Josie thought for a minute. "Um, there aren't any signs that say 'no sex' or nothing."

"That's true," Granny offered. "I was just at the hospital last week, and I didn't see any signs about sex. And I would have remembered that."

Megan shuffled everyone into the dining room, the sex discussion forgotten. As we were entering the dining room, Jack, Megan's husband, came through the back door. He made a beeline for his wife, planted a kiss on her lips, and then dropped to his knees to kiss her belly. Love radiated off the two of them and lit up the room. We all took our seats and gave them some privacy.

Jack was our age and had gone to school with us. He was a goofy, scrawny kid that got picked on and didn't have much luck with girls. The years had been kind to him though. Now at just under six feet, with deep brown eyes and dark brown hair, he could turn every female head when he walked into the room. He had a lean waste, wide shoulders, and lots of swagger in his walk. He always looked like he just had sex; his hair was always ruffled, and he usually had stubble on his jaw. He smelled like expensive cologne and motorcycles. He looked like sex personified, and he loved my best friend more than life itself. They were about to become parents and I couldn't be happier for them.

Jack spotted Granny and raised an eyebrow at Megan. Megan shrugged and pointed to me. "Um, Granny is going to be keeping Stacy company for a few days."

Jack eyed me speculatively and I shrugged. Man, I could have used a drink. Jack gave me a hug and whispered in my ear, "I'll try to get you out of this." I mouthed a silent "thank you" and took my seat at the table. I loved Granny, but I didn't know that I could live with her...even short term.

As Jack was greeting everyone, the doorbell rang and Megan rushed to answer it. We all looked at the door in excited anticipation. This must be Mickey's date. The door opened and there was a six foot Christina Aguliera standing in the door way holding a bottle of wine, flowers, and a duffle bag. My mouth dropped open. I was not sure what I was expecting, but this wasn't even on the list.

Mickey gestured to his friend and did a quick introduction. "Everyone, this is Matt. Matt, this is everyone."

Matt smiled shyly and waved. "I'm sorry I'm late everyone. Rehearsals ran long." He gestured to his bag. "May I change somewhere?" Matt asked, and Megan led him to the guest room. He gave a curious glance at the crystal ball and tarot card display, but said nothing.

Back in the dining room everyone took their seats as if Christina Aguliara came to eat dinner with us all the time. I took the seat between Megan and Granny; that put Christina, or Matt, between Josie and Mickey, with Jack at the head of the table.

Matt emerged from the guest room looking like a regular guy clad in jeans and a polo shirt. His face was free of makeup, his blond hair pulled into a tight ponytail. He looked very handsome, and even a little boyish. He handed Megan the wine and gave Josie the flowers. Mickey shook his head and pointed to me, and Christina-Matt changed course, held the flowers out to me, and smiled a self-conscious smile. "Hello," he said to me, and to be polite I returned his greeting. Why was Mickey's date bringing me flowers?

Jack started passing food around and everyone filled their plates. Megan was an amazing cook. On the menu tonight was pork tenderloin, with sweet potato puree, stuffed mushrooms, and asparagus. Everything looked incredible, and I realized I was starving. Everyone dug in and surprisingly conversation was kept to a minimum, which was fine with me. No "Stacy, you need a date" or "Seeing anyone new, Stacy?"

"So Matt," Granny said, breaking the silence. "I have a question for you." I braced myself, and Megan let out a strangled sigh.

"What is your question, Miss…?"

"Granny," she replied. "Everyone calls me Granny."

"Okay, Granny?"

Granny leaned forward and lowered her voice. "How do you get your boobies to look so perky?"

Megan gasped. Granny continued. "Do you buy them that way, or is that a special trick?"

Matt blushed and Mickey tried to save him. "Granny, they aren't real," he said, and Granny dismissed him.

"I know they aren't real, Honey Bun. I mean, I know his mama didn't give them to him, but I was wondering where he got them." She reached down to her waist, grabbed one, then the other, of her old grandma boobs, and pulled them up. All around the table mouths were open and everyone except Megan was gaping at Granny. Megan was eating, shoveling it in. Nothing came between pregnant Megan and food.

Adjusting her boobs, Granny continued. "I've been thinking of getting some work done. Maybe one of those booby lifts or some of those implants." Jack kicked Megan under the table and Megan shrugged. Matt looked mortified.

"Granny," Mickey said. "They aren't implants, they are inserts. Matt can take them out and put them in whenever he wants to."

Granny was intrigued. "Really? Can I see them?" Matt looked at Mickey, who turned to Megan, who shrugged. Matt said, "Sure," excused himself, and went off to retrieve the fake boobies. Jack started grumbling about Granny, but stopped when Megan reminded him that Granny was going home with me.

Oh hell. I had forgotten about that. Granny couldn't come live with me. I'd go insane. I gave Megan the death stare and she smiled sweetly, or as sweetly as one can with a mouth full of sweet potatoes.

Matt returned and passed the fake boobies to Granny, who turned them over in her hands. "Hmmm," she said, and then stuck one hand up her shirt while using the other one to pull her shirt at her neck so she could see down her shirt. She positioned the first insert then repeated the process for the second. "What do you think? How do my bazoombas look?" she asked everyone, and everyone concentrated on the food, except for Josie, who jiggled her own boobs and gave Granny a thumbs up.

"They look good," Matt said. "You can keep that set, I have more." Granny was ecstatic at the thought and I just cringed. I was going to have to see these bazoombas for the next couple of weeks. I offered up a silent prayer that she could return home soon. Megan's dad couldn't stay mad forever. Right?

"So, are you single?" Josie asked Matt.

"Yes," he answered politely.

"Gay?" she asked. Jack choked, and Megan smacked him on the back.

"No," Matt replied.

Granny frowned. "But you dress like a girl."

Matt shrugged. "That's just for my job."

Granny's eyes lit up. "Want to go out on a date?"

She stood up and grabbed her boobs, and one of the inserts fell out and landed in Megan's sweet potatoes.

Megan didn't skip a beat. Jack pushed his plate away. "I'm done," he said, and Megan scooted his plate over to hers and started eating off his plate.

"Granny!" Mickey shouted, but Matt interrupted him. "Miss...um, Granny...I can't go out with you tonight, because I'm already on a date."

That's right, Matt was Mickey's date.

But wait a minute. Matt said he wasn't gay....

"Oh, Honey Buns?" Granny said, referring to Mickey. "He won't mind if we go out. We share everything, right Mic...? Hey, but I thought you aren't gay?"

"Umm...," Mickey started, but seemed to lose his thought. He looked guilty as hell. I looked to Josie, but she was busy texting. She smiled sweetly and wiggled her eyebrows.

"I'm not," Matt said again, and I began to get a bad feeling about this evening.

"So, who's your date?" I asked, and Mickey said, "Pass the wine."

Matt looked directly at me with a surprised look on his face. Then it all made sense. Him giving me the flowers, the looks he had been giving me all throughout dinner. The gazillion times he had offered me wine. I gave Mickey my best I'm-going-to-kill-you look, and he pointed at Megan, who flipped him the bird and threw the booby at him. He ducked and the booby hit the wall and slid down it, leaving a trail of sweet potatoes in its wake. Matt belted back his wine and poured another glass. Granny retrieved the fallen boob, dipped it in her water glass to rinse it off, then replaced it lopsidedly in her bra. Matt was speechless, Josie stopped texting long enough to fix Granny's boobs, and Megan was still eating, having finished her plate and most of Jack's.

I stood to start clearing the table. "Mickey, you want to give me a hand?" I asked.

Mickey shook his head and said, "Looks like you got it, girl." I leaned down and whispered in his ear.

"You wouldn't!" he said, his eyes locked on mine.

I grinned. "You bet your sweet ass I would, Honey Buns."

Mickey looked mortified, which was exactly what I was going for. He jumped out of his seat, started grabbing plates and glasses, and followed me to the kitchen. Once there, I unleashed on him, barely controlling my anger.

"You set me up!" I hissed, and Mickey held his hands out and backed up.

"I did," he admitted. "But I was only trying to help."

"Help?" I couldn't believe what I was hearing. "How does setting me up with a drag queen help me?"

"It gives you a potential date for Josie's wedding. That way you won't be so sad about Thad."

I blew out a deep breath and counted to twenty-seven. "Mickey, I don't date boys that dress up like girls. I like my men rough and rugged, and...oh jeez, I just remembered I swore off men." I started counting again.

Mickey didn't skip a beat. "That's the beauty of dating Matt," he said. "For those days you've sworn off men, he makes a smoking hot chic. So it's like you have the best of both worlds." He gave me a palms up gesture. I faked a smile and headed back to the dining room to collect Matt and Granny's plates, then headed back to the kitchen. Megan stopped me from passing by her. She stabbed a sprig of asparagus off Granny's plate and a medallion of pork loin from Matt's. I hustled back to the kitchen with the dishes as Megan called after me "Dessert?"

***

I finished my dessert and began rinsing dishes to go in the dishwasher. Megan was having a popcorn craving and needed movie theater popcorn, so Jack was on a mission to the theater to satisfy his wife's hunger. Granny was reading Matt's palm. Josie was lounging on the couch talking to her reflection in the crystal ball, and Mickey was helping me with the dishes while Megan sampled ice cream toppings for her popcorn.

Since Mickey and Megan were the matchmakers tonight, I knew I had to talk to both of them about all the surprise blind dates. First of all, if I was going to have a date I would at least like to know about it before hand so that I could dress accordingly, wear my sexy special lingerie, shave my legs, pluck my eyebrows, paint my toenails. I didn't want to date boys who dressed like girls, especially if they looked better than me in drag. I wanted to steer clear of mama's boys, criminals, carnival or circus workers, midgets, and vegetarians. I didn't want a boyfriend who was unemployed, a workaholic, gay, arrogant, dishonest, or homeless. Bottom line was, *if* and *when* I decided to go on a date, I wanted to pick my date and have the courtesy of knowing that I was on an actual date. No more surprises. No more set ups. I knew my friends meant well, but this had to stop.

I started the dishwasher and joined Megan and Mickey at the breakfast bar. Mickey was sipping a beer while Megan was expertly applying caramel and sprinkles to sour dill pickles.

"How can you still be eating, woman?" Mickey asked, and I wondered the same thing.

She patted her belly. "The baby is hungry." She leaned down and talked to her belly. "Aren't you, Precious?"

"Are you sure there is only one baby in there?" I asked. "Because, no offense Meg, but you are huge."

"There is only one baby," she said.

Mickey said, "One big ass baby."

Megan squirted Mickey with caramel. "For your information, Michael, the doctor said my baby weighs about five and a half pounds right now."

Mickey licked the caramel off his arm. "Then what is the other fifty pounds you've gained?"

Megan pouted. "I have only gained forty seven point two pounds, and in case you are wondering, some of the weight is fluid and stuff. I pretty much have a swimming pool in my tummy for my baby to swim in." She narrowed her eyes. "Wait a minute! Are you calling me fat?" she said, and I knew I had to stop this before it got out of hand. It could have gotten ugly quick.

I jumped between them and called a time out. Thankfully, Jack arrived, planted a kiss on his wife's lips, delivered her popcorn, and escaped to his man cave to avoid Granny and her fortune telling. Megan, distracted by the popcorn, forgot about the argument with Mickey, and another potential food fight disaster had been averted. Megan juggled the popcorn, caramel, sprinkles, and pickles and joined Jack in the den. Mickey and I finished cleaning up and joined them.

In the den, Jack was watching a television show about guns, Megan was eating caramel popcorn with a side of pickles, her bowl balanced perfectly on her baby belly, and Mickey stretched out on the couch and put his size thirteen shoes on the coffee table. He closed his eyes, but I was pretty sure he wasn't going to sleep. I retrieved Josie from the living room and prayed Granny wouldn't follow. The last thing I needed was Granny predicting my love life for me. If I listened to her, I would be living in a bubble on Mars with a unicorn.

Once the gang was all rounded up, I stood in front of the TV, which Jack politely muted for me.

"Okay, look guys; first off, I love each one of you very much, and I know you mean well, but we have to talk about this blind date thing. You have to quit setting me up."

Josie frowned. "But Stace, we hate seeing you so lonely."

"I know, and I get that. I know your intentions are good, but I'm okay with being alone now," I lied.

"No you're not," Megan said. "And we know that Mr. Right is out there."

"I'm not interested in Mr. Right."

Josie's eyes lit up. "How about Mr. Right Now? Because I know a guy—"

"No! No more set ups, blind dates, or matchmaking. I am done with men!"

"Oh well, now I get it," Josie said, and I rolled my eyes.

"I'm not into women either, Josie."

"Oh," she said, then scrunched up her eyebrows. "Then what exactly are you into? 'Cause I am confused." It didn't take much to confuse Josie.

Jack spoke up. "I think what Stacy is saying is that right now she just wants to focus on being alone. If Mr. Right happens to show up, then that's fine. But she isn't looking for him right now."

"Exactly," I said, and Mickey opened his eyes.

"Well, you have to put yourself out there at some point," he said. "I mean, Mr. Right isn't going to show up on your doorstep and ring your doorbell."

I changed tack. "What do I need a man for anyways? I have cable TV, great friends, and good books."

Megan smiled a sad smile. "What about companionship and sex?"

I swallowed hard. Megan had cut right to the heart of it. I did miss the companionship and the sex. I missed it a lot. "I have you guys for the companionship and...." I blinked back tears and cursed quietly. "...and I'm going to get me a pet. A hamster or an iguana, or maybe a fiddler crab. And as for sex...well, I'm beginning to believe that sex is overrated."

"You're just saying that because you aren't getting any," Josie said, and of course she was right. "You just need a friend with benefits. You know, someone you can just have sex with but no relationship." All eyes went to Mickey. I shook my head in horror.

"What you need is one of those handy dandy vibrating peckers," Granny said, joining the conversation. "They come in different colors and sizes, and they run on batteries. Batteries last longer than most of your relationships, and when they run out they are easy to replace. Unlike men. I have a magazine where I can get you one."

"Granny, I don't need a vibrator."

"Well, neither do I, but it is a pleasant way to pass the time. Mine is purple and —"

Jack bolted out of his chair. "Okay, enough! Megan, deal with your Granny. Josie, and Mickey, no more matchmaking. Stacy, get rid of your date."

My date? Oh hell! I had forgotten about Matt. He was standing in the doorway, an amused smile on his lips.

"Would you like to offer me a drink?" he asked.

"Nope." I started towards the door.

"Would you like to invite me to stay the night?" Was this guy for real?

"Nope." I grabbed his duffel bag and dropped it over his shoulder.

"Do I get a goodnight kiss?" I wanted to kiss his balls with my right knee.

"Not on your life." I turned him around and pushed him out the door, slammed the door, and looked through the peephole. He was still standing there. He rang the doorbell, and I opened the door. "What?" I asked, and he produced a business card. There was a picture of him dressed in drag talking on a phone, and underneath the picture it said, "Call me Christina." Below that was his cell number and a link to his Facebook page. "I wanted to give you my card so you can get ahold of me for our next date." Geez! I took the card and slammed the door.

I threw the bolt and turned to walk away, and the doorbell rang again. I checked the peephole and surprise surprise, it was Matt. "What now?" I asked, my frustration radiating off me.

"You didn't give me your number," he said, and on impulse I jotted down Granny's phone number on the card he gave me. I then slammed the door in his face. I waited a beat and checked the peephole. He was still standing there. Oh well, he could stand there all freaking night...I was done. I was going to bed. This day had been hell.

I took three steps and the doorbell rang. Resisting the urge to reach out and strangle him, I calmly opened the door and smiled sweetly.

Matt looked me directly in the eye. "I just wanted to let you know that I will not be calling you, and you have blown your chance for a second date."

I tried to seem disappointed.

"I just don't want you up all night waiting for the phone to ring." Fat chance of that happening.

I slammed the door one last time and slid the bolt. The doorbell rang but I ignored it. There was knocking on the door but I ignored that too. Jack joined me at the door, an amused smile plastered on his face.

"Want me to handle it from here?" He asked.

I waved to the door. "Be my guest," I said, and sauntered off to my bedroom.

AMY JOHNSON

Chapter 3

Cooper Carson was at his desk doing paperwork. He had his blinds closed and had left his shiny red Corvette at home, just in case Kayla happened to show up again. He'd tried to wait her out yesterday but she'd threatened to kick the bathroom door down, so he had reluctantly come out and faced the music. He gave her the usual spiel and tried to let her down easy. She nodded her head that she understood as she blinked back tears. She seemed to take it well, but Cooper was sure he could see a carefully reined in spark of crazy in her troubled blue eyes. He still didn't trust her and had the feeling he wasn't home free yet. If only she hadn't been so hot. He shook his head to clear it. It was thoughts like that that had got him into trouble in the first place.

Colleen entered his office and threw a file on his desk. "I need you to do a service call," she said, and Cooper didn't even glance at the file.

"Send Ed," he said distractedly.

"I already have," Colleen said as she took a chair. Ed was a good technician. Cooper looked up. "He's been out there twice. Can't seem to satisfy the customer." She gave Cooper a teasing smile. "Since that's more your specialty...."

"Stop right there. You know I never mix business with pleasure."

"That's only because most eighteen to twenty-four year olds aren't home owners."

"That's not an accurate statement. I usually draw the line at twenty-two."

Colleen rolled her eyes. "Anyways, this woman is pissed. She's already spent a small fortune with us. She wants management. I already told her you would be there."

Cooper opened the file. "Okay, I'll go."

"She sounds hot," Colleen added.

Cooper smiled. "And how would you know that?"

"Well, it is a hundred degrees outside. Duh!"

Cooper laughed. "Didn't I fire you yesterday?"

"Yep, but you know you can't live without me." She batted her eyelashes.

"Whatever," Cooper said, then turned his full attention to Colleen. "Anything else?"

She handed him a stack of Post It notes. "I have your messages." The one on top was from Kayla. He cringed. What was it going to take to get rid of this girl? He raised an eyebrow at Colleen. She was still sitting comfortably in the chair having made no attempt to move. "And you need to sign pay checks." She handed him another folder. He signed the checks and returned them to her. She was still sitting, eyeing her perfectly sculpted fingernails.

"Next?" he asked, and she put her hands flat on his desk and stood to face him. "Okay, so there's this thing." He groaned. She held her hands out. "Just hear me out!" He motioned for her to continue. "It's super easy and you don't really have to do anything." He doubted that, but let her go on. "There's this charity auction where they are auctioning off eligible bachelors..."

He shook his head. "No."

"...and all the money goes to Autism Speaks. And you know how important that is to me." Colleen was a single mom of a five-year-old boy named Max who had autism. She was all about raising awareness and did everything she could to aid the cause. Cooper participated in every fundraiser and donated money regularly. Max's dad had hit the road shortly after his diagnosis, and Cooper did all he could for Max, including taking the boy for ice cream and frequent trips to the park. He'd even gotten the boy a puppy. "...and you get a free meal and you can take a date. And there will be tons of women there. And—"

"Okay," Cooper conceded. "I'll do it for Max. When is it?"

"Next Saturday. And I even have a date lined up for you—"

Cooper cut her off. "No on the date, but yes to the fundraiser. Now, do you have anything else for me?"

"Yeah. Where's my fish?"

"Pet store," he said, fished out his wallet, and threw a twenty on the desk. "And get Max one too. Only let him name it something cool, like Raider or Jett."

Colleen scooped up the cash. "And the cappuccino machine?"

"Don't push your luck," Cooper said, as Colleen laughed and left his office.

***

I woke up with a start having just had a bad dream. I dreamed that all my friends and Granny thought I was so desperate to find a man that they set me up with all sorts of misfits just to get me laid. All the while I had no clue what they were doing, and I made an ass out of myself every time.

Oh wait…that wasn't a nightmare…that was my life at the moment. Great! And happy Wednesday to you, too!

Remembering that I had a repairman coming to my house, I dressed quickly and headed home. I did not want to miss the AC guy. My house was unbearable without air conditioning. While I loved Megan, her house was a zoo. If you weren't crazy when you arrived, you would be crazy when left.

It was a beautiful morning so I decided to jog the short distance to my house. Mickey's truck was parked in my driveway behind my Bug, and my front door was wide open. I heard a noise that sounded like a quack, quack, and then Josie appeared in my doorway.

"You can't go in yet," she said by way of greeting.

"Why not?" I asked, and I took a second to determine if I really wanted to know why.

Josie lowered her voice. "Because you will ruin the surprise," she explained, and shut the door in my face. Now I could've just keyed my door open, but the truth was I was in no hurry to enter my house. For one thing, it was probably hotter than the depths of hell after being closed up with no air conditioning for the night. And then, of course, there was the whole Josie surprise thing. While she meant well, her surprise would probably not be a happy surprise. I was in no hurry to encounter whatever mayhem awaited me inside.

I sat on the porch and admired Mrs. Murray's flowerbeds next door. I thought I could have flower beds like that too if I had nothing better to do all day but build the beds and tend to the flowers.

Shit.

I realized I didn't have anything better to do. No job. No boyfriend. No sick relative to make soup for.

I looked at my pitiful yard. Sure, it was mowed and maintained, thanks to Jack, but it really had no curb appeal. I vowed to remedy that. After the repairman left, I was going to go to the nursery and buy a plant. Or a bush. Or some seeds or something.

Feeling ridiculous, I knocked on my own door. Josie answered the door wearing short shorts, a bikini top, and a snorkel. Yep, it was going to be one of those days. "Surprise," she said.

I walked into my house and was greeted by a little yellow duck. "Quack" he said, and pooped on the floor. Josie informed me that the duck was named Paddington. She scolded the duck and handed me a pair of arm floaties. "We are having a pool party," Josie informed me, and I did a ten count. I probably should have just left then. I could've just moved away and started over. I could have become Amish or joined a convent. "Here, put these on," she said, and for some unexplainable reason I put the floaties on my arms.

I entered my house and everything looked normal. I started to relax. Maybe it wasn't as bad as I thought. "Quack," said the duck, and I was reminded that it probably was as bad as I thought. I ventured into the kitchen following the duck, and ran right into a swimming pool where my dining table used to be. I slipped on a puddle of water, lost my footing, and landed in the pool. "Quack, Quack." Josie picked up the duck and gently placed it in the pool.

Let's assess the situation. I was face down in a child's wading pool in the middle of my kitchen. I had Paddington the duck swimming around me, pecking at my hair, and floaties on my arms to keep me from drowning myself, as tempting as that option sounded. The house was about 150 degrees, and Josie was standing over me with a beach ball yelling "Surprise." I was afraid to open my eyes because I was sure I was in Hell. Thank God I had a swimming pool to keep me cool.

I picked myself up and climbed out of the swimming pool, water sloshing all over the kitchen floor, and was standing there speechless when Mickey approached me. He was appropriately dressed in swim trunks, lime green bikini top, goggles, and a hot pink Band-Aid on his thumb. He was holding two daiquiri glasses with colorful umbrellas sticking out, and informed me that mine had no alcohol in it. I took a drink, and suddenly I wished there was alcohol in it. I had a feeling after this whole surprise ordeal I would need several daiquiris.

I took a deep cleansing breath and exhaled it very slowly. I was at a complete loss, and had no idea where to begin.

"Okay, spill it," I said as Josie led me to a lounge chair and dropped a floppy hat on my head. "Start with the duck."

Mickey and Josie looked at each other, probably contemplating who should give the explanation.

Mickey spoke first. "Well, we went to the pet store to buy you a kitten."

"Okay."

"And while we were there we decided to throw you a surprise pool party, because that would be a great way for you to stay cool with your air conditioner problem," Josie said, and waved her hand to indicate the pool. "Cats don't like the water, so then we started looking at animals that went with the water theme, and we decided on a turtle."

Mickey held up his thumb. "But the turtle was a biter. So we scratched that idea."

"Then we looked at frogs, but they were all slimy and gross, and you had to buy a habitat thingy for them, and we were kind of in a hurry because of the surprise thing."

"So you bought me a duck?"

Josie nodded and Mickey corrected me. "Actually, it's a duckling. But it will grow up to be a duck."

Great! I downed my virgin daiquiri.

"And all it needs is water and food, so it is easy to keep alive. Just feed it and give it water," Josie added excitedly. "We bought it a pool and some food, so you are all set."

Sure, except for the part where I had a duck roaming freely about. I applied a palm to my forehead to help tame the headache I had coming on, did the deep breathing thing again, and looked up at the ceiling. When I had regained my composure, Mickey was standing beside me with another drink.

"Josie, I appreciate the thought, but I'm not sure I will make a good duck parent. I mean, I don't know anything about ducks."

She reached in her bag and came out with a book. "That's why we bought you this," she said and handed me a *Ducks for Dummies* guide. Really? Was this really happening? I took the book and tossed it on the counter.

I tried again. "Okay, here's the deal. I don't want a duck! And I can't have a swimming pool in my kitchen. I'm pretty sure it's unsanitary, and probably not good for the floor underneath."

Mickey nodded. "Yes, we thought about that, and we are going to move Paddington outside as soon as you plant him a shade tree and get him a pond."

I banged my head on the wall.

"We were going to plant the tree for you but we couldn't, because Mickey is wearing heels and I just got a manicure," Josie said, and showed me her nails.

There was a knock at the door, and I was relieved to have the distraction. Expecting the repairman, I opened the door without checking the peephole and regretted it instantly. Granny was standing in the doorway clutching her overnight bag, a large suitcase beside her. Megan's dad was pulling out of my driveway. He waved and floored it when he saw me.

I finally lost it. I couldn't take anymore. I had reached my limit. This was not going to be good. "Out!" I yelled, and everyone just looked at me, but nobody moved. "Out! Everybody out!" I repeated, and Josie laughed. Mickey grabbed Granny's suitcase and started laughing too. Granny joined in the laughter and Paddington quack quacked. "What the hell is so funny?" I asked as the laughter got louder.

"Nothing, it's just that you kind of look like a crazy person, all waving your hands around and stuff."

I was appalled. "Me? I'm the crazy one? You two are the ones that bought me a freaking duck and put an outdoor pool in my kitchen!"

Josie frowned. "Well, when you put it that way—"

"We thought you would find the humor in it, Stace," Mickey said. "We were just trying to cheer you up. You know, make you laugh a little."

"Yeah, you need to laugh more Stacy. It keeps you young," Granny added. "Laughter and sex. And we all know you aren't getting any sex, so you better be laughing double time."

Mickey playfully slapped me on the behind. "Go put your suit on and grab a water gun. Let's have some fun."

"I'm not putting my suit on, but I will try to have some fun." I aimed a water gun at Josie and shot, squirting her in the face. She squealed with delight and squirted me back. Before I knew it, I was actually having fun, laughing, and cooling off.

***

The ringing doorbell halted our play. I ran to the door armed with my squirt gun and answered the door breathlessly. Holy Mary, Mother of God! I was ill prepared for what I saw. At first I thought Josie and Mickey had pulled a prank on me and hired a stripper to pose as a repairman. But judging by the truck and tool bag, he seemed to be the real deal.

I opened the door completely, and standing before me was a gorgeous specimen of a man, about six feet tall with sandy blond hair and blazing blue eyes. He had the sexiest lips, which curved into a curious smile when he saw me holding the squirt gun. The small gap between his two front teeth was beyond adorable. He was dressed in jeans and a polo shirt that was stretched tight across his chest. From what I could see, this boy was all muscles and hard lines, and I was rendered speechless.

"Hello," he said, and I searched for my voice.

"Hi," I breathed.

He offered his hand. "I'm Cooper Carson. I'm here to take a look at your air-conditioner."

"Yes, of course. Come on in." His voice was like warm honey, and I tried to hide my attraction to him. Failing miserably, I blushed and he smiled an innocent shy smile.

39

I moved aside so he could enter and closed the door behind him. And what a behind he had. His jeans fit snugly and hugged his ass perfectly. He took two steps, and stopped when he saw the duck. He smiled and shook his head, and I led him to the back yard through the kitchen, where Mickey and Josie were lounging by the pool. Granny was in the pool sipping a daiquiri. If Cooper thought any of this to be bizarre, he had the good manners not to say anything. When we entered the kitchen Granny began fanning herself. Josie mouthed, "Oh my God," and Mickey gave me a thumbs up. Apparently, I wasn't the only one overcome by this man's looks.

When Cooper was outside and out of earshot, Josie ran up to me and said, "When I told them to send eye candy I was only joking, but I think they took me seriously. That man is to die for!" She squinted at me, eyeing me suspiciously. "And you noticed him too!" she exclaimed. I blushed darker.

"Did not," I retorted, trying to sound convincing.

"Oh yes you did. You like him," she insisted.

Okay, she was partly right. I liked what I saw, but geez, who wouldn't?

"How can I like him?" I asked. "I don't even know him. I just met him, and after he leaves I will probably never see him again. Plus, he is *way* out of my league."

"Nonsense!" Mickey said. "You are smoking hot, and don't think Mr. Repairman didn't notice. I saw the way he looked at you."

My heart beat faster. "How did he look at me?"

"Like he's starving and you are lunch," Mickey said, and Josie nodded.

"Go talk to him," she urged.

"I can't just go strike up a conversation with him. And besides, he's working. I don't want to bother him."

"Okay," Josie said, her eyes lighting up. "I have a plan." Oh hell! "It's crazy hot outside. Go offer him a bottle of water, or some lemonade or a soda."

I frowned. "That is so lame. Besides, I'm not even remotely interested in him. I'm done with men!"

"Well, I'm not done with men," Granny said. "I'll handle this. Now help me out of this pool, Honey Bun. I have got a date with destiny."

I threw my hands up. "Wait! Okay. I'll do it. Just keep Granny in here."

I ran to the bathroom and fluffed my hair, added lip-gloss and a little mascara, and pinched my cheeks for a little bit of color. Staring at my reflection in the mirror, I wondered again why I was doing this. I really didn't want, need, or desire a man.

Who the hell was I kidding? Any woman in their right mind would want *that* man! Of course, I had a duck and a swimming pool in my kitchen, so it was very questionable as to whether I was in my right mind.

"You going to go talk to Hot Lips, or are you going to puss out?" Granny asked, and I rolled my eyes.

"I'm going! Keep your pants on!"

I bounced outside, where Mr. Hot Repair Guy had some sort of gauges hooked up to the big air conditioner thingy behind my house. He looked very professional, and capable, and busy. Probably this was a bad idea. He was probably married or gay. I caught a glimpse at his left hand and saw no ring. Yep, probably gay.

I turned around to head back in the house, tripped over the water hose, fell flat on my face, and before I could stop myself the word "fuck" flew out of my mouth. Embarrassed, I tried to stand, but found that putting weight on my left leg was not a good idea. I'd twisted my ankle and it hurt like hell. I tried standing again, this time putting all my weight on my other foot, but suddenly felt big strong arms surround me. I looked up and came face to face with Mr. Sex on a Stick, and I melted. My Lord, I could have looked into those eyes for an eternity. And his smell. He smelled like fine cologne and sweat. It was intoxicating.

"Hi," I breathed, and I knew it sounded lame, but it was all I could manage. I was just mesmerized by this man.

He helped me to a standing position. "Are you okay?" he asked, and I again tried to put weight on my injured ankle and my knee buckled. "Let's get you sitting," he said, and gathered me up into his arms and carried me to the patio. Once he had me sitting down, he knelt in front of me and took my foot in his hand, removing my shoe then my sock. I crossed my fingers and hoped my feet didn't stink. He bent my foot forward at the ankle and I winced. He frowned and gently tried moving it side to side. I took a fast breath as the pain hit me.

Wasn't this just my luck? Mr. Strong and Handsome shows up on my doorstep and I answer the door with a squirt gun, have a duck pond and a drag queen in my kitchen, and a granny that is itching to get in his pants. And then to redeem myself, I come out to ask him if he would like anything to drink and I bust my ass and drop the "f bomb." Yep, real classy, Stacy.

"Can you move it at all?" he asked. I tried, but it hurt no matter which way I moved it. "You should probably get it x-rayed," he said, and I shook my head.

"Nah, I think I just twisted it. I'll be fine."

He inspected it for swelling or bruising, and when his eyes finally found mine there was a heat so intense, I had to look away. Where in the hell did *that* come from? I felt about a thousand butterflies fluttering in my belly, and I had trouble keeping my breathing even. I felt a blush spread across my face and prayed that he didn't notice. The intensity in his eyes increased, and I knew he knew what effect he was having on me. "Ice," he said, and gently placed my foot on the ground. Before I could protest he was gone, but he returned a few minutes later with a first aid kit that he'd retrieved from his truck. He found the ice pack, banged it on the ground to activate it, and gently applied it to my ankle while he cradled my foot in his hand. His touch ignited me while my ankle was throbbing. It was a strange sensation of pleasure and pain, and I felt like I was going to combust.

He took my hand and brought it to my ankle. "Hold this," he said, and busied himself with the first aid kit. He found a bottle of antiseptic, sprayed some on my knee, and using gauze he cleaned the wound. I looked down at my knee. I was in so much pain with my ankle and so enamored by this magnificent man that I didn't even know I'd hurt my knee. Gently he applied ointment and a Band-Aid, then brought two fingers to his lips, kissed them, and gently applied them to the Band-Aid covering the wound on my knee. My heart stopped. He smiled shyly. "Family trick, seal it with a kiss" he explained, and I was rendered speechless. He had kissed my booboo. Well, he didn't actually kiss it with his lips, but damn it, it was close enough. How freaking sweet was that? His hand moved slowly from my knee back to my ankle, my skin on fire from his touch. He sat on the ground, put my sore ankle in his lap, and re-applied the ice pack.

"Thank you," I said, and because I was worried about his job, I added, "I can take it from here if you need to get back to work."

He seemed perfectly content sitting on my patio holding my foot. "Nope. Work can wait."

"But will you get in trouble?"

He chuckled. "For helping a damsel in distress? Of course not."

Oh. Well, if I'm a damsel then that would make him my knight in.... Nope. Don't go there, I reminded myself.

"Don't you need to call your office and check in or something?"

"Nope, they will call me if they need me."

Oh.

"So how long do you suppose we should keep the ice pack on?" I was actually very thankful for the ice, because it was helping balance the fire I felt in my crotch. Maybe Granny was right. Maybe I needed to get laid. No! I couldn't do casual sex and I was done with relationships. Been there, done that! But I took one long look at Cooper and decided that maybe I could start tomorrow with being done with stuff.

Focus Stacy!

"I think they say twenty minutes on and twenty minutes off," Cooper said, and I barely heard him. He could apply ice to that ankle forever as far as I was concerned. Hell, I'd trip and injure the other one if I had to. I just wanted this feeling to last.

"So… sure is hot out today," I said, trying my hardest to get my mind out of the gutter and away from all these crazy sensations I was feeling.

He blinked and stared up at me through long, thick lashes. "Extremely," he said, and he released my foot and searched in his first aid kit again. "You need to take something for pain and swelling," he said. "Can you take ibuprofen?" I nodded and he shook out three tablets. "I need to get you something to drink. May I go inside?"

With a drag queen, Granny, and Paddington the duck? Um, hell no!

"No."

Cooper smiled. It was a lovely sight. "No?"

"Um, I'm kind of having issues with my kitchen right now," I said, which was totally true.

This got a chuckle from him. "Really? I didn't notice."

"Yeah, crazy story. You would never believe it." Hell, I barely believed it. "But I have an idea. We can use the water hose."

He looked at the small lawn covered in dead grass. "You actually own a water hose?"

"I do, and last time I used it, it worked and everything."

"And when was that?" He seemed amused.

I counted on my fingers. "Um let's see…about eight months ago."

Cooper laughed. "That I believe." He went off in search of the hose and I got a good look at him from behind again. I fanned myself. I didn't know if it was this dry heat or this crazy, hot man, but I felt like I was just moments away from a heat stroke. He found the water hose and followed it to the spigot, which was covered in weeds. He turned it on, and as I predicted it worked just fine. Kinking the hose, he brought it over to me, unkinked it, and let the water flow.

Cooper handed me the ibuprofen and I took them with a drink of water from the hose. I opened my mouth and stuck my tongue out to show him I had been a good girl and taken my medicine. He kinked the hose again and shut the water off, then walked back to the patio and sat on the ground in front of me and took my injured foot in his hand once again. Slowly and very gently, he caressed my foot, drawing teasingly little circles on my flesh. I knew I should have protested, but I didn't because I loved the sensation his touch awakened. I didn't know what was going on between me and this man, but good God almighty it was intense. I closed my eyes and allowed myself to enjoy his touch. I was still done with men, I swore…starting tomorrow! But right now? Well, right now didn't count!

"Have you got a sprinkler?" he asked, and I opened my eyes, confused.

"Sprinkler?" I was freaking melting over here, and he was talking about a damn sprinkler?

"Yeah you know, plugs into a water hose, water shoots out of it."

Smart ass! I cocked my head to the side and pursed my lips. "I know what a sprinkler is."

His glorious smile returned. "Well, do you have one?"

"Nope. I sure don't."

"Then how do you water?"

Did I really need to answer that question? "Um, I don't." Well, I did up until the whole depression thing. And then there was the Thad disaster. My lawn just wasn't a priority. My main priority was staying sober, and remarkably I had managed to do that.

"You should," he said. "This is a perfect little patio for a picnic, or for some romantic, late night stargazing." That was true. It would be amazing if I had someone to do those things with. If I hadn't sworn off men tomorrow, I would rush right out and buy a sprinkler.

"If I water it then I will have to mow it," I said playfully. "And I don't have a lawn mower."

He took my foot in his hand and reapplied the ice pack. "I'm sure you will have men lined up to the street offering to mow it."

I blushed and laughed. "I doubt that."

"I don't," he said seriously, and I saw that heat in his eyes again.

I broke eye contact, unable to take it anymore. Sure, the flirting had been fun, but I couldn't let it continue because I didn't want to lead this man on...and I was in no shape to start a relationship. I was a disaster with a capitol D. And casual sex? While it would probably be loads of fun, I just couldn't do that again. I was an emotional creature and I needed to be loved. I fell too hard and too easily and sex without some emotional commitment was just something I couldn't do. Thad had taught me that lesson and I'd come too far to fall now. But dear Lord, there was something about this man.

"What are you thinking about?" Cooper asked, and I looked away to avoid eye contact.

"I'm thinking about buying a sprinkler."

"Just thinking?" he asked, and I nodded. "Let me know what you decide, Miss Dupree." Before I could form a response his phone rang and he fished it out of his pocket. He excused himself and took the call. It was probably his work wondering where in the hell he was. He was probably in trouble and it was all my fault. I felt absolutely horrible. After he left I would call the company and tell them what a wonderful job he did on my air conditioner. Maybe I would even write a letter or post a testimonial on their website. He returned and slipped his phone back into his pocket.

"Sorry," he said, and resumed ice pack duty.

"If you need to get going, I can handle the ice pack."

He didn't move. "I'm in no hurry, Miss Dupree."

"Stacy."

"Stacy," he said, and the sound of his voice saying my name drove me wild. Why did this man have such an effect on me?

"You should go," I told him, because I couldn't take any more of the crazy chemistry that was going on between us. If he didn't go I might say or do something I would regret, and I couldn't deal with the guilt. Thank God I had a houseful of misfits most likely glued to the window watching my every move. If it weren't for them, I would have probably been naked.

"Should I?"

No! "Yes!"

He frowned. "But I haven't fixed your air-conditioner."

"I don't want you to get in trouble or lose your job. You've gone far beyond the call of duty and I greatly appreciate it, but I think you should just fix my air conditioner and go."

He took my hand and placed it over the ice pack. My whole body ignited from his touch. "If you insist, Miss Dupree."

"Stacy."

"Stacy," he whispered.

Chapter 4

Cooper, the crazy hot repairman, agreed to leave only after he helped me inside. Josie, Granny, and Mickey pretended to be busy in the kitchen while Cooper carefully sat me on the couch. He raised my left leg, placed it on the ottoman, took my hand in his, and brought it to my ankle, skimming my skin along the way. He placed the ice pack on my ankle and slowly released my hand.

"Twenty minutes," he said, and I saluted him.

He didn't move. He just stared at me with those amazing blue eyes, and again it was I who broke eye contact.

"Thanks again, Cooper," I said, and my message was clear. I was dismissing him. He told me this repair was at no charge, had me sign a work ticket, and gave me a copy.

"You're welcome Stacy." He winked and smiled. "Don't hesitate to call me if you have any more trouble with your unit. And keep ice on that ankle." And with that he exited through the front door.

"You can come out now!" I hollered, and Mickey, Josie, and Granny stumbled into the living room.

Josie fanned herself. "Oh! My! God! Stacy!" Tell me about it. "That man is so dreamy, and he is totally into you!"

Mickey gave me a thumbs up. "Score," he said.

Granny pushed her way through and asked when we were going on a date.

"We're not," I informed her, and she sagged onto the couch.

"Well, why the hell not?" she wanted to know, and I didn't want to have this conversation.

"He is obviously wildly attracted to you," Josie said, and I gave her a dismissive wave.

"He's just a nice guy."

"That wants to throw you down in bed and make you scream his name," Josie said, and I entertained the idea for a second. "And you want it too. You guys were totally connecting." She was right, we did connect. But was a connection enough? My head said no, but the tingle in my tummy said yes.

"Look, I fell and he helped me. End of story!"

Mickey shook his head. "Babe, he kissed your owie!"

I pointed my finger at the three of them. "So you *were* watching!"

Josie looked at me like I had two heads. "Um, duh! Of course we were watching!"

"Yeah, and we saw everything!" Granny added, and wiggled her eyebrows at me.

"There was nothing to see," I insisted.

Mickey raised an eyebrow. "Babe, there was plenty to see. He couldn't keep his hands off you. If there had been any more chemistry your head would have exploded."

"Oh my God!" Josie exclaimed. "This is just like a porno. You know, the pretty girl, home alone, the hot repairman shows up on a service call, and before you know it, he is servicing the girl."

"Boom chicka wow wow," Granny said, her eyes glazed.

I rolled my eyes. "He didn't service me! And I wasn't home alone. You guys were here and you saw everything."

"And thank God for that!" Mickey said. "If we weren't here he *would* have serviced you!"

"No he wouldn't have!" I protested. "I am not a slut! Geez!"

"You're a little sluttish," Josie said.

"I am not!"

Mickey held his thumb and index finger a millimeter apart.

"I am so not a slut," I insisted. "If anything, I am the anti-slut!"

Josie giggled. "Anti-slut? Really?"

"Yes, really!" I applied the ice pack to my head. These two were giving me a headache already. "When have I ever acted like a slut? Why, I've never even had a one-night stand. I have a five date rule!"

"Me personally?" Granny slurred. "I have a one date rule. I could be dead in five dates. I say you got to go for it. You only live once." She threw the peace sign and shouted "Yolo!" Okay, Granny was hammered. I gave Mickey the stink eye. The last thing I needed to deal with today was Megan's drunk Granny.

"It's a dumb rule anyways," Josie said. "And it's not like you always follow it."

"Yes I do!"

"Well, you didn't with Thad," Mickey pointed out.

I frowned. I knew this was coming and I really didn't want to go there. "And look how that turned out!"

"So what? That was Thad. That's old news. That has nothing to do with this."

"I've learned my lesson from the Thad debacle."

"Debacle?" Mickey said, his voice calm and smooth. Typical Mickey. Nothing got him excited. "There was no debacle. You and Thad dated. You laughed, you cried, you came. You had some really great sex, spent some time getting to know each other, and realized you weren't meant to be. Big whoop! That's life, Stacy. Time to get over it and move on."

Easier said than done.

"I am over it! But just because I'm over it doesn't mean I have to break my own rules and act like a slut."

"It also doesn't mean you have to lock yourself up and swear off men." Mickey took the ice pack off my head and placed it on my now swollen ankle. His tone softened. "Everyone deserves to be happy, Stace. And you will find that special one. I'm not saying go sleep around or settle for Mr. Right Now. I'm just saying keep an open mind."

He was right. "Okay," I conceded. "I will keep an open mind."

"Good enough," Mickey said as Megan bustled through the door. She visibly relaxed when she saw Granny. Granny was asleep sitting up, her head thrown back, her mouth wide open.

"Oh thank God," she said breathlessly. "I woke up and couldn't find Granny, and I was scared to death. You can't imagine the thoughts that went through my head."

"She's fine," I assured Megan. "She's shitfaced. But she's totally fine."

Megan looked at her watch. "It's only 10:00 A.M. How is she drunk?" I pointed to Mickey, who made a run for it. Megan waddled after him and they disappeared into the kitchen.

"So what are you going to do about Cooper the sexy service technician?" Josie asked, and I rolled my eyes.

"Nothing! I'm not going to do anything about him."

Josie's face lit up and I knew she was up to something. "You should call him."

"He isn't interested. If he wanted me to call him he would have given me his number."

Josie grinned. "So if you had his number you would call him?"

Yes...no! "I don't know! Maybe! Yes!"

Josie offered me her pinky. "Pinky swear?"

I squeezed her pinky with mine. She squealed with delight and produced the work ticket I'd signed. At the very bottom in the left hand corner were four tantalizing words. "Call me sometime, Cooper," followed by a phone number.

I slapped my forehead. "You tricked me!"

"You pinky promised!"

"Didn't count. I had my legs crossed." And that's the way I planned to keep them!

***

For as long as I could remember, the girls, Mickey, and I had always made time to have lunch together once a week. We would go to the same place and sit at the same table every time. We talked about everything under the sun during our lunches, and today would probably be no different, although today I was sure Mr. Sexy and I would be the main topic. I thought about skipping lunch, but the truth was I kind of wanted to talk about Mr. Sexy Pants. I almost felt human again with him. Something about the way he looked at me and talked to me awakened something within me. I didn't feel quite as depressed today, and was kind of excited to start my day. And why not talk about him? It would be better than talking about how I still didn't have a date to Josie's wedding. Or the fact that Scott and the dog walker had moved in together. Yes, Mr. Cooper was a perfect topic for the day. That brought a smile to my face, and I remembered those four little words he'd left for me. Of course, I'd never actually call him, but at least I'd gotten the invitation.

And why shouldn't I call him? I mean, this was the year 2013…women did it all the time; and he did give me his number. What harm could come from giving him a call? It could be fun.

There was, of course, the dilemma of what I would say once I made the call. I had no clue how to start a conversation with that man. Hello could only take me so far. And if I called him it would imply that I was interested in him, which would imply that I wanted to have sex, which would imply that I was a slut. Which I was not!

Ugh. I was over thinking this when there was nothing to think about at all. I was not calling him. I would never see him again. He was just a nice guy doing the right thing for a clumsy girl. End of story!

I had a couple hours before I needed to meet the girls, so I decided to pamper myself. I checked on Granny and found her still passed out on the couch. I hobbled into the bathroom, ran a hot bath, dumped in some lavender bath salts, and set my iPod on shuffle. For the next thirty minutes, I was not going to think about weddings, babies, ex-husbands, boyfriends, sluts, or handsome repair guys. I was just going to clear my mind and go to my happy place.

I was lost in the land of relaxation when the bathroom door opened. Instinctively I covered myself with my hands.

Granny shuffled in and waved. "Don't mind me. I just have to tinkle," she said, and I stared at her open mouthed.

"But I'm in here," I said.

"I know that, but you aren't on the pot."

"But I'm naked!"

She sat and began to tinkle. "So? Naked people don't bother me. I've seen lots of naked people."

Yuk! "Granny, you know I have another bathroom, right? Why didn't you use it?"

"No time. At my age, when you gotta go, you gotta go. I don't have time to mess with stairs." She finished her business, tucked her shirt into her hip hugging jeans, and washed her hands. "All done," she announced, and left the bathroom.

51

I sat in the bathtub in shock. Granny was just too much. She couldn't stay here. I would go crazy...well, crazier! And I could handle a lot. I could handle a pool party in my kitchen. Hell, I could even handle a pet duck. But Granny peeing on my happy place was just too much. I had to talk to Megan. She had to talk to her father and get Granny back home. Soon!

I did the whole deep breathing thing and massaged my temples. I tried thinking happy thoughts. Sunsets and beaches and fluffy little puppies. My breathing slowed and my body began to relax. I was almost back in my happy place when Granny knocked on the bathroom door. Well, at least she knocked.

"Those Bahama Mamas went right through me. I think I need to make a number two. Best you get out while you can." The words weren't even out of her mouth before I was up and out of the tub, wrapped in a towel, and through the bathroom door.

"Do you have any reading material?" she asked. "Preferably, large print?"

***

Back in my room, I dressed in my usual attire; low slung jeans, white peasant blouse, clunky belt, and earthy sandals. I blow dried my hair and then decided to really go all out and curl it. Choosing the sultry, smoky eyes look, I gobbed on the eyeliner, mascara, and eye shadow. Staring at my reflection in the mirror, I applied lip-gloss and puckered my lips. Not bad for an average girl. I didn't have drop-dead looks, but I was, for the most part, happy with what I did have. I dabbed perfume on both wrists and in my cleavage. I looked good, I smelled good, and for the first time in a long time, I *felt* good. Today was going to be the most magnificent day! My smile turned to a frown as I remembered that Granny was downstairs blowing up my bathroom and I had a duck roaming about my house. Oh well. Not going to let it bring me down. After lunch, I would buy a tree, plant that sucker, and move Mr. Paddington outside. One problem solved.

Then, there was Granny. Well, I would figure out the Granny thing. I would talk to Megan and we would work it out. Granny had lived with Megan's parents for over ten years, and Megan's dad got pissed and kicked her out about every couple of months.

He always let her go back. We would just have to wait him out and butter him up. Everything would be a-okay.

I hollered at Granny through the bathroom door. "You okay in there?"

"All systems go," she responded, and I told her I was running to my neighbor's house for a minute and I would be right back.

I limped over to Mrs. Gentry's house. My neighbor yanked open the door before I even had a chance to knock. Mrs. Gentry was in her late seventies or early eighties. She had blue-grey hair teased high and sprayed into place with enough hairspray to cause spontaneous combustion. At barely five feet tall (hair included) I felt like I towered over her. Her voice reflected the fact that she smoked two packs a day, and she had about thirty cats. Mrs. Gentry only left the house twice a week to buy cigarettes and cat food. She never had visitors, but burned up the phone lines; she knew everything about everybody, and was usually the source of most neighborhood rumors, frequently embellishing the truth for the sake of gossip.

Squinting at me with beady little eyes, she stood in the doorway and lit a cigarette.

"What do you want, Ms. Stacy Dupree?" she croaked in her smoker's voice.

Okay, this old lady gave me the creeps. Maybe this wasn't a great idea. "Um, well, I was wondering if you had a kitty crate I could borrow for a couple of days."

She raised a drawn on eyebrow. "You got a kitty?"

"I'm, umm, watching one for a friend," I lied, and she flicked the ash from her cigarette.

"Ahh, Mr. Underwear Model repair man, huh?"

I blushed. I could only imagine the rumors Mrs. Gentry would spread. As soon as I left she would be on the phone. "No, actually, it is for my friend Josie."

"Oh, the slut!" She took a drag of her cigarette. "She doesn't come across as a cat person to me."

"Oh, she loves cats!" I lied, but Mrs. G. looked skeptical. "She has a bunch of cats. She might even open up a cat rescue."

"What's the kitty's name?"

"Huh?"

"The kitty you are watching. What is its name?"

Oh geez! Just give me the damn kennel already! "Paddington. His name is Paddington."

Mrs. G stubbed out her cigarette and squinted at me. "That's a stupid name for a cat."

"I agree. So do you have a kennel I can borrow or not?"

She eyed me suspiciously. "For how long do you need it?"

"Three days. Maybe a week, max."

She disappeared in her house and left me standing outside the door. She returned carrying a medium sized kennel. She handed it over and lit another cigarette. "Make sure you clean it out before you bring it back."

I took the kennel. "Yes, of course. Thank you. I will see you in a few days." I turned and trotted off before she could say anything else, as quickly as I could with a bum leg. I made it back to my door as Granny was coming out. I almost knocked her down getting in the door. I closed the door and peeked out the window. Mrs. Gentry was still standing on her porch smoking a cigarette and watching my house, but she made no movement towards me so I thought I was good. I knew she was a lonely old lady and I should respect her and be nice to her, but she was batshit crazy and nosy, and the last thing I wanted was her and Granny getting together. That would be a complete disaster. Each of them individually could be manageable, but together? I shivered. I didn't even want to think about it.

"Okay, grab the duck," I told Granny. The plan was to get the duck tucked away in the kennel, go to lunch with the girls, buy a tree, plant that sucker, move the pool and Paddington outside, and find a new home for Granny. Then all I had left to do after that was decide what I wanted to be when I grew up, find a man, get married, start a family, begin a career, buy a mini-van, and live happily ever freaking after! One thing at a time, I reminded myself.

I rummaged through my kitchen cabinets until I found a small Tupperware dish that could serve as a make shift pool in the kennel. I placed a small saucer with food on it next to the pool. I didn't know much about ducks, but Josie said they just needed food and water, and Paddington now had both. He would no longer roam free, pooping wherever he pleased.

Granny hollered from the hallway "Incoming," and I saw Paddington waddling my way. I leapt up, forgetting about my bad ankle, and put my weight on that leg. My ankle twisted and my knee buckled. I tried to catch my balance and reached for the wall, but I misjudged the distance and fell face first into the doorjamb. I slid down the jamb and landed on the floor. Paddington watched me curiously then waddled away. Granny ran into the kitchen and grabbed an almost empty roll of paper towels. I took what was left and held them to my now bloody nose and tilted my head back. So much for my most magnificent day!

After a little thinking outside the box and innovation, I got my nosebleed under control, caught Paddington, stored him in the kennel, and gathered Granny. We were late for lunch, and I wanted to get out of the house before the nosy old bat across the street wanted to come over and check out my kitty story. I walked out the door just as Cooper's truck pulled to a stop in front of Mrs. Gentry's house. I tried to hustle to my car, but found it very difficult with my swollen ankle. Cooper saw me and waved, and I returned the wave. I made it to my car and thought I was home free.

Think again.

Granny was taking her damn sweet time, and I was a sitting duck waiting for her in the car. Cooper chose that moment to stroll over and chat. I honked the horn to hurry Granny. I fluffed my hair and plastered my sexiest smile across my face. He reached my car and I politely rolled down the window. He took one look at me and his cheerful smile turned into a concerned frown.

"Hi," I said.

"Ms. Dupree, are you okay?"

I nodded. "I told you, call me Stacy."

"Stacy, what the hell happened?" His frown deepened and he touched my cheek.

I flinched at his touch. "I walked into a door jamb."

The look on his face told me he didn't believe me. I'm not even sure if I would have believed me.

"True story," I insisted, but he didn't appear to be buying it.

He looked toward the house. "Who are you waiting for?"

"Granny."

He raised an eyebrow. "No jealous husband or boyfriend?"

I laughed. "Um, no and no!"

He seemed relieved that there weren't any abusive men in my life beating me and hiding out in the house.

"And I know it sounds unbelievable, but I really did walk into a door jamb. I was chasing the duck, and then I slipped on my sore ankle and I tried to catch myself, but I overcorrected and I biffed it into the door jamb."

"Okay," he said and nodded slowly.

"Then my nose started bleeding, and Granny got me paper towels, only I ran out because my nose wouldn't stop bleeding, so I got inventive." I waved my hand toward my face to indicate the creative use of absorbent tampons I had cleverly shoved in my nostrils to stop my nose from bleeding. "I had to reshape them a bit so they would fit, but they did the trick. So voilà. I even left the strings on so I can pull them out with ease."

He chuckled. "You are quite a mess, Ms. Stacy Dupree."

"Hey, I resemble that remark," I said, and stifled a sob. I laughed unconvincingly to keep from crying, because he was right. I was a mess…a crazy, pathetic, lonely mess. I'd had a good run of bad luck lately, and there seemed no end in sight. Where were those speeding buses when you needed one?

"Are you headed to the hospital?" he asked, and I looked at him, surprised.

"No, why would I?"

He sighed and tried to hide a smile. "Ms. Dupree…." I cocked my head and he corrected himself. "Sorry…Stacy. You have an injured ankle that probably needs to be x-rayed, and now you have a busted nose and two black eyes."

"What?" I grabbed the rearview mirror and adjusted so I could see it, and sure enough, I had the beginning of two black eyes in addition to my purple and bloody nose.

"You probably need to have your nose looked at, and at the very least it might need repacking, only this time from a trained professional. As a matter of fact, I don't even know that I want you to be driving. It appears that you are quite dangerous all on your own. Who knows what damage you could do behind the wheel of a motor vehicle?" He playfully made a grab at my keys.

His eyes lit up and he smiled, and I felt that flip-flop flutter in my belly.

"So what brings you back to my neck of the woods?" I asked, trying to change the subject and calm my nerves. This man affected every nerve and hormone in my body.

"I am here on official business, Ms. Dupree." I laughed and gave him a skeptical look, and he threw my words right back at me. "True story. Mrs. Gentry called in and needs a repair, and I thought I could fix her up and stop in and check on you and see how your ankle is doing. Make sure you have been icing it like you promised."

Oh my! What I would give for an ice pack right about now. "Oh," was all I could manage to say.

He shrugged. "Plus, I brought you a present."

I couldn't hide my shock. My mouth fell open. "A present?"

"Close your eyes," Cooper ordered, and like a kid at Christmas I obeyed. I felt an object being placed in my lap, and when I opened my eyes I discovered a bright yellow sprinkler. I was speechless. I picked it up and turned it around in my hands. Cooper was smiling from ear to ear, and his eyes had a mischievous twinkle in them.

"You bought me a sprinkler?"

He nodded. "I sure did."

"Thank you!"

"You're welcome." He took the sprinkler from me, and then took my hand and used it to point to the place where the hose went. "Now Stacy, you screw the hose into here." I rolled my eyes and stuck my tongue out at him. He didn't hide his laughter. It was a magnificent sound. "Then you set the sprinkler where you want the water to go." He set the sprinkler back in my lap and ran his hand along my skin, from my fingertips to my elbow. My breath caught. "Then you turn it on." His eyes never left mine, and I knew that we were no longer talking about the sprinkler. I parted my lips and looked for a sharp retort, but found none. He had his eyes fixed on me, his expression amused. I was concentrating on slow, deep breathing when I saw Granny peek out the window, and I knew that she was hanging back because of Cooper. I was relieved and scared at the same time; relieved because I wanted this moment to last, but scared because I didn't know where this crazy attraction was going, and I was having a hell of a time controlling my hormones. I had never felt this drawn to or attracted to anyone in my life. The chemistry between us was crazy scary, and I suspected he felt it too.

He pointed to my window. "We have an audience," Cooper laughed, and waved at Granny, who promptly disappeared from the window.

"Yes, she is under the firm belief that I need a boyfriend."

His eyes heated and I blushed. "And what do you believe, Stacy?" His voice was soft and low.

"Well, I just barely got a sprinkler. I believe I need to take baby steps. I believe that when Mr. Right shows up I will know it. Until then...."

"And how will you know?" he asked, and tucked an unruly curly lock of hair behind my ear.

I felt my body heat rise. "I don't know. I just will." Or at least I thought I would. I again tried to change the subject. "What about you? Wife or girlfriend at home?"

"Nope." He shook his head, his eyes never leaving mine. I honked the horn again for Granny.

"Well, Cooper, it was good seeing you again."

His voice was smooth as molasses. "Are you trying to get rid of me, Ms. Dupree?"

"No, of course not!" I lied. "I just don't want you to get in trouble at work. I mean, don't you have to call in when you get to a job and stuff?"

"Nope," he said, and opened my car door. "Let me see your ankle." I turned in the seat and swung both legs out of the car. I was wearing flip-flops, so removing my shoe was a breeze. He gently pushed on my ankle and inspected the swelling. I had a nasty purple bruise forming, and my ankle was sore to the touch. I flinched as Cooper touched the bruise. He frowned.

"It's just bruised," I assured him.

He shook his head. "Can you put any weight on it?"

"Yes," I lied, and I had no idea why I was being dishonest with this man. He seemed genuinely concerned, and it wasn't like I hadn't been flirting with him all day.

"Prove it!" he said, and took my arm to help me out of the car. I willed my ankle to cooperate and tried to put weight on that leg, but it was just too painful. My knee buckled once again and my breathing became shallow. Cooper scooped me up into his arms and shut my car door with his hip.

"Hey, I have a lunch date!" I protested. He was heading to his truck, and I was trying not to enjoy the feel of his skin against mine or his intoxicating scent.

He paused and frowned at the word date, but other than that was undeterred.

"Where are you taking me?" I demanded. He answered that question by opening his truck door, sitting me in the passenger seat, and buckling me in. I opened my mouth to protest and he closed the door on me, shutting out my protests. For the second time in about twenty minutes, I was speechless. Cooper climbed into the truck and cranked the engine.

"Hey! Wait a minute!" He turned to face me. "Where are you taking me?"

"Hospital."

"But I don't want to go!" I argued.

"Tough."

Now I was pissed. I felt my face flush with heat and I was almost yelling. "So you are just going to kidnap me?"

He locked the doors. "Yep."

"Are you freaking crazy? You can't take me somewhere I don't want to go." I was full on yelling at this point, and Cooper was, for the most part, ignoring me.

"You need to go," he said in a low, controlled voice.

Okay, he could be right. I might need to go, but that should be my decision. I looked to the house for Granny. Why in the hell hadn't she come out?

"Wait! I can't leave Granny."

Cooper grinned. "If I go get Granny, will you let me take you to the hospital to get checked out? Granny can be a chaperone."

That got a full chuckle from me. He obviously didn't know who he was dealing with. Granny was by far the worst chaperone I could think of. A porn star would have made a better chaperone.

And it wasn't necessarily that I didn't trust Cooper. He seemed like a good guy. It was really that I didn't trust myself. Cooper was obviously interested in me, although I had no idea why. And I would be lying if I said I wasn't attracted to him and interested in getting to know him better, but the timing was just all wrong. And besides, how did I know that he didn't flirt with all of his female customers like this? Aside from being gorgeous, he was very charismatic. I was quite sure women fell at his feet.

So why was he wasting his time buying me a sprinkler and tending to my injured leg?

"Stacy?" Cooper said, snapping me out of my thoughts.

"Okay," I heard myself say. "But no hospital. I hate hospitals. My physician has an urgent care center. We can go there."

"That's fair enough. I will go get your grandma." He leapt out of the truck and returned minutes later with Granny in tow. He opened the back passenger door for her and helped her climb in. She was beaming, and I knew she was up to no good. She buckled her seatbelt and gave me a thumbs up.

"You can just drop me off at my granddaughter's house. It's just two streets over." I glared at Granny and she wiggled her eyebrows at me.

"Granny, I need you to go with me to the urgent care clinic."

"No can do, Stacy. I have a hot date to get ready for."

Great! Eighty-year-old Granny had a date, and I hadn't had one in over three months.

"Date? With who? Is it with Herbert from the post office?"

"Pfft," Granny sputtered. "Herbert is seventy-five years old. He is almost dead! He's way too old for me."

I rolled my eyes. As much as I shouldn't ask, I couldn't help myself. "Who is your date with then?"

"Matthew." When I shook my head, not understanding, she continued. "Matt, Christina, something or another."

My eyes went wide. "Granny, you have a date with a drag queen?"

"Yes! I'm so excited. And I have got to look the part. Josie is going to help me out." Granny was getting more excited by the minute. "Honey Bun is going to put pink streaks in my hair, and Josie has a bustier and boa she is going to let me borrow." Cooper was quietly laughing and I was mortified. "We are going to one of them drag queen shows. Matt is performing. Then afterwards, we are going to a gay and lesbian bar." Granny grinned. "Granny might get lucky," she said, and I closed my eyes and imagined being anywhere but there.

Cooper put the truck in reverse and off we went. Granny pointed him in the direction of Megan's house, and we pulled up in the drive. Megan came out the door before Cooper had time to put the truck in park. She approached the truck, took one look at me, stifled a smile, and introduced herself to Cooper. Granny brought her up to speed.

"I hear you took good care of my friend earlier," Megan said to Cooper.

Cooper smiled. "It was nothing really."

"Granny says it's pretty bad. She thinks it is broken." I opened my mouth to protest but Megan shushed me. "Stacy, you know darn well Granny was a nurse for over forty years. If she thinks it's broken, it probably is. Either way, I'm glad you are getting it checked out."

"Would you like to go with me?" I pled.

She shook her head. "Can't, Stace. I have lunch with the crew. Then I have to help Granny get glamorous for her date. And Jack and I kind of have a date tonight. You know, the baby will be here before too long, and we won't get many more date nights."

Ugh! Everyone had a date! Even my married friends had dates.

"Looks like you are stuck with me," Cooper said, a playful smile on his lips.

"That's what I'm afraid of," I muttered.

Chapter 5

After a two hour wait, and a handful of x-rays, it was determined that Granny was right...my ankle was indeed broken. The doctor said it was a clean break and should heal nicely, but I needed to see a specialist to confirm that. In the meantime, I was given a boot to wear, crutches to help me get around, some heavy-duty anti-inflammatory medication, and a prescription for pain medication. I was instructed to take it easy, stay off my ankle as much as possible, and take my meds around the clock.

My nose, however, was not broken and would heal up just fine. It did not require being repacked, and the doctor said the swelling and bruising should subside within a few days. Thankfully, the medication would help with both injuries.

After we left the urgent care, Cooper asked me which pharmacy I used and we filled my prescriptions. Cooper fished out a pain pill, dropped it in my hand, and gave me a bottle of water.

"Take this," he said, and I didn't argue. I literally had pain from my head to my toes. If the pain pill could just take the edge off, I would be happy.

"Now we need to feed you," he said. "What do you feel like eating?"

I frowned. "I really don't feel like eating anything."

"Wrong answer," he said, and I just wanted to punch him in the arm. He was so demanding. He definitely liked to be in control. His tone softened. "Stacy, you have to eat. Remember what the doctor said. If you don't eat, the medicine can make you sick to your stomach."

"I have cereal and Pop-Tarts at home."

"That's not a meal. You need real food. Now, where to?"

I surveyed my surroundings. There were a couple of fast food restaurants, a Chinese buffet, and a pizza place. As much as I loved Chinese food, I didn't think I could navigate the buffet line in my new highly fashionable "boot" that the doctor had so graciously prescribed. Cooper had been adamant about picking it up as soon as we left the urgent care. I had waited in the truck, and as soon as he reached me he'd had me turn sideways and he gently and carefully put it on my foot. It was big and bulky and was proving to be a real pain in the ass. Just like Cooper. I chuckled, and Cooper gave me a bewildered look.

"What's it going to be, Stacy? I'll get you anything you want."

Okay, so he was a *sweet* pain in the ass. "Pizza. Pizza will do just fine."

Cooper looked relieved and put the truck into drive. "If pizza is what the lady wants, that's what she shall have." He drove to the pizza place and idled in the parking lot. "Shall we go in or do you want to take it to go?"

I really felt like hell. I just wanted to go home. "Do you mind if we take it to go?"

"Nope, I'd actually prefer that as well. How do you take your pizza?"

"I'm easy. I like everything…lay it on me."

He laughed. "One kitchen sink coming right up!" He exited the truck and entered the pizza place. I leaned my head on the windshield and closed my eyes. It had been a hell of a day. I had a headache from hell, my nose was swollen and sore, my knee was busted all to hell, my ankle was broken, and my eyes were ringed in a lovely shade of purple. One thing was for sure, today couldn't get any worse. I couldn't wait to get home, strip down, and crawl into by big comfortable bed.

I opened my eyes and stole a glimpse of Cooper from behind. And wasn't that just a feast for my eyes? I took in his long legs, broad shoulders, and perfect butt. I admired his confident posture and the graceful way he moved. Man oh man, why did he have to be so damned handsome? He had me wanting to break all of my own rules. Of course, they were probably just a bunch of dumb rules anyways. I mean, they'd served me well so far. No man, no job, no um… life. I sank back into the seat. Geez, I really was a mess.

I decided not to focus on me and instead turned my focus back to Cooper, who was waiting patiently for the pizza. He had looked back at the truck and caught me staring. A curious smile played across his lips, and he gave me a little wave. Like an idiot, I waved back.

That's when I saw movement in the side mirror of the truck. I heard squealing brakes, and saw a black van cut off a little red car. The passenger from the van, dressed in all gray, exited the van, opened the door on the little red car, jerked the driver, a young girl, out, and attempted to throw her in the van. She put up a fight, though, and I knew that I had to help her. I jumped out of the truck and hobbled as fast as I could to the girl's aid. The girl was holding her own, clawing at the gray man's eyes.

I did a quick assessment of anything I could use as a weapon. I had nothing on me…no keys, no purse, no belt. Nothing. Although I did have a boot. I took it off, silently limped up to the scene, and smacked Mr. Scumbag in the back of the head with the boot as hard as I could.

At first, I thought it stunned him. Turned out, I had just pissed him off. He threw the girl to the ground and charged at me, taking me down at the waist. My boot went flying and I hit the ground hard. I managed to connect my heel with the jerks nuts and his knees buckled. I rolled over and tried to get in a fighting stance, but it wasn't necessary. Cooper was running across the street to the scene and the thug had hauled ass to his van. Seconds later, the van sped away. The girl from the red car was dazed and in shock, and I was trying to get to her. Cooper made it to me, hit his knees, and picked me up off the ground. I pushed him away.

"Help the girl," I said, and Cooper locked eyes with me and nodded once. Hesitating for only a second, he went to the girl. A crowd was forming and people were on cell phones, presumably calling the police.

I managed to stand up and hopped over to Cooper and the girl, whose name was Avery. Besides being scared, she was crazy pissed. Her attacker should be glad he escaped when he did. Had he not she probably would have pummeled him. Cooper calmed

Avery down enough that she was able to call her father as we heard the faint sound of sirens. Help was on the way.

Cooper turned his attention back to me. He ran his eyes over the length of my body, checking for new wounds or injuries.

"You're okay?" he asked me.

I nodded. Cooper ran his hands roughly through his sandy brown hair, then paced back and forth a couple of times, rubbing his neck. Finally, he shook it off and retrieved my boot.

"Sit," he said, and I shook my head.

"Can't. My ass hurts."

"Come again?"

I frowned. "Well, I would sit but my ass hurts. When that guy took me down I landed flat on my ass. I think it's broken."

Cooper smiled. "You broke your ass?"

I scoffed. "Well, *I* didn't do it, and I'm not even sure it's broke. It just feels like it's broke."

"Let me take a look at it," Cooper said, a note of mischief in his voice.

That got a smile out of me. "Yeah right! You just want to gawk at my ass."

Cooper flashed me the choirboy smile. "Me? Never! I'm insulted." He didn't look insulted. He looked like he was having a blast. "Here I am genuinely concerned about you and your ass, and you accuse me of gawking." He grinned. "But for the record, I have already gawked, and I have to say you have a truly amazing ass."

I rolled my eyes and waved him off. "Please, you're going to make me blush."

His tone turned serious. "That was very brave of you, Stacy. I mean, you're in a boot, for goodness sake, and that guy out weighed you by at least seventy-five pounds. You could have been really hurt. Worse than a broken butt."

I looked at the ground. "I know that, but I would rather me be hurt than that girl. She needed help, so I helped her. I didn't really think about it. I just did it."

"And you are sure you are okay?"

I took a deep breath and nodded. "Yep. For the most part I think I'm fine. My ass hurts and my pride is a little hurt because the guy got away, but all in all I'll live."

"Did you get a good look at him?"

I frowned. "It all happened really fast. I mean, I saw him but I'm not sure I really saw him, if you know what I mean."

The police had arrived and swarmed Avery. A black Escalade skidded to a stop and a frantic man jumped out and ran to the girl. I assumed this had to be Avery's father. Poor guy. His daughter had narrowly escaped being kidnapped, and here I was whining about a broken butt. He spoke to his daughter for a moment and she pointed him to me. He made his way over to me and graciously thanked me for helping his daughter. I told him it was no problem, I was just doing what anyone else would have done.

After he returned to his daughter, Cooper leaned me against his truck and raised my foot. He fastened my boot back in place carefully and gently lowered my foot. I had quite the issue. It hurt to stand up and put weight on my ankle, but the way my butt felt I was pretty sure sitting wasn't an option either. I was such a mess.

"After the police are done with us, I am going to feed you and lock you up in a rubber room," he laughed. "You are an accident waiting to happen."

I sighed. "I have had a hell of a day," I admitted, and rubbed my forehead.

Cooper laughed. "You can say that again."

Before I got the chance, a round, middle-aged officer with kind eyes and a gray goatee approached me. His badge said Officer Redman. He introduced himself and we shook hands.

"I hear you were a hero today," he said.

I shook my head and waved him off. "No sir. Not a hero. I just helped someone who needed help."

His weathered face wore a skeptical look. "If it weren't for you her assailant could have succeeded in kidnapping her. You may very well have saved her life."

I felt my emotions getting the best of me. I sucked it up and soldiered through. I would cry, but I wouldn't do it here in front of two men I'd just met.

"I was just in the right place at the right time. That's all. I did what anyone in my shoes would have done."

Officer Redman smiled and took a notepad from his pocket. "Ms. Dupree, are you okay to answer a few questions?"

"Yes of course," I replied, and looked for a place to sit. As bad as my butt hurt, my ankle hurt worse. Boot or no boot, my ankle was throbbing and I couldn't take it anymore.

Officer Redman pointed me to a bench on the sidewalk. I gently lowered myself down on the bench, and abandoned that idea as soon as my butt hit the metal. Cooper explained to the officer that I had gone down ass first, and Officer Redman had to stifle a laugh. Cooper sat on the bench, spread his legs apart, and pulled me to a sitting position in his lap. I was kind of just hanging there, my butt not touching anything, my legs thrown over his and my low back resting on his other thigh. Cooper rested one large hand in the small of my back and loosely draped the other across my legs. I felt my temperature rise and my cheeks flush, but I was too comfortable to move. Truth be told, I was very much enjoying being this close to this crazy sexy man. Breathing in his scent and feeling his warmth was making me dizzy, and I was finding it hard to concentrate on Officer Redman.

It wasn't easy, but I was eventually able to focus and get through Officer Redman's thorough questions. Turned out I had actually seen more than I thought I had. I was amazed with how Officer Redman was able to coax those details from my memory. After declining Officer Redman's offer to get me an ambulance and giving him all of my contact information, Cooper and I were free to go. Cooper hefted me up and carried me to his truck. I opened the door and he gently sat me in the plush leather seat.

Just as we were about to pull out of the parking lot, Megan's car skidded to a stop and she tried unsuccessfully to jump out. Her belly was trapped by the steering wheel. After realizing her problem, she tilted the wheel up, turned sideways in her seat, and levered herself out of the car. She waddled to Cooper's truck in a bathrobe and slippers and yanked the door open. Her hair was wrapped in a plush pink towel and she had a huge frown on her face.

She hugged me tight. "I came as soon as I heard. Are you okay?"

I laughed. "Yes, Megan. I'm fine. Little sore, but other than that I'm just fine."

Megan breathed a sigh of relief. "Oh, thank God. I was worried sick."

I already knew the answer but had to ask anyways. "How did you find out?"

Megan gave me a look that said "duh." "My mom called me. She said Mrs. Phillips was leaving the bookstore when she saw a black van try to run you over. Then she saw the man throw you on the ground and try to steal your boot. She said you kicked him in the gonads and then some hot guy, presumably um...you...." She gestured to Cooper. "Restrained you from continuing to kick the bad guy's ass. She said you got beat up pretty bad." Megan took in the busted nose, black eyes, and boot. "Of course, you pretty much kicked your own ass before this latest scuffle, so it's kind of hard to tell." She laughed.

"You should see the other guy."

"From what I heard he hauled ass the minute he got to his feet."

"Yes, it's a bummer really. I was just getting started. You know I'm a badass."

Megan smiled and rubbed her belly. "I'm sure he was scared shitless, Stace." She turned her attention to Cooper. "And once again, thank you for taking care of my friend. She isn't usually so reckless or destructive." Megan pursed her lips. "Although, she always has been quite the scrapper." Somehow that little tidbit of information didn't seem to surprise Cooper.

Turning her attention back to me she said, "You should probably call your mother. By now she has probably already heard, and I'm sure the story has been embellished quite a bit."

I moaned. After the day I'd had, the last thing I needed was a conversation with my mother, but I dutifully reached into my back pocket for my phone and came up empty. I searched around the truck, and still no phone. Cooper offered to retrace our steps to see if it had fallen out of my pocket during the scuffle, and I asked Megan to call my cell number so that maybe we could hear it ring. When she tried it went straight to voicemail, indicating that it had been turned off. Cooper returned empty-handed, shaking his head.

Which meant the kidnapper had probably taken it with him, which meant I had no phone and had lost all of my contacts.

Again. Geez. I really needed to learn more about technology and backing up my data...I was getting tired of doing everything the hard way.

"I'll call your mom for you," Megan said, and I breathed a sigh of relief.

"Thanks Meg."

"You're welcome. Now how about you? Do you need me to do anything else? Are you okay?" She glanced towards Cooper, no doubt sending a small signal that she would rescue Stacy from Cooper if need be.

I squeezed Megan's hand and gave her a small smile. "No Meg, I think I'm good. Go get ready for your date tonight."

Megan nodded. "Okay; if you need me call me."

"I will. Thank you," I said. And then as Megan was walking away, I added. "Come back, I need you to write down your number."

Cooper laughed and found a piece of paper and handed it to Megan. Megan jotted her number down and gave me a hug before leaving.

"Love you, Stace," Megan said.

I buckled my seatbelt. "Love you too, Meg."

***

Cooper settled into the driver's seat and fastened his own seat belt. He started his truck, and then turned his attention to Stacy.

"How long have you two been friends?" Cooper asked.

"Since age two," she said, smiling at the memories Megan and she had made together.

"And you don't know her phone number?" Cooper asked, amused.

"Hey, what can I say? I'm bad with numbers."

"What are you good with?" he asked playfully.

"Wouldn't you like to know?" Stacy said, and Cooper thought he would like to know indeed.

***

It was just dinnertime. He was just going to cook her something to eat, make sure she took her medicine, and then he was out of there. He would not have sex with her. This was the conversation he was playing constantly in his head. He mentally listed all the reasons why he shouldn't fuck her, trying to convince himself.

She was too old for him. He usually liked them under twenty-five. She was a brunette, his preference was blonde. She was thick and curvy, he was more into the stick thin look. She was a walking disaster, and he was trying to cut the drama out of his life. She was the type you made love to and cuddled with after; he was more of a love 'em and leave 'em kind of guy. She was so not his type.

Oh, who was he kidding? She was beautiful and hot, and she would for sure keep him on his toes. She was funny and witty, and he was pretty sure she had a stubborn streak a mile wide. She intrigued him with those big hazel eyes that he could get lost in, and that perfect set of pouty lips that begged to be kissed. She had an amazing rack and that ass that was sheer perfection. He just wanted to throw her down and lose himself in her. He was in trouble. Bigtime.

Trying to rid the thoughts of her from his mind, he focused on the task of gathering the ingredients for dinner. He grabbed the pasta and what he needed for his famous Alfredo sauce and headed to the checkout. The cashier was young and cute, and on any other day he would have left the store with her phone number. Today though, he wasn't interested in pursuing her, which was weird. He was always interested in beautiful women. At that moment, his thoughts were consumed with the crazy, accident prone mess of a woman in his truck. She was like a one-woman wrecking ball. She was clumsy, feisty, goofy, and sexy as sin, even with a couple of black eyes and a busted nose. What the hell was wrong with him, and why was he letting this mess of a woman get under his skin? He knew better than to get involved with a woman like Stacy Dupree. The cashier was more his type, and maybe, just maybe, she could help him forget all about Stacy.

He gave the perky little cashier his best panty dropper smile. She blushed, and he knew at that moment he could have her number in a heartbeat. But surprisingly, he didn't want it. All he wanted was the crazy mess in his truck...although, getting the cashier's number didn't mean he had to call her. It was always good to have a backup plan. And she *was* super hot!

He was pondering this when he heard someone call his name. He looked towards the source and cringed. A blonde headed, blue-eyed college girl that he'd spent a wild sex filled night with was making her way over to him. She was wearing an apron, but he couldn't see her nametag, and when she began sacking his groceries, he had nowhere to run. He was so screwed. He searched his memory bank for her name, and although he knew it started with a ck sound, he was at a loss otherwise.

"Hey Cooper," she said in a flirty tone.

"Hello, Candice." He thought that was her name. At least he hoped so. It would be embarrassing if it wasn't.

"It's Kelsey," she said, deadpan, then undeterred she flipped her long blonde hair over her shoulder and leaned in close, whispering in his ear. "You never called," she said, and he stepped back to put some space between them.

"Yeah, I'm sorry about that. This is my busy time." He used his standard summer excuse.

Kelsey bit her bottom lip. "Um, that was like six months ago."

Oops. Okay, time for excuse number two. "Well, I broke my phone and lost all of my numbers."

"I thought maybe you lost my number, that's why I called you and left you voicemail," she said, and Cooper shifted his feet. Not only did he want to get back to Stacy, who was waiting for him in the truck, but he also didn't want to blow his chances with the cashier. "Four times," she added. Shit. How was he going to wiggle out of this one?

The cashier smirked at him and gave him his total. He dug his wallet out and, thankful for the distraction, busied himself with the task of sliding his card and entering his pin number. Kelsey continued to bag his groceries, cramming his purchases in the plastic bag with more force than necessary. The cashier was biting back a grin. Cooper paid and made an attempt to scoop up his bags, but Kelsey beat him to the punch. "Allow me," she said.

He responded with, "Thanks, but that's not necessary."

"I insist," Kelsey replied, and having no other choice, Cooper relented and allowed her to place his bags in a cart and push it out to the parking lot. He led her to his truck and helped her put the groceries in the back. Kelsey glanced in the cab of the truck, eyed Stacy, and shot Cooper a dirty look. She removed a pen from her pocket, took Cooper's hand, and scribbled her number on his palm. She then held her palm out for Cooper to do the same. Cooper placed a five-dollar bill in her hand, thanked her for her assistance, and slammed his tailgate. Kelsey pouted and stomped away.

Cooper quickly climbed into his truck and got the hell out of there, hoping Stacy hadn't seen the little exchange between him and Kelsey. If she'd noticed, she didn't mention it. She had her head rested on the window, her eyes closed and her lips slightly parted. She looked so damn cute he couldn't resist touching her. He lightly brushed her cheek with the backs of his fingers, and she smiled, opened her eyes, and stretched, causing the fabric to pull tight against her breasts, and he knew at that moment he had to have her. There was something about this girl, and he wouldn't be satisfied until he had fucked her out of his system.

***

Cooper and I were sitting in his truck in front of my house. To say the moment was awkward would be an understatement. After the whole kidnapping incident, we had, at Cooper's insistence, gone to the Sprint store and got me a replacement phone. The pain medicine was really working at that point and making me drowsy, so I told Cooper I just wanted to go home. He still insisted on feeding me, and I was too hungry to argue. When he had offered to cook me dinner I was shocked, but I was enjoying his company, and since I never cooked anything more than a Pop-Tart, a home cooked meal sounded amazing.

That was then.

Now, I was having second thoughts.

Cooper looked too good, smelled even better, and don't think my body wasn't responding. My sex-o-meter was on full alert and I couldn't keep my mind out of the gutter. This whole being a good girl thing was for the birds.

Cooper was looking at me, obviously expecting me to exit the truck and invite him into my home. Since I couldn't trust my body and mind, I needed to set a few things straight before our evening could progress.

"Um, Cooper," I said, not knowing how to say this without coming across as a bitch or a lunatic.

Cooper turned to face me. "Yes?"

I fidgeted in my seat and unbuckled my seat belt. "Before we go in we need to talk."

Cooper turned off the truck and nodded slowly. "Okay."

I folded my hands in my lap and stared at them. "I, um...well, I just wanted to let you know that this is not a date."

Cooper smiled. "Of course it isn't."

"And I don't put out, so there will be no sex."

His eyes glittered as his smile reached them. "Never crossed my mind."

"And I don't want or need a man," I continued. "As a matter of fact, I am done with men, so if you have any expectations, now would be the time for you to make your exit."

Cooper shook his head. "I owe you dinner."

"And I'm looking forward to it. I just don't want to lead you on."

"And I appreciate that, Stacy," he said. "And for the record, I have no expectations other than having dinner with an attractive woman I would be happy to call my friend."

I relaxed. "Then what are we waiting for? I'm starving. Feed me already!"

***

Cooper moved around my house with a relaxed ease. It was obvious he knew his way around a kitchen, and he looked good while doing it. He'd been quite the gentlemen all day, and even more so since we arrived at my house. After helping me out of his truck and into the house, he had brought in all the groceries and gone about familiarizing himself with my kitchen. He took in the lawn chairs, the wading pool, and the squirt guns with a smile. I, on the other hand, was not happy to see those things, and although they had helped lift my mood earlier, they were no longer having the same effect. I opened a cabinet, took out a pitcher, and opened the back door. I then filled the pitcher from the pool and tossed the water out the back door. I repeated the process while Cooper stared at me, his eyes glittering with humor. I limped back to the pool to fill the pitcher again, and Cooper wordlessly went out the back door. I continued bailing water from the pool and threw it out the back door without looking and heard Cooper curse. I peeked out and found him standing just outside the door, soaking wet, holding my water hose.

"I'm so sorry," I said, and tried to move quickly to the counter to retrieve a hand towel.

Cooper shook his head to rid the excess water from his hair. "It's alright, Stacy. It's hot in here anyways. I needed to cool off." He seemed to take it in stride but I was devastated. This had been the most embarrassing day of my life so far. I just wanted it to end. I felt the tears start, and this time I didn't fight them. Cooper dropped the water hose and steered me to a lawn chair. His expression was of compassion and concern, and I couldn't help but notice the smoldering intensity in his eyes. I was truly mesmerized and had completely lost control of my tears. I was full on crying now, and Cooper knelt in front of me on his knees, his hands on my thighs.

"Don't cry, Stacy," he said softly, and that made me cry even more. He pulled my chin to face him. "What's wrong, honey?" he asked, and I just shook my head.

"Can you please just leave?" I ground out between sobs. He looked me in the eye and his expression was even hotter than before.

"I can't leave you here like this, alone." He rubbed my cheek and wiped my tears. "You need to eat and you're upset. Just tell me what to do and I'll do it. How can I help?"

"You can run out of here as fast as you can and never look back."

"And what will you do?"

"I don't know...go to bed and sleep the rest of this wretched day away before I can break anything or embarrass myself any further."

Cooper unfolded another lawn chair and sat facing me. He took my hands in his. "Why are you embarrassed? You have nothing to be embarrassed about. You've had a rough day. You're entitled to cry."

"It's not just that, Cooper." I wiped my eyes. "I'm a mess! A huge mess. I mean, I have a freaking wading pool in my kitchen and a duck pinned up in a cat cage. I have a broken ankle, busted nose, black eyes, and a possibly broken butt. And I've achieved almost all of that on my own. Add to that the fact that I will be thirty in a month and I have no career, no man, no kids, and can't even keep a plant alive. I can't cook, suck at math, sweep dust under the rug, and my driving is horrible." Cooper used the opportunity to pull me into his lap when I stopped for a breath. "My last date was with a drag queen, my toes are crooked, and I still wear my retainer. I—"

Cooper stopped my words by covering my mouth with his. His kiss was explorative and took me off guard, and while I didn't kiss him back, I didn't exactly pull away. I loved the feel of his stubbled jaw against my wet cheek, his sweet scent, and the warmth of his body pressed against mine. I knew this was a bad idea, but at that exact moment, I didn't care. I fisted my hands in his hair and gave into the kiss, claiming his mouth greedily. He deepened the kiss and his hands explored my neck, my back, and my waist. He pulled me even closer, as if he couldn't get me close enough. I felt the same way, and experienced the desire to connect completely with him.

And then I came to my senses. I broke the kiss, but couldn't bring myself to leave the comfort of his lap. He rested his forehead on mine and we each took a deep breath.

"I'm sorry," he said, and I shook my head.

"No, I'm sorry. That was my fault."

"I'll go," he said, but made no move to leave, and I honestly I didn't want him to go. I didn't want him to stay either. I really didn't know what I wanted. I hugged him tighter.

"I don't want you to go," I told him.

His fingers drew tiny little circles on my back. "I'll stay then."

I inhaled his intoxicating scent once again. "I don't want you to stay," I breathed, and he laughed.

"What exactly do you want, Ms. Dupree?"

You! "I don't know," I said.

Cooper laughed again and I loved the sound. "I knew you were going to say that!"

I cocked my head. "And how did you know that?" I asked playfully. "Are you a mind reader?"

That got me a sweet but innocent smile. "Yes ma'am."

I readjusted myself in his lap. "Okay, tell me what I'm thinking right now."

His bottomless blue eyes burned into mine. "You're thinking, 'I'm starving! Feed me already!'"

I smiled, my tears forgotten. "Wow!" I exclaimed. "You really are good at this."

We spent the next hour cleaning up the mess in my kitchen. Cooper retrieved the water hose and used it to siphon the water out of the pool. I let Paddington the duck out of the kennel to take care of his little ducky business, refreshed his water and food bowls, and laughed as Cooper ran all over the yard trying to catch him so he could be returned to the kennel. After that chore was done, Cooper retrieved a floatie from the pool, sat it on a barstool, and plopped me on top of it. He turned me sideways, propped my boot on another bar stool, and ordered me to stay put. He made me a large glass of iced tea and went about preparing dinner as I sat and watched.

And watching Cooper move about in my kitchen was no hardship. He was big, at least six feet tall with broad shoulders and a lean waist. I placed his weight at right about two hundred pounds. His arms were well toned, his biceps tugging on his T-shirt as he moved. His hands were large, calloused, and tanned...a working man's hands. I closed my eyes and remembered the feel of those hands exploring my body from our kiss moments ago and I shuddered. Ugh! Why was this so difficult? Why did I have to be the self-proclaimed anti-slut? I mean, I could have died that day. Wasn't I entitled to a little fun? And I had no doubt in my mind that Cooper would be a little — scratch that — a lot of fun.

Cooper stirred his Alfredo sauce and added a dash of salt. He threw a little over his left shoulder for good luck, and I had to laugh. I hadn't seen anyone do that since I was a kid working in the kitchen with my mother. Speaking of which, I really needed to call my mom. Though we weren't too close anymore, I did owe it to her to let her know what had happened and that I was okay. Gossip spread quickly in our town, and I would hate for her to hear about the whole incident from someone else.

I searched for my phone and then remembered that I didn't have any of my contacts. My address book was in my nightstand all the way down the hall in my bedroom. I felt like hell and hurt from my head to my toes. I didn't have the energy to go get my address book. I would call her before bed, I decided. Bed...Cooper...I shook my head. No, I definitely wasn't going anywhere near a bed while Cooper was there.

Cooper tasted his sauce, cocked his head, and closed his eyes. "Yum," he said and filled a spoon with sauce for me to taste and fed it to me.

"Mmm," I heard myself mumble, and felt my mouth water for more. I didn't know if my reaction was a result of the sauce or the fact that Cooper had seductively fed it to me. Happy with his sauce, he dropped the penne into boiling and seasoned water, then searched through the drawers of my kitchen.

"What are you looking for?" I asked, although I rarely used my kitchen so I probably wouldn't be much help to him.

He pulled a bottle of wine out of the grocery bag. "Corkscrew?" he asked, and I shook my head.

"I don't have one," I said, and he looked surprised. I didn't want to get into the issue of my sobriety, so I simply said, "I don't drink. Sorry. I have tea and soda though." He nodded, tucked the wine back in the bag, and filled a glass with ice for tea. He didn't ask me to expand about the drinking, and I didn't offer anything else. I didn't know him well enough to feel comfortable discussing my struggles with alcohol with him. I liked that he didn't pry, and I liked that the silence between us was comfortable.

The food was cooking and didn't need his immediate attention, so he turned it to me. "So," he started. "Stacy Dupree. Tell me about yourself."

I laughed. "There's not much to tell." He gestured for me to go on. "Well, let's see, I'm almost thirty and divorced, no kids. Not even a dog. I'm an only child. I grew up here, but out in the country. My mom is...well, my mom is just a little different."

"Different can be good," he offered.

"Well, in my mom's case it just means that she kind of beats to her own drum. She's a hippy, actually. She lives off the land and is big into recycling and living organic."

"Are you close?" he asked, refilling my tea glass.

"We aren't exactly close, but we aren't distant either." I looked up at the ceiling, trying to figure out how to word this in the short version. I didn't think "My mom is a pothead stuck in the '70s" was information I should reveal on a first date. I mentally slapped myself. This is NOT a date, I reminded myself. I decided turning the tables to him was my best option. "What about you, Cooper? Parents? Brothers or sisters?"

He nodded and peeled cloves of garlic. "My parents are still putting up with each other...just celebrated their fortieth wedding anniversary. I have three sisters, no brothers."

"Oh, so you are the only boy? I bet you are spoiled rotten, being fawned over by all those women."

His guilty grin said it all. "Me spoiled? Nah!"

I didn't believe that for a second. "Marriage? Kids?"

"Nope and nope," he said, and combined the garlic with some butter and began to whip it. "Although I do have four nephews and a niece."

"That's the best kind, I've heard. Spoil them, then send 'em home." I couldn't wait for Megan and Jack to make me an auntie.

"Oh, I do my fair share of that," he said with a smile. "What do you do for a living? Well, I mean when you aren't foiling kidnappings or chasing ducks."

I sighed. I had asked myself that same question repeatedly since my divorce. "I am still trying to figure out what I want to be when I grow up," I said, and laughed. "Right now I'm thinking stunt double, but that could change if Hollywood doesn't call soon. I was fired from the circus so...."

Cooper laughed again, and I decided that I absolutely could not get enough of that magical laugh. Actually, it was growing painfully obvious that I couldn't get enough of Cooper period. The man had quite the effect on me.

He had begun to cut the french bread into slices, and I thought that maybe I should offer to help. Of course, I would probably just chop a finger off or catch the house on fire or something. "I'm actually thinking about going back to school," I said, breaking the silence.

Cooper raised his eyebrows. "Really? What for? Any idea?"

"Promise you won't laugh?"

"Cross my heart."

"Cake decorator." Cooper kept his promise and didn't laugh. On the outside. I was quite sure he was laughing on the inside though.

"They teach that in college?" he asked, keeping his humor in check.

"Well, I'm not sure, but probably. I mean, they have classes for everything these days."

"Can you bake?" Cooper asked skeptically.

"Um, no." I was quite sure he knew the answer to that since I didn't even know how to turn the oven on to preheat for the bread.

"Are you the artsy type?"

I laughed. "Nope again. But I love cake! I'm a cake connoisseur." Cooper's expression was skeptical. "Really! I am! And I know a lot about it because I watch the shows about it on TV."

"Have you ever baked a cake?"

"Well, no, but it can't be that hard. My friend Josie baked me a cake once, and if she can do it, anyone can. What about you, Cooper? Can you bake a cake?" I was sure he probably could. I found it hard to believe there was anything he wasn't good at.

He covered the bread with the garlic butter spread. "Sure. I baked my mom a cake for her birthday."

I was impressed. What a sweet gesture. "So you can teach me?"

He put the bread in the oven. "Sure. I'd love to."

I smiled. "Then it's a date," I said before I had a chance to think about what I was saying. "I mean, it's not a date date, but...well, it's just a figure of speech."

Cooper's expression turned serious and his eyes burned through me. "Can I ask you a serious question?"

No! "Sure."

"What have you got against dating?"

"Oh, I've sworn off men," I said offhandedly.

"Mind if I ask why?"

I tried to answer carefully. "I just...well, I don't have the best track record when it comes to men. I tend to attract assholes." Cooper looked disappointed. "Not that I'm calling you an asshole," I said in a rush. "And of course this isn't a date, as you know." Cooper busied himself with draining the pasta. "And I didn't mean to imply that I'm attracted to you. I mean I could be.

If I hadn't sworn off men." I frowned. Okay, that sounded incredibly lame. I was just digging myself a hole.

Cooper abandoned the pasta and leaned with both elbows on the counter, his mouth inches from mine. "Well, I am attracted to you, Miss Stacy Dupree." I swallowed hard and prepared myself for the kiss I knew was coming. "And I'd like to get the chance to take you on a real date and show you I'm not an asshole." He cupped my chin and raised my face to his. Gently he placed a whisper of a kiss on my lips. I closed my eyes, ready for more, but he ended the kiss as gently as he'd started. I felt a twinge of disappointment. I opened my eyes and my focus went directly to his mouth. He lowered his gaze to my lips and I had to look away. The raw attraction in his eyes was intense. This chemistry, this magnetism between us, was becoming too much for me to handle.

I blushed beat red and cleared my throat, and Cooper turned his attention back to the food. My stomach growled, and I was glad for the distraction as he began plating our dinner. I had to admit that I was crazy hungry and looking forward to experiencing Cooper's cooking. After refilling my tea glass, Cooper placed a delicious looking plate in front of me and announced that dinner was served.

"This looks amazing!" I told him truthfully.

Cooper raised his glass and I did the same. We clinked glasses. "Cheers," he said, and then I followed suit.

***

I woke up about 3:00 A.M. in my bed, fully dressed minus my boot. My phone was beeping at me, indicating I had a text message. At 3:00 A.M.? Who in the hell could be texting me at this hour? My room was pitch black, the only illumination from my alarm clock. My head hurt like hell and I felt hung over, although I hadn't had a drink in over three years. My heart hammered in my chest as I tried to recall how I had gotten there. The last thing I remembered was eating dinner with Cooper.

Dinner had been tasty, and I had had a second helping of everything. Mid-way through dinner, Cooper had reminded me that I needed to take my pain medication, and I did what I was told. The doctor at urgent care had said tomorrow would probably be the worst day, and had advised me to stay ahead of

81

the pain by taking my meds around the clock. I reached around on my bed for my cell phone, and almost jumped out of my skin when my hand landed on a large lump on the other side of the bed. I traced the lump with my hand…the lump rolled over, a big hairy arm swung around my waist, and a stubbled cheek nestled in my chest. Cooper!

I panicked. What on earth had I done? I was embarrassed, and then I became pissed. Really pissed! I thought he had been such a nice guy, maybe the last one left on earth, but he had taken advantage of me the first chance he got. That son of a bitch! I was going to kill him! I broke away from my uninvited bedmate, positioned myself where I was laying sideways, and drew my knees into my chest. I let out a disgusted sigh, took a deep breath, and then kicked the lump with all my might, which subsequently made my ankle burst with pain.

I heard a yelp and then a thud as my unwanted sleeping companion catapulted to the floor. I jumped out of bed, grabbed my pillow, and started beating the hell out of him. I heard my name whispered and then scrambling on the floor as Mr. Asshole tried to get away. I felt around with my toes until I located my intruder, and I swung my foot in that general direction. He caught my foot with his hand and I tripped, falling on top of him. He growled "oowww," grabbed my hands, and wrapped his legs around me to hold me in place.

I screamed at the top of my lungs and hoped my nosy neighbor Mr. Sanders would hear my screams. He was a card carrying member of the NRA, and would probably show up packing heat. Suddenly, the door creaked open, and the room was flooded with faint light from the hallway. Granny stood there in her housecoat, a bottle of moonshine in her hand. I still couldn't see my intruder's face, but I was on top of him trying to claw his eyes out while he was slapping at my hands. I yelled at Granny for help, and she swung the moonshine bottle and hit me in the back of the head. I saw about a thousand little stars and then felt a cold sweat come over me.

My pillow fight partner rolled me to my side and wrapped his arms around me, pinning me in place. After what seemed like forever, he released me and I jumped up, only to fall back down. I got a little dizzy and then everything went black.

I woke up moments later to find Mickey's scraggly face staring back at me, asking me how many fingers he was holding up. Granny was in the kitchen talking to herself, making me an ice pack. Mickey had picked me up and propped me up in my bed. I sat rubbing my head, wondering what the hell had just happened. Granny returned with the ice pack and Mickey applied it to my head.

"What the hell happened?" I asked, taking the ice pack from Mickey.

"Um, where do you want me to start?" Mickey answered with a laugh.

Geez, my head hurt! "Start at the beginning, but give me the short version."

"After Granny's date, I picked her up and brought her here," Mickey started. "Matt offered to bring her home, but I didn't think you would want him knowing where you lived."

"Thank you."

"You're welcome. Anyways, we came in the back door and the hot AC guy was doing your dishes. We asked where you were and he said you had passed out in your pasta. He figured it was the pain meds working."

I winced. So this super-hot sexy guy makes me dinner and I face plant into a plate of pasta. I tried to run my finger through my hair, but couldn't because my hair was all tangled with pasta sauce in it. I made a gesture for Mickey to continue.

"Cooper said he cleaned you up the best he could and put you on the couch to sleep it off. He said you had had a rough day and needed the sleep. So his plan was to stay and sleep in your chair in case you needed anything throughout the night, but me and Granny told him he could go and we would handle it from there."

"So he's gone?" I frowned, confused. "Who was in my bed then?"

Mickey raised his hand. "That would be me."

I breathed a sigh of relief and felt a little twinge of disappointment. Somehow the thought of Cooper in my bed, his strong arms around me, sounded like a great idea.

Mickey continued. "Cooper refused to leave until you were tucked away safely in bed, so I carried you in here and Cooper tucked you in. He fiddled with your phone for a few minutes, made sure your medicine was on your night stand along with a glass of water, and then he left."

I looked at my nightstand, and sure enough those items were there lined up neatly, along with a note.

"So get to the part where you decided to sleep with me."

"Well, you pretty much decided that for me." I raised an eyebrow. "You were sawing logs, and I mean really getting it done. I've never heard anyone snore that loud —"

I waved my hand, trying to hurry Mickey along. "So I was going to crash in the spare room, but Granny was in there passed out, so I went to the couch and tried to get comfortable, but my head and feet were hanging off. So I opted for the floor. I was sleeping peacefully, dreaming of Coronas and sandy beaches, when you started screaming at the top of your lungs. I ran in here and found you air fighting with some imaginary fiend. I jumped in bed with you and calmed you down, and you wrapped your arms around me and went back to sleep. I tried to extricate myself from you, but you held on for dear life, and you were once again sleeping peacefully, so I stayed."

I was relieved. "So Cooper was never in my bed?"

Mickey shook his head. "Sorry to disappoint ya babe, but it was all me."

"Maybe he isn't an asshole after all," I mumbled.

"So next thing I know, I'm back to dreaming about beaches, and then I was thrown to the floor and you were beating the piss out of me. I whispered your name, trying to get you to stop without waking Granny, but you weren't having any of it. You were feeling around and your foot almost connected with my nuts, so I grabbed your foot to stop you. I guess you lost your balance, and that's when you fell on me, knocking the wind out of me. When your fists and claws came out, I screamed."

Granny took a pull on the moonshine and burped. "I heard Honey Buns screaming and thought somebody broke in or something, so I came a running."

"Why'd you hit me on the head?"

"Because in my haste to help Honey Buns, I forgot my glasses and all I could see was someone on top of him, so I swung." She took another swig of moonshine. "I gotta work on my swing more. I didn't even break the bottle."

And thank God for that, I thought. I rubbed my head. "Everybody out! I'm going to bed. Alone!"

Granny shook her head. "Can't do that, Stacy."

"Why the hell not?"

Granny belched and high fived Mickey. "You could have a concussion. I can't let you sleep if you have a concussion."

I rolled my eyes. "I don't have a concussion. I'm fine! Now get out!"

Mickey clapped his hands and squealed, "You know what this means?" and he and Granny both yelled "Pajama Party!" at the same time. I closed my eyes and took a deep breath. It was going to be a long night, and arguing with these two would be pointless. I kicked my covers off as my cell phone vibrated again. Irritated, I grabbed it to silence it, and when I read the text message my stomach flip flopped. It was from Cooper. It read *Time to take your pain pills. Then go back to sleep and dream of me* ☺. I couldn't help the goofy grin that was plastered on my face. Granny and Mickey moved in closer, anxiously waiting for me to spill the beans. I giggled and hugged my phone. He wasn't an asshole! He was a remarkably sweet guy that had definitely earned a first date.

Granny was getting impatient. "Well?"

Mickey inspected his nails. "Isn't it obvious? It's from Cooooper!" He drew Cooper's name out playfully.

Suddenly, I wasn't the least bit tired. In fact, I felt completely refreshed. I jumped up, grabbed a pair of pajamas, and escaped to the bathroom, taking my cell phone with me. I wanted to respond to Cooper, but I didn't want an audience.

I poised my fingers to type out a text and froze. I had no idea what to say. "Thank you" sounded lame, although I did feel it was necessary to thank him. I mean, it was a workday and he was obviously having his sleep interrupted to take care of me. "You're sweet" didn't quite cut it either. I wanted to say something fun and flirty, but nothing came to mind. My brain just didn't function at 3:00 A.M.

I was still debating what to say when my phone rang in my hand. I stared at the display in dismay as Cooper's name popped up. He must have programmed his number into my phone after I passed out on him.

I answered on the second ring. "Hello."

"Good morning, Wrecking Ball."

"Wrecking ball?"

He laughed. "Well, you do seem to leave a trail of destruction behind you."

I frowned. "Not usually I don't. Usually, I'm just plain old, sensible Stacy."

"Honey, there's nothing about you that's plain."

I couldn't help but smile. I laughed nervously. "Thank you."

"You're welcome." His tone turned serious. "How are you feeling?"

I felt my throbbing head. "Fine," I lied.

"That's good. I'm glad. I won't keep you. I just wanted to remind you to take your pain medicine so you will be able to get a good night's sleep." So much for that! I was wide awake now with about a million butterflies fluttering about in my belly.

"I will take it right now."

"It's on your night stand."

"I know. I saw it."

"Take it now so that I can sleep knowing you won't be hurting." Could he be any sweeter?

I shook a bottle from my medicine cabinet, jiggled it, and made an exaggerated swallow.

"Good girl," Cooper said, and like a love struck schoolgirl I smiled that silly, sappy grin.

"Cooper?"

"Mmm?"

"Thank you. I mean, thank you for everything. For taking care of me, and dinner, and…well, just everything."

"That's what friends are for," he said, and I winced at the "f" word. I was the one that insisted on the whole no dating thing. The "friend" word was mostly my fault. "Well, I'll let you get some sleep, Wrecking Ball."

I wasn't sure that I liked the little nickname he had for me, although it was fitting. "Goodnight Cooper."

"Goodnight."

"Oh, and Cooper?"

"Yes?"

"My dreams have never been sweeter."

He laughed, and I felt that now familiar tingle throughout my body making me shiver. "Goodnight, Ms. Dupree."

"Goodnight, Cooper." I hit the end button and sighed. Oh man, I was a goner. Why oh why did he have to be so sweet, and handsome, and attentive? I had really meant it when I said I was swearing off men. And I was perfectly happy with that decision until Cooper waltzed right in and renewed my faith in the male species. Now what was I going to do? I could sit and debate this all night but it wouldn't get me anywhere. I needed coffee before I could even attempt to figure this out.

I changed into my pajamas and opened the bathroom door, stepping aside so Mickey and Granny wouldn't knock me down. I figured they were leaning on the door, and of course I was right. Mickey batted his eyelashes at me and said in a mocking voice, "My dreams have never been sweeter."

I slapped him playfully on the arm. "Shut up!"

Granny adjusted her hearing aid and it let out a sharp shrill. "What did I miss?" she slurred. "I couldn't hear a thing." She adjusted her glasses and tried to focus, then took them off and cleaned them on her gown. "And I can't see so good either."

Probably she couldn't see because she was drunk. "Maybe it's the moonshine," I suggested. I tried to remove the bottle from her hand and she growled at me. I had busted my ankle, almost died during a kidnapping, lost a fight with a wall, and been smacked in the head with a bottle of moonshine. My luck wasn't looking so good today. The last thing I needed was to have Granny kick my ass. I relinquished my hold on the bottle and gathered my manicure kit. Girl time was about to begin.

***

It was 11:30 in the morning and some over achieving asshole was out mowing their yard. I tried putting a pillow over my face to drown out the sound...no luck. I scooted further under the covers and covered my ears with my hands, but it was no use. I was awake and wouldn't be able to go back to sleep. Oddly, for being up half of the night I felt pretty good. I had this anxious excitement pulsing through me. Cooper came to mind, and I quickly kicked out from under my covers and grabbed my cell phone to check for a text. I tried not to frown when there wasn't one.

Aside from the phone call from him at 3:00 A.M., he had sent me a text at 8:00 to remind me to take my medicine. I had still been up at that point, having pulled a Channing Tatum marathon with Mickey while Granny snored away in the guest room. I had taken Cooper's advice and took my medicine, and then decided to turn in. I didn't feel like I had a concussion, so I figured it was safe to sleep at that point. But sleep didn't come easily. I tossed and turned and couldn't get Cooper off my mind. It seemed I liked everything about him. His scent, his smile, those smoldering eyes, the earring he wore in his left ear. He had this bad boy vibe that he seemed to reign in, but it was there just begging to come out. And I wanted it to come out. The whole bad boy thing was so not my style, but I had to admit it was a huge turn on. I was tired of being the sensible, level-headed girl. Of course, the last time I let down my guard my heart had been broken and my world had come crashing down around me. Cooper didn't seem like the type to get what he wanted from me and then discard me with a text message, but neither had Thad. Thad had started out sweet and attentive, and I'd thought he hung the moon. We all knew how that turned out, and it was downright devastating...even worse than my divorce. I couldn't go to that place again. So even though I was crazy attracted to Cooper, I had to remind myself to be cautious and take it slow. Of course, I could be getting ahead of myself. He may just be a nice guy and not interested in me at all. If he was smart, he'd run.

I closed my eyes and thought about that kiss. That kiss was not a friendly kiss. That kiss was explosive. It was hot and passionate, and definitely not the way I would kiss somebody I wasn't interested in. But what if all he wanted was sex? Then what? I couldn't do that. I had to have more, and I didn't know if I was ready for that. Ugh! In typical Stacy fashion I was over thinking this whole deal. Hell, I might never even hear from him again.

I smelled coffee and decided I would think about the Cooper thing after a cup of coffee.

I climbed out of bed and went to the bathroom to brush my teeth, caught my reflection in the mirror, and winced. The good news was I didn't have black eyes anymore…nope, they were a lovely shade of greenish purple. My nose was still swollen, and I had the worst case of bed head ever. Oh well, I didn't have anybody to impress, so who cared?

I brushed my teeth, carefully ran a brush through my hair, and followed the scent of coffee to my kitchen. Granny was scrambling eggs and frying bacon, and Mickey was impatiently waiting for the toaster. As I entered the kitchen, he grabbed me a cup, tossed in some sugar and coffee, and slid it in front of me.

"Morning, sunshine."

"You're up early," Granny teased.

I took a long sip of coffee. "Not by choice, Granny." I nodded toward the back door. "Somebody decided to mow their lawn and interrupt my beauty sleep."

"Honey, you'd need to sleep for days…," Mickey mumbled.

"What?"

"Oh, nothing Stace. You look bitchin!"

I rolled my eyes. "Sure that's what you said."

Mickey batted his eyelashes at me and gave me a cheesy grin. "So?"

Granny turned the heat off the eggs and quickly took a seat, hollering, "Wait, wait! Don't start without me?"

"Start what?"

"You know what," Mickey said, giving me a knowing look

I blushed. "I have absolutely no idea what you are talking about." My cell phone vibrated and I snatched it off the table. I couldn't help but be disappointed when I saw it wasn't Cooper. It was Megan checking on Granny.

Granny was leaning forward, waiting for my response, and Mickey was urging me on. "Seriously, I have no idea—"

Granny was impatient. "Just spill it sister. We want to know about you and Mr. Sexy Pants."

"There's nothing to spill. He texted me a couple of hours ago and reminded me to take my pain medication, and I haven't heard from him since."

It was the truth, but they weren't buying it. "I swear!" I added.

"So are you going to see him again?" Granny wanted to know.

I blew on my coffee. "I don't know. Maybe. I haven't really thought about it." Actually, it was all I could think about. My heart actually sped up at the thought of seeing Cooper again.

"Well, do you like him?" Granny asked.

Yes! I shrugged my shoulders. "He's okay."

"Okay?" Granny asked. "Sweetheart, if that boy was any hotter he would be on fire."

She was right of course. "Really? I hadn't noticed."

Mickey threw his head back in laughter. "Stacy, you've noticed alright. We are just talking about him and you are blushing and your nipples are hard. You almost fell out of your chair trying to get to your cell phone. And at the mere mention of his name you get that goofy grin. Yep, you've noticed alright!"

"Hell, I can't see squat and I noticed," Granny said.

Mickey eyed his manicure. "Yep, that boy is H-O-T hot! And he's crazy about you, Stacy." He pointed at me. "And I'm pretty sure you like him too."

I couldn't lie. "Okay, I like him." I held my finger and thumb a tiny bit apart. "Just a little bit."

"You should call him!" Mickey said.

"And say what?"

"How about 'Hello, how are you?'" Mickey suggested.

"Um, that's lame."

Granny's eyes twinkled. "How about 'Hello Big Daddy. I wanna hop on your love stick'?"

I rolled my eyes and sighed. Granny was a handful. "Nope, no way. I've sworn off men and sex."

Mickey tried again. "How about 'Hey sexy, thanks for mowing my lawn.'"

What? It took a moment for Mickey's words to register, and then I heard the lawn mower again. I ran to the kitchen window and looked out, and sure enough, there was Cooper wearing shorts, a T-shirt, and a ball cap, pushing a shiny red lawnmower. His jaw was lined with stubble and his shirt was soaked with sweat. He looked delicious, and I just wanted to devour him. My body was reacting in every way imaginable, and my heart thudded in my chest. "Oh my God! He's here!" I snatched the curtain shut. "What do I do?" I asked in a hysterical voice.

Granny handed me a glass of ice tea and shooed me towards the door. "He looks pretty hot." Boy, did he! "Take him this."

I pushed the glass away. "I can't go out there like this. I look like hell. I'd send him running, and he isn't done with my lawn yet."

Mickey laughed. "Babe, he's seen you with your face buried in pasta! I'm pretty sure that was worse."

I panicked. "Mickey, you've got to help me!"

"With what?"

"You have to make me look hot." I frowned. "Or at least presentable."

Mickey threw his hands up. "Honey, I'm a drag queen, not a magician." I kicked him in the shin. He held out his hands to put some distance between us. "Okay! Okay! I'll give it a shot!"

***

Mickey had done a fair job on my hair and make-up. The lump on my head prevented me from being able to do much with my hair, but a little fluff here and some scrunching there and it looked okay. Mickey complained about not having all of his make-up supplies, but he begrudgingly made do with what we had. He had wanted to go get his supplies but there was no time. With a fair amount of concealer and some creative shading, my eyes went from purple bruised to sultry smoky. I added strawberry lip-gloss and puckered my lips. Not bad. Not great, but definitely presentable.

"Wardrobe!" Mickey called out, and I laughed. I could get used to having my very own drag queen for hair and make-up. Too bad he wasn't for hire.

Mickey had selected a denim mini skirt, chunky heels, and a low cut hot pink lacy tank top. I vetoed the mini skirt and exchanged it for a pair of cut off shorts, and kept one heel and put my boot on my other foot. I paired the tank top with a black undershirt that somewhat tamed my boobs, and added a spritz of perfume to my neck and my cleavage.

"Bicthin'," Mickey proclaimed, happy with his handiwork. He clapped his hands and ushered me out of my bedroom. I made it to the kitchen just as the lawn mower became silent. I peeked out and saw Cooper undoing the gas cap of the mower. Perfect timing for him to take a little break. I adjusted my boobs

91

and patted my hair, thankful I had shaved my legs yesterday. I grabbed the tea and made my way to the backyard, making a beeline for Cooper.

"Hey," I said, giving him a little wave.

"Hey yourself." He accepted the iced tea and drank half of it in two swallows, never taking his eyes off me. As I got closer, I could smell his delicious scent of cologne and sweat and Cooper. My heart hammered away in my chest and my stomach knotted. The sun glinted off his earring, and I saw a tattoo peeking out from his shirt sleeve. Ah, there was that bad boy just begging to come out and play.

"How are you feeling?" Cooper asked me, and I had to take a deep breath to quiet the excitement in my voice.

"I'm good. Thank you for taking such good care of me."

He finished his ice tea and I took the glass. "It was my pleasure."

I gestured to the lawn. "And thank you for mowing my grass."

"Correction: weeds."

I laughed. He was right.

"You look...gorgeous," he said, and I felt a slow blush come on.

"Thank you. There are perks to having a drag queen as a best friend." I indicated the make-up.

His smile was sincere and sexy as hell. "You were beautiful before, Wrecking Ball."

I smiled as words evaded me. Even though I had already thanked him a gazillion times, it was all I could think of to say.

"Why do you keep doing that?" he asked me.

"What? Saying thank you?"

"No." He closed the space between us and cupped my face with his big hands. "Looking at me like that, chewing on your bottom lip and playing with your hands. I just have this crazy desire to kiss you every time I set eyes on you. I want to taste you and feel you, and I'm afraid once I start I won't want to stop."

I felt the heat rise on my cheeks and between my legs. "Oh!" It came out as a breathy whisper. My gaze dropped to his lips. He had beautiful delicate lips. I wanted those lips on mine.

"Stacy Dupree...why do you have this effect on me?" He released my face and tilted his head, and delivered a whisper of a kiss to my lips. I looked him directly in the eyes, our gaze full of heat and lust. He pulled me into his arms. "Ah Jesus, Wrecking Ball. You are going to wreck me. You know that, right?"

I didn't answer him. Hell, I didn't know what to say. I was having a hard time forming intelligent thoughts. I was on sensation overload. His arms were wrapped around me, his hands intertwined, resting on my lower back. His scent enveloped me, his lips planted tender kisses on the top of my head, and when I looked up to meet his gaze, I was pretty sure my heart stopped. I leaned in closer, enjoying the feel of his body pressed to mine, and I felt his growing erection press into my stomach. I tried to speak, to stop this madness, but before I could form a single thought, Cooper grabbed me with both hands on the back of my thighs, lifted me up, and backed me up against the house. And I was toast. Any rational thought was gone. I gave in to him and parted my legs, wanting to feel his body as close to mine as possible, and he took the hint and positioned himself between my legs, his sex even harder, straining against his zipper. His mouth found mine, and this time he didn't hold back. He kissed me with everything he had, and I was suddenly grateful that he had backed me up against the wall because I wouldn't have been able to support myself after that kiss. I was breathless, speechless, and I didn't want him to stop. I wanted him to take me right then and there.

And then I came to my senses. Sort of.

I pushed him back and cleared my throat. He leaned his forehead on mine, closed his eyes, and quietly cursed. I wrapped my arms around his neck and we stayed like that for what seemed like an eternity, staring into each other's eyes. I could see his internal struggle of lust and desire. He probably thought I was crazy because I was sending him mixed signals. One minute I wanted him pressed into me as close as possible while I devoured his mouth, the next I was pushing him away. I was so torn. The good girl inside of me was whispering "take it slow," while the slut inside me was screaming "Jump on this boy's love stick right here, right now." Cooper kissed me on the forehead, and then gently on my swollen nose.

"I'm not a slut!" I blurted, and Cooper smiled. "I mean okay, so right now, I mean the way I was kissing you and stuff, might have seemed a little sluttish, but usually I'm not so slutty." Cooper kissed my forehead again. "I think it's almost time for my cycle and my hormones are clogging up my brain." I smacked myself in the face, which sent pain shooting through my nose. I could not believe I had just said that out loud. I winced at the pain and opened my mouth to speak, but Cooper was gazing into my eyes with those blazing blue eyes, and his perfect lips were stretched into the sweetest smile and…. Oh hell. To hell with the good girl, the naughty slut won this little struggle. I covered Cooper's mouth with my own and I devoured him. I drank him in as our tongues intertwined playfully, and my lady parts did the happy dance. My knees went weak and I felt dizzy. My heart was pounding in my chest and my entire body was on fire. At that moment in time, I was pretty sure the man could do anything he wanted to do to me and I would completely surrender to him.

Cooper's hands explored my body greedily, and when he slipped his hand under my shirt and cupped my breast, I thought I was going to explode. He kneaded softly as a deep growl resonated in his throat. His touch, his kiss made me want to break all of my rules and just let him make me feel good…really good. I was in big trouble, and at the moment I didn't care. All I cared about was being wrapped in Cooper's arms, his lips on mine, the tingle low in my belly, and the heat between my legs. It occurred to me that Granny and Mickey were probably spying on me, and believe it or not, I didn't care about that either. Sure I would probably have my title of "Anti-Slut" stripped from me, but at that particular moment, that was the least of my concerns. I wanted this man…now!

And then I heard a piercing shrill coming from my kitchen. I opened my eyes to follow the sound and saw the smoke.

Cooper's mouth was hot on my neck and I wanted nothing more than to let him stay there forever. What he was doing felt amazing, but the smoke billowing out of my kitchen window was a problem.

I tried to wiggle away from Cooper, which just made him press his body against me tighter.

"Fire!" I said, as Cooper pulled my shirt up, revealing my breasts covered in a thin sheaf of black lace.

"Yes, I am on fire too, baby," Cooper whispered. I shook my head and closed my eyes as he pulled the lace cup down and exposed my aching breast, my nipple swollen and puckered from his attention there moments ago.

"No, you don't understand. Smoke!" I almost shouted as Cooper covered my nipple with his mouth. If my house wasn't on fire, I would have come right then. He teased my nipple with his tongue, swirling it slowly around.

"You said it, Stacy! You are smoking! Incredibly smoking fucking hot! God, I want you so bad!" he said, and as much as I hated to, I pushed him off me and pointed to the smoke coming out of my kitchen window.

"Cooper, my house is on fire!" I yelled, and he quickly surveyed the situation. I pulled my shirt down and we ran to the back door. As soon as we opened it, smoke enveloped us, making me cough. Cooper ran to the stove that was on fire and removed a flaming pan of bacon, discarding it into the sink still flaming. I ran to the pantry, grabbed the fire extinguisher, pulled the pin, and sprayed the flaming skillet, not even registering the fact that Cooper was in the line of fire. I covered the fire and Cooper in a thin layer of white powdery foam. Cooper was coughing and gagging, and wiping the foam from his eyes, but thankfully the fire was out. I dropped the extinguisher and ran to Cooper, trying to wipe his face free of foam.

Granny and Mickey ran into the kitchen and took in the scene. Mickey went into the bathroom and returned with a damp towel. He tossed it to me and I went to work scrubbing Cooper's face. "Are you okay?" I shouted frantically over the shrill of the smoke alarm.

"I'm fine," he hollered, looking around the kitchen. "Is everyone else okay?"

I checked Granny for injuries and Mickey nodded that he was fine. "I think we are all okay," I said to Cooper, and to Granny and Mickey, "What the hell happened?"

"Granny burned the bacon," Mickey said matter of factly. I rolled my eyes. He reached up and ripped the smoke alarm out of the ceiling, the broken device suddenly silent.

"That much I figured out. But where in the hell were you guys while my house was almost burning down?"

Granny poured Cooper a glass of water and held it out for him. He took it graciously and took a long pull on it. "We were in the bathroom," she said, as if that explained everything.

Knowing I wouldn't want to know the details, I didn't ask her to elaborate. "Did you not hear the smoke alarm going off?" I half shouted, before realizing I didn't have to shout any longer.

"Of course we heard it, Stacy. Hell, Megan probably heard it from her house," Granny said.

I looked from Granny to Mickey, an incredulous expression on my face. "And it never occurred to you to put the fire out or get out of the house?"

Mickey crossed his hairy arms across his chest. "We couldn't," he said.

Okay, this was going nowhere. I was pretty sure I didn't want to know what had been going on in that bathroom, but it was obvious if I wanted any answers I was going to have to find out. I waved my hand for Mickey to continue.

Mickey spread his hands out and laughed. "You are going to find this really funny, Stace."

I winced. "Oh, I'm sure I will," I said, knowing that I probably wouldn't.

"Mickey saved my life!" Granny dramatically declared.

Mickey shrugged. "It was nothing really."

I had had all I could handle. I tried the whole slow breathing thing and shot a pleading glance at Cooper. If these jokers hadn't tried to burn my house down, I could still have been in Cooper's arms, his mouth on me, my body sizzling from his touch. He could have been inside me, filling me with pleasure and.... My thoughts were interrupted by loud banging on my front door.

I groaned when I went to the door and saw three fire trucks parked in front of my house. "Who called the fire department?" I shouted, and Granny raised her hand and winked at me. I sighed, opened the door, and wordlessly stepped aside as my house was stormed by firemen. I informed them that the fire was out, but they were already past me, surveying the damage.

"We got a call about a fire," said a tall, green-eyed kid of about twenty-five. I couldn't see much of his body because of his gear, but his face was model quality and his teeth were perfect and gleaming white. He looked like he should be on the cover of a magazine. We were joined by other firemen carrying various pieces of equipment, looking around, obviously trying to figure out what the hell was going on. I wanted to know the same thing.

Cooper wrapped a possessive arm around my waist and addressed the firemen. "We had a small grease fire, but Ms. Dupree put it out and everyone is okay."

Granny was fanning herself. "Actually, I feel as though I might faint. I think I inhaled too much smoke. I can't breathe. I might need mouth to mouth." I did another eye roll as two capable firemen rushed to Granny and eased her down into a chair. Granny winked at me, smiled, and then went back to her fainting act.

"I'm glad everyone is okay," Mr. Green Eyes said. "But could anyone tell me what happened?"

"Yeah, anyone care to fill us in?" I said expectantly to Mickey and Granny. I was standing in front of Cooper, and he had both of his arms draped around me, his hands resting just below my breasts. I was having trouble concentrating and my breathing was ragged. Before it was all said and done, I might need mouth to mouth too. I shivered at the thought of Cooper's mouth on me. On my lips, my breasts, lower on my sex. Oh Lord, I was toast. I suddenly couldn't wait to get everyone out of my house, except for Cooper. If he touched me like he did earlier, I was locking him up in my house and making him my sex slave.

"Well?" I said, prompting Mickey and Granny.

Granny was receiving oxygen through a mask, so I looked to Mickey. He smiled. "Well, Granny was making breakfast, and then Stacy went outside to um...."

"I was assisting Cooper," I said in a rush. "We were, uh...doing yard work."

"Yeah, okay Little Miss Naughty Pants," Granny said around her oxygen mask.

"Anyways," Mickey continued. "Granny and I were keeping an eye on Stacy because she is quite accident prone. When we didn't see her for a few moments we were afraid something might have happened to her, so we went into the bathroom to look out the window for her."

"Why didn't you just go out the back door?" the fireman asked.

"Well, because we didn't want to be rude. I mean, she is a grown woman after all. We didn't want her to know we were spying on her. But she did suffer from a concussion yesterday, so we didn't want to take any chances."

Cooper looked down at me questionably. "I did NOT have a concussion!" I insisted.

Mickey laughed. "So, like I said, we were keeping an eye on Stace and we forgot about the bacon, and Granny couldn't see out the window because she is too short so I gave her a boost so she could see, but after a few minutes my hands went numb and I dropped her."

Everyone's eyes landed on Granny. She removed her mask. "It's okay, I was fine. I didn't get hurt or nothing, but I did lose a booby." Mouths dropped and looks of confusion spread around the room. "Don't worry, it wasn't my real booby. It was one of those handy dandy booby inserts. I get a full cup size out of those babies."

Everyone looked at her chest, and sure enough she had one perky mound on the left side, but the right side was pretty much flat.

"So anyways, we looked everywhere for the boob and we couldn't find it, and then finally Granny spotted it in the toilet and she jammed her hand in there to get it, but it just made it go down further in the hole."

"And I had to have my booby," Granny said. "I have a date tonight and I need both of my boobs on full display because I'm wearing a leather corset, and it wouldn't look right with the b cups God gave me." Someone kill me now.

"So Granny went in after the boob and that's when she got her hand stuck in the toilet. About that time I heard the fire alarm. I knew Stacy was outside and safe so I wasn't worried about her, but Granny was stuck and I wasn't about to leave her behind to die in the fire."

Granny smiled and put her hand over her heart. "Thank you, Honey Buns!"

"So she called 911 with her free hand while I tried to get her other hand unstuck."

"Why didn't you just go into the kitchen and remove the pan from the stove? Or put the fire out?" Cooper asked, which was a very logical question. If we were dealing with logical people there would be a simple answer. But we were dealing with Granny and Mickey, so I braced myself for the answer.

Mickey looked at us all like we had two heads. He fluffed his hair. "Honey," he said, addressing Cooper in full on drag queen voice, and I stifled a laugh. "It takes about a gallon of hairspray to hold all this luxurious hair in place." His hair was frizzy and stiff, and stuck up haphazardly on his head. His hair looked like he'd taken about a hundred thousand volts straight to the head. But of course that's the way his hair always looked, so I was used to it. "So, hairspray and fire don't mix," he continued. "If I had walked into that kitchen I would have gone up in flames. Like poof! I just concentrated on getting Granny out of the house. So I got behind her and grabbed her around the waist and pulled."

"Which was pretty interesting. I kind of enjoyed it," Granny said. "I haven't had a man behind me like that since 1997. I mean sure, I've had a few men, but most of them can't do it that way because they might throw a hip out."

There was a collective cringe as everyone in the room was probably trying to erase the mental image in their heads and hope it wasn't permanently engrained in their brains, a memory that would be triggered anytime doggie style was being blissfully enjoyed.

"So finally Granny was able to twist her hand and get it unstuck, but I was still pulling on her, so then we were propelled into the wall where I landed ass first. Now my ass was stuck in the hole in the wall, and Granny had to pull on me to get me out, and we both crashed onto the toilet." He laughed. "Told you it was funny."

I didn't think it was funny. In fact, I thought it was anything but funny. It was outrageous and crazy and what I guessed I got for surrounding myself with crazy people. I mean seriously, these people were nuts! They needed to be in a put in the crazy house. I had to get new friends. And Granny had to go! I had a hard enough time dealing with the crazy shit I got myself into. I couldn't handle Granny's craziness too. As soon as everyone was gone I was calling Megan. Or maybe I would just drop Granny off somewhere and move to a secret location, lock my doors, and collect cats.

Green Eyes was trying not to laugh. "So, everyone is okay and the damage is minimal. Unless there is anything you need from us, Ms. Dupree, we will be on our way."

"Thank you for coming," I said, because I didn't know what else to say.

"We are here anytime you need us," Green Eyes said, and then he and all but one of the other firemen filed out of the house. Granny followed them out. No way was she going to stay in the kitchen when there was that much eye candy outside.

I waved. "See you next time," I said cheerfully.

The fire fighter that had stayed behind had arrived late and hadn't heard the whole story. His name was Preston and he had responded to fires at my house before. He smiled at me and took his hat off. "What did you try to cook this time?" he asked playfully.

I blushed and my face heated. This might not go too well with Cooper wrapped around me. Preston and I had a history...kind of. "It wasn't me this time. I swear!"

"This time?" Cooper said incredulously, his eyebrows raised.

I shifted in his arms. "I've um...well, I've had a problem with my stove before. It's not the first time the fire department has come." Cooper laughed.

"It's actually my third time responding to this address," Preston supplied helpfully. "I was off duty that other time."

Cooper turned me around in his embrace and placed a kiss on my forehead. "Remind me to never let you cook, Wrecking Ball," he said, his eyes sparkling with humor.

Preston shifted on his feet and cleared his throat. "Um, actually Stacy, I'm glad we got the call. I mean, I'm not glad your house caught on fire...."

"Again," Mickey said, and I shot him a rot in hell look.

"...well, you know what I mean. I just...." He looked at Cooper and swallowed hard. "It's just that you never called me after that date, and when I tried to call you a Chinese Restaurant answered and they had never heard of you." He shifted on his feet again. "You must have written the number down wrong or something."

Sure, that's exactly what happened. Cooper's smile lit up the room and he chuckled, obviously finding this whole thing hilarious. I jabbed him in the ribs and he tried unsuccessfully to wipe the smile off his face.

When I didn't say anything, Preston continued. "Anyways, Stacy, I just wanted you to know that I really like you and I would love a second date." He stood there looking at me expectantly, and I knew I had to say something, but I couldn't think of anything to say. I was dumbfounded, and Cooper was enjoying this little exchange way too much. "I'm off Thursday," Preston added helpfully.

"She's busy," Cooper said.

Preston, bless his heart, was undeterred. "Oh okay, how about Saturday?"

Cooper looked at me and I shrugged my shoulders. Since he was enjoying this so much, I thought I'd mess with him a little bit. "Um, hold on a second Preston. Let me check my schedule." I turned to go into the other room to check my imaginary calendar when Cooper scooped me up, brought his lips to mine, and kissed me silly. I felt a flush spread across my body and leaned into the kiss, just as Cooper broke it and sat me back on my feet, a satisfied smile on his lips.

"I'm busy," I told Preston, and saw Cooper's smile twinkle in his eyes. "As a matter of fact, I'm going to be really busy, Preston. I have a lot going on. I don't know if I will have any free time for a while."

"Oh, okay," Preston said with a frown. "Well, can I at least get your phone number? This time I will write it down and repeat it back so I won't get it wrong."

I smiled and rattled off a phone number. Preston wrote it down, repeated it, and put it in his wallet. He smiled, and I almost felt bad for duping the poor guy. "I'll be in touch Stacy!" Preston said excitedly.

"See ya," I said, and Cooper and I waved, both of us trying to hold in our laughter. As soon as Preston was out of earshot, we both busted out laughing.

"I know that's not your number," Cooper said. "I've committed your number to memory." He pointed to his head. "I've got it right here. So whose number did you give him?"

I laughed and a wicked smile formed on my lips. "Oh, you know, just a little Cuban restaurant I like."

Cooper laughed again, and I decided I wanted to hear that laugh every day for the rest of my life. "Why is it you can't remember your best friend's phone number, but you can rattle off the numbers to restaurants at the drop of a hat?"

"Hey, this fat kid has got to eat!" I smiled sweetly. "And I don't cook because every stove I get catches on fire. They just don't make them like they used to."

Cooper laughed loudly and pulled me back into his arms. "Oh Wrecking Ball, what the hell am I going to do with you?"

I smiled against his chest. I had a few ideas of what he could do with me. And what I wanted to do with him!

Chapter 6

The aftermath of the fire was chaos as was everything else in my life. Megan had rushed over as soon as the gossip chain had reached her mother, which took all of about fifteen minutes. She waddled into the house, asked me what I tried to cook, and immediately went to work cleaning up the mess in the kitchen. I tried to stop her but she wouldn't listen. She said she was "nesting" and needed to be busy. I let her have at it because in all honesty, I wasn't looking forward to cleaning up the mess anyways. Cooking, cleaning, all that homey wifey stuff, wasn't really my thing. I wasn't sure what my thing was, just that it wasn't that.

Megan told me Jack would be over shortly. She pulled a dust mask over her face, gloved up, and armed herself with a bottle of cleanser. She went to work on the stove, and because I felt like I needed to do something, I made more coffee. I had begged Megan to take Granny for the night, and at first she had been reluctant, but after searching mine and Cooper's faces and seeing the intensity there, she caved. "One night" she told me, holding up her index finger. I didn't argue. I would take whatever I could get. I doubted one night would be enough for me to get my fill, but it would at least let me sample the goods and give me time to hatch a plan to drug Granny or sell her in the black market sex trade. Surely there was a demand for an eighty year old woman with the boobs of a sixty year old who knew the lyrics to Lil Wayne songs.

Cooper had been amazing. He was still covered in powder from the fire extinguisher, but that didn't stop him from helping with the cleanup. By the time he and Megan were done, the kitchen looked normal again. Jack arrived, carrying a large box labeled "Stacy Code Orange," just as Megan finished mopping the floor. He tried to side step the wet spots, almost toppling over. He sat the box on the dining room table and dropped a kiss on his wife's forehead, then turned to me, drug me into his arms, and gave me a big brother bear hug.

"Do I even want to know?" he asked.

"Nope," I answered, then gestured to Cooper. "Jack, this is Cooper." Jack and Cooper shook hands. "Cooper, this is Jack, Megan's husband. He's kind of like a big brother to me." The men nodded at each other, and if Cooper minded Jack sizing him up, he didn't say anything. Jack's chocolate brown eyes turned serious. "If you make her cry, I'll hurt you. But if you make her drink, I'll kill you."

My eyes grew wide and I gasped. I had planned on telling Cooper that I was a recovering alcoholic, but I was saving that discussion for later. Much later. Cooper glanced my way and smiled. "I'll take that into consideration," he said.

Jack opened the box and pulled out a shiny new fire extinguisher. He went to the pantry, retrieved the used up extinguisher, and replaced it with the new one. Cooper laughed as he eyed the box.

"Code Orange?" he asked, amusement in his voice.

Megan lowered her dust mask. "That's Stacy's fire box," she explained. "We keep a fresh fire extinguisher, smoke alarms, burn gel, and whatever else we think she might need on hand. Whenever there is a fire...." She paused and eyed Stacy. "Which does happen from time to time...we come over and Jack replaces everything so that Stacy is ready for the next Code Orange."

Cooper laughed and shook his head, probably trying to figure out a way to ditch me quickly without coming off as a complete asshole.

"We have other code boxes too," Jack offered helpfully. "Ya know, just in case."

"There's Code Blue for a broken heart," Megan supplied. "Code Red for —"

I shot Megan a go to hell look. "Enough! Cooper doesn't want to hear about this."

Cooper's smile was infectious.

"And then there's my favorite," Jack said. "The Code Black and Blue Box. That's the one I pull out when some asshole hurts Stacy. It contains brass knuckles —"

"Jack!" I shouted.

"...baseball bat...."

I flushed with embarrassment.

"...shovel...." Jack grinned as he continued. If looks could kill, Jack would have been using the shovel to dig his own grave. "...Chinese throwing stars, buck knife —"

"Seriously, that's enough!" I pleaded. Jack would have continued, but Josie flew in the house, grabbed me, and hugged me, saying, "I came as soon as I heard. Are you okay?" I assured her I was fine. "Did you inhale smoke? Are you dizzy? Do you need to go the hospital? Should I call Jon to make a house call?"

"Josie, I'm totally fine. It was just a small grease fire, but Cooper and I put it out."

Josie looked at Cooper as though she'd just noticed he was there. "Why are you both covered in white stuff?"

"He was in the line of fire when I extinguished the fire. And I, well...."

"Megan, Code Pink! Stat!" Josie hollered. "That means right now, for those of you not in the medical field."

"What's a Code Pink?" Cooper wanted to know, and I had a feeling I never wanted to know.

Megan screwed her face up in confusion. "I don't have a Code Pink."

Josie threw Mickey the keys to her car. "It's in the trunk. I carry it with me. I call it the 'Boom Boom Box.' You never know when a Code Pink might come up. Better to be prepared." Josie looked up wistfully. "I used to date a Boy Scout, and although he batted a zero in bed, he did teach me the importance of preparation. I mean this one time —"

"Josie!" Megan and I yelled in unison.

"Well, I'm curious." Mickey muttered, and went to retrieve the box.

Granny came into the kitchen, announcing she was packed and ready for her sleepover with Megan. All eyes went to Jack when Granny made that little announcement, because although Jack could put up with a lot, he usually drew the line at Granny.

Actually, everybody with a brain drew the line at Granny. "I'm all set, but I'm not leaving without my booby."

Megan looked at me, horrified, and I just shrugged. Jack winced, realizing that he was stuck with Granny. "Long story," I said, and Megan rolled her eyes and crossed herself, mumbling, "Lord help us all!"

Cooper and I had unfinished business, and I was anxious to get everyone out of my house. I threw Cooper my best puppy dog eyed pout, chewed on my bottom lip, batted the lashes of my bedroom eyes, and like a rocket he was gone. "One booby rescue coming right up," he said as he disappeared down the hall. As soon as he was out of earshot, Josie ran up to me, grabbed my hands, and started jumping up and down. "You better get that boy naked and let him fuck you until you forget your own name."

"Josie!"

"Look, I know about boys like that. I've dated boys like that."

"You've met him once, Josie," I argued.

"I'm very observant, Stacy, and if there's one thing I know, it is men." I rolled my eyes and she continued. "For instance, I know he is at least nine inches and he tucks it to the right. I know he will bite your bottom lip when he kisses you, and that the come ratio between you two will be at least three to one in your favor."

That got my attention. It had been a long time since I had had an orgasm. To say I was frustrated was an understatement. "He's the type that will paint your toenails, give you a massage, and pull your hair from behind. He's going to make you laugh, make you cry, and make you scream with pleasure. He'll make you wonder where he's been all your life, and you will fear going a day without him. He's your prince, Stacy. Give him a chance."

I was speechless and my mouth was hanging open. And I wasn't the only one. Everyone in the room was in shock, and all eyes were on Josie. Megan nodded and blinked back tears.

"Woah," Mickey said, having returned from retrieving the box. He bumped fists with Josie. "That shit was deep, girlfriend."

Josie smiled, her whole body radiating love. "What can I say, I'm a hopeless romantic."

"Since when?" I asked, and she put her hand over her heart.

"Since I met my Jon, Stacy. He's my prince, my lover, my everything." Megan was full on sobbing now, and Jack was cradling her in his arms. "That's why I'm taking him off the market by marrying him. I may be a dumb blonde, and I may not be real smart, but I know love when I see it, and sister, I'm seeing it now."

Cooper picked that moment to return, waving the fake booby in the air victoriously. Granny clapped her hands and said, "My hero." She grabbed the booby, hiked up her shirt, and put it in place. She adjusted her cleavage, gave Megan a thumbs up, and blew Cooper a kiss.

Josie clapped her hands. "Okay, enough with the mushy shit, let's get down to business. Mickey, Code Blue, dump that box."

"Um, babe, Code Blue means dead."

Josie raised her eyebrows. "Mickey, I know what it means. I am marrying a doctor, after all."

"So? Why a Code Blue? Stacy isn't dead."

"No," Josie said. "But her sex life is." She shooed him towards the table. "That's why we need the 'Boom Boom Box' STAT!" I was horrified. No matter what I had to do, I could not let that box be opened in this house. Josie leaned over, whispered to Cooper, and he laughed. He looked intrigued, amused, and damn sexy. His lips were curved in a mischievous smile, and his eyes glittered with promise. Oh damn! Heaven help me!

Jack grabbed Megan by the shoulders and tried to usher her out the back door. Granny stepped in front of it and blocked the way. "Granny, let's go," Jack said.

Granny shook her head. "No can do, Loverboy! I ain't leaving until I see what's in that box." Jack's face flushed with panic. Knowing Josie, there was absolutely no telling what was in that box. And knowing Granny, she would want a demonstration of each item. Having to view the contents would be embarrassing, and if I was being honest, probably a little educational for me. Viewing the contents with Granny would be a disaster. Megan tried sweet talking Granny but she wouldn't budge. Jack threw his hands up and took a seat. Megan sat in his lap, and everyone else gathered around the table as Mickey carefully placed the box in the middle of it. I was scared and excited at the same time.

Josie crossed her arms across her chest and shivered with excitement. "Oh my gosh, Stace, I have been waiting so long for this. I mean, I have been gathering these things slowly and putting them in this box, just like my gramma has been saving things for me in a hope chest." I was quite sure Grammy's hope chest didn't contain a sex swing and nipple clamps. "I mean, I have been carrying this box for months now in the hopes that one day my little Stacy would spread her wings and fly."

"Oh for the love of God, just open the damn box already!" Granny cried, and launched herself past Mickey towards the table. She grabbed the box, opened the flaps, and dumped it out on the table. There were gasps and sighs and shocked expressions all the way around.

Nobody spoke for what seemed like forever.

Granny was the first to speak. "Where is the kinky stuff?"

"Yeah Josie, I thought this was the 'Boom Boom Box,'" Mickey added.

I heard Megan start sobbing again and Jack quietly curse.

I was glued to my spot with my eyes tightly closed. If I couldn't see it, it didn't exist. Right? Don't get me wrong. A little part of me wanted to see what was in that box, but not in front of Cooper and everyone else. What if I didn't know what something was or how it worked? When it came to sex toys, I was clueless. I had never had one. Hell, I'd never even seen one in real life except for that one time in high school when I snuck into the porn shop on a dare and bought breath mints that were shaped like penises. My mom found out, gave me the sex talk, and put me on the pill. It was a very awkward time for me, and I emotionally blocked it out, which meant I still didn't know what a vibrator looked like.

"That's so sweet, Josie!" I heard Megan say, and I opened my eyes because my curiosity got the better of me, and I couldn't believe what I saw. I looked at Josie in confusion.

Granny was holding the box upside down, tapping it as if there were some hidden contents. When nothing came out, she tossed the box and pouted. "Where's the good stuff, Josie?" she asked. "What about the whips and chains, the vibrating peckers, the cock rings?"

Jack choked and told Megan he would be waiting in the car. A part of me wanted to join him. The other part of me wanted to stay and explore this box. With Cooper. All night!

Granny was tapping her foot and eyeing Josie expectantly. "So?" she said.

"Granny, all that fun, kinky stuff is in the 'Boom Boom Kaboom Box.' That's more of an intermediate box. This here is the beginner box."

"Lame," Granny said, crossing her arms over her chest.

"Bor-ing!" Mickey said, then clapped Cooper on the shoulder. "I'm out," he added, then walked out the back door. Megan tried to get up, stuck her hands out, and Cooper and I helped her out of the chair. "Come on," she said to Granny.

Granny slumped her shoulders. "But I wanna see the Kaboom box!" she pouted as Megan opened the back door and gently pushed her through it. I looked at Cooper, his blue eyes sparkling, and felt excitement building in my belly.

Josie threw her Louis Vuitton over her shoulder and kissed me on the cheek. "You kids have fun!" she said over her shoulder as she headed for the back door.

Cooper and I were the only people left in the house...finally! I was staring at the items on the table, and suddenly I was extremely nervous. I fidgeted with my hands and chewed on my bottom lip. Cooper came up behind me and wrapped his arms around me. "Finally alone," he whispered, his breath hot on my neck.

I picked up the item closest to me and turned it over in my hand. It was a DVD titled "Sensual Love Making" and it showed a tastefully naked couple in a loving embrace. Not at all the type of viewing material I had pictured Josie picking out. I fingered the next item...massage oil, honeysuckle scented. I opened it and smelled it, and Cooper took it out of my hand and placed it back on the table. He tucked a runaway curl behind my ear, his fingers lingering on my neck. He tilted my head, and before I knew it his lips were on mine, gentle at first, then his kiss became more intense and hungry. He bit my bottom lip and I saw stars. Josie was right. I already wondered where he had been my whole life, and didn't want to experience a day without him or his touch, or his kisses that drove me crazy. I was in way too deep.

Cooper ended the kiss and tilted my head up to face him, his eyes full of heat and promise. My heart skipped a beat. I was really going to do this, throw caution to the wind, break the rules, and just surrender to this man. I was nervous. I was scared. I was extremely worried that I wouldn't be able to bring him pleasure like I was sure he would bring me. But I was going to give it one hell of an effort. I threw the bolt on the door and took a deep breath.

"Stacy?"

"Yes?" I breathed.

He sat in the chair and pulled me into his lap. "Talk to me. Tell me about this 'Beginner Box.'"

I surveyed the contents on the table. "Well, let's see here. There's the DVD, lotion, candles, silk rose petals, condoms, massage oil, lubricant, and um…feathers." The feathers confused me a bit. I had no idea what the hell to use them for, but everything else I was good with.

Cooper laughed, his eyes laced with humor. "I know what everything is. I wanted to know why your friend Josie would give you a 'Beginner Box.'"

I blushed beat red. "That doesn't matter. She was just playing." I waved him off, desperate to change the subject. The last thing I wanted him to know was how inexperienced I was. I began to fidget and wring my hands, my resolve quickly fading.

He stilled my hands and his voice took on a serious tone. "It matters to me Stacy," he said, and I felt my stomach fall. When he found out what a lousy lay I was, he would probably decide I wasn't worth the trouble. As much as I wanted to lie to him, I chose to be honest and decided I would not cry when he got up and left. I should have just stayed with the whole sworn off men thing.

"Okay, Cooper, what do you want to know?" I bit my lip as I anticipated his response.

He tried to keep his tone even. "Well, you aren't a virgin, right?"

I laughed, a hearty chuckle that ended with a snort. Wow, really sexy, Stacy! "No, I'm not a virgin. As a matter of fact, I have had tons of sex." I winced at his surprised expression. "Okay, that came out wrong. I mean, I have had lots of sex, I just haven't had many partners." I looked down at my hands intertwined with his. "And according to Josie, I've never had a real orgasm."

Now that got his attention. The challenge had been established. "Okay, so tell me about these partners." I was uncomfortable talking about this, and I wasn't sure this was the kind of conversation everyone had before they had sex, but Cooper had asked and I was sure he had good reason to do so. I swallowed hard.

"Okay, so I was twenty-two when I lost my virginity. On my wedding night. To my high school sweetheart. We spent seven years married, until he told me he was no longer attracted to me and found someone else. I was devastated, but there were signs along the way that I had missed because I was dealing with my own issues."

"The drinking?" he asked softly.

I nodded. "Yes, but I don't want to talk about that right now."

"Okay." He gestured for me to continue.

"So I accepted that my marriage was over, and Scott and I divorced amicably. We still remain friends. He felt horrible about how things turned out, so he agreed to a healthy divorce settlement and a generous amount of alimony."

Cooper was running his fingers up and down my back, his touch light and soothing. I felt so comfortable in his lap and sharing my life story with him. Even though we had only met a few days ago, it felt as though I'd known him forever. I felt safe, and suddenly I wanted to share everything with him. "And then there was Thad," I continued. "I'd known him forever, was reintroduced, and I fell really hard, really fast. He used me for sex, got his fill, and dumped me three months later via text. On Valentine's Day. He was a major douchebag, and I realized later that I never really loved him. I just loved being with him because I hated being alone. The irony is, I felt more alone with him than I had ever felt before. It was a bad time for me."

"When was that?"

"About four months ago."

"And then?" Cooper asked, urging me to go on.

"That's it. That's all there is. That's my whole story."

Cooper looked at me, incredulous. "You've only been with two guys?"

"Yep. That's it. I wasn't kidding when I said I wasn't a slut. Plus I have a five date rule. I just haven't found anybody I wanted to go on that many dates with, so nobody else has gotten past second base." He brought my hand up to his lips and brushed tender kisses across my knuckles.

"And you've never had a real orgasm?"

I frowned. "I don't know. Okay?" Cooper looked confused, so I tried to explain. "I mean, I've gotten really turned on and came a little here and there, but nothing like the mind blowing, life altering explosions that Josie and the girls talk about."

Cooper's blazing blue eyes sparkled. "Well, we will have to change that, Ms. Dupree." I shivered, my tummy full of butterflies. "When I make you come, you will damn well know it." I swallowed and nodded. I had a feeling sex with Cooper would be earthshattering. I would probably be ruined for any other man. Probably I would have to ask Josie if she had a "Hans Solo Box" so I could take care of myself, because after Cooper I doubted anyone else would measure up.

Cooper's gaze was heated. "What are you thinking right now, Stacy?"

I laughed and flashed him a flirty smile. "I thought you could read my mind," I teased.

Cooper swept the items on the table to the floor. He lifted me out of his lap and sat me on the table facing him. His hands at my waist, his lips found mine. Our tongues danced playfully until he deepened the kiss and made love to my mouth in a way I had never experienced before. I melted into him desperately, needing to feel him closer to me. I slipped off the table and straddled him in the chair, and felt his erection, long, hard and poking my backside. I wanted to see it, feel it, taste it, and more than anything, I wanted it inside me.

Cooper slipped one hand under my shirt and expertly released the clasp of my bra. He then pulled my shirt up to expose my breasts, and I helped him out by yanking the shirt over my head and discarding it in the floor. He stripped me of my bra and his eyes feasted on my naked breasts. "Oh sweet Jesus," he said before burying his face in my hair and inhaling my scent. He nipped my ear, my neck, and then dipped his head lower, his tongue swirling my swollen, hardened nipple. He nibbled gently, and I arched my back to give him better access. He unfastened the button on my shorts, his mouth never leaving my over sensitized breasts. His hands cupped my ass, and he laid me on the table and rid me of my shorts, leaving me in a black lace thong. Thank God I wasn't wearing granny panties or period panties.

"You should never wear clothes, Stacy. It's a crime to cover this beautiful body. I just want to feel you, to taste every inch of you, to make you come over and over again until you cry out my name and beg me to stop."

Oh-kay. Well, that sounded like a good plan to me.

Cooper slid his finger into my panties and groaned when he found my sex free of hair. Okay, confession time. Not that I believed any of Granny's fortune telling mumbo jumbo, but I did see that love card come up several times, and I wanted to be ready just in case. There's nothing sexy about needing a weed whacker before you can go down on a woman. And in all honesty, I wasn't going for the whole bald thing, but I messed up while shaping the bush so I chose to take it all off instead of having a lopsided landing strip on my hoohah. That was so not sexy.

Cooper slid my panties to the side and ran his finger along my folds, making slow sweeping motions. I was completely turned on and wet for him. I wanted him naked too. I wanted him inside me, hard and fast. I wanted to squeeze every drop of come from him and feel him pulse inside me.

Cooper sat in the chair and pulled me toward him. He dropped whisper kisses to my ribs, my abdomen, my hips. He slowly slid my thong down first one leg, then the other, his fingers skimming my heated flesh along the way. I shivered and felt goose bumps invade my smoldering skin. Even after seven years of marriage and three months of what I considered great sex, I had never been this turned on. Cooper held my bootless foot in his hand and placed sensual kisses along my arch, my ankle, behind my knee, and then—oh sweet Jesus—the inside of my thigh. And then the moment I had been waiting for...Cooper licked the folds of my pussy, not touching my clitoris.

"Delicious!" he said. His tongue stroked me slowly, and then his tongue was flicking at my swollen sex, and it took every ounce of resolve I had not to bolt up from that table and jump on his cock. His fingers were working my nipples and his tongue was doing its magic, and I was so close to what I knew was going to be earth shattering and magnificent. Then his mouth covered my clitoris just as he inserted a finger inside of me, and I couldn't hide the moan that escaped my lips.

"That's right baby. Come for me."

His finger was sliding in and out as he nipped at my swollen nub, his other hand caressing my breast. It was sensory overload and still I wanted more, and he gave it to me. He slipped another finger in and I cried out in pleasure, and I couldn't lie still any longer. I began moving with his finger, setting the rhythm I needed. Eyes closed, bottom lip between my teeth, I felt my body starting to shatter as Cooper kept building and building my orgasm, getting me almost there and then taking it back a notch until I couldn't take anymore. With his fingers still moving inside me, he covered my clitoris with his mouth and sucked hard, and I cried out as wave after wave of ecstasy shook my entire body, and I came violently and harder than I ever had before.

Cooper didn't stop. He kept doing what he had been doing, harder and faster, and I felt the pressure building again. This time when I came, I cursed and shouted his name, and wrapped my legs around his neck to stop him because I couldn't take anymore. Cooper smiled and looked up at me, a satisfied and sexy grin on his face. He caressed my breast and I trembled as the aftershocks of my orgasms overtook me.

"Wow!" I said when I found my voice.

Cooper pulled me into his lap, my body limp. "Yeah, wow!" Cooper agreed.

I stared into his sea blue eyes, and all I could think of to say was, "Thank you."

Cooper laughed. "It was my pleasure, Ms. Dupree."

"Um, actually the pleasure was all mine. Literally."

Cooper kissed my jawline, my cheek, my lips. I tasted myself on him, and that turned me on even more. I wanted Cooper to slide inside me, fill me, and stroke me more than I had ever wanted anything in my life. And he was more than ready. His cock was swollen and hard and teasing me through his shorts. I fingered the button on his shorts and he stopped me. I frowned, confused, and slid my hands up his shirt instead, desperate to feel flesh on flesh. His whole body stilled and his breath caught. He caught my hands and stopped me. "Stacy," he said. "Baby, I want today to be just about you. I want to please you."

"Well, it would please me to have you inside me!" Here I was naked and in his lap. What kind of red-blooded American man refused sex in a situation like this?

Cooper looked conflicted and his breathing was ragged. I could tell he was trying really hard to keep himself in control. Although I admired his restraint, it was really starting to piss me off. I started to wonder if it was me. Did I not turn him on? Did he not like curvy, take charge women? Did I have something in my teeth? A puss filled zit on my forehead?

Cooper gathered me in his arms and pulled me even closer to him. He buried his nose in my hair and groaned.

"Is it me?" I whispered. I hated how needy my voice sounded, but I had to know.

"Yes," he replied, and pulled my chin up so he could look in my eyes. I tried and failed to keep the disappointment I was feeling inside from showing. The rejection hurt, but I was a big girl. I could handle it.

Suddenly, I felt very uncomfortable being naked in his lap. I looked around the kitchen for something to cover up with. Finding nothing, I had decided to leave his lap when he tilted his head and kissed me gently. This was so confusing. His actions said one thing and his words said another. This was Thad all over again. I broke the kiss and abruptly jumped out of his lap. He reached for me to come back to him, and I shook my head, blinking back tears. "Stacy —" he began, but I cut him off.

I covered my body as best I could with my arms and hands. "I think you should go, Cooper."

"You don't understand," he said, and he was right, I didn't understand. But the one thing I did understand was hurt, and I would not let him hurt me. My face was flushed red and I was angry. I knew I shouldn't have, but I lashed out at him. "Look, thanks for the orgasms. They were awesome. But I don't want to be some charity case that you took pity on and threw a little fun at so you can feel like you accomplished something."

He reached out for me again and I took a step back. "That's not what happened, Stacy. And I could never think of you as a charity case."

"Well, you said it was me!" I shot back.

"It is you." He took a step towards me. "It's you that makes me so crazy that I just want to throw you up against the wall and make love to you every time I see you. It's you that I want to taste, to touch, to feel, and kiss. It's you that makes me want to break all of my rules, let down all my walls, and just lose myself in you." He took another step forward, and his knuckles brushed my cheek. "It's you that is consuming my every thought, invading my dreams, and making me walk around with a constant hard on like a lovesick teenager." He tucked a curl behind my ear and kissed my nose. "It's you that I can't get enough of, and that scares the crap out of me. When I'm near you I have to touch you, and I know that if I make love to you I will never want to stop."

I was speechless. "Oh."

"I want to be perfectly honest with you, Stacy."

I swallowed. "Yes, please do."

"I like women. And women like me. I don't really do the whole relationship thing. I've never found anybody I wanted to be in a relationship with. Sure, I go on dates, and some of those dates do end with sex. But I am a perfect gentleman and I'm always upfront and honest with the other person. I always use protection and never make any promises."

"Okay, so you want no strings attached sex. I get that. I'm fine with that."

"That's the problem." The look in Cooper's eyes was so tender. "I don't want that with you." I opened my mouth to protest and he held his hands out to stop me. "Let me finish please." I closed my mouth. "There's something about you, Stacy. You're different. I don't want to just have sex with you a couple of times, then move onto the next girl. I don't want to have a little fun with you then leave before you wake up." He pressed his body into my mine and brought his forehead to mine. My eyes were locked with his electric blue eyes, and my heart was in my throat, my nakedness forgotten. "With you, I want so much more.

I want to hold you all night and watch you sleep. I want to wake up with you wrapped around me, your hair a mess, your make up gone. I want to make you laugh, wipe away your tears when you cry, and bring you pleasure until your body can take no more. And to be honest with you, it scares me to death. I have never felt this drawn to anybody, and just the thought of screwing up or hurting you has my stomach in knots."

The tears were streaming down my cheeks and I didn't bother to try to stop them. "Cooper, seriously, I'm a mess. I mean I'm a major work in progress."

Cooper laughed and kissed me on top of my head. "You are a mess Stacy. You are a beautiful mess. And I would love to make you my mess."

"I would like that too," I admitted. "So what's the problem?"

"The problem is, although I want to throw you down on that table and fuck you silly, I don't want you to break your rules for me. I want to take it slow and do it right. I want to get to know you. I want our first time to be special and perfect, and I don't want to just have sex. I want to make love to you. I want to connect with you; I want to share my day with you. I want to be on your mind all day long, and I want you to crave me as much as I crave you." He found my lips with his and his kiss was like a loving caress.

"I want that, too," I said, and he released the breath he had been holding. His eyes sparkled and his luscious lips curved into the sexiest smile I had ever seen. His words and his touch were the sweetest things I had ever experienced. I fell for him completely at that very moment, and I knew the risks. I knew I might get hurt. I was trusting him with my heart, and after Scott and Thad, I knew that was a very dangerous thing to do, and at that very moment I didn't care. All I cared about was right now, being in his arms, my body pressed to his, his lips on mine.

"So let me get this straight," I said, wrapping my arms around his waist, enjoying the feel of his erection poking me in the stomach. "You want to date me?"

His hands caressed me back. "Yes."

"But no sex?" I asked doubtfully.

"Not for five dates."

I rolled my eyes. Me and my stupid rules!

I kissed his jaw. "But we can still make out, right?" I moved my lips to his neck and nipped lightly.

"Absolutely!" We were so close I could feel his rapid heart rate and hear his ragged breathing.

I gave him a coy smile. "And you will make me come like that again?"

His breath caught and his hands slipped lower, cupping my ass. "Guaranteed!" he said with promise. He then scooped me up and sat me on the counter. My ass was still sore, but I forgot all about that when he began delivering teasing kisses to my neck. "Over," he dipped lower. "And over." His mouth found my breast. "And over." He nipped with his teeth, and I threw my head back in pleasure. "And over again."

I was dripping wet, every nerve in my body on high alert. I was close to coming again and he had barely touched me. "Cooper," I breathed, and slid his hand to my sex. He inserted one finger and then…the freaking doorbell rang! Whoever was at my door was going to die. I was going to kill them and then revive them so I could kill them again.

Cooper continued to slide his finger in and out of me, painfully slowly. "Ignore it," he whispered.

The thought was tempting. Whoever was at the door gave up on the doorbell and started knocking. As I was about to push him away and find my robe and answer the door, he slid another finger in me and I couldn't move. I opened my mouth to protest, but was rendered speechless when his fingers curved and found my g spot. The knocking got louder. I was getter closer. Cooper had found the perfect rhythm. "Cooper, we have to stop." His fingers stilled as the knocking went to banging. "What are you doing?" I half shouted. "Don't stop!" Cooper laughed and found his rhythm again. The pressure was building and I was close to exploding bliss. I closed my eyes and bit my lip to keep a moan from escaping my lips. Cooper was prompting me, his voice low and sexy. I felt the first wave of sheer pleasure hit me and Cooper took it up a notch, working his fingers faster and harder, and I was on the brink…and then I heard Granny's voice outside my back door.

"I know you are in there, Stacy! Open up! I need my dancing shoes!" There was still loud banging on the front door. I was surrounded! Shit!

"Oh God!" I moaned, because what Cooper was doing felt so good, but I knew at any moment that door was going to fly open and Granny was coming in. I did a quick assessment of my options, all of which sucked. My clothes were by the kitchen table, which was by the back door. Couldn't get to them without being seen. My robe was in my room, but I had to pass the front door to get to it, and I had no doubt whoever was knocking the door off the hinges was probably snooping through the window. I was screwed. I jumped off the counter and pulled Cooper down with me.

"You locked the door right?" he asked, amused.

"Yes, but that won't stop them. We don't have much time."

"So? I'll just go get your clothes." He started to stand and I yanked him back down behind the counter.

"No, then they will see you with my clothes and know I'm naked." I was panicked.

"Um babe, I'm pretty sure they are going to know that pretty soon anyways."

"NO! We have to do something."

Cooper was finding our predicament humorous. I would make him pay for that later. "Look, we are consenting adults. It might   be   embarrassing   but...."
"I've got it!" I said, and opened a drawer. "We will just set the house on fire."

Cooper looked at me like I was nuts, and in all honesty I probably was. "They won't come in, the firemen will, and they'll wrap me in a blanket, and no one but you and the firemen will know I was naked."

"That's a horrible plan," Cooper pointed out.

"Got a better plan?"

"Stacy, if we are going to be roommates, I'm going to need a key." Granny hollered as she jiggled the doorknob.

"Do you have an apron?" Cooper asked, and I looked at him with an incredulous look. "Okay, right. Shit. Well, I'm out of ideas."

I opened a cabinet in search of a trash bag, but found the aluminum foil and thought of a better idea. I grabbed the foil, got on my knees, and started wrapping the lower half of my body with foil. I now had a foil mini skirt. Cooper helped me repeat the process with my top half.

He had just ripped the foil off the roll when the front door opened and Josie bounced in. She entered the kitchen and laughed when she saw me and Cooper on our knees behind the counter. Knowing we were busted, we both stood.

"Aluminum foil, huh? Kinky." Her lips formed a devilish grin. "I like it."

"It isn't what you think," I told her, and she giggled and let Granny in.

Granny took in the scene and whistled. "You know, if you are going to do the dirty with Mr. Sexy Pants in in the kitchen, you need to hang a bra on the door knob. That's like roommate code for 'Do Not Disturb. Sex in Progress.'"

"We aren't roommates!" I ground out, and Granny waved me off. "And besides, the door was locked! That's universal code for 'Keep out!'"

"We were afraid you might have been kidnapped," Josie said. Right, because the kidnappers were on a rampage these days.

"And I needed my dancing shoes! I'm going clubbing with Mickey and Matt, and I can't go without my sparkly shoes," Granny added.

"How did you get the door open?" I asked Josie. "I thought you lost your key."

"I did." She dug around in her bra. "I used these." She pulled out a set of lock picks.

"You're a locksmith?" Cooper asked, and Josie laughed.

"Of course not! But I used to date this guy. He was a burglar. He taught me all the tricks of the trade. When he went to prison, I broke into his house and stole his tools. You never know when you might need to do a B & E. That means Breaking and Entering in felon talk," she added.

Cooper's mouth was hanging open. I, on the other hand, had known Josie since kindergarten. Nothing she said or did surprised me anymore. "And you just carry burglar tools with you wherever you go? That's dumb Josie. You can go to jail for just having them."

She waved me off. "Oh please, do you know how many judges I've dated?"

I gave up. I would never win this argument.

"What's with the foil, Stacy?" Granny wanted to know.

"Oh, it's a new treatment for cellulite," I lied. "Cooper was kind enough to help me wrap myself in it."

Granny was intrigued. "Cellulite? Really. I got some of that." She picked up the aluminum foil. "Tell me how it works."

I thought fast. "It, um...well, the aluminum reacts with chemicals in your body that breaks down the fat cells that cause cellulite. All the celebrities are doing it."

"You don't say?"

"Yep, I saw it on TV. Thought I'd give it a try." I was lying my ass off and Cooper had turned so that his back was to me. I could see his shoulders shaking and knew he was laughing. I could have used a little help, but obviously he wasn't going to rescue me.

Granny's eyes sparkled. "Hey, I just got a great idea!" She kicked off her shoes. "I'll strip down and you can wrap me up. I'll wear it to the club tonight and make a fashion statement while I'm burning off some cellulite. That foil will go with my shoes perfectly. I'm going to start a new trend. Maybe those paparazzi people will see me and I'll be on TV. I'll be the next big thing!"

"No!" We all yelled in unison as Granny unbuttoned her pants. She stuck her bottom lip out and pouted. "Why do you youngens get to have all the fun?" She trotted off to her room, muttering along the way. "It's no fair! Getting old is a bitch."

Josie shot me a menacing look and followed Granny. "I'll wrap you in foil when we get back to Megan's, Granny. Don't you worry about a thing. You will look great."

Cooper took a deep breath. "That was close," he said. I nodded. "We need to find a secure location," I told him. "One that nobody knows about, because my house is a mad house."

He laughed. "I've noticed."

I heard the front door open and figured it was Megan. "I'm in the kitchen," I called out, and was surprised when Old Lady Gentry from across the street walked in. She gave me a long look, appraised Cooper, and opened her mouth to speak. I cut her off. "What can I do for you, Mrs. Gentry?"

"I just came to check on you. I saw the firemen here. What did you cook this time?" I knew she wasn't there to check on me. She'd hated me ever since I moved in. She was there to check out Cooper. Not wanting to argue with her, I said, "It was just a small grease fire, but I put it out quickly. Everything is fine now. Thank you for checking on me, but you can go now. You are probably missing your shows."

She reached for a cigarette. "I have DVR, and this here looks more interesting than my shows anyways. What's up with the foil outfit?"

"Oh, this?" I said. "This is called a detoxification wrap. It's a new way to get rid of toxins in your body from smoke inhalation. The firemen recommended I give it a try, since I have inhaled quite a bit of smoke here lately. It works. I am feeling better already."

Mrs. Gentry scrunched up her eyebrows. "It looks like regular Reynolds Wrap to me."

I kicked the foil box out of sight. "Oh no, this here is special stuff. They are using it at NASA now for the astronauts...for, you know, when they are exposed to toxins on other planets and stuff." Mrs. Gentry was staring me down and I took a step closer to Cooper. In all honesty, that crazy old lady gave me the heebee jeebees.

We stood in a stare down for a moment, and then Granny re-emerged with her small suitcase in one hand and her bottle of moonshine in the other. She sat her things on the counter, walked right up to Mrs. Gentry, and slapped her across the face. She then took her shoes off and removed her earrings, but before she could do any more damage, Cooper grabbed her and held her back.

"Let, me go, Mr. Sexy Pants!" she yelled. "I have been waiting patiently for my opportunity to whip her ass since 1992, when I found out she kissed my man!" Granny was flailing her hands around, trying to break free. Cooper held on tighter.

"Well, if you had kept him happy at home he wouldn't have come knocking on my door," Mrs. Gentry yelled, inches from Granny's face. "And he wasn't your man anyways. He was mine first!"

"Ladies!" I shouted, stepping in the middle of them. And I was using the term "ladies" loosely. "That's enough. Nobody is going to kick anybody's ass. We are all friends here, right?" Okay, so nobody was friends there, but that was beside the point. I just wanted all of these crazy people out of my house as soon as possible. "Now Granny, will you behave if Cooper lets you go?"

She was still squirming. "Hell no, I won't!"

"I got your back, Granny," Josie told her, and started removing things from her bra.

"You want a piece of me?" Mrs. Gentry asked, waving a fist in Granny's face.

Granny spit at her. "Sure, why not? Everybody else has already had a piece."

Old Lady Gentry's eyes bulged and she attacked Granny. Cooper wisely let go and let them have at it. There was a lot of slapping and some hair pulling. After about thirty seconds they were both worn out. Granny had her hands on her knees, breathing heavily. "Tramp!" she shouted, and then Mrs. Gentry, also huffing and puffing, called Granny a home wrecking whore bag. This got Granny all fired up again, and they were at it for round two. It was Granny's Gone Wild in my kitchen. Cooper looked to me for guidance and I just shrugged and took a seat at the table. Josie examined her nails like she was bored. In a very short time, they were both worn out again, although their mouths were still going full force.

"If it weren't for my bum hip, I would have destroyed your skank ass," Granny said, to which Mrs. Gentry responded with a whole new barrage of insults. After they had called each other every name in the book, they began to compare aches and pains and complain about their arthritis. Granny retrieved her "medicine" and took a long pull, and then passed it to Old Lady Gentry, who was lighting up a cigarette.

"I didn't mean everything I said," Granny told her. "I mean, I meant most of it, but that comment about you being a pig fucker? That was crossing the line."

"It's okay," Mrs. Gentry said. "I shouldn't have said you had the herpes. Even though you probably did have them a time or two." They passed the bottle a few more times, and then Granny told Mrs. Gentry about her date tonight and invited her to come along. Granny said they could double date like they used to before Mrs. Gentry turned into a back stabbing heifer. Mrs. Gentry complained about how she didn't have anything to wear, and Granny explained the foil club attire. For a brief second I was consumed with panic at the thought of two naked old women in my kitchen wrapping each other in foil, but Cooper saved the day by grabbing the box of foil, emptying it, and holding it up for them to see that it was all gone. Granny suggested they go to Megan's, and although I hated to dump them off on Megan, I hated them being in my kitchen even more. Josie offered to take them to buy foil and then to Megan's. I waved and relaxed when I heard the door close.

I only got a second of relief though, as Mrs. Gentry re-entered. "I almost forgot, Stacy, I came over for the cat."

"What cat?" I asked.

Mrs. Gentry narrowed her eyes. "The one you are watching for your friend." When I still didn't get it, she added, "The slut? You know the one you borrowed a kennel from me for?"

Cooper's grin was infectious. "You have a slut in a kennel around here and you haven't told me?"

"No," Mrs. Gentry said. "The slut is driving the car. But Stacy is watching her cat. And I'm not leaving without that cat. Stacy is dangerous. She catches things on fire. I'm not going to stand for that poor little creature being stuck in a crate with no means of escape the next time she catches the house on fire."

Oh shit! Paddington! I had forgotten all about him. He was probably dead already. I was a horrible person. "Oh, that cat?" I said. "Yup, funny thing. It must have run away when the firemen were here, because I haven't seen him since."

"Smart cat," Mrs. Gentry mumbled. "Well then, give me my crate back and I'll be on my way."

I couldn't give her that crate with a maybe dead duck in it. "I have to clean it out." Josie was laying on the horn. I gave her my best smile. "I'll get right on that and leave it on your porch. Now run along. You don't want to be late for your date."

Mrs. Gentry pointed a bony finger at me. "I've got my eye on you, Stacy Dupree," she said before leaving for the second and hopefully the last time.

CHAPTER 7

After the Grannys Gone Wild smackdown in my kitchen, Cooper and I checked on Paddington the duck, who thankfully was still alive. I was so relieved that I hadn't killed him. We let him outside to do his little ducky business and refreshed his food and water, and made plans to put in a little pond for him and plant him a shade tree. I was a horrible duck parent and couldn't even keep a plant alive, but by God, I was hell bent on keeping the little guy. I even entertained the idea of getting him a little playmate so he wouldn't get lonely.

Cooper had a meeting he had to get to, but promised to return promptly at 6:00 P.M. to pick me up for our first date. The man had seen me naked and made me come. I had dry humped his leg. He had seen me with tampons in my nose, but yet I was crazy nervous about our date. We were just going to do the whole dinner and a movie thing…no big deal. Cooper was honoring my stupid five-date rule, so there was no pressure for sex, although to be honest, I would have willingly put out. I didn't know what was wrong with me, but ever since Cooper Carson walked into my life I had been walking around with sex on my brain constantly. I'd gone four months without it and really hadn't missed it, but now it was all I could think about. *He* was all I could think about. I wanted him more than I had ever wanted anything in my life, and the thought scared the hell out of me and excited me at the same time. I had never felt this way before, not with Scott, and definitely not with Thad. I was in way over my head with a guy that was way out of my league. I had it bad and I knew it. I needed help. I needed Josie. If anyone knew about men and sex it was Josie. She wrote the freaking book on it.

Josie picked up on the third ring and promised to come over just as soon as Granny and Mrs. Gentry were done at the beauty shop. It was only 3:00. I had three hours until our date and I was antsy, so I decided to get rid of some nervous energy on the treadmill. I used to work out all the time and it relaxed me. I hadn't been in my workout room in months, but I was pretty sure I was still in relatively good shape. I was wrong. My plan was to just hobble along at a brisk pace. Just like walking right? After three minutes, my legs were on fire, my booted foot was throbbing, and I was gasping for air. I turned that sucker off and got the hell off it. But since I had burned fourteen calories I decided to reward myself with ice cream and strawberry cheesecake.

Josie showed up about thirty minutes later. Her hair was a mess, her shirt was backwards, and her lipstick was smeared. She rushed in, breathless, grabbed a bottle of water, drank it in one long swig, closed her eyes, took a deep breath, and then turned her attention on me.

I raised an eyebrow. "I thought you said you were at the beauty shop."

"I was." She patted her hair down and smoothed out her shirt, revealing a mountain of boobs.

"Are you sure you weren't in the elevator with Dr. Ross?" I indicated her shirt.

She took it off, turned it around, and slipped it back on. "No, we did it in my car." I rolled my eyes and she held out a hand. "No, listen, I know what you are thinking. You're thinking that I was off having sex with my fiancé while you were having a crisis, but that's not what happened. This was an emergency! If you had experienced what those old ladies put me through, you would have needed some reassurance sex too."

I so didn't want to know the details, but I couldn't help myself. I asked anyways.

Josie's eyes grew wide and she put a hand on her heart. "It was horrible, Stacy. I am traumatized. I might require therapy, although Jon said I should be fine when the shock wears off."

I wanted to slap her. "What happened? When you left here you were going to get foil."

She exhaled a long breath. "Well, that was the plan, but then Granny told Mrs. Gentry that her hair looked like a rats nest, so when we passed a salon they made me double back and take them there for a quick cut and style."

"Okay, that doesn't sound too bad."

"Oh, it gets worse." She paused for effect. "So Granny and I were just sitting there flipping through magazines, and Granny saw a sign for body waxing."

"Uh oh."

"Yeah, big uh oh. So she decides she wants a Brazilian wax, just in case she gets lucky tonight at the club."

I stopped her. "Okay, I've heard enough. No need to explain any further."

"Jon said talking about it will help." I really didn't want to know what happened next, but I signaled for her to go on.

"So anyways, Granny asked me if I've ever had a Brazilian and I said 'Yeah sure,' and she asked how they did it, so I told her and she said that didn't sound too bad, so she decided to do it. And I told her to go for it. I mean, you only live once, right?"

"Right. YOLO!"

"So she goes in and I'm flipping through Cosmo and then I hear her screaming my name. I ignored her, but she was scaring the other clients, so the lady came and got me and asked me if I would go in and stay with Granny for moral support."

I closed my eyes. "Oh God!"

"Yeah, so I go in and I see it." She grabbed my hands. "I see it Stacy! I see her old eighty-year-old vagina. It was horrible. It scared me to death. I ran to the bathroom and splashed water on my face. And then I got curious and needed to know if my kitty looked like that. So I grabbed my compact and stuck it between my legs to see, but I couldn't get a good enough angle, so I texted Jon and told him it was an emergency, and he texted back that he was going on break. So I rush up there and tell him all about it, and he assures me that mine doesn't look like that. So he offers to help me get a better angle so I can see for myself, and then I finally see that mine doesn't look like that. It's actually kind of pretty. Mine has—"

"Josie! I don't want to know!"

"Right, okay, so I see for myself and I'm okay, but then Jon starts touching and petting it, and then...well, one thing led to another, and you know what happened next."

"I get the picture."

"But," she continued. "I knew you needed me so I made Jon hurry. I only got off twice."

Josie had no filter or concept of too much information. "Thanks."

She put her elbows on the table and rested her head in her hands. "So, what do you need, Stace? You know I'm always here for you."

"I know." I stopped, at a loss for words. I really didn't know how to proceed. I was not even sure what I needed help with. I was a grown woman, for God's sake. I was quite capable of making my own decisions. I laughed nervously, took a deep breath, and smiled at Josie. "So, you know Cooper right?"

"Mr. Beefcake with a side of delicious? Yes, we've met." She batted her eyelashes. "Now, confession time! Tell me all about it!"

I squirmed in my seat, remembering the feel of his hands touching me. "There's really nothing to tell." Josie shook her head. "Yet!" I added.

"Well, why the hell not? That boy is crazy about you!"

That brought a sappy grin to my face. "Josie, I'm crazy about him too."

"Duh. I've seen you two together. Ya'll are crazy about each other. You need to just give it up and get it over with. You know you want it."

Boy did I? "Well see, I already have. Sort of."

"There's no sort of. You either do it or you don't."

"I've tried, but he is only interested in making me come."

"And that's a problem how?" Josie asked. "Just lay back and let that boy make you feel good."

"I have, but I want more."

Josie threw her hands up and shook a finger at me. "Oh no you don't. Don't start with that love shit. Just have some fun and see where it goes."

"When I said I wanted more, I didn't mean love. I meant I wanted to go further, like sexually." I needed to just say it, but all of a sudden I felt shy. "Like, I want him to fuck me sideways," I blurted, and felt my cheeks heat.

Josie looked confused. "So, again I ask, what's the freaking problem?"

"He doesn't want to have sex with me."

"But you just said —"

I didn't let her finish. "Josie, he wants to *make love* to me." I held my hands up. "His words, not mine. He says he feels this crazy connection, and he wants to take it slow and honor my five date rule."

"Which is a stupid rule to begin with," Josie said.

I nodded. "It probably is, but it has served me well so far. It's helped me weed out the assholes." I thought about Thad. If I'd stuck to my rule I might not have been hurt by him.

"Okay?" Josie said, obviously not following. "So, go on five dates with him."

I frown. "That's the thing, I don't want to."

Josie raised a brow, obviously perplexed. "Well then, what the hell do you want? Do you even know?"

I ran my fingers through my long brown hair. "I just want sex from him. I don't want to fall in love, get married, or have babies. I just want sex. Lots of it. But, I want to leave my heart out of it." As if I hadn't already started to fall for the man. "I don't want to get attached to him."

Josie nodded, understanding now. "So you just want to use him for sex?"

"Yes," I lied, and I felt horrible about it.

Josie's expression softened. She covered my hand with hers. "Oh honey, you shouldn't feel bad about that. Sex is natural and necessary. As long as you lay down the ground rules with him there's nothing wrong with it." She brightened. "I mean, guys do it all the time, Stace."

"Yeah, but I kind of feel dirty about it."

"Dirty is fun!"

"But I feel like I'm a slut or something."

"Oh my gosh, Stacy, you are over thinking the hell out of this. Geez woman! You're killing me here. Okay. Slow down a second. Are you attracted to Cooper?"

I gave her an incredulous look. "Yes, very."

"Okay, and we both know he is attracted to you. So there are no worries there. Do you want to let him make you feel so good you forget your own name?"

"Yes," I fanned myself. "And he is very, very good at that."

"Okay, so just pretend you are a guy. Go on the dates, court him, hang out and have fun, get him in the sack, and keep him there until you get your fill."

She made it sound so easy. "But what if he develops feelings?"

"So? You make no promises. If you feel it, great; if not, oh well, at least you got a good lay out of the deal."

I sighed. "But what if I develop feelings?" I was afraid I already had. "I'm afraid of getting hurt."

"Then you go with it. Look, Stacy, not all men are Thad. You can't hold something against Cooper that isn't his fault. Thad hurt you and I get that, but that doesn't mean Cooper will. Girlfriend, you have to kiss a few toads before you find your prince. Take me and Jon for example. Do you know how many toads I had to kiss? And yes, in the process you might break a couple of hearts." She rolled her eyes. "Big whoop. They'll get over it. That's why you play with men and not boys. And anyways, if he just wanted in your pants he could have already been there and done that. You said so yourself."

"Well, there's the other problem too," I said, knowing this was more Josie's area. She signaled for me to go on. "Um, I've only been with Scott and Thad. I'm pretty inexperienced. Cooper told me himself that he dates a lot, and I'm pretty sure he's been with quite a few women. I'm afraid I might not measure up. And I want to be memorable. I want to please him like he pleases me. I want him to want me."

My cell phone buzzed and I checked the screen. Josie snooped and read the message upside down.

Cooper: "Can't wait to see you Gorgeous! Only 2 more hours."

"You've already made an impression, Stacy," Josie said. "He's counting down the minutes. Trust me, Stacy. When it comes to men, I'm not the dumb clueless blonde. I know my shit. And I know that Cooper has got it bad, and I also know that he has the goods to satisfy you beyond your wildest expectations.

Just go with it, Stace. Don't think about it. Don't worry about it. Don't stress yourself out. Just go with it."

"And you don't think I'm a slut?"

"Honey, you have a long ways to go to reach slut status." She giggled. "Just close your mind and open your legs and good things will come."

"I'll try. But I don't know if I can wait five dates."

"Then take it up a notch. Make it as hard on him as he is making it on you," she said with a wicked smile.

"How do I do that?" I was so not good at this whole sex thing.

"Ah, you'll think of something." She stood. "Now go ye forth and get laid! I've got to go. I promised Megan I'd go to that silly breathing class with her."

"You mean Lamaze?"

She threw her purse over her shoulder. "Yeah, something like that. Jack is working late so I'm standing in. I don't even think the whole breathing thing is necessary. I mean, seriously, when you are squeezing something the size of a watermelon out of something the size of a penny, is breathing really going to make that big of a difference? I think they should have a class about drugs. Fuck the natural birth crap. Give me drugs! Anyhow, I've got to go. Love you." She blew me a kiss and then she was out the door.

**

I took a hot bath and shaved the parts that needed attention. I soaked in pomegranate bath salts until I looked like a prune. I was so relaxed I could have easily passed out for the evening. I kept thinking about what Josie had said about making it hard for Cooper to resist me. I loved the way he looked at me with that hunger in his smoldering eyes. I loved the way his body responded to my touch, and the way his voice got low and husky and irresistibly sexy when he was fighting for control. It seemed I loved everything about him. Although I had only known him a short time, we had spent a lot of time together, and I had told him personal things about me that nobody else knew except my girlfriends. When he wasn't with me he was on my mind, and of course there was the sweet and sometimes suggestive texting we did throughout the day. With all my might I wanted to keep my heart out of this equation and just let loose and have some fun. I wanted to be free and spontaneous, not sensible and responsible. I wanted to live recklessly and just not overthink things like I usually did. But there was something about Cooper that just made my heart sing. As scared as I was to get close to him, I was even more scared not to. I couldn't let my anger or hurt from Scott or Thad get in the way of something that could be great. I also needed to proceed with caution. I couldn't take another heartbreak.

"Ugh" I growled at myself in the mirror. "Just stop over thinking it! This is just a date!" I told myself. I crossed my eyes and stuck my tongue out at my image in the mirror. I thought about what Josie had said about making him want me as bad as I wanted him. I wasn't sure how I was going to achieve that, but I was going to give it one hell of a shot.

I wasn't sure where we were going to dinner, so I didn't know how to dress. I decided to play it safe and go with a short but tasteful mini skirt, black V neck blouse, knee high black boots, and chunky black and gray necklace with earrings to match. Underneath I was sporting black lace from Victoria's secret. I took extra care to make sure my make-up was flawless, and let my long brown hair fall into soft ringlets that cascaded down my shoulders.

I had fifteen minutes to spare and it seemed like time was ticking by at a snail's pace. With every tick of the clock I got more nervous and excited and was on the verge of a panic attack. I hadn't dated since high school. The last date I had been on was with Scott when I was in my twenties. Thad and I had never "dated." We made dates, but we always just ended up at his place or mine having sex. I thought about sex with Cooper and my heartbeat sped up, and I was overcome with anxiety and excitement. I tried to control my breathing. I needed to calm the fuck down! A glass of wine sounded sublime and would help calm my nerves, but I refused to take even one drink of alcohol. Not that I had any in my house anyways. I took my sobriety very seriously. I would not throw three years down the drain. I flipped through the channels and found nothing worth watching. I decided to grab a good book, curl up on the couch, and lose myself in some chick lit until Cooper arrived.

***

The clock on the wall said 5:15 and Cooper was lacing up his boots, almost ready for his and Stacy's first date. He was freshly showered, shaved, and dressed in faded ripped jeans and a black t-shirt that pulled taut across his chest and biceps. He gelled his hair, spritzed on cologne, and put his earring in. Grabbing his cell phone, keys, and wallet, he made a mad dash for his truck. He had wanted to take Stacy something, but she didn't seem like the flowers type. He racked his brain trying to think of something, but was coming up blank. He decided to make a quick stop at the department store for some inspiration.

As he was browsing the aisles he made a mental list of the things he knew about Stacy. She was sexy as sin with those pouty lips and bedroom eyes. Her curvy figure was the stuff wet dreams were made of. Those killer legs of hers led to an ass that made his knees weak. Stacy was sex personified. She had this shy innocent side that made her beyond adorable, and he loved the way she blushed beat red every time she was around him. And when she bit her bottom lip and batted those eye lashes, it took all the restraint he could muster not to throw her down and bury himself inside her. He remembered how she made the softest sweetest sounds when she came, and he loved the way her body shivered at his touch. She tasted delicious, and he ached to taste her again. She had a smart mouth, a stubborn streak, and was as ornery as the day was long. He knew she was a walking disaster, an accident waiting to happen, and she surrounded herself with crazy people, but she had a great sense of humor, and an awesome personality to boot. Stacy was also probably the kindest person he had ever met and her heart was made of gold. Although she was so not his type, she was all he wanted. She consumed his every thought, turned his insides to mush, and had him walking around with a permanent hard on. He was so fucked!

Never had a woman had this effect on him. Cooper was scared to death, intrigued, and excited all at the same time. When he wasn't with her, he couldn't stop thinking about her, and when he was with her, he could barely keep his hands off her. He didn't know if it was love or lust, but he did know one thing. He had to have her. She had to be his. He wouldn't rest until he felt her come while he was inside her, feeling her shatter around him. His dick was getting hard just thinking about her and he was running out of time. If he didn't hurry he was going to be late. He had to find something quick and get to her house to pick her up. Everywhere he looked he saw something that reminded him of her, so he just started grabbing things and throwing them in the cart. Ten minutes and a small fortune later, he was back in his truck hauling ass to her house. Cooper couldn't get there quickly enough.

***

At 6:00 on the dot Cooper pulled into my driveway. I had planned on playing it cool and letting him knock while I lazily took my time opening the door, as if I hadn't been sitting there counting down the seconds to his arrival. But one look at Cooper and that plan went down the drain. I threw the door open and ran—okay hobbled—to him and threw myself into his arms. He smiled, wrapped me in his arms, and lifted me off the ground. Setting me back down, he delivered soft kisses down my neck.

"Happy to see me?" he asked.

"No, not at all," I lied. "Why would you think that?"

"Oh, I don't know. Maybe because of the way you bolted out the front door as soon as I pulled up."

I scrunched up my face. "Oh that? That was just a coincidence."

"A coincidence? Really?" He raised his eyebrows and gave me that lazy, sexy smile. "Do tell, Ms. Dupree."

I kissed his jaw. "I was having a fire drill and you just happened to show up."

His hands found my waist and his teeth nipped my ear. "A fire drill, huh?"

"Yep, I was practicing for next time my house catches on fire." Cooper's laugh was intoxicating. "You can never be too prepared for these things, you know."

"This is true, Ms. Dupree." He trailed tender kisses down my neck.

"I have the evacuation part down, but I still need to work on the other part." I untucked his shirt and ran my hands up his chiseled abs and grazed over his nipples. I could barely hide my excitement when I found that they were pierced. Cooper's breath

134

caught and he gripped my ass, lifted me, and carried me inside my house, kicking the door shut behind him. He slammed me up against the wall and used his legs to support my weight. His lips found mine and his hands explored my body greedily.

"What's the other part?" he asked, and it took me a minute to figure out what he was talking about. Every time I was around this man my brain turned to mud. I bit his bottom lip.

"Stop. Drop. And Roll," I said between kisses. "Let me demonstrate what I've mastered so far. Stop," I said, and pushed him off me. "Drop." Using slow deliberate moves, I dropped to my knees. Gripping his ass, I ran my hands down the back of his muscled legs, put my mouth up to his growing bulge through his jeans, and blew out a hot breath. His breath caught and I smiled. I ran my hands up his shirt and grazed my nails lightly along his rib cage. With purpose, I brought my hands to the button on his jeans, and he grabbed both of my hands in one of his and rolled me onto the floor, with him on top of me. Jamming his knee between my legs, he ground himself into me. I was dripping wet for him and so ready to feel him inside me. His lips mauled mine and his free hand was working my already hard and swollen nipple. Cooper had me close and he hadn't even taken my clothes off. I moved my head from side to side and arched my back, trying to get closer to him, seeking my release. He then rolled me over to where I was straddling him. Cooper rolled his hips, his erection digging into my sweet center. "And that, darling, is how you roll." Then he lifted me off him and stood, reaching a hand out for me to follow.

"I think I need more practice," I pouted. "I'm a slow learner. And you know my stove is defective. My house is like a ticking time bomb. It could catch on fire any minute. Screw the date…let's practice some more."

Cooper pulled me into his arms and kissed my forehead. "Oh, we will practice Stacy. That, I can promise you." He kissed my nose. "We will practice over and over and over." He fisted his hand in my hair and pulled my head back, revealing my neck. "And we will keep practicing until we master every step." He ran his tongue from my earlobe to my collarbone, making my whole body shake. I stuck my bottom lip out and snaked my arms around his waist, leaning into him. He laughed. "You are so cute when you pout."

"Is it working?" I asked.

"Nope." He kissed the top of my head.

"Well, when can we practice?" I asked, not even trying to hide my frustration.

He responded, "On our fifth date." I kicked him in the shin with my boot.

"Ouch!"

"Fuck five dates! I mean, seriously dude, what's your deal? I want you. You want me. What's the damn problem?"

He frowned and sat me on the couch. "You're right Stacy. I do want you. I want you bad. But as bad as I want you, I don't want to screw this up with meaningless sex. I don't want you to break your rules for me. I want to do this right. I want to make love to you. I want you to need to feel me inside you just like you need oxygen to breathe. I want you to crave me." His eyes searched mine and my frustration melted away. "And I want to take my time. I want to touch and taste every inch of you. I don't just want sex with you. With you, I want much more."

"And you're serious about this five date crap?" I asked.

"Absolutely! If on our fifth date you can still stand me, I promise I'll put out." He held up two fingers, symbolizing the scout's honor.

I let out an exasperated sigh. I stood, smoothed my skirt down, and grabbed my handbag. "Well, let's go then. The sooner we get these dates over with, the sooner we can get to the fun stuff."

Cooper removed my handbag from my arm and tossed it back on the couch. "Not so fast baby." He pushed me back down on the couch. I looked at him with a mix of anger and confusion when he gently claimed my mouth, his tongue delicately intertwining with mine in a slow, sensual rhythm. He moved down to my neck again, and I was just about to protest when he moved my panties to the side and slid one finger inside me. "We have some unfinished business babe." I closed my eyes and bit my bottom lip. He yanked my shirt down, exposing my breast, and swirled one swollen nipple with his tongue before nipping down lightly with his teeth. Just when I thought I couldn't take anymore, he slipped a second finger inside me and gave me what I needed. "You are always so wet for me baby." I arched my back and moved my hips with him. I was amazed at how in tune with my body he was. He seemed to know exactly what I needed, most of the time before I did. I opened my eyes and found his electric blue eyes fixed on mine. The expression in his eyes was pure contentment, as if making me come was the only thing that mattered to him. I knew it was soon and I knew it was crazy, but I was quite sure that I was falling for this man. "Come for me baby," he prompted and sped up his rhythm, moving harder and faster. Staring into those eyes I lost it and gave him what he wanted.

I closed my eyes and lay there, limp and satisfied. He helped me up and slapped me softly on the ass. "Okay woman, let's get this show on the road. Let's get date number one in the bag."

I stood and smoothed down my skirt, and caught a glimpse of myself in the mirror. I had "just fucked" hair and my make-up was trashed. "Give me five minutes," I pleaded, and Cooper told me to take my time, saying he needed to get something out of his truck anyway.

Ten minutes later I was walking out of the bathroom at the same time he was walking in the door carrying several bags that he sat on the couch. His lips spread into a mischievous grin and he looked like a kid at Christmas. "Okay, so I wanted to bring you something, but you don't seem like a flowers and chocolate kind of chic. So I went to the department store for inspiration, and that's when I came up with this brilliant plan."

"Cooper, you didn't have to bring me anything." I kissed him softly. "You are all I want."

He sat me down and busied himself opening the bags. First, he pulled out a large first aid kit. "Here, I thought this might come in handy, and it could remind you of the day we first met." I took the kit and smiled, remembering Cooper icing down my ankle. Next, he gave me a stick of cherry chapstick. "You are going to need that because I plan on kissing the hell out of those luscious lips." I don't know if he knew it, but cherry was my favorite.

"And now on to the good stuff," he said, and opened a bag and took out cake mix, icing, and all the ingredients needed to bake a cake. I felt a lump form in my throat. "I thought for date number two, I could teach you how to bake a cake."

"Oh Cooper."

"Wait, there's more." He told me to close my eyes, and when I opened them there was an iPad in my hands. I didn't know much about the whole iPad thingie, but I did know that they were expensive.

"Cooper, this is too much. I can't accept this." I tried to hand it back to him, but he wasn't having it.

"Sure you can. I want you to have it. Besides, we need it for date number three." At my confused look he continued. "This thing is awesome. You can sync your phone to it, and it will store all of your contacts. No more lost phone numbers." Okay, so maybe I would keep it.

Cooper wasn't finished. "And it has a calendar, so if that asshole firefighter shows up or calls, you can consult your date book and let him know that you are busy." He handed me the iPad, and I noticed that every day had his name typed in the box. "I went ahead and took the liberty of penciling me in."

I laughed. "I see that."

"Here's the best part. I saw all the books around the house so I know you like to read. Well, this is also an e-reader. You can download any book you want in a matter of seconds. And since you said you are technologically challenged, I thought date number three could be me teaching you how to use it."

I cracked a coy smile. "Well, I do have you scheduled in my date book."

"Damn right you do." He disappeared behind the couch and reappeared, carrying a large box with a picture of a telescope on it. "I saved the best for last, gorgeous. Check this thing out."

"You bought me a telescope?" I was giddy with excitement. I had always wanted a telescope. How in the hell could he have known that? He set the box on the couch and I launched myself into his arms. I kissed him sweetly and he pulled me closer, nuzzling his nose in my hair. I felt content and complete, and I didn't overthink it or fret over whether Cooper felt the same way. I just relished the moment and gave my heart to him. I fell hard and way too fast, but I just accepted it for what is was. I was in love with this magnificent man, and I didn't know what on earth I did to deserve him, but I was not going to let him go.

"I sure did," he said. "For stargazing, baby. Date number four."

"Cooper?"

"Mhmm?"

"I can't—"

He pulled away and put a finger on my lips, shushing me. "I don't want to hear any arguments."

"But—"

"Zip it, woman."

I giggled. I liked the way Cooper called me woman. "I wasn't going to argue. I was just going to say I can't believe you did all this. Thank you." His smile was so sincere and so genuine that it brought tears to my eyes. Cooper kissed them away. "I do have a question though."

"Okay, shoot," he said.

"What did you get us for date number five?"

He dug around in the bag and pulled out a family size bottle of extra strength Advil and handed it to me. I turned it around in my hand, a little confused. "Um, okay," I said. Cooper offered no explanation. "Okay, I give up," I said. "I don't get the Advil."

"Honey, date number five I am going to make you scream. We are going to stop, drop and roll, rock and roll, and catch the sheets on fire. I am going to make love to you until we both pass out from exhaustion; and trust me, Advil will be your best friend."

I wasn't scared. "Big ego, Mr. Carson?"

"You could say that," he said, then he took my hand and placed it over the zipper of his jeans, where my fingers ran the length of him. I gulped. He felt huge, and although the thought of him filling me completely excited me, I must admit I was now officially scared. I was scared of what he could do to me. I was scared of losing him. I was scared of not being enough for him. And I scared of spending a day without him.

CHAPTER 8

Our first date was awesome. Cooper told me he would take me anywhere I wanted to go, and I was in the mood for some good old fashioned BBQ so we hit up my favorite little BBQ shack. There were peanut shells on the floor and the waitresses called you baby. The food was phenomenal and the sweet tea was to die for. We talked and laughed and had an incredible time. By the time we left, we realized it was too late to make it to the movie, so Cooper suggested a walk in the park and I happily agreed. We held hands and walked through the park, enjoying the beauty of nature and one another.

At sunset we sat on a park bench. Cooper had his arm around me, and as I lay my head on his shoulder, we took in the red and orange hues of the day coming to an end. It was beautiful and perfect, and felt so right.

As stunning as the sunset was I only had eyes for Cooper. He turned to me and caught me staring, and pulled me into his lap. It had started to sprinkle, the rain cooling my heated skin. Cooper's kiss was like a gentle caress, and it left me dizzy and wanting with need. A few passersby saw us and gave us looks, but we ignored them. It was like there was nobody there but me and Cooper. We were all that existed and all that we needed.

I would have been content sitting there all night long in Cooper's arms, but the rain had other plans. It began pouring, and we quickly tried to make our way to his truck, but with my boot running was difficult, so Cooper scooped me up and carried me. He ran to the driver's side, deposited me in the seat, and then got in beside me. We both had rain dripping off us, and Coopers eyes were ablaze with desire. He cupped my face and crushed my mouth with his. My whole body heated from his kiss and his touch. I wanted him to take me right there. My body shivered with lust and Cooper broke the kiss, asking me if I was cold. I shook my head no, but he turned and started his truck and turned the heater on. I missed his touch immediately.

"Let's get you home and in some dry clothes," he said.

"I'd rather be in no clothes," I replied, and with one arm around me and my head on his shoulder, we pulled out of the park and made way to my house.

***

When we arrived at my house, we found my door standing wide open. It could have been nothing. Granny could have come by for something, or one of the girls could have stopped by...everyone had keys to my house, so I tried to convince myself that it was no big deal, but in my gut I knew something was wrong. I could feel it and I couldn't hide my alarm. Cooper sensed it too, and he reached across me, opened his glove box, and retrieved a shiny, deadly looking gun. He loaded the clip, put one in the chamber, and turned to me, his demeanor deadly serious.

"Stay here," Cooper ordered in a voice I had never heard before. I swallowed hard and nodded, and Cooper got out of the truck and motioned for me to lock the doors. I did so and he made his way to the door, his movements slow and deliberate, gun in hand. I sat in the truck, scared, imagining all kinds of horrible scenarios. What if somebody was still in the house? What if Cooper got hurt? What if Granny was in there? The what ifs were killing me, and it took everything I had in me to keep me seated in that truck. Finally, after what seemed like an eternity, Cooper emerged and came to the truck, rubbing the back of his neck, his expression tight. I unlocked the door for him and turned in the seat to get out. He stopped me by putting his hands on my thighs. His expression was grim, and he looked as though he was struggling with what to say.

I placed my hands on top of his, needing to touch him. "Just tell me, Cooper."

He pulled me close to him, and I felt his heart hammering in his chest. I prompted him again. "Just say it, Cooper. Tell me what's going on."

"It appears that someone ransacked your house. It's a mess, Stacy."

I nodded, my eyes wide. I tried to push him out of the way so I could go in, but he stopped me. "We need to call the cops, baby. We need to let them do their thing before we go in." I nodded again. He was right. "I don't know much about this kind of stuff, but I do know they might be able to get prints or something." He took his phone out of his pocket and dialed 911. He then softly and calmly spoke to the dispatcher, giving them all the necessary information. The rain had stopped falling, but I was still soaking wet and began to shiver, both because I was cold and out of fear. I had absolutely no idea who would destroy my house or why. If I hadn't agreed to a date with Cooper, I would have been there and Granny could have been there too. The thought gave me the chills.

Cooper pulled away from me and rubbed my arms to warm me. "It's okay, baby. I'm here," he cooed, and I felt myself fall into him. He reached into his back seat and retrieved an old battered leather motorcycle jacket. He motioned for me to raise my arms and I obeyed so he could peel my wet shirt over my head and put the jacket on me, then zip it tight. "We will get you some pants as soon as we can go in." He then reached around me, started his truck, and let the heater blow full blast. We sat there for what seemed like forever, but was actually only about five minutes before the first car arrived, followed by a frantic Jack. Cooper talked to the police officer while Jack made his way over to me. He grabbed me, pulled me into a bear hug, and then pushed back, eyeing me carefully.

"You're okay, right?" he asked.

"Yes." I felt suddenly calm now that Jack was there. I had become so dependent on Jack lately. He was like the big brother I never had. It seemed he was always rescuing me, and unfortunately I seemed to always need to be rescued. "I wasn't here when it...." I waved towards the house. "Happened. I was on a date with Cooper." Jack's face flooded with relief. I had a sudden panicked thought. "Granny?"

Jack held out his hands. "She's fine. She's with Mickey." His expression softened. "Was it a burglary? Was anything taken?"

I frowned and let out a small sob. "I don't know. Cooper got his gun and went in and said it was trashed, then he stayed out here with me until the cops got here. I haven't been inside yet." And I wasn't sure that I would ever be ready to go inside. The thought of someone entering my home, invading my privacy and destroying my things, was scary. And in all honesty, it thoroughly pissed me off. I would be sleeping with a baseball bat that night. And a knife. And I would for sure borrow Granny's Taser thingie. She said it shot fifty thousand volts. Take that to the nuts, asshole!

Cooper joined us, slid between my legs, and pulled me into his arms. He and Jack exchanged grim looks.

"What are you thinking, Cooper?" Jack asked, going into security, protector mode, which wasn't a stretch since he was a private investigator.

"I'm not sure. It doesn't appear to be a robbery. I mean, I don't know if anything was taken, but there were things in plain sight that weren't. Like, I bought her an iPad earlier and it is right there where we left it, as well as her TV's and things like that. I checked her bedroom, and her jewelry boxes seem intact and don't appear to have been gone through."

"So they were there for her then?" Jack surmised, and I felt my stomach contract.

Cooper eyed me warily. "I don't know about that, but based on what I saw she wasn't robbed."

"Do you have any idea who would do this, Stacy?" Jack asked, and I shook my head.

The cops came out to talk to me and I followed them into the house. Cooper offered to go with me, but I told him to stay. Odds were I was going to be a crying mess, and I would prefer to do that alone. Cooper huddled with Jack and I took a deep breath before entering my front door.

Cooper had said it was a mess. That didn't even begin to describe it. My house had been turned upside down. Lamps were knocked over, dishes were broken, my couch cushions had been cut up, and stuffing was everywhere. Drawers had been removed, the contents thrown onto the floor. Windows were broken, books were everywhere, the pages torn out. As Cooper had said, it didn't appear that anything had been taken, just destroyed.

The kind officer led me to my bedroom, which was in the same state of disarray. All of my clothes were thrown out of the drawers, and my bed was wrecked. He led me to my dresser and pointed to the writing on the mirror. As soon as I read it, the tears burned my eyes. In big, bold, red lettering, it said, "You talk again and you die bitch." There was a red lipstick with the lid off sitting on my dresser.

I felt my knees give way and the officer grabbed me to steady me. Cooper and Jack chose that moment to enter. Cooper was by my side in an instant and guided me on wobbly legs to my destroyed bed.

"Do you know what this means?" the officer asked, pointing to the writing.

I shook my head, the tears coming faster now. "I have no idea," I said, and Cooper and Jack exchanged a knowing glance. Jack introduced himself and Cooper to the officer, and he motioned for Cooper to take it from there. I looked from Jack to Cooper, and then it hit me like a ton of bricks as I put two and two together.

Cooper addressed the officer. "Ms. Dupree witnessed and foiled a kidnapping recently. She saw the kidnapper clearly, but he was able to get away. We filed a report yesterday."

The officer began writing in his notebook. Jack spoke next. "We believe the perpetrator made off with her iPhone, which had all of her personal information in it."

"Oh my God! Facebook!" I said, mentally kicking myself for not listening to Jack. He had warned me about putting too much personal information on there.

The officer raised an eyebrow and Jack explained. "Stacy has had some...issues...recently. We stay in close contact. My wife checks her Facebook every night before bed, so instead of Megan calling Stacy to check on her, Stacy would just do the check in thing on Facebook and Megan would know she was home safe and she wouldn't worry."

"And the kidnapper could have easily logged onto Stacy's Facebook from her phone. I'm sure she stayed logged in instead of logging out each time," Cooper added.

"Yes," I admitted. "It always came right up. I never had to enter the password. Hell, I can't even remember the password."

The officer excused himself and made a phone call. I stood staring at the wreck that was once my neat little house. Cooper had his arms around me, rubbing my back.

Jack's expression was grim and he looked like he might explode any second. "Pack a bag!" he said. "You're going home with me."

I shook my head. "No way, Jack! I will not put Megan and the baby and Granny in danger."

He stepped closer until he was inches from my face. "Well, you aren't staying here."

I opened my mouth to argue, but Cooper beat me to it. "She's going home with me," he said, and Jack and I both looked at him as his words sank in. "I have a gun, a security alarm, and a Rottweiler. Trust me, I won't let anything happen to her." When this date started I had entertained the idea of going home with Cooper. Not quite under these circumstances, but hell, why not turn this negative into a positive?

Jack and Cooper were arguing about me like I wasn't even there. I held both hands up to silence them. "Jack, I love you, but I'm going home with Cooper," I said. He tried to protest but I talked right over him. "If something happened to Megan or the baby, I would never be able to forgive myself. It's too dangerous. It's easy to link me to you and Meg. I've checked in on Facebook from your house." Jack frowned, and I knew he was pissed. But he also knew I was right. I had put his wife and child in danger. I let the tears fall. I hadn't meant to endanger them. Who knew this could happen? "It's not quite as easy to link me to Cooper. Hell, I don't even know where he lives and we just started seeing each other, so he's pretty new to the scene."

"Wait, we are seeing each other now?" Cooper asked, and I punched him in the arm.

"Yes, we are seeing each other. We just went on a date, and I'm going home with you."

Cooper smiled. "Sweet," he said, and I punched him again. He ruffled my hair. "I'm just trying to lighten the mood baby." I wrapped my arms around his waist and kissed his cheek.

The officer came back into the room and explained that the detectives would be arriving shortly. He cleared me to pack a bag, but asked me to disturb as little as possible. Since my clothes were everywhere, that was easy for me to do. I just grabbed what was laying on top. I quickly grabbed my toiletries, a few necessities, my gifts from Cooper, and Paddington the duck.

"You will take care of her?" Jack asked for about the twentieth time.

Cooper answered Jack patiently. "I promise I won't let her out of my sight. My house is secluded and secure. I will take off work and keep her safe. I promise."

Jack was about to speak when Megan's car skidded to a stop in front of my house. "Stacy!" She ran to me and we hugged awkwardly, her bulging belly in the way. "Stacy, what the fuck is going on? First you get all banged up, then you get beat up by a kidnapper, then the house catches on fire again, and now this. Geez sister. I swear I'm going to have you confined to a rubber room or put you in a bubble. You are going to give this pregnant woman a heart attack."

"I'm fine Megan. I wasn't even here."

"And thank God for that," she cried, not even trying to stop the tears from rolling down her face. "Well, you can't stay here. It's not safe!"

"We've already established that Meg. I'm going home with Cooper." I held up my bag. "I'm all packed and ready to go."

She looked from Cooper to me to Jack, and then back to Cooper. "You will keep her safe?" she asked, and I rolled my eyes. I was beginning to feel sorry for Cooper. He was getting the third degree from everyone today. He smiled and wrapped his arm around my shoulder. "Yes ma'am. I will guard her with my life."

She conceded wearily. "And you will have her check in everyday so I know she is okay?"

"Yes ma'am," Cooper said again.

Megan seemed to debate the situation for a second. Jack wrapped his arms around her and kissed her temple. "Honey, you need to go home," he told her. "We have everything under control here."

"Okay," she said, but she reached for my hands. "Stacy, are you alright? I mean, you've been through a lot. What can I do? How can I help?"

147

Oh, how I loved my best friend. "Meg, I'm fine. Go home and stop worrying. We don't want that baby coming early." I frowned. "But you are going to have to keep Granny for a couple of days. I'm sorry."

Megan waved me off. "Granny's no problem. She will be fine. I'm sure my dad has cooled off by now anyways."

"We can only hope," Jack said.

Megan glanced at him. "What did you say?"

Jack smiled sheepishly. "Nothing, darling. I didn't say anything."

Megan rubbed her belly. "Well, I guess we will go if you don't need anything from us."

"Wait!" I shouted. "How did you know what happened? Please tell me your mother didn't call you."

She laughed. "Nope, I heard it on the scanner, but it's only a matter of time, Stacy. You gotta call your mom and tell her what's going on. By the time the gossip mill gets to her you could be having alien babies with Elvis. You know how stuff gets twisted."

I cringed, but acknowledged that she was right. I needed to talk to my mom. I would do that first thing in the morning. Right now I was tired. Okay, that was an understatement; I was flat out exhausted. I wanted a hot shower and a warm bed. I thought about being in Cooper's bed, and the wetness between my legs had nothing to do with the rain.

Cooper loaded my bags into his truck and dealt with the detectives that had arrived. Megan and Jack stayed with me until Cooper and I were able to leave. After I promised Megan again that I would check in and promised Jack I wouldn't drink, they finally let me go. Megan held me close and Cooper and Jack had a hushed conversation where they exchanged phone numbers. Finally, they left in their respective cars and I climbed into Cooper's truck.

His blue eyes were full of concern. "You okay baby?" he asked, and I leaned my head on his shoulder and nodded. I intertwined my arm with his and held on to him. That's when it all came crashing down on me. The events of the past couple days overwhelmed me, and I began sobbing. Cooper pulled me close, held my head in his hands, and lightly kissed my forehead. "It's okay baby," he whispered, and I tried to stop crying, but the tears continued to fall.

"I'm so scared," I admitted, and Cooper pulled my head away so I could make eye contact with him.

"Listen," he said, his voice low and steady. "You have nothing to be afraid of. You are safe. I would die before I let anything happen to you."

I shook my head. "You don't understand. I know you will take care of me. I'm not scared about that."

He searched my eyes. "What are you scared of baby?"

I lowered my eyes. "I'm scared of you, Cooper. I'm scared I'm falling for you."

Cooper pulled my hand to his lips and kissed my knuckles. "Honey, I fell the minute I saw you."

***

The ride to Cooper's house was quiet. It seemed we were both lost in our own thoughts. I was angry and worried about my house and the people that wanted to hurt me, but I knew Cooper would keep me safe. The look in his eyes had said it all. He *would* protect me, or die trying. I didn't doubt that for a second.

At a time when my physical safety and wellbeing should have been my main concern, it wasn't. What was troubling me was my admission that I was falling for Cooper, and his acknowledgment that he was falling for me as well. I could handle being beaten and bruised. That hurt but it healed. Heartbreak didn't, and I was scared to death. This was crazy. I had known Cooper all of about a week. We'd only been on one date, and although he had brought me loads of pleasure, we had never even been intimate. It just didn't seem possible for me to love him so much so quickly. But yet I did. I loved him more than I ever thought it was possible to love someone. I had no idea what I would do if he didn't feel the same. The pieces of my heart would never be able to be put back together. I tried not to think about it and focus on what I was going to do about my house and the bad guys, but Cooper was everywhere. He was by my side, his arm around me, our bodies pressed together. He was in my thoughts and in my heart. I inhaled his scent with every breath I took, and his voice poured over me like warm honey.

With my head still resting on his shoulder I tilted my eyes up and took him in. Cooper was so beautiful he literally took my breath way. His hair was a sandy brown cropped short in the back, and longer and tousled playfully in the front. Deep, piercing blue eyes sparkled with just a hint of golden specks. Perfect lips accentuated his strong jaw line, which was freshly shaved, and his goatee was neatly trimmed. His intoxicating scent was a mixture of expensive soap and fresh rain. He looked dangerous and delicious. He was perfect.

His gaze met mine and he caught me staring. I smiled shyly, and he pulled the truck over to the shoulder. I immediately thought something was wrong, but Cooper told me everything was fine. Bending his head slightly, his lips met mine and tenderly consumed my mouth. It was the sweetest, most delicate kiss we had shared, and I drank him in. I tried to deepen the kiss, but he wouldn't let me. Cooper kept it light and gentle, and literally made love to my mouth.

When he broke the kiss and I opened my eyes, I met his intense stare and knew in that instant that things between us had changed. We had somehow skipped a few steps and were treading in dangerous waters. We were both in deep and there was no turning back. The intensity of his gaze told me he knew what I was feeling, and he felt it too. I lovingly caressed his cheek. I wanted to tell him I loved him, but I bit the words back. Although no words were spoken, we had expressed everything that needed to be said.

Slowly he put the truck back into gear and veered back onto the road. I nestled next to him and couldn't help the smile that spread across my face. He took my hand in his and kissed my knuckles as he drove us down the winding road to his house.

***

Cooper's house was gorgeous. It was about ten miles out of town and sat back from the road. He had a huge lawn that was green and manicured, and trees surrounded his modest brick home. The landscaping was earthy with a lot of gravel and stone. It was masculine, but charming at the same time. "Home sweet home," he said, and hit the button on the clicker that opened the garage door, revealing a well-used but organized space. He parked in his spot next to a shiny red convertible sports car, which I recognized immediately as a Corvette. One of my mom's old boyfriends had had one, and he used to let me drive it down the back roads when I was a kid. Of course, it wasn't as pristine as the one sitting beside me. Cooper's was old, classic probably, and it was waxed to perfection...I could see my reflection in it.

"That's Lucy," Cooper said. "When I got her she was rusted and banged up. I restored her. Brought her back to life."

"She's beautiful," I said honestly. I got out of the truck and ran my fingers over the shiny red paint.

"Honey, she's nothing compared to you."

He was sweet. He was also a liar. "Do you need to have your eyes checked?"

He ran a finger down my cheek. "Nope. I have perfect vision."

I hadn't seen a mirror, but I knew I had to look rough. My hair was matted to my head from the rain, and I was pretty sure the crying had caused a nice set of raccoon eyes; and that was not even counting all the various colored bruises on my face and around my eyes. I stood on tiptoe and kissed him lightly on the lips. "You're sweet. You're a liar, but a sweet one."

"You really don't see it, do you?" he said, his tone soft.

"See what?"

"Your beauty, Stacy. You are absolutely gorgeous. You are stunning. Sheer perfection."

I blushed. "You're kidding, right? I mean, look at me. At my best I'm just an average girl."

He reached for me. "Baby, nothing about you is average." I shook my head. "Trust me. I'm just surprised you're hanging out with me. You are so out of my league."

I raised my eyebrows and tilted my head, eyeing him suspiciously. I had already said I wanted to have sex with him. He could stop now. "And you are cute as hell when you blush." I chewed on my lip. He pulled me to him and tilted my head up to look at him. "And when you do that, I just want to devour you."

"So put your money where your mouth is, big boy." I shot him my sexiest smile.

"Oh, I plan to." He buried his head in my hair. "Right after our fourth date." Before I had a chance to kick him, he quickly stepped back and laughed. "But if you are a really good girl, I will be sure to go to third base on every date." He ducked from my punch and chuckled.

He retrieved my bag and Paddington, shut the garage door, and we entered his house. He set my things down and turned to me. "Okay, so what first? Shower, food, movie, sleep?"

I was starving, although it wasn't for food. But I needed a bath or a shower even more. "Can I take a hot bath? I just want to soak the day away."

"You bet. Follow me." He took Paddington's kennel with one hand and my hand with the other. I was a little confused. I was not sharing my bath with the duck. Don't get me wrong...I loved the little guy. He was really starting to grow on me, but he was not going to be my bath buddy. I hesitated, and Cooper tugged on my hand. "C'mon. I have something to show you."

I followed him through a set of sliding glass doors to a paradise of a back yard. Off to the corner of the yard was a large pond that had a beautiful stone waterfall. A weeping willow shaded the pond, and it was filled with colorful and beautiful coy fish.

"Oh my gosh, Cooper, this is beautiful." I could imagine me and Cooper sitting out there at night, enjoying the sound of the water falling and the cool summer breeze.

"Thanks. I love it," Cooper said with pride, and busied himself with freeing Paddington from the kitty crate. The duck waddled to the water and dove right in. He swam, stuck his head under, and reemerged, causing a splash. Cooper smiled at me. "I think he likes it," he said, and I nodded in agreement.

Cooper scooped me up and carried me inside. "Now, let's get you in the bath, and then I'll give you a tour." We went through a large hallway and into what I assumed was his bedroom. It was large and had one wall that was basically all windows. He had a beautiful view of the countryside and a charming old barn. A king size bed made of dark wood took up most of one wall, with matching dresser, armoire, and night stands placed tastefully around the room. Two of the walls were painted a neutral brown, and the one that housed his bed was painted deep, chocolate brown. There were light blue accents interspersed about, and his closet was as big as my bedroom. If I didn't already love this man, I would have fallen hard just for the closet.

Cooper left me alone to browse and went into the bathroom and began running me a bath. He busied himself laying out fresh towels, washcloth, and a robe. "Lavender or vanilla?" he asked, and I went into the bathroom, not understanding what he said. When I walked in he was holding up two bottles of bubble bath. I selected vanilla and he dumped a generous amount into the bath. He left the room, returned with two candles, lit them, and placed them on the edge of the bathtub. Next, he dimmed the lights. He unzipped his motorcycle jacket, discarded it on the floor, and removed my boot and helped me out of my pants. I stood there in only my undergarments, which were pink and black lace.

"Awe Christ," Cooper said as his gazed flowed over my body. He undid my bra, allowing my heavy breasts to fall, and I smiled at the curse he bit off. He got down on his knees and slowly pulled my panties down, and I held on to his shoulder for balance as I stepped out of them. His face lingered at my center and he inhaled my scent. "Jesus, baby," he said, then picked me up, cradling me in his arms, and kissed me passionately. I could feel his growing erection pressing into me, and at that moment I would have been happy to forego the bath and go straight to bed.

He carefully sat me in the bathtub as if I were made of glass. He left the room and returned seconds later with a large cup, and knelt down beside the bathtub and used the cup to pour water over the areas that weren't submerged. He pushed a button and I jumped as the jets began massaging me. I closed my eyes and sunk down as deep in the water as I could, and just let the water and Cooper wash away the stress of the day.

I reached for Cooper. "Join me," I said, and I saw the struggle play out on his face.

"I can't, baby." He rubbed the back of his neck and frowned.

"Please," I said, and he shook his head.

"Baby, I am already teetering on the edge of control. If I get in this tub with you and feel you naked and wet against me, I'm going to lose it. And I don't want to do that. I want to make it special for you."

I sighed. "It's already special to me. You're special to me." I couldn't hide my disappointment.

"I'm honoring our agreement," he said, and motioned for me to sit up. I did, thinking maybe he had changed his mind and was going to join me, but instead he tilted my head back and used the cup to wet my hair. "I'm sorry, baby, but all I have is man shampoo."

"That's fine, Cooper, but you don't have to wash my hair. I can do it, you know."

"I want to. I want to do everything for you." He squirted shampoo into his palm and began massaging it into my scalp. This was a new experience for me. I had never had a man wash my hair before, and it was one of the hottest sensations I had ever experienced.

He found my lump from Granny's midnight moonshine swing and was careful not to cause me any discomfort. After rinsing the shampoo out, he repeated the process with the conditioner. I closed my eyes and enjoyed the feel of Cooper's hands on me. He used the washcloth to cleanse my arms, shoulders, breasts, neck, and face. "Feeling better?" he asked, and I nodded. "Relaxed?" I nodded again, my eyes still closed, savoring every moment.

He lifted one leg, washed it, then the other, placing kisses on my ankles. Next, he moved down to my most intimate places, and instead of using the washcloth to clean me, he slid two fingers inside of me. I stretched to receive them, and he used the other hand to caress first my face, down my neck, and then to my breast. He rolled one swollen nipple between his fingers as he kept up a rhythm that was driving me insane. "That's right," he whispered. "Just let go baby. I want you to come for me." I leaned back to give him better access. "I love it when you come for me, baby. You are so sexy when you come." He sped up his rhythm, and using his other hand he expertly worked my clit, and that was all it took. I came so hard my whole body shook, causing water to slosh over the side. Cooper removed his fingers and slowly slid them up my body, stopping to cup my face. His tongue invaded my mouth, and then he bit my bottom lip and pulled away. "Oh God, Stacy. You are killing me. You know that?"

I didn't have the energy to speak. I was so relaxed and sated and utterly speechless. Cooper pulled the drain and helped me stand. My ankle was getting better, but it was still really difficult to put any weight on it. He wrapped me in a bath sheet and dried me off. He then wrapped me in a luxurious robe that I knew was his because it smelled just like him. I snuggled it to my nose and inhaled his scent. It was delicious, but it would smell better on Cooper. He led me to his bed and sat me down on the edge.

"You can put your stuff wherever you want. Just make yourself comfortable," Cooper said, taking a fresh towel and towel drying my hair. "I don't have a blow dryer, but if you want we can take the 'vette out with the top down."

I laughed. "I think this will do fine. Besides, it rained today. It's not Corvette weather. A good Corvette owner would never take it out in inclement weather."

Cooper's eyes sparkled as his smile spread. "Finally, a woman that understands my relationship with Lucy. Where have you been all my life, woman?" He pushed me down on the bed and covered my body with his. He kissed me senseless, and his erection dug into me once again. I wished he would just give it up already. I was growing increasingly impatient and I was running out of ideas. I wanted him inside me. Now. "Cooper, please," I pleaded, and he flopped on his back and stared at the ceiling, groaning.

"No," was all he said, but he said it in a playful tone.

I climbed on top of him and straddled him, letting the robe fall open. I ground on his hard cock, closed my eyes, and bit my bottom lip. "What's a girl got to do to get laid around here?" I batted the lashes of what I hoped was my best set of puppy dog eyes. He covered his face with his arm and did some creative cursing. "Well?" I prompted, and lazily caressed my breast.

"Three more dates," he said, and I blew out an aggravated sigh. "That's what you've got to do baby. Three more dates." He pulled the robe shut. "It may fucking kill me. My balls might get so blue they fall off. But I'm honoring that fucking five date rule."

I gave up. This was one stubborn man I was dealing with. But he had met his match. I could be just as stubborn, and when I wanted something, really wanted it, I usually got it. Game on!

**

Cooper left me in his room and said he was going to pop some popcorn and find a movie for us to watch. I dressed in yoga pants and a tank top, foregoing a bra. I brushed my hair and piled it on top of my head, and decided that even though I desperately

155

needed it, I would skip make up. Cooper had seen me without it and battered and bruised, and for some reason he couldn't stay away and could barely keep his hands off me. Excitement pooled in my belly at the thought of Cooper's hands all over me. I loved the way he touched me and I loved the dark, dangerous intensity that flashed in his eyes when he brought me pleasure. I giggled just thinking about it. There was no mistaking it now. I had for sure had an orgasm. I had had several and I figured that was just the tip of the iceberg. Feeling Cooper inside me would probably cause me to explode. I couldn't imagine the ecstasy that would bring. And I would find out. I was wearing him down. He was fighting for control and doing a damn good job of it, but I still had a couple of tricks up my sleeve.

I joined Cooper in the living room and found him on the phone. From the sound of it he was taking tomorrow off work, and I hated the thought of him doing that for me. I didn't want him to get in trouble. He had already done so much for me. I would never be able to repay him, but I would sure try like hell. He noticed me, ended the phone call, and held up two movies. "Comedy or drama?" he asked.

"I'll take comedy. I think I've had enough drama lately."

"Okay, how about *Step Brothers*?"

I laughed. "You're kidding me, right? That's my favorite movie. I've seen it about a million times."

"It's one of my favorites too," he admitted. Crazy how much we had in common. "*Step Brothers* it is," he said, and inserted the movie in his DVD player. We nestled together on the couch, and Cooper pulled my legs out from under me and rested my feet in his lap. He gently massaged my feet as we watched the movie, and I gobbled down popcorn, lovingly feeding him some every now and then. Everything felt so comfortable and so...so right. It was like I was right where I had belonged all along. I had found what I was missing my whole life, and I didn't ever want to let it go. I wanted him to be mine and me to be his. I wanted to share everything with him, and I wanted to be his everything.

The movie ended and I yawned. It had been a long day. Cooper clicked off the TV, stood, and stretched his massive muscles, pulling his t-shirt taut. Holy Mary Mother of Christ, the man was built like a God. He reached for me and helped me off the couch. "Let's get you into bed," he said, and my stomach did that whole flip flop thing. Bed. With Cooper. Yes please! He took my hand and led me to his bedroom, flipped on the light, and pulled the covers down, motioning for me to get in. "I've wanted you in my bed ever since the first second I laid eyes on you."

I pulled my top over my head and tossed it behind me on the floor. Cooper's jaw clenched. I shrugged. "Sorry dude, but I sleep naked." I lost my pants. Cooper's eyes were everywhere and his hands were fisted. I wanted him in this bed with me and inside me, and I would play dirty if I must to get him there. I inched closer to him and licked his ear lobe, and his breath caught. I nipped playfully, and he picked me up and plopped me in the bed. He covered me up to my chin and tucked me in, placing a tender kiss to my forehead.

"Are you going to read me a bedtime story too?" I asked, laughing, and pulled my hair free so that it cascaded down around my shoulders.

"Sleep tight, Wrecking Ball." Like I was going to let him off that easy.

"You aren't going to join me?" I lowered the blankets, exposing my breasts. I licked my finger and then used it to pinch a pink nipple.

Cooper swallowed hard. "Stacy, I'm a strong man and I can take a lot of things. But you naked in my bed, touching yourself, isn't one of them. You keep doing that and you won't be able to walk in the morning."

I licked my lips. "Promises, promises." He covered my breasts with the blanket again and I pouted.

He held up three fingers. "Three dates, darlin'." He blew me a kiss. "I'll be in the living room right next door. If you need me, holler." He took one last long look at me and turned to exit the room.

"Cooper?" My voice was low and husky. "I won't be able to sleep. I forgot Oscar and I can't sleep without him."

Cooper raised his eyebrows. "Oscar?"

"Yes, he's my Pillow Pet. He's a monkey and he's adorable. I never sleep without him."

Cooper's face showed his amusement. "You are twenty nine years old and you have a Pillow Pet?" He shook his head and laughed.

"Yes! And don't laugh. It's just that I don't like to sleep alone. I like to snuggle with something." Or someone, I silently added. I would get him in this bed with me. This was one round I would win.

"Do you want me to go get him for you, baby? I will if you need him." Nope. I had a different plan.

I pulled the covers back again and patted the bed beside me. "Will you be my Oscar tonight?" Cooper closed his eyes and rubbed his neck. "I swear I'll behave, and I won't take advantage of you. We can just cuddle." I smiled sweetly. "Please?"

Cooper stood stock still. He didn't move and he didn't speak. After he gathered his thoughts, he went to his closet, pulled out a black Harley t-shirt, and dropped it over my head. "You have got to wear clothes, Stacy. My control is fading fast. You naked beside me... nope, I don't even want to go there. Not tonight anyways." He tossed me my panties and told me to put them on. He then rifled around in his dresser and found a pair of sweats. He shed his jeans and pulled on his sweats so fast I didn't even get a good peak at his goods.

He crawled into bed with me and I held my panties up. "Ditch the shirt or the panties stay off," I told him. He gave me the evil eye and off went his shirt. His body was a feast for my eyes. The tattoos that started just above his elbows went all the way up his arms and continued to his chest, covering his pecs. They were intricate and colorful, and I wanted to lick every line. His chest was smooth and shaved and his nipple rings glinted in the dim light. His shoulders were wide, his waist was lean, and oh Lord, his abs had abs. He was flawless. My eyes grazed his hips and the way his sweats sat low on them. And then I allowed myself to look lower to the enormous bulge between his legs. I licked my lips. I wanted to touch him there, to feel him expand in my hand. I wanted to taste him and bring him pleasure like he had brought me. I wanted every inch of this man, and I was getting impatient. I was getting tired of waiting. His little hard to get act was cute at first, but now not so much. Too much had changed between us. We had already thrown all of our rules out the window, so why honor the dumb five date thing? I knew he was on the edge and it was taking everything he had in him not to maul me. I just needed to kick it up a notch.

I lay on my side, threw my leg over his, and nestled into him, my head on his chest. I traced the lines of his tattoos and let his heartbeat lull me to sleep. Before long I was in dreamland dreaming of Cooper. After all, he *was* my dream come true.

***

Cooper lay in bed staring at the ceiling. The clock on the nightstand said 2:13. He was exhausted, but there was no way in hell he would be getting any sleep tonight, not with this amazing woman wrapped around him snoring softly in his ear. He'd dreamed of having her in his bed, but this wasn't exactly how it played out in his head. No, sleep was not on the agenda, and all he could do was hold her close and watch her sleep. She made the cutest little sounds when she snored, and here in his arms, her hair fanned out around her, her lips slightly parted, she was the most beautiful thing he'd ever laid eyes on. She was hell on wheels and she was probably going to kill him, but it was a risk he would take. He couldn't walk away and he was afraid he'd never be able to. He was just going to have to make her his. Deep down he'd known this the minute he saw her, but he'd tried to tell himself that it was lust, that she was just another hot chic to conquer. His heart knew different though. She was the one, the one that would turn his world upside down and change life as he knew it. This was a new experience for him and he'd be lying if he said he wasn't afraid. And he didn't only want her, he needed her. He needed her so much he didn't know what he would do if she said no; or worse, if she was taken from him. Just thinking about what could have happened if she'd been home tonight when her house was broken into, the thought of losing her, or anyone causing her harm, cut him to his soul. Cooper had meant it when he said he'd do anything to protect her. He and Jack had come up with a few ideas to make her house more secure, but after having her in his bed like this, he had a better idea. He'd just never let her go home. It felt so right, and he knew this was where she belonged. His bed would never be the same without her. Hell, his life would never be the same without her. In such a short time she had become his world. He didn't know how it had happened, but it had. He'd fallen in love with her and he hoped like hell she loved him too.

Cooper was pondering this when she shifted her hip and snuggled closer. Her red hot center pressed into him, and he felt her heat. Yep, she would be the death of him. His hand roamed to her ass, and just as he suspected, the little rebel woman had not put her panties back on as he'd instructed. His lips curved into a smile and he moved his hand back up to her hip. He wasn't going to grope her while she slept. He wasn't a pervert, but he was, however, horny as hell, and he wasn't going to be able to hold out much longer. He knew it, and he was pretty sure she knew it too.

Cooper knew she was frustrated too. And he wanted her that way. He wanted her to want him so bad it hurt. He wanted her to need him like she needed her heart to beat, to miss him when he wasn't near and crave his touch. In all his life he'd never had to work so hard to get laid, and it wasn't even her that was putting up the fight. Sure, he was using her five date rule as an excuse. In all honesty, he'd bedded many women who said they didn't put out on the first date. He was not a stranger to one night stands, and women didn't usually tell him no. He knew he looked good, he was financially stable, and he was extremely charismatic. He knew how to turn on the charm and get what he wanted. But the crazy thing was, he didn't want sex with Stacy. Well he did, but more than that, he wanted to make love to her. And that's why he was honoring her stupid rule. Cooper was afraid. Never before had he felt this way about a girl, and he'd never been in love. Hell, he'd never wanted to be in love and he damn sure didn't go out looking for it. Usually as soon as the "L" word came up he was gone, but not this time. Not with Stacy. With Stacy, he could barely keep the words from rolling off his lips. With her, he wanted it all. To just get lost inside her and never leave. He never wanted to live a day without her in it, or spend a night without her wrapped in his arms. He wanted to give her everything she ever desired and make her smile every day. He wanted to protect her, provide for her, and make her dreams come true. Being with her made him want to be a better man, and his sole mission in life was to love and cherish her for as long as she'd have him; which, if he had any say in the matter, would be forever.

Having accepted his destiny, he lay watching her sleep until his eyes became heavy and sleep finally came.

CHAPTER 9

At 6:30, Cooper woke with a start. He was still tangled in bed with Stacy. The arm she lay on was numb, and there was a puddle of drool on it. She was sleeping peacefully and he didn't want to disturb her, so he carefully pulled his arm free and eased out of bed.

He jumped in the shower with a spring in his step. Although he'd only had a couple hours sleep, he had had a revelation and now had a plan, and he felt completely refreshed. After his shower he shaved and dressed in ripped jeans and a white T-shirt. He glanced at his bed and found Stacy in the same position she was in when he'd gotten up. He resisted the urge to crawl back in bed with her and absorb her warmth. He had things to do.

He went into his kitchen and started the coffee pot. While the coffee was brewing, he called his office and checked in with his secretary. She put him on speakerphone and he outlined the day for his crew. He told his secretary to call if she needed him, and then he dialed Jack's number.

Jack answered on the second ring, his voice thick with sleep. He put Cooper on hold while he went into his office so he wouldn't wake his sleeping wife. He sounded like he had had a rough night too. Once he was out of Megan's earshot, he explained that she had been up most of the night having Braxton Hicks contractions. Since this was their first baby, they were both concerned. He said he'd finally fallen asleep around three in the morning, and Granny had picked that time to come in from clubbing and set the alarm off. Jack, already on edge, had gone to investigate with his Glock in hand, only to find Granny lining up belly shots of moonshine with Cher and Dolly Parton Drag

Queens. After Jack ran them off, Granny huffed upstairs, slammed her door, and stuck her headphones in her ears, then attempted to rap the lyrics to every Eminem song she had...loudly! Luckily Megan, who was exhausted, had slept through most of it, but Jack was not so lucky. Jack told Cooper he would probably end up in jail if Granny stayed there another second, to which Cooper offered to bail him out and Jack told him not to bother. He'd rather be in jail than with Granny. Cooper offered to let Granny stay with him and Stacy, and as good as that sounded to Jack he wanted Cooper's sole focus to be Stacy's safety. They would figure something out with Granny. They always did.

"I did have one of my guys stay at Stacy's to give the appearance that she was there, hoping those pricks would come back, but they didn't." Jack's voice was full of disappointment. "I would have loved a minute or two with them before the cops came."

"Me too," Cooper admitted. After spending the night with Stacy in his arms, he knew that he would annihilate anyone that even thought about causing her harm.

"We will try again tonight," Jack offered. "Maybe we'll get lucky." He cleared his throat. "The cops did offer to place Stacy in police protection."

"No way," Cooper answered firmly. Until all of this was over, he was not letting his little wrecking ball out of his sight. No one could protect her better than he could. If anything happened to her...hell, he couldn't even finish the thought. The mere thought twisted his guts.

"That's what I figured. I told them we had her somewhere safe. She still sleeping?" Jack asked, and Cooper acknowledged that she was. "You get any sleep?"

"No, not really. I wasn't too worried about anyone finding her here. I live kind of out of town, and I was careful getting here. I know no one followed me. I did load my gun and have it ready, and my dog would have barked if anyone was lurking around. I was on alert all night. I managed to catch a couple of hours though. I know you had an eventful night, but have you found out anything about the people that are after her?"

"I canvassed the neighborhood, talked to the neighbors, and a couple of them reported seeing a dark van driving slowly in front of Stacy's house. Probably casing it."

Cooper frowned. "The kidnapper was in a dark van."

"Yeah, that's what my contact at the PD said. And Stacy remembered three of the letters on the plate, so it will take some time, but it will help narrow it down some. We just have to keep her safe until we get these assholes." Jack's voice was tight; it was evident that he cared a great deal for Stacy.

But so did Cooper. "You don't have to worry about that, brother. I won't let anything happen to her. I won't leave her side or let her out of my sight."

Jack laughed. "Good luck with that one. She's stubborn as hell. She doesn't exactly play well with others."

It was Cooper's turn to laugh. "Tell me about it."

"She is a great girl though," Jack said. "And she's crazy about you. I just hope the feeling is mutual. I don't want to see her get hurt again."

"I won't hurt her," Cooper said honestly. "And it's definitely mutual. I'm way beyond crazy for her. I'd do anything to make her happy."

"That's good to know," Jack said. "She deserves the world."

"I'll do my best to give it to her," he said, and he meant it. He would give his all.

Jack got back to business. "Look, I know Stacy, and she isn't going to want to stay gone from her house for long. She'll look at it as she's letting the bad guys win. So we need to prepare for that. I've got a guy I know in security coming at 10:00 to install an alarm, and I will be changing the locks as soon as the hardware store opens. But that's about all we can do. Sit and wait. Who knows if and when these guys will come back? And who knows what they are willing to do keep her quiet? It would be best if you could just keep her there."

That's exactly what Cooper planned on doing. He would handle Stacy.

"I'll keep her here as long as we need to." Forever sounded even better.

"Well, good luck bro," Jack chuckled. "She can be a handful. Call if you need anything, and I'll call with any new developments. Hopefully this will all be over soon."

Cooper disconnected the call and whipped up some omelets. He didn't know Stacy's food preferences, but he did know that she had a healthy appetite, and he liked that. He loved the fact that she was curvy and that she embraced her curves.

After finishing the omelets, he cut up some fruit, poured two glasses of orange juice and two cups of coffee, and using a cookie sheet as a tray, he headed toward the bedroom.

Stacy was still asleep with a smile on her face. Whatever she was dreaming must have been wonderful. He hated to wake her, but when she found out why she wouldn't be able to stay mad at him.

He lightly tapped her shoulder and she slept on. He gently shook her, and she opened her sleepy eyes and smiled when she saw the coffee.

"Breakfast is served, beautiful." He kissed her forehead and sat the tray in her lap.

"Awe, thank you, Cooper. You are too sweet." She went straight to work on the coffee, then put away the omelet in record time.

"Do you want me to make you another one?" Cooper asked.

"Oh no, I'm not hungry anymore," she said, then with a coy smile added, "For food, that is."

He knew the feeling and had the solution. He finished his omelet, and as much as she tried to drag him back to bed, he held firm.

"Baby, I have a big day planned for us."

She yawned. "Can we start at about ten-thirty or so? I function so much better after ten."

"Nope," Cooper pulled her into arms. "We need to start now."

She snuggled into him and kissed his jaw. "You sure we can't just stay in bed?"

The offer was very tempting, but Cooper pulled out of her embrace. "Nope. Up and at 'em, woman!"

Stacy groaned but reluctantly complied. "Okay, I'm up. So what do you have planned?"

"Speed dating." He winked at her. "Brilliant, huh?"

Stacy was confused. "Speed dating? Isn't that where you go on like fifteen dates with different people in one setting?"

Cooper's eyes glittered. "Well, in theory that's how it goes, but I figure we can change it up a bit."

Stacy lay back down. "I don't want to date other guys. I'm going back to sleep."

Cooper dragged her back out of bed. "Just hear me out." She rolled her eyes. "Do you want me, Stacy?"

She nodded. "Of course I want you, you know that."

He sat on the bed and pulled her to his lap. He was already hard, and he made sure she knew it. "I want you too, baby, but we have three more dates to go, right?"

She ground herself against him. "I guess. So?"

"So we bake a fucking cake, figure out the iPad, check out the sky, and then make love until we can't move. If we start now we can be back in bed by ten. And I promise I will keep you there until you are totally, completely, and happily satisfied."

He let his words sink in. Abruptly Stacy jumped up and tugged on Cooper's hands. "C'mon. Hurry up. Let's do this."

Cooper stood and pulled her close. "Are you sure you want this, baby? I don't want to rush you, and I want it to be all you've ever dreamed of."

"Yes, it's what I want." She kissed him lightly on the lips. "You are what I want. I know it hasn't been long and we are progressing fast, but I have never been so sure of anything in my life." She grabbed his junk and looked him dead in the eyes. "I. Want. You. Now."

That was good enough for Cooper. He caressed her fabulous ass and dragged her to the kitchen, but not before he gave her a little taste of what she would be getting later.

***

I had slept better last night than I had in a really long time. I felt safe and secure and completely whole in Cooper's arms. It was the only place I ever wanted to be. Cooper was so sweet to bring me breakfast in bed, and I admired his creativity of how to get around our five date rule. He wanted me as much as I wanted him, and the thought of that sent shivers down my spine. It seemed like I had been waiting forever for him. I just wanted to

167

get that boy naked and keep him that way until I got my fill...which would probably be never. With every second that passed, my need and desire for him increased, but the wait was almost ever. I was relieved, and so excited I couldn't help the silly smile that stayed on my lips, or the wet heat that burned between my legs.

I escaped his wandering hands and dashed to the bathroom to freshen up. I brushed my teeth and washed my face, noticing that the bruises were more faded today. That was a good thing. I dabbed on some foundation and gunked mascara on my lashes. Strawberry lip gloss coated my lips, although I was sure it wouldn't last long. Anytime Cooper was near his lips found mine. But I wasn't complaining. I loved his kisses.

I brushed my hair and let my natural curls fall to my breasts. Cooper seemed to love my hair down, and I wanted him to find me irresistible, because even though he promised me that today was the day, I was going to use everything I had to hold him to it. The waiting had gone on long enough. I tossed Cooper's shirt onto the pile of towels from last night. Looking sexy hadn't been my main priority when I was grabbing items from my wrecked home, so my choices were limited. After rummaging around a bit I settled for a pair of gray yoga pants, which did wonders for my ass, and a gray tank top. They didn't quite match, but it was close enough. Hopefully I wouldn't be wearing them for long. Underneath I wore a turquoise lace thong with matching bra. Looking in the mirror I felt confident and happy, and found myself in a playful mood. For the first time in a long time, I was excited to face the day. I puckered my lips and blew the sexy bitch in the mirror a kiss. Today was going to be epic.

I found Cooper in the kitchen setting out ingredients for the cake. You could tell he'd spent some time in the kitchen. He looked completely relaxed, and it was obvious he knew exactly what he was doing. He was humming to himself, and when he saw me standing there, he grabbed my hands, held me close, and danced me around the kitchen. It was sweet and romantic, and a little awkward with my boot, but it wasn't getting me any closer to getting him naked.

I pulled out of his embrace and clapped my hands. "Alright, Buster. Let's get this cake baked." I slapped his ass and a slow smile spread across his face. I sashayed away, looking over my shoulder, and found Cooper's eyes glued to my ass. I clapped again. "Like now, big boy! Let's do this."

I stood at the counter and he came up behind me, his hands first caressing then roughly grabbing my ass. I leaned into his touch and he nestled his face in my neck. "Oh, baby, you are so fucking hot! I can't wait to get inside of you." Well, he was the one wasting time dancing!

"We could skip the cake baking lesson," I teased, but in all reality, I really wanted that damn cake. I wanted sex with Cooper too, but cake was cake.

"Nope," he responded, his voice low and husky. "I have ulterior motives, baby. I'm going to cover you in cake batter and lick it off of every inch of your body." As good as that sounded, I still wanted the damn cake. My inner fat girl was pouting. It was lemon pound cake, for crying out loud.

I stuck my bottom lip out. "So no cake? I really love cake, Cooper."

Cooper laughed and caressed my lip with his thumb. "And I really love your pouty face." He pecked my cheek. "Okay, we'll bake the cake, but I get to lick the frosting off you."

I licked my lips. "Deal."

The cake-baking lesson was a disaster. I got eggshells in the batter, and since I'd never used a mixer before, I didn't know you had to start slow and build up speed. I just wanted to get the cake in the oven so we could get to the icing licking part. So, I turned the mixer on high and was promptly covered in cake mix. I tried to turn it off, but the buttons were covered and I couldn't find the power switch. The dry ingredients were flying everywhere and Cooper was lazily leaning on the counter, holding his belly and laughing hysterically. Not knowing what else to do and wanting to stop the cake massacre, I jerked on the power cord, unplugging the demon possessed mixer. It stopped whirling and swinging cake batter all over the place, and I breathed a sigh of relief. This baking stuff was harder than it looked on TV. Cooper continued to laugh, tears falling down his cheeks.

"A little help would have been nice," I huffed.

"Then I wouldn't have gotten to do this," he answered, licking cake batter off my neck.

"Mmm," I responded, melting from his touch.

He placed my index finger in his mouth and sucked. "This shirt is all dirty. We should probably get rid of it." He lifted my arms and the shirt was history. He traced the lace of my bra. "That's much better." He lowered his mouth to my breasts and pulled my bra down, exposing my hard pink nipples.

"Um, Cooper?"

"Mhmm?" His mouth never left my nipple and his hands were gently kneading my ass.

"There's no batter there," I said playfully, and Cooper dipped his finger in the mixing bowl and covered my nipple with it. This time he licked softly, then sucked hard and nipped with his teeth. I cried out in pleasure and directed his hand to my red-hot center. He worked my clit through my thin yoga pants, and I ground myself into his hand and moved with him, trying to speed up his movements, needing to feel him harder and faster.

The oven dinged, letting us know it had finished preheating. I couldn't have given two shits. Cooper's mouth moved to my lips. He parted them and bit my bottom lip hard. He then released me, plugged in the mixer, and set it to low. I was sitting on the counter dumbfounded. He had never left me hanging before. He had always made me come. He enjoyed making me come. What the hell?

He told me to grease the cake pan, tossed me a stick of butter, and winked at me. I caught the butter and held it in my hands, trying to figure out what the hell had just happened. Cooper must have thought I didn't know how to grease the cake pan, because he peeled the paper back and demonstrated how to do it...like I didn't know that. I was not an idiot. Okay, so I didn't know that, but I did know lots of other stuff. So, I went to work on greasing the pan and Cooper finished the batter. We then poured the batter into the pan and put it in the oven. Cooper set the timer for twenty-eight minutes.

"It takes almost thirty minutes to bake a cake?" I asked, incredulous. I really wanted that cake.

"Yep, but don't worry, I'm sure we can find something to do to pass the time." He grabbed me by the ass and lifted me back onto the counter that was covered in flour. He lay me down, and I offered myself to him like I was a buffet. "Damn," he said, and his eyes roamed all over me.

He opened the frosting and made good on his promise to lick it off every inch of me. I lay back with my eyes closed, enjoying the wet heat of his tongue everywhere. Somewhere along the way I had lost my pants, and while Cooper was licking frosting off my belly he inserted two fingers inside me. He started out achingly slow, then sped up, giving it to me faster until I was almost there, and then he slowed it back down, not giving me what I needed. I opened my eyes, and his eyes never leaving mine, he removed his fingers from inside me and sucked my wetness off them. "You taste so good, baby." That was twice he had taken me to the brink and then stopped. I didn't know what he was doing, but if he did it again I knew I might have to kill him. I literally couldn't take it anymore.

"Cooper, please," I panted just as the oven timer went off.

"Saved by the bell," he said, and grabbed a potholder. I stuck my tongue out at his back, threw him the finger, and pulled myself off the counter. If he was trying to drive me wild and insane with need, he was succeeding. I was a woman on the edge.

He set the cake pan on a hot pad to let it cool. "Date number two is now complete. Go get your iPad."

I blew out a sigh of frustration, but I went and got the damn thing. I handed it to Cooper and he powered it up. He showed me how to get on the Internet and check my email, how to get to the calendar and how to download music. I really could have cared less about all of it. He then opened an icon that said "notes," and informed me I had a note waiting to be read.

I took the iPad from him and read the note. In big bold letters it said: **STACY DUPREE, I REALLY DIG YOU. WILL YOU GO STEADY WITH ME? XOXOXO COOPER**. I rolled my eyes and chuckled. That was so cheesy, and so Cooper.

I figured out how to type on the note, and in big letters I wrote YES! NOW QUIT BEING A TEASE AND MAKE ME SCREAM.

His eyes glittered with promise. Starting at my ankle, he began to kiss his way up my body. "Oh, baby. The things I'm going to do to you." He stopped at my core, moved my thong to the side, and delivered sizzling kisses there. I fisted my hand in his hair and pulled him closer still. He took his time and explored every inch of my dripping pussy. Just when I thought I was going to explode, he laid his cheek on my throbbing flesh and smiled up at me.

Okay, that was the last straw. This was war. I was on to his little game. He was good, I'll give him that. And he had the home field advantage. But I had learned a lot about him in the last week, and I formulated a plan. He was denying me an orgasm because he wanted me aching with need. Well, I wanted him to just lose control and fuck me already. And I would win. He would not be able to resist what I was about to do.

I stood and retrieved the telescope box, as I assumed it needed to be assembled. "Okay, that was date three. All we have is number four and then its game time." I sat on the floor beside him, leaning my back on the couch. "All you have to do is assemble this baby, we'll take a gander at the sky, and then you can carry me to bed…where, if you know what's good for you, you will make good on your promise to make me scream."

Cooper's blue eyes were burning with lust. "Oh, I always keep my promises, Ms. Dupree."

"You'd better, Mr. Carson," I said. "Now get that thing put together," I unsnapped my bra and let it fall down my arms onto the floor. "And hurry." I cupped my heavy breasts and licked the tops of them. Cooper swallowed hard, his eyes wide. "Because you have been denying me all day." I moved one hand lower to my panties. "And since you wouldn't let me come and I really need to, I'm just going to do it myself." It was Cooper's turn to be surprised. "And if you are a good boy, I'll let you watch, but you can't touch me."

Cooper shook his head. I shimmied out of my thong and tossed it to Cooper.

"If you touch yourself, baby, all bets are off. I won't be able to control myself. I told you if you go there you won't be able to walk tomorrow."

I moved my hand lower and began to massage my folds painstakingly slowly. Cooper reached for me and I slapped his hand away. "No touching," I reprimanded. I was taking control of this situation. I handed Cooper the directions for the telescope. He held them open upside down, his eyes never leaving my hands. I slipped a finger inside myself, parted my lips, and let out a small moan.

"Fuck," Cooper croaked, and ran a hand through his hair. With my other hand, I kneaded my breast and tugged on my nipple. "Stacy," he breathed, and I ignored him. I closed my eyes, threw my head back, and inserted a second finger. "Baby, I have to touch you. You are killing me here." Good. He had been killing me all day...hell, all week.

I sucked on my finger. "You can touch, baby." He leaned into me and I pushed him back. "Right after we complete date number four," I said. His eyes smoldered blue gray, and I knew I had him. I spread myself open for him and circled my clit, increasing my rhythm until I was on the edge. I could feel my orgasm building, and let out a sexy moan and bit my bottom lip, and that was his undoing. In one swift motion he had me over his shoulder in a fireman's hold.

He carried me to his bedroom, threw me on the bed, and dug around in his nightstand for a condom. I jerked it out of his hand, backed him up against the wall, unfastened his pants, and pulled them, along with his boxers, low enough that his impressive cock sprung free, and I slowly rolled the condom down his enormous length. I attacked his mouth with a passion I didn't even know I possessed. It was like I was a wild woman. Cooper roughly grabbed the back of my thighs, turned me around, and backed me up against the wall. His mouth claimed mine, and he lifted me up by my hips and slammed into me. I cried out in pain as my body stretched to receive him. Cooper stood stock still, his pulsing cock still inside me.

"Cooper, don't stop," I breathed.

He was fighting for control. "Baby, I don't want to hurt you."

"You aren't hurting me." I cupped his face and kissed his lips. "I know you won't hurt me Cooper. I trust you."

"You'll tell me if it's too much?" I nodded.

Cooper slowly began to thrust into me, giving me what I wanted. With each thrust I was able to take him deeper, and the pain was now mixed with delicious pleasure. I wanted all of him, but I wasn't sure I could take all of him. He was massive and he was in the driver's seat. All I could do was keep my legs locked around his waist, my arms around his neck, and enjoy the ride.

And what a ride it was. As my body began to accommodate him, Cooper started driving into me harder and faster, and with every thrust he hit my g spot, leaving me quivering, filling me completely. I dug my fingernails into his back as I felt my body coming undone. My orgasm shook me to the core. I cried out and held on to Cooper tighter as he slammed into me, taking my orgasm even higher and higher. The other orgasms Cooper had given me were good, but him inside me was off the charts. I came violently, my juices covering that magical cock of his.

"Baby, you feel so good," Cooper said, and I wanted to tell him how wonderful he felt too, but my words were swallowed by his kiss. His kiss was hungry and rough, and the sensation made me even hotter. I liked the way he was struggling for control. I just wanted him to let go and give me all he had. He carried me to the bed, still inside me. He lay me down and threw my legs over his shoulders, pounding into me with more force now, and I could feel another orgasm building. His eyes were on mine and the lust and desire and...love I saw there was all I needed.

"Baby, if you are going to come, you better do it." I arched my hips upward, taking him impossibly deeper. "You are so wet and tight, and the way you are stroking me has me on the edge. I can't take much more."

"Cooper," I said, biting back the words "I love you." "Oh God." My entire body tensed as I shattered. I came undone beneath him, my eyes never leaving his. He continued to move inside me, making my sensitive core quiver, prolonging my orgasm. As amazing as he felt, I wasn't sure how much more I could take. I was pretty sure if I came again I would pass out.

I clenched down hard on him and he lost it. "Fuck baby," he ground out, and with one last thrust he threw his head back and found his release. Still inside me, he collapsed on top of me, supporting his weight on his elbows. Using my nails, I traced small circles on his back and he shivered.

He lovingly caressed my cheek as we gazed into each other's eyes. No words were spoken. None were necessary. We both knew what the other was thinking.

Or so I thought. Cooper was the first to break the silence, and his words surprised me.

"Stacy, baby, I'm sorry," he said, and I couldn't hide my confusion.

"Sorry?" I asked, blinking back tears. Was he sorry he'd made love to me? "Why are you sorry? For making love to me? I'm not sorry."

Cooper pulled out of me and flopped onto his back, covering his face eyes with his arm. "Honey, I didn't make love to you."

"But—"

"I fucked you Stacy. And I'm so sorry." I rolled to my side and moved his arm so I could look into his eyes. There was so much conflict in his blue eyes that words escaped me. I had absolutely no idea how to respond. "I lost control, Stacy, and I'm sorry."

Although I wasn't sure I wanted to know the answer, I had to ask anyways. "Are you sorry you had sex with me?" My voice cracked. "Was I not good enough?"

Cooper pulled me on top of him, took my head in his hands, and looked at me incredulously. "What? No! You were amazing. You are amazing. That just wasn't how I envisioned our first time to be. I wanted to make it special for you and take my time. I wanted to slowly and gently and tenderly make love to you." My tears started to fall. "I didn't want to rush and be rough and hurt you." I shook my head to let him know he hadn't hurt me. "I know I hurt you, and I'm so sorry baby." He pulled me down to him and kissed my tears away. "I lost control like a horny lovesick teenager. You are so just incredibly hot, and you had me so revved up that I just had to be inside you."

"But it was all I ever dreamed it would be, Cooper. You made me feel so good. You made me feel….loved, and desired." I lay my head on his shoulder.

"Thank you for saying that, but I feel like I failed you." Now the tears were flowing again, but they weren't from sadness. "Next time baby, I swear I'll take my time and do it right. I won't let my dick control me. I will be slow and gentle and…." Cooper stopped and I let the silence linger for as long as I could.

"And what?" I finally asked.

Cooper rolled to his side, taking me with him. His hungry eyes pierced my soul and his arms held me tightly. "Next time baby, I will show you how much I love you." He looked as surprised as I was at the words that tumbled out of his mouth.

"You love me?" I asked, my chest tight.

Cooper took a deep breath. "Yes, Stacy Dupree. I fucking love you, okay? I loved you the second I laid eyes on you." He kissed me hard on the lips. "I have fallen completely and deeply in love with you. I tried not to. I tried to fight it, but I just couldn't. I know it's crazy and soon, but I can't change how I feel. My heart belongs to you, if you'll have it."

My heart melted. "Oh Cooper! Of course I'll have it, because I love you too. I love you more than I ever thought it was possible to love another person."

Cooper searched my eyes and frowned. "And don't you ever think you aren't enough, baby. You are more than I deserve."

"Cooper, I'm a mess."

That got a smile out of him. "Yes, you are Stacy Dupree. But you are *my* mess." He kissed my nose. "You hear that? You. Are. Mine."

"I'm yours." I acknowledged, and Cooper took my mouth with the sweetest, most tender kiss I had ever experienced.

"Mine," he repeated, his arms holding me tightly. His. I was his. I was happy and scared and I didn't know what the future held for us, but I did know one thing. As long as I had Cooper, I had all I'd ever need.

***

After they'd had sex, Stacy went to take a shower. Cooper wanted to join her but he resisted the urge, telling her he had to make some phone calls for work. That was partly true. He did need to check in at the office, but the real reason he didn't join her was because he knew if he was that close to her naked body he wouldn't be able to keep his hands off her. He would have had her against the shower wall, unable to control his need to be inside her. And he swore to himself that the next time he was lucky enough to bury himself inside her glorious body, he was going to do it right and make love to her the right way, the way he'd wanted to from the start.

Already he felt like a complete asshole. He had wanted to give Stacy so much, flowers and candles and massages, the whole romantic nine yards. Instead, he'd lost his head, both of them, and given her a rough fuck that had lasted all of about five minutes. He'd roughly impaled her, and he knew he had hurt her. She wouldn't admit to it, but when he had slammed into her and she cried out, that was a cry of pain. Her entire body had tensed, and he had felt the fear radiate off her. She'd told him to continue, desperate to please him, and he had. But he was kicking himself now. At that very moment he'd wanted her so badly that he had put his own needs before hers. Like an idiot, he'd treated her like he did the other girls he had sex with. He was not the type of man to "make love," and viewed sex as a necessary and enjoyable physical need. He had always been honest and up front with women, and took pride in the fact that he always made sure his partner enjoyed the experience as much as, if not more than, he did. But it was always just sex. Two consenting adults making each other feel good for a little while, nothing more to it than that. No emotional connection, no commitment, no promises.

Until now.

Stacy Dupree had changed all of that. She'd gotten into his head, under his skin and stolen his heart. He wasn't lying when he told her he'd tried to resist, he had. He'd told himself she was no good for him and tried to convince himself that it was just physical attraction, and that after he got her out of his system he would move on to the next girl like he always did. He tried to stay away, but he was so drawn to her that he just couldn't. She was such a mess and so in need of being rescued, and she was exactly the type of woman he generally stayed away from. He didn't like drama and avoided crazy. She had plenty of both. He'd never had a real relationship, and although he knew when the right girl came along he would be happy to put in the work, he just wasn't sure he wanted to put in as much work as this woman would require.

Cooper had begun falling and feeling things for this girl the moment he saw her, and that's something he'd never experienced before, that made him want to spend every second with her, protect her, and do everything he could to make her happy. He'd tried to convince himself it was just infatuation, but he knew he was wrong.

Very wrong.

He knew that the second he slid inside her. Sliding inside her wet heat had been like going home. His heart had swelled, he had a lump in his throat, and he knew at that second where he belonged. With her. Inside her. For as long as she'd have him. And he hoped like hell that was forever, because he didn't know if he'd survive a day without her.

He shook his head to clear it. He may not be able to control how his heart felt about Stacy, but there were a few things he could control. Like keeping her safe, finding out who was after her, and making them pay. Yes, that was a much better plan than worrying about all this love stuff. That would all work itself out. Priority one was protecting her. Priority two was keeping her in his bed and finding a way to be inside her every night.

His phone buzzed and he read the screen and saw that it was Colleen. He answered just as Stacy came in from the bathroom, towel drying her hair. He held up a finger to signal that he would just be a minute, and she waved him off and plopped down on the couch. She was finger combing her long, thick mane, and the sight of her with those wet curls framing her beautiful face made his dick come to full attention. She had her hands in her hair, her lips parted, and she was obviously not wearing a bra. Every move she made caused her magnificent breasts to jiggle. Her perfect nipples were hard and erect, straining against the cotton fabric of her tank top, and Cooper was having a hard time keeping up with the conversation with Colleen.

Unable to resist touching her, he sat backwards on the arm of the couch and ran his fingers through her hair. She smiled and laid her head in his lap. He absently caressed her scalp as he finished his call with Colleen. When he got off the phone, Stacy pulled him into her lap. He laughed and tried to get up, but she pouted and pulled him back down, and he settled his back across her thighs and nestled his head in his favorite place, her heavenly breasts. She ran her fingers through his hair and stared at him with more love in her eyes than he could ever deserve.

"Cooper," she said softly. "I need to talk to you."

He had closed his eyes and was enjoying her head massage, but at the tone of her voice he opened his eyes and met her gaze. "What's wrong, baby?"

She smiled. "Nothing's wrong. In fact, it feels like everything is right."

He ran a calloused thumb across her jaw, fighting the urge to smother her in kisses. "What do you want to talk about then?"

"That phone call…that was work, right?"

No longer able to resist those luscious lips, he tilted her head down and planted sweet, tender kisses on her mouth. "Yes."

"Are you going to get in trouble for missing so much work?" she asked, and he laughed. It was adorable that she worried about him. He was beside himself for fear of her safety, but here she was worrying about him.

"Nope, I can pretty much run things from my phone. I have a great crew, and Colleen, although she is a little firecracker at times, is really good at what she does. She's been with me seven years, and she can pretty much read my mind most of the time."

She had moved her hand from his head to his face, softly caressing his temples, cheeks, jaw. "So you are the manager then?"

"You could say that." Cooper slid his hand under her shirt, seeking out a pretty pink nipple.

She squirmed. "But don't you have to answer to someone? You've missed quite a bit of work already, and who knows how long I'll have to hide out until the bad guys are caught." He found her nipple and gently tugged, and she closed her eyes and moaned. "I just don't want you to lose your job or have issues with your boss because of me. I can take care of myself. I took a self-defense class in junior high, and I got skills. Well, I have like a skill, but it's enough to get me by. Plus, Jack has showed me some stuff. I'm a total badass."

He laughed, raised her shirt, and tenderly caressed her breast. "Really?"

"Yeah." She bent her arm and flexed her muscles. "Check out these guns! And these fists? They are like lethal weapons. I probably should register them or something."

Cooper smiled and his tongue swirled on her nipple. "I'm shaking over here."

"You should be. I'm like a highly trained ass kicking machine." She closed her eyes as Cooper lightly nipped at a swollen peak. "Okay, so I'm not highly trained, but I am capable of taking care of myself. So tomorrow, you are going back to work so you don't have to get in trouble with your boss."

Cooper brought his tongue to her other nipple. "Honey, I *am* the boss. I own the place. I can come and go as I please, and trust me I have everything under control. If I need to go into the office I'll take you with me, but Colleen can handle damn near anything, and I know she's got my back. Between email and speaker phone I can take care of just about everything that needs to be done, and I don't have to leave your side to do it." His mouth claimed hers and she let out a little moan. "And whatever skills you have, feel free to bring them to the bedroom. I have a few skills myself I might show you."

Stacy bit his bottom lip. "Or maybe you might learn a thing or two." She was in a playful, cocky mood, and he loved seeing her this way. He loved the fact that she was confident and independent. He had no doubt that she *was* quite capable of taking care of herself, but that was his job now. She was *his,* and he would spend his dying breath protecting her. He didn't know exactly how it had happened, but somehow this little wrecking ball had become his whole world.

He got up from her lap and sat beside her, then pulled her into his arms, fisted her shirt, and yanked it over her head. He buried his nose in the nape of her neck and took in her scent before splattering sensual kisses down her neck and collarbone. His erection was painfully straining against the soft cotton of his pants, and he was suddenly glad he was wearing sweats. And speaking of pants, why was she still wearing hers? He took first one nipple and then the other in his mouth, his hands running along her hips and ass. How he'd gotten so lucky he didn't know, but he knew one thing for sure; he was going to do his best to show her every second of every day how much he loved her, starting right now. He was going to take her to bed and make love to her. Really make love. Take his time and worship her.

Cupping her ass, he stood. She wrapped her arms and legs around him, her mouth warm and wet on his neck. She was so gorgeous and so sexy, and the little sounds she made almost did him in. He had barely touched her and he was already fighting for control. She affected him like no other woman ever had.

He had almost made it to the bedroom when his phone rang. Cursing and still carrying her, he returned to the living room and retrieved it. He read the screen and told her it was Jack. He answered the call and they spoke for a few minutes, then he hung up and continued to the bedroom.

"Is Megan okay?" she asked, her voice thick with desire.

"Yes, she's fine. She wants you to call her though." Cooper gently laid her on the bed and busied himself lighting candles. "I guess she's been calling and texting, but you haven't answered. She was about to send out a search party."

"My phone is dead and I don't have a charger."

"We have to go into town later anyways. We will stop and grab one." He grabbed the waistband of her yoga pants and slowly pulled them down her legs, revealing his own little piece of heaven. The sight of her was always breathtaking, but seeing her like this, primed and ready and offering herself to him, her eyes hooded with desire, her lips parted, was just about all he could handle. He had to be inside her.

Ditching his own sweats, he sat on the edge of the bed and just took her in. She looked like an angel. His angel. He caressed her curves and let his eyes feast on her. She had told him repeatedly that she was just average, but she was so wrong. She was perfection. He wanted to worship her body, lick every curve, and make her come slowly and sweetly. His needs could wait. This time it was all about her.

He started at her feet, taking her delicate foot in his hand and bringing it to his lips. He delivered whisper kisses to her toes, and the arch of her foot. He kissed the cross tattoo on top of her foot, and licked his way up the inside of her thighs, skipping over her sex and bathing her hips and ribs with tender kisses. Slowly and softly he licked and nibbled on her breasts, then up her neck and behind her ear. She was squirming and moaning and breathless beneath him. His mouth took hers and she tasted so sweet, and he wanted her so badly he had to fight himself to keep the kiss slow and gentle. He just wanted to consume her, to claim her, but he had promised to do it right this time, and by God that's what he was going to do. It might kill him, but he would make love to her.

She deepened the kiss, reached for his cock, and began stroking him. She tried to position him to enter her while she was whispering, "Please Cooper."

"Not yet, baby," he said, and kissed his way back down her body, past her breasts and belly until he was at her center. He took his time and licked every inch and fold of her pink flesh. She writhed beneath him, but he pinned her down with his forearms on her hips. As he felt her getting closer, he increased his momentum and blew on her clit before taking it in his mouth and nipping lightly. Her whole body tensed as she found her release, and he lapped up every drop of her sweet nectar, feeling so whole and so complete from making her happy.

She tugged him towards her and attacked his mouth and grabbed his sex, and this time she wasn't taking no for an answer. Cooper rolled on a condom and she directed him into her and arched her hips up to give him better access. He wanted to ram into her, and he was pretty sure that's what she wanted too. But he didn't give it to her. Instead, he moved in and out of her painfully slowly. She tried to speed him up, but he set a slow rhythm and stayed with it. Kissing her softly and holding himself up on his elbows, he continued to move slowly and gently, his eyes burning into hers. "I love you," he told her, and that sent her over the edge. She closed her eyes and moaned his name, and her sex clenched down on his cock, stroking and milking him, bringing him dangerously close to finding his own release. But he didn't want to come yet. He was enjoying making her come; he was pretty sure by this point she could honestly say she had had a real orgasm, and he planned to keep them coming. Slowly he pulled out of her and she whimpered, trying to pull him back.

"Cooper," she said, her voice thick with arousal. "I don't want to stop. I want to make you feel good."

Cooper scooted her up the bed and threw the pillows out of the way. "Honey, just being inside you is the most incredible feeling in the world."

She reached for him. "But you didn't come."

"I told you, this time is all about you." He lay beside her and gathered her into his arms. "I told you the next time you let me get inside you I was going to make love to you. I was going to do it right." He caressed her shoulder as she rested her head on his chest. "With you baby, I want to do everything right."

She was drawing small circles on his chest with her fingers. He lay staring at the ceiling, enjoying the feel of her next to him. She began to lick his nipple and tug lightly on his nipple ring, while her other hand caressed his balls. If she kept doing what she was doing, there was no way he would be able to hold out. She lowered her head to his cock and removed the condom. He groaned and covered his face with his hands. This woman was gonna be the death of him. He tried to tug her back up, but she smiled and shook her head.

"My turn," she said, and starting at the base of his dick she licked the length of him. She swirled his velvety tip with her tongue, and then she took him in her mouth while she stroked him with her hand. She relaxed her throat and took him deeper, and all he could do was close his eyes and enjoy the ride. She took him in and out of her mouth slowly, then, as he was on the verge of losing control, she scraped her teeth lightly along his length, and that was all he could handle.

He grabbed her and pulled her toward him with more force than he had planned. She climbed on top of him, and was directing him to her entrance when he stopped her. "Condom," he breathed, and she reached into his nightstand, retrieved one, slid it on his hard shaft, and hopped on top of him. She took him impossibly deep, and he busied himself with her heavy breasts. She rolled her hips with each stroke and found the rhythm that she needed, and he held her at her hips as he slammed into her. Her eyes were heavy, her scent lingered everywhere, sexy moans were escaping her lips, and she felt fucking amazing. He knew right then that he needed her like he needed air to breathe. If he wasn't able to experience this with her every day, there was no reason to live.

She reached down and cupped his face. "I love you, Cooper," she whispered, and he lost it. He thrust into her harder and deeper, causing her to cry out with pleasure, and then as she shattered on top of him, bathing him in her warm, sticky juices, he came violently, his orgasm lasting forever as she continued to stroke him with that amazing pussy.

When they were both sated and limp, she collapsed onto him and lay listening to the rapid beat of his heart. He held her tightly and stroked her head, and he knew that life as he knew it was over. And as much as that had scared him before, the fear was gone. It was replaced with love, and he felt it to his soul.

***

Cooper had decided to grab a shower, and I cleaned myself up and got dressed in jeans and a plain turquoise V neck t-shirt that hugged my breasts. I blew out the candles and tidied up the bed, and then remembered I needed to call Megan. I also needed to call my mother, but I was holding off on that as long as I could. My mother was hard to deal with, and I already had enough on my plate.

I searched the bedroom for Cooper's phone since mine was dead. I didn't have Megan's number committed to memory, but I knew Jack's number would be in the recent calls list. Not finding the phone anywhere, I opened the bathroom door and peeked my head into the shower.

My breath caught at the sight of Cooper's magnificent tattooed body. He was tall and lean, tanned and muscled, and the sight of the water dripping off him had my hoohah doing funny things. It hadn't been ten minutes since we had made love, and I already wanted to do it again. He had wanted me to crave him, and boy did I. I could just live in his bed from now on and I still would probably never get enough of him.

He was humming softly and lathering up his hair when he finally saw me. I smiled and he leaned his head towards me and kissed me.

"Miss me already?" he asked, and I shook my head and gave him a smirk. "Want to join me?" he offered, and although it did sound tempting I declined by shaking my head. Truth was, as much as I wanted him, I didn't know if I could take him again. He was rather large and I was pretty sore. I knew eventually my body would become accustomed to his size, but that hadn't happened yet.

I ran my finger along the lines of a tattoo on his bicep. "I just wanted to know if I could use your phone. I need to call Meg and check in with her."

He pointed to the counter by the sink. "Go ahead, baby. Let her know you are fine. I know she is worried about you."

"I'm worried about her too. The last thing she needs right now is stress. And between me and Granny, she's probably about reached her limit."

"Why don't you offer to bring Granny out here with us and give her and Jack a night to themselves?" Cooper said, and I laughed. He so didn't know what he was getting himself into with that one. But he was sweet to offer.

"I'll mention it to Meg," I said, then left the bathroom to let him finish his shower.

I scrolled through Cooper's recent calls in search of Jack's number. There were several calls from "office," two from Jack, and about twenty from someone named Kayla. I frowned at the screen and instantly felt guilty. I shouldn't be snooping through his phone. I tried not to let it bother me but I wanted to know who the hell this Kayla was and why she called him so many times. I shrugged it off. First of all it was none of my business, and secondly, Kayla could be anybody. She could be his sister, or his accountant, or a spiritual advisor.

I was scrolling back to Jack's number when Cooper's phone vibrated in my hand, indicating that he had a new text. It was from Kayla, and I knew then that I should just drop the phone and call Megan later. But nosiness won out and I opened the text. I immediately wished I hadn't.

'Coop, I get out of class at 2:00 and I want you inside me by 2:30. You game?'

I froze, staring at the screen. Kayla was definitely not his accountant, and sister wasn't looking good either. She was his what? Girlfriend? Booty call? I'd asked him if he had a girlfriend and he had said no. Had he lied to me? Was he just playing me? Did he tell Kayla he loved her too?

Quickly, I closed the text box and found Jack's number again. Trying to keep my voice steady and even was hard, because my emotions were in my throat. A wave of nausea overtook me as well as confusion, anger, and hurt. I took a deep breath as I waiting for Meg to come to the phone, and told myself I was probably over reacting. Cooper and I had only started going steady that day, and we'd only spent a week together doing

185

whatever we were doing before. Dating I guess. And he was handsome and successful, and of course he had women in his life. Probably I should just give him the benefit of the doubt and ask him about it later.

I heard the shower cut off just as Megan came to the phone, and I assured her I was fine and that Cooper was taking good care of me. We talked about the baby and she said that the doctor had put her on bed rest. She didn't sound happy about it, and I knew Jack would have his hands full trying to keep her down. She asked me what was going on between Cooper and I, and I told her I wasn't sure but I was pretty sure I was in love with him. She was quiet for so long I had to ask her if she was still there. When she finally spoke it was in a concerned voice. "Stacy, please take it slow," she warned, and I thought, Oops. Too late for that.

I said, "I will, Meggie, don't worry about me." The last thing she needed was to be worried about me. Even though I wanted to tell her everything, I knew now was not the time.

I offered to take Granny for the night and she gratefully accepted, so we made arrangements for me to pick Granny up at the bingo hall around 8:00. I asked Megan if Jack had found out anything about the bad guys that wanted to hurt me and she said they hadn't, but Jack was still on top of it. She made me promise her I would get a phone charger and keep my phone powered on and handy, and agreed to check in with her daily. Geez, she was in total mommy mode. I told her I loved her, and hung up just as Cooper entered the bedroom wearing only a towel around his lean waist. His hair was damp and lay seductively down his forehead. His torso was bare save for the intricate tattoos that covered him. The scent of soap and sex intoxicated me.

He smiled and sat at the foot of the bed, pulling me into his arms. "Everything okay?" he asked, his voice laced with concern.

I swallowed the lump in my throat. "Yes, everything is okay. Meg is now on bed rest and we have to pick Granny up at the bingo hall at 8:00." I wanted to tell him he had gotten a text, but I didn't want him to know I had snooped. I felt extremely guilty about it, and I was having a hard time controlling the thoughts going through my head.

"And what about you? Are you okay?" He had turned me and tilted my head up so he could look into my eyes. I tried to hide the storm raging inside me.

I put on a forced smile and nodded my head. "Yep, I'm good. Never been better." I kissed his lips and remembered the feel of his lips on me, inside me, everywhere. I wanted that again and I was willing to fight for it. This Kayla bitch didn't know who she was messing with. I *was* a badass, after all, and Cooper was mine. He had claimed me and I had let him, and little Miss Kayla would just have to take a hike.

Cooper's phone vibrated again and I knew it was a text from her. It took all I had in me not to jump up, grab that phone, and tell her to back the fuck off. In fact, that was exactly what I was going to do the next opportunity I got, but I wasn't going to keep it from Cooper. I needed to come clean. I didn't want to come off as a crazy possessive bitch, but I didn't want to be the stupid girl that got played, either. Like my Gramma Estelle always said, honesty was always the best policy.

"Cooper, can I ask you a question?"

He licked my ear lobe. "Sure."

"Who's Kayla?" His body tensed and he went still. I could feel the anger radiate off him.

"What did she do?" he asked, and lifted me off his lap and looked out the window.

"She didn't do anything except…well, she sent you a text that sounded an awful lot like a booty call." Cooper looked at me with wide eyes, and I knew instantly he was pissed that I snooped. I held my hands out. "Look, it's not what you think. I didn't set out to go snooping. I couldn't remember Meg's number, but I knew you had Jack's so I went to your recent calls to find Jack's number and I saw a bunch of calls from this Kayla chic, which got me curious. Then I decided it was none of my business and went back to Jack's number, when a text came through from her and I saw it. That's all that happened, I swear."

Cooper came back to the bed and sat down on his haunches in front of me. He took my hands and his intense gaze stole mine. "Kayla is just a girl I used to date. We went on a few dates and it didn't work out so I cut her loose. She has just had a hard time accepting that."

I didn't want to know the answer to my next question, but I had to ask anyways. "Did you sleep with her?" The thought of him touching another woman broke me.

He nodded, his eyes bluer than I'd ever seen them. "Yes, Stacy, we slept together. I told you, I dated a lot before you."

"Yes, but you told me you had never had a real relationship before."

He caressed my jaw. "And I haven't. That wasn't a lie." He tenderly kissed my lips. "Stacy, I will never lie to you. Yes, we dated, and yes we had sex, but it's over. I've made that perfectly clear to her. She just won't give up. She will eventually though."

"And you promise it's over? That you aren't seeing her anymore? That you weren't seeing her when you met me?" I was rambling like a mad woman and I knew it, but I just couldn't control the stupid words coming out of my mouth. Between Scott and Thad my heart had been shattered, and I just couldn't take another heartbreak. I loved Cooper, but I had to protect myself.

Cooper took both of my hands in his. "Stacy, baby, it's over with her. It was long before you came along. I promise you. Hell, I haven't even seen her in weeks, except from across the street where she sometimes camps out watching for me."

"She sounds a little stalker-ish," I told him.

Cooper closed his eyes. "Yes, she is, but it's complicated."

I wanted to know. No, I needed to know. "I'm listening."

"Look, she's eleven years younger than me and she has quite the temper. She busted up an ex-boyfriends car and then tried to run over him. She's on probation. Colleen suggested that I get a restraining order, but if I do she will probably go to jail."

"So?" I didn't see what the problem was.

"So, she is a sweet girl and I am good friends with her dad, who is a big contractor that I do business with." He held out his hands. "And before you go there, let me just say that I didn't know who her father was, nor did I know about her arrest. As soon as I found out I told her it wasn't working, and I have avoided her since."

"Okay." I felt tears sting my eyes and he wiped them away.

He searched my eyes. "Okay?" He stood and pulled me into his arms. "Baby, it's the truth. Yes, she's crazy, but deep down she is a sweet girl and she has her whole life ahead of her. I don't want to mess that up for her. If she does it on her own that's her bad. But I don't want to carry the guilt."

"And you don't want her?" My voice was squeaky and I hated that it showed my every emotion.

"No, I don't want her." He pulled me back so he could see me, and tucked a curl behind my ear. "I want you baby. And only you."

I stood up on tiptoes and kissed his cheek. "Okay, I believe you Cooper. Just promise me you will never lie to me. I have had my heart ripped up and I've had to stitch it back together. I can't go through another heartbreak."

His eyes were intense and they bore right into my soul. "I will never intentionally hurt you baby, and I will never lie to you."

I believed him. "Okay, but you need to tell that little hooker what a badass I am. After all, I am highly trained and all that."

Cooper laughed and I melted into him.

"I'm serious," I said, enjoying the sound of his laughter in my ears. "I mean, I could wrestle a bear right now. Okay, so not a real bear, or maybe not even a dead stuffed one. Those things give me the creeps. But give me a teddy bear and that sucker won't stand a chance. I will own its ass!"

"I will be sure and warn her," he said, winking at me.

"Okay, and I'll try to hide my crazy from now on."

"Honey, you couldn't hide your crazy if you tried, but luckily you are my kind of crazy."

"I'm sorry I got upset, Cooper. I love you."

"I love you too, my crazy Wrecking Ball."

CHAPTER 10

We spent the rest of the afternoon running errands and just being together. We made a quick stop at the cell phone store and got me both home and car chargers for my phone. We stopped at his office for a minute, where he returned to the truck with a hard hat tucked under his arm. He made an appearance at a couple of jobsites, and checked progress on a few projects. The sight of him in those snug jeans and a hard hat made my knees weak. That man was my definition of absolute perfection. I had to hold myself back from mauling him the second he got back in the truck.

We hit the grocery store, and since it was such a beautiful day, Cooper suggested we have a picnic. We bought food from the deli, and Cooper retrieved a blanket from behind the back seat of his truck and spread it out in front of the lake at the park. We ate and talked and laughed like we were two lovers with not a care in the world. The only reminder of the dangerous reality we were living in was the compact pistol Cooper kept close at all times. I was pretty sure the kidnappers had given up on me by now, but Cooper and Jack weren't taking any chances. Freaking men! They all think they are GI Joe and all of us women are helpless little Barbies.

Cooper had left his phone in his truck and mine was there charging, so we had no interruptions. No Crazy Kayla and no work emergencies. We were just two people in love enjoying the sound of the water washing up on the bank, the sun shining in the sky, and the company of one another. As I lay in his lap, his hand lightly caressing my scalp, I took the time to count my blessings. I was thankful I had tripped and broken my stupid ankle. I was thankful I hadn't been injured worse or killed by the kidnappers. I was thankful for my friends and for this amazing man that had walked into my life. Hell, I was even thankful for the torment Scott and Thad had caused me, because it made me appreciate what was developing between Cooper and I all the more. I could have stayed like that all day, but when the sky opened up and bathed us in a light, gentle rain, we packed everything up and headed for the truck.

Cooper opened my door for me, then stowed the food and blanket in the back. We still had about four hours until we needed to get Granny, so we decided to go back to Cooper's house and relax...or make love, if I had any say in the matter. We held hands the whole way to Cooper's, and made small talk about nothing at all. It amazed me how natural and easy our conversations flowed, and how much we had in common.

We arrived and I helped Cooper put up groceries, and then I made a beeline for the bathroom. As I opened the door, my heart lurched through my throat when I heard the shower going and I could make out a female form behind the glass. My eyes were wide and my mind went into overdrive. Please God don't let this be Crazy Kayla. I was only kidding about the whole badass thing.

I searched around the bathroom for a weapon just in case my badass skills failed me. There wasn't much so I settled on a toilet bowl cleaner and a can of shaving cream. I didn't know what the hell I would do with them, but you've got to work with what you have. Taking a deep breath, I told myself it was now or never. Either I was going to stake my claim and run this crazy bitch off for good or let her have him. My mind flashed back to self-defense class, and all I could remember was "kick em in the nuts." Okay, that didn't apply so I'd have to wing it.

I remembered seeing Cooper's motorcycle helmet on his dresser, and I thought, *What the hell?* Safety first. My badass skills may not kick in. Better to be protected. Grabbing the helmet, I slipped it on and opened the visor so Miss Crazy Stalker Bitch could hear every word that came out of my mouth. Slowly, I opened the glass door and pointed the toilet brush at a screaming brunette, who was trying to cover herself with her hands. I stood there frozen as the mysterious brunette grabbed a towel and covered herself.

"You must be Kayla," she said, and I let out a hysterical laugh. She really was crazy. What was she using, some reverse psychology bullshit? Aside from that, she was really fit and looked like she was going to hand me my ass. I looked around for a better weapon but came up empty.

Keeping my weapons in hand I told her how it was going to be as I heard the door open. "Now, look Kayla. Cooper is with me now and I don't want to hurt you so I suggest you leave before I go zombie ninja on your ass." I was hoping to scare her off with words because I really didn't want to get beat up by a naked chic while I was waving around a toilet cleaner wand. The ER would seriously lock me up if I showed up beaten and bruised with another outlandish story. On the plus side, I probably wouldn't suffer another concussion since I had head protection.

The brunette laughed, and if I hadn't just painted my nails the other day I would have punched her. I felt someone grab me from behind, and turned around and slammed right into Cooper. He stashed his gun in his waistband and, smiling, drug me out of the bathroom and shut the door.

"Hey," I protested. "I was about to go all Karate Kid on her ass." Laughing, Cooper pulled me to the bed. "Hey, it's not funny mister. I am a serious threat. Who does she think she is...?"

"My sister," he interrupted.

"...that she can just show up and take a.... Your sister?"

He nodded as the bathroom door opened and the pretty brunette stepped out wearing a short satin robe. "I'm Josslyn," she said, and stuck out her hand for me to shake.

Embarrassed, I removed the helmet and offered her my hand. "I'm Stacy," I said, and she looked at Cooper, her eyes dancing with amusement.

"I thought Kayla was the crazy one," she said, and I knew I deserved that comment. I was acting pretty crazy. I couldn't help it though. Cooper brought out the crazy in me. Okay, that was a lie, but it sounded better than admitting that I might be a little bit bat shit crazy all on my own. Just a tad.

"She is," Cooper admitted.

Josslyn waved her hand in the air. "Okay, I'm totally confused. So you have *two* crazy women now, Coop?" She shook her head. "Dude, seriously, you gotta slow down. Someday I'm going to come home and find you dying in the bathtub, covered in honey, with ants crawling over you." We all cringed at the mental image.

"You are supposed to call first," Cooper told her.

"I did. You didn't answer. I was only going to be here for about half an hour, and I figured you were probably at work or in a meeting. I would have been gone by the time you got home."

"I had some things to take care of, and I left my phone in the truck."

"Well, there ya go. Anywho, I'll be outta here in a few. I just needed a shower and a change of clothes." She wiggled her eyebrows. "I've got a hot date tonight, so don't wait up."

"How long are you here for?" he asked at the same time she noticed the gun in his waistband.

"Eight days," she said, and then, "Why do you have your gun out?"

Cooper pulled me into him. "It's a long story. Here, join me for a beer and I'll tell you all about it."

Josslyn gestured for us to exit first. "This I gotta hear," she mumbled.

**

So Cooper, Josslyn, and I sat around his dining room table as Cooper filled her in from the beginning. Turns out she was a traveling nurse, and when she was off she stayed with Cooper. She was young and it gave her the opportunity to travel and see the country, and since she wasn't ready to settle down, it was kind of a no brainer for her. She loved what she did and she loved to travel. It was a match made in heaven. She only worked twenty-one days a month, and she spent the time off visiting her family. It made no sense for her to rent or buy a home that she would only spend a week a month in, and her parents were too old fashioned too accommodate her social life, so she stayed with Cooper. Now she sat there with an amused twinkle in her eyes, fiddling with the label on her beer bottle as Cooper told the whole wild story. Except for a couple times when she stopped him and asked him to clarify, she didn't say much. When he was done she laughed, and I mean really laughed...like grabbing her belly laughing. Like any of this was funny!

"Okay, so let me get this straight. You meet like they do in porno, you break your ankle and my brother rescues you, and in the process you fend off some kidnappers that are out there looking for you right now? So you are hiding out here, speed dating, falling in love, and now you want to have babies?"

When she said it like that it did sound kind of crazy.

"No babies," Cooper said, and Josslyn ignored him.

"But we do have a pet duck," I added helpfully.

"Meanwhile, Crazy Kayla is still out there stalking you?"

Cooper took a pull on his beer. "Yep."

"Want me to take care of her for you, Coop?" Josslyn asked, and I hoped to hell he said yes, because ass kicking wasn't exactly my expertise. I talked a good game and all, but backing it up was a different story.

"No," Cooper said. "I can handle Kayla. What I want you to do is stay at Mom and Dad's until this whole thing is over."

There was a glimmer of mischief in her dazzling blue eyes. "No way, brother! I'm staying here. Mom and Dad's house is boring. No way I'm going to miss out on all of this craziness."

"Really it's been pretty quiet, all things considered," I said.

"I'd really feel better if you were at Mom and Dad's. I'm already concerned about Stacy's safety. I don't need to add you to the mix."

She waved him off. "Coop, please. I can take care of myself and you damn well know it. You've taught me well. I can help."

Copper rolled his eyes and sighed. "You aren't going to leave, are you?"

She finished her beer in one long swallow. "Not on your life. In fact, I'm canceling my date. I don't want to miss a second of this."

"Okay, well, nobody knows she is here, so keep your mouth shut. And don't tell Mom and Dad."

She tilted her head and eyed her brother. "So you really love this one, Coop?"

"I do," he said honestly.

"And she's actually over twenty-five and has an actual brain?"

Geez, what kind of bimbos did Cooper usually date?

"Yes to both," Cooper said.

She turned her blue gaze to me. "You truly love, my brother?" I nodded. "And you aren't really crazy?"

"Not usually." I thought about all the craziness that followed me around. "Well, not most of the time anyways."

"And you actually did this whole five date rule thing?" Cooper nodded. "Okay." She collected her and Cooper's beer bottles, tossed them in the trash, and grabbed them each another. She offered me one and I held up my water bottle, letting her know I was fine. "Well, that's good enough for me. I mean, crazier things have happened. Our parents went on two dates and got married, and they've been married over forty years. If my brother's happy, I'm happy. If he loves you, I love you too."

Cooper went into the kitchen to begin dinner, and Josslyn and I sat at the table getting to know each other. She was a really sweet girl. She was five years younger than Cooper, and had a wild side that reminded me a bit of Josie. She was telling me about her crazy adventures when my cell phone rang. I picked it up off the counter and saw that it was Granny. It was only 6:45. Either she won big or she'd been kicked out of the bingo hall. I answered on the third ring.

"You've got to come get me, and you can't tell Megan," she yelled into the phone.

"What did you do?" I asked, lightly banging my head against the table.

"I had an Alzheimer moment and went bowling for trolls. Now I'm in jail and you are my one phone call! Hurry!"

"You're in jail?" I asked, but she had already hung up. Cooper stopped what he was doing and raised an eyebrow. And to think I had almost convinced Josslyn that me and my crew were perfectly normal.

"Umm, Cooper? Can I borrow your truck?"

He turned off the stove and grabbed his keys. "No, I'll take you. You aren't leaving my side."

"It's okay, Cooper. I'm going to the police station. I mean, how dangerous is that?"

He was shaking his head. "Not happening baby, you are stuck with me."

Josslyn grabbed her phone and shoes. "Me too. I'm going, too. I'm not missing this shit!" Cooper gave her the evil eye. "Plus, I can keep an eye out for Crazy Kayla."

I sighed and threw on a pair of flip-flops. We all piled into Cooper's truck, and off to the police station we went.

***

We made it to the police station in record time. I had no idea what Granny had gotten herself into, and I just hoped I could get her out of it. If Megan found out the shit was going to majorly hit the fan. Jack was about at his wits' end with Granny, and if she got kicked out of there, odds were I would be stuck with her permanently. I groaned and Cooper rubbed my leg.

"I'm sure she's fine, baby. Try and relax." I wasn't all that worried about Granny. She could definitely hold her own. I was more worried about the craziness that she would bring with her.

We pulled up at the police station and Cooper stowed his gun and locked up the truck. We found Granny sitting opposite a police officer at an old tattered desk, drinking coffee. She smiled as we walked in, and grabbed her handbag and a large tote.

"Well, Harold, it was good talking to you, but there's my ride." She stood, threw her tote bag over Cooper's shoulder, and winked at him. "Let's get out of here, Mr. Sexy Pants."

"Not so fast," the officer said. "I can't just release you, ma'am. I have to have a family member or responsible party sign for you."

"I'll sign for her," Cooper said, and he huddled with the officer signing the necessary forms.

I asked Granny what happened and she pointed to the cameras and said she couldn't confirm or deny anything. I rolled my eyes, and as soon as Cooper was done we got the hell out of there. Well, we tried anyways.

Granny, as usual, was on the prowl and wouldn't pass up an opportunity to flirt with a man in uniform. Or a man period, for that matter. She wrote her phone number on a piece of paper and winked at the poor officer. "If you felt anything you liked when you frisked me, give me a jingle." She handed the stunned officer her number, and I grabbed her and drug her out to the truck.

In the truck I introduced her to a smiling Josslyn and asked her what happened. She said she would tell me when we got to

197

Cooper's, because she didn't want to have to start and stop when we got there. I figured she was trying to embellish the truth and get her story straight. We made it back to Cooper's and all took a seat at the table. I gave her a bottle of water and got one for myself. Cooper and Josslyn both had another beer. I had a feeling I would probably need a beer by the night's end.

"Okay, Granny, spill it," I said, pinning her in place with my gaze.

"Okay, it's really a funny story."

Oh boy. "I'm sure it is. Let's hear it," I prompted her.

"Well, I was playing bingo with Miss Gentry and minding my own business," she started, and already I knew she was lying. "I had my crystal ball out and I was predicting the numbers that the announcer was calling, only they weren't matching up. Something was off with my juju."

Josslyn stopped her. "Wait, you have a crystal ball?" Granny pulled it out of her tote and handed it to Josslyn. "Wicked cool," Josslyn said as she turned it over in her hands. "Okay, go on."

"So anyways, something was messing with my mojo and I couldn't figure out what it was. I checked my aura and I knew it wasn't me. Then I looked around, and that's when I spotted the problem. Old lady Demspey had a bunch of trolls standing there in front of her, smiling their demonic smiles. She thinks they bring her good luck."

"Granny, old lady Demspey is thirty years younger than you, and you aren't allowed to go near her."

"I didn't go near her! I sat clear at the other end of the table. And anyways, I was there first. *She* sat near *me*."

I knew this wasn't going to end well, but I had to know what happened next. "Okay, whatever. Continue."

"Well, since I can't get near the old bat, I wrote her a note, nicely asking her to put away her trolls and their bad juju, and then I passed the note to the person sitting next to me just like we used to do in grade school. When the note finally got to her, she opened it and read it, and then she turned to me with a sneer and flipped me the bird."

"Oh God," I said, and Josslyn, all smiles, said, "What happened next?"

Granny drank some water and cracked her knuckles. "Well, I won't tolerate being disrespected, and I was speaking for the whole table when I said those demon trolls had to go. So since my crystal ball was useless at the moment, I stood on the table, held the ball between my legs, swung it and let it go, and knocked her trolls down like bowling pins." I put my head in my hands. "I did pretty good, too. I got seven out of nine. Not bad considering I haven't bowled in years. So anyways, the old bat got pissed and threw my ball at me, but I ducked and it hit the glass case where all the balls come from, and the bingo balls went flying everywhere. That's when it got bad."

I groaned. There was no way Megan wouldn't hear about this. Megan's mom was probably on the phone fielding calls right now.

"It was like bingo pandemonium. I barely made it out of there alive. Only I couldn't go anywhere because I was on foot." She turned to Josslyn. "You run a guy on a bicycle over one time and the cops take your license. They say I can't see. I'll tell you this though. They are full of shit. I see just fine with these babies." She tapped her trifocals. I signaled for her to go on. "So I go back inside, and people are yelling and running around and it's just pure craziness, and the announcer guy is trying to get control of the situation so I helped him out."

I glared at Granny. "What did you do?" I demanded.

"All I did was fire a warning shot into the air, that just happened to hit a chandelier, that just happened to come crashing down on the snack bar lady." She shook her head. "She was fine though. It just grazed her. I knew the popo was on the way, so I wiped down the gun, ran to old lady Dempsey's side of the table, and dropped it in her bag. I was home freaking free, too, until that crazy bitch Miss Gentry threw me under the bus and told the cops that I was responsible for exciting a riot."

"You mean inciting a riot?" Cooper asked.

"Well, whatever you call it. The point is that backstabbing old bitty sold me out." She hit the table with an arthritic fist. "Next time I see her I'm going to break her nose all over her face."

"Granny!" I shouted. I didn't mean to shout, but it just came out that way. "You can't go around shooting guns. Where did you even get a gun?"

"I got it from my pharmacist," Granny said, and I picked up the phone.

"Okay, I'm calling Megan."

"No wait," Granny said. "I'll tell you the truth, but I can't give you any names."

Cooper fished another beer out of the fridge and I took it and applied it to my now aching head. Josslyn scooted up closer to the table and encouraged Granny to continue.

"I got the gun from my moonshine supplier." She turned to Josslyn. "I use my moonshine for medical purposes only. That's why I call my contact my pharmacist."

Josslyn gave her a thumbs up. "Gotcha."

"Granny...." I started, but I had no idea what to say. She had gone too far this time. This was worse than her starting an underground strip club in the nursing home.

"Hey, I only carry it for protection. And according to my ball I was supposed to win big. I couldn't walk out of the joint with a wad of cash and not be strapped." She waved a hand in the air, dismissing the matter. "It's really not a big deal. Nobody got hurt."

I felt like I was dealing with a child. "That's not the point, Granny."

Josslyn got another beer for herself and one for Granny. "So what happened when the cops got there?" she wanted to know.

"Oh, you'll love this," Granny started, and I seriously considered that beer. "When the cops got there I used the old Alzheimer's act and pretended that I didn't know who I was or where I was at. I kept insisting that I was at the bowling alley with Scott Baio. You know, the dude from *Happy Days*. He's such a hottie. If I was going to go bowling with someone it would be with him. But that's beside the point. Anyways, the Alzheimer's act worked and the cops talked the bingo hall out of pressing charges on me, as long as I paid for the damages to the ball thingie and the chandelier. So as long as I pay the repair bill I'm home free. They even called the judge and everything."

I suddenly had a great idea. If she didn't pay the bill she would go to jail, which would mean she wouldn't have to stay with me, which would be awesome. And Granny was tough. She could hack it in jail. Hell, she would run the joint before they let her out.

"What about the gun charges?" I asked hopeful. Surely they could get her for the gun.

"What gun?" she asked innocently. "I wiped it and they can't trace it to me. I watch CSI. I know my shit."

"Right on, Granny!" Josslyn said, and her and Granny bumped fists.

"The only bad part is this." Granny placed her foot on the table and showed off her pretty house arrest tracking bracelet. "Until I pay that bill, I'm still facing charges, and since I did the whole Alzheimer's bit, they are gonna make me wear this. They said it's for my safety, but really I think it's because that fine piece of ass police officer wants to know where to find me at all times. He said he was just frisking me. You know, standard procedure? My ass! I'm getting my groove back." She jiggled her boobs. "I can feel it."

Josslyn tapped the neck of her beer bottle on the edge of the table. "You go, Granny. Bump bump, get it get it." She and Granny toasted to that and downed their beers. Cooper had downed his as well. Everyone was pretty much speechless.

I rubbed my face and mouthed, "I'm sorry" to Cooper. He pulled me into his lap and kissed my temple. We had had such a normal, quiet day. I only went a little bit crazy, and then Granny happened.

Granny clapped her hands. "So what's for dinner? I'm starving."

Cooper lifted me out of his lap and led me to the kitchen, leaving Granny and Josslyn to get acquainted. In the kitchen, I wrapped my arms around Cooper's waist and told him how sorry I was.

"You have nothing to be sorry about, baby," he told me, but I felt sorry anyways.

"Well, I'm sorry about Granny. She's just...well she's—"

He silenced me with a kiss. "Not your fault, sweetheart," he whispered.

There was also the matter of Josslyn. "I'm also sorry I went crazy after your sister." He laughed and pulled me closer. "It could have gotten bad if you hadn't come in." I smiled up at him.

"I mean, I was about to be all over that ass. She's lucky you dragged me out of there."

The corners of his eyes crinkled and his eyes sparkled. "I'll be sure and let her know that."

"She looks like she might be a bad ass too. Maybe we should let her handle this Kayla chic." That way Kayla would be gone and Cooper wouldn't know I was a wimp.

Cooper danced me around the kitchen. "Let's worry about Kayla tomorrow. We've had enough excitement for one day." I nodded into his chest. "Let's feed the troops and then get you naked and in bed." He pulled away and turned on the stove.

Sounded like a good plan to me.

***

Dinner was steaks, baked potatoes, and veggies. I didn't realize how hungry I was until Cooper slid a plate in front of me. I inhaled it and got seconds. We talked through dinner and thankfully nothing catastrophic happened. Granny had two beers and a couple swigs of her medicine…she would be asleep before her head hit the pillow, thank God. Currently, she was reading Josslyn's palm while Cooper and I cleared the dishes.

"Hey, you cooked, I got dishes," Josslyn hollered.

We made a second run at the table gathering dishes. "Thanks sis," Cooper told her.

She wiggled her eyebrows. "You two lovebirds just go have some fun. Granny and I got this."

I shook my head. "Oh no, I can't leave Granny with you."

She winked at me. "Nonsense. Granny and I will get along just fine. You guys run along. I'll sleep with headphones on, so don't worry about me. Just pretend I'm not even here."

"Woot, Woot. Get some!" Granny slurred, and pumped her fist in the air.

Cooper bent down and kissed his sister on the cheek. "Set the alarm," he told her, and she nodded.

"You hear that, Granny? Josslyn is going to set the alarm, so don't try sneaking out," I scolded.

She held up her ankle. "House arrest, bitches! I ain't going nowhere."

That still didn't make me comfortable. Josslyn stood and cleared the rest of the dishes. "Seriously guys, I got this. Don't worry about a thing."

"You're sure?" I asked one more time.

"Positive. Your granny is a riot. She's crazy cool." She lowered her voice. "Plus, she's plastered. I'm pretty sure she'll pass out midway through doing the dishes." I nodded. She was right. Granny would be out like a light. "I'll let her have my room and I'll take the couch." She shooed us away. "Now run along."

We walked arm in arm to Cooper's bedroom, and as soon as the door shut I unsnapped my boot and discarded the annoying thing. Cooper dimmed the lights and turned some music down low. He lit a couple of candles and gathered me into his arms. Being in his arms felt amazing and I wanted to stay there forever.

Cooper's phone buzzed in his pocket and he fished it out. I was sure it was probably Crazy Kayla, but I was wrong. It was Jack. He had heard about the bingo hall incident and wanted to know if we had everything under control. Cooper assured him that we did, and Jack told him Megan was having false labor again, and that under no circumstance was she to know what happened with Granny. We swore to secrecy and told Jack goodnight. I sent Megan a quick text, telling her goodnight and that I loved her. I felt like I should be there for her, but unfortunately being there would just put her and the baby in danger. Tears stung my eyes and I wiped them away quickly. Cooper took my face in his hands.

"Don't cry, baby," he said tenderly.

"I'm sorry. I'm just...well, I think everything is finally catching up with me. I mean, the kidnappers, and Granny, and now Megan is hurting and I can't be there to help her. And that's what hurts the most. Megan has always been there for me, and I feel like I'm failing her."

"Shh, baby. She wants you safe. You are helping her by staying safe. She's not worrying about you, and we took care of Granny."

I sniffled and nodded. "I guess you're right." I found his eyes. "But what about you? Are you ready to run yet?" He shook his head. "'Cause in case you haven't noticed, I'm a train wreck."

He sat beside me on the bed. "No you aren't. You are a beautiful, sweet, kind hearted, amazing woman." I shook my head. "Honey, we all come with some baggage. Look at me, I've got Crazy Kayla. And trust me, I'll take Granny over Kayla any day." He tilted my head up. "I'm not going anywhere Stacy. I love you, and I'm here as long as you will have me."

"I love you too, but I'm not sure I deserve you."

"You're right." He ran his fingers through my hair. "You deserve far better than me."

I wiped away my tears. "Cooper?"

"Yes baby."

"Make love to me."

"It'll be my pleasure, Ms. Dupree," Cooper said as he slowly undressed me.

"Actually, it's usually all my pleasure."

"As it should be," he whispered as he put me into bed and gently made love to me until I fell asleep in his arms.

***

Cooper lay staring at the ceiling, wrapped up with the only woman he'd ever loved except for his mom and sisters. Yes, she was a mess, but she was his mess. He knew life with her was going to be chaotic and crazy, but he was all in. He wanted her and everything that came with her. The baggage of a bitter divorce, a bad break up, kidnappers, Granny, drag queens, broken bones, and pet ducks. It didn't matter; as long as he got to hold her like this every night, he could deal with anything life threw at them. He needed her like he needed oxygen to breathe. She was his everything, and the thought of laying there in the bed without her made him feel hollow inside. He didn't know how he would keep her there, but he knew he could never let her go home. He would feel empty without her.

He glanced down at her sleeping silhouette, and was so consumed with love that it choked him up. He always knew he would fall in love someday, but he didn't know it would drop kick him in the nuts. It happened before he could stop it, and now the thought of going back to his old life, filled with casual dates ending in meaningless sex, had lost all of its appeal. Hell, he couldn't even think about other women. Stacy had consumed his body, mind, and soul.

She was smiling in her sleep, and he hoped she was dreaming of him. He needed to get up and blow the candles out, but he didn't want to disturb her slumber. He kissed the top of her head and whispered "Mine." She was his. He was hers. That was all that mattered.

She stirred beside him and called out his name. Her eyes were closed and her lips were parted and he smiled, knowing she was dreaming of him. He slowly untangled her from his body so he could blow the candles out and turn off the music. He took a moment to capture her beauty in the candle light, and when she moaned his name and began touching herself he came undone. She was grinding against her hand and making the sexiest little noises, and he didn't want to wake her, but damn it, he couldn't control himself when she did that. Her dreaming of him and touching herself was the sexiest thing he'd ever encountered, and although he would feel like an asshole later, he had to have her now.

He went into the kitchen and grabbed the Advil and a bottle of water. When he came back, she was grinding harder and breathing heavily, her release near. It took everything he had in him not to touch her. He let her finish, and once she did she opened her eyes and found him staring at her. She was soaking wet and her skin was flushed. She reached for him and asked him what was wrong.

"Nothing's wrong baby. I was just admiring you and trying to figure out what the fuck I did to get so damn lucky." He handed her three Advil and opened the bottle of water for her.

"What's this for?" she asked in her sleepy voice.

"Baby, you are going to need those, because I plan on making love to you all night long."

She felt her wetness. "Did we just make love? Did I sleep through it?"

"No baby, that was all you. You were asleep—"

"I was dreaming about you, Cooper."

"And you were touching yourself, and you came. That was the sexiest thing I've ever seen. I had to practically sit on my hands to keep from touching you, but now it's my turn. You are mine and I want you right now. I have to be inside you, baby. I need it like I need air to breathe."

"Why do I need Advil?"

"Because you have me so primed right now, slow and simple isn't going to cut it, and I don't want you hurting in the morning. You might not be able to walk, which would be fine with me. Keeping you in my bed all day sounds amazing, but I don't want to hurt you."

She took the Advil with a big gulp of water. "You talk a good game, Cooper, but are you going to back it up? Or should I just take care of myself?" She gave him an evil, sexy grin, and he lowered himself to the bed and attacked her mouth, his hands everywhere.

"Stacy?" he said, his voice thick with desire. "Can you do me a favor, baby?"

She would do anything to have him inside her, filling her completely. "I'll do anything you want, Cooper. Just hurry up and get inside me."

He planned to do just that. "Will you get on the pill for me? I would love to be inside you without the barrier of a condom."

She smiled a slow sleepy smile. "Cooper, I've been on birth control for months. And I got tested for everything after my divorce. Scott cheated on me and I had to know I was clean, and I am. I'm good to go. You said you are always safe, right?"

He nodded. "I've never had unprotected sex with anyone. And I do get tested on a regular basis. Joss pretty much insists. She is under the impression that I'm a man whore."

"Wonder where she got that idea."

He gave her that innocent, shy smile that made her knees weak. "I haven't a clue."

"Well, you were a man whore. Those days are over, Mr. Carson. Are you okay with that?"

"Honey, you've ruined me for all other women. I'm totally and completely yours."

That evil grin returned. "So now you are my very own man whore."

He slid a finger into her red-hot center. "At your service, baby."

She drew his face down to hers and bit his bottom lip while she lightly tugged on a nipple ring. "Then fuck me already, will ya?"

"I thought you'd never ask," he said, and took her mouth in a hungry kiss that had her holding on for dear life. He was a man on the edge and she wanted him to lose control. She began massaging her clit while he was working his fingers inside her, and she saw the moment he unraveled and knew this would be a hell of a ride. He picked her up, positioned her on her knees, and he roughly entered her from behind. He slipped a pillow under her belly and threw the other pillows out of the way. Making love with Stacy had been amazing every time, but doing it with no condom, where he could feel her velvety smooth pussy, was earth shattering. If he wasn't careful he'd blow his wad before she even had a chance to get there. All this time, she'd been telling him she wanted all of him, so he finally gave it to her. She cried out but met him thrust for thrust as she took him deeper and deeper still. He fisted his hand in her hair and tugged gently. "Who do you belong to?" he rasped.

"You Cooper. I'm yours."

"That's right baby. You. Are. Mine. And I'm never letting you go." He was pumping into her harder now, and they were both close to their release when a piecing shrill rang out throughout the house. Cooper jumped off Stacy, and when he opened his eyes there was smoke everywhere. In their urgency to make love, he had thrown the pillows out of the way, and one of them landed on a candle and was now on fire. He grabbed it, ran to the bathroom, and shoved it in the shower.

Suddenly, the bedroom door swung open and Josslyn came in with a baseball bat and a can of mace. Granny was hot on her heels with her stun gun and a pair of brass knuckles. Stacy did her best to cover herself with the sheet as Cooper emerged from the bathroom, using the burnt pillow to cover his junk.

"Where are they?" Granny asked, squinting around the room. "I got something for them. If I can find 'em, I'll zap em in the gonads."

"Yeah Coop, is everything okay?" Josslyn had lowered her baseball bat, but still had her mace ready to go.

"It's fine. It was just the fire alarm," Cooper told everyone.

Granny's eyes lit up and she dug around for her phone. They both yelled "No" at the same time, and she pouted. "So no firemen, and I don't get to zap anyone? This is bullshit. I'm going back to bed." She turned and left the room.

Josslyn was holding back laughter. "Dang Bubba, talk about setting the sheets on fire. You go boy!"

"Joss, seriously, get out," Cooper told her.

She was laughing but trying to keep it together. "Okay, okay. Geez. Nite, Coop, Stacy."

"Goodnight Joss," Cooper said, and locked the door behind her. He tossed the pillow and climbed on top of Stacy. "Okay baby, where were we?"

"We were on fire!"

"Yes we were. That seems to happen a lot with you," he said as he rolled her to her side and reentered her.

"Cooper, shut up and make love to me." And that's exactly what he did, twice before morning.

CHAPTER 11

I woke up satisfied and well rested. I don't think I had ever slept better than I did in Cooper's arms. The clock said 11:13, and I didn't have to glance over to see that Cooper was already up. It didn't take long for me to figure out that he was a morning person. As I lay warm and comfortable in his big bed, I took in his room with the large, masculine furniture and neutral brown tones. Everything was neat and tidy and so...Cooper. I could get used to waking up there. Shaking the thought from my head I told myself to get a grip. I mean, I was getting way ahead of myself. We had only been together a week, but it seemed like so much longer and I had gotten so attached to him in that short amount of time, and in my head I knew I needed to slow the hell down, but my heart was telling me the opposite. A part of me knew that as soon as the kidnappers were caught I would have to go home, and the thought of falling asleep without Cooper holding me made me frown. I wanted to share my day with him and let his heartbeat lull me to sleep at night. Suddenly my comfortable little condo felt empty and lonely. I decided not to dwell on the matter and just live everyday with Cooper to the fullest. We would make it work.

The smell of coffee wafting from the kitchen perked me up, and since I didn't have any more clean clothes, I dug in Cooper's dresser and found a soft, worn pair of sweats and a t-shirt. I had to roll the sweats up at the waist and the shirt hung to my knees, but they would do until I could wash my clothes or go to my house to pick up more. I padded to the kitchen, poured a cup of coffee, and sugared and creamed it to perfection. The first sip was sheer bliss, and I closed my eyes and savored the magnificent flavor.

I glanced out into the driveway and saw that Cooper's truck was there, so he must be there somewhere. The house was dead quiet, no sign of Granny or Josslyn anywhere. I peered out the back door and heard music coming from the back garage. Cooper said he had had it built to house his home gym, and I assumed he was out there working out. I imagined him shirtless, his muscles bulging, his body glistening with sweat, his tattoos on full display. As sore as I was from our marathon lovemaking, I still craved him inside me.

Coffee in hand, I grabbed a piece of bread and made my way out the back door. I sat my coffee down on a rock near the pond, tore the bread into pieces, and fed Paddington. He seemed to be happy swimming around in the pond without a care in the world. He quack quacked and dunked his head underwater to retrieve a piece of bread.

Laughing, I scooped up my coffee and went to find Cooper. I found him in his gym wearing low slung sweats and nothing else. He looked delicious and I wanted to jump him then and there. He was lying on his weight bench lifting, and when he saw me he rose and toweled the sweat off his face. He reached for me, I straddled his lap, our lips found each other, and before long we were both breathless and panting.

"Let's go to bed, Cooper," I pleaded.

Cooper kissed my forehead. "Baby, you are insatiable."

"Only for you," I answered. I stood and signaled for him to follow me.

He groaned. "No," he said. "We need to take a day off."

My smile was coy. "Can't hang, Mr. Carson?"

I saw the challenge register in his eyes. "Oh, I'm not worried about me. I can hang all day baby. I'm more worried about you. I know you are sore, and the last thing I would ever want to do is hurt you."

"I'm okay," I assured him, but he wouldn't budge.

"As much as I want nothing more than to be inside you, I'm not going to do it. I want making love to always be a pleasurable experience."

I licked my bottom lip. "So, you want to play hard to get, huh?" If I really wanted to play dirty I could. All I had to do was touch myself and it would be game over. But truth is I *was* sore, and I thought it was so sweet that he was concerned about me. It made me feel special and loved beyond anything I'd ever felt before. I changed the subject. "Where are Josslyn and Granny?"

"Joss took Granny to Megan's, and then she was going to go run the beach with Gus." Gus was Josslyn's dog that she and Cooper shared. Since she didn't have a permanent residence he lived with Cooper. Gus was seven years old and about a hundred pounds, but he thought he was a lap dog. He was always bouncing with energy and loved to give big, sloppy kisses.

"Have you talked to Jack today?" I asked, and he shook his head.

"But don't worry, between Jack and the cops they will get this guy."

I nodded. "I know, it's just I hate hiding out. And I feel like I'm imposing on you and Joss."

He stood and dragged me into his arms. "Honey, you are anything but an imposition. I love having you here. And Joss is crazy about you." He kissed my temple. "Hell, we may not ever let you go home."

I smiled into his chest. "I don't know that I ever want to go home."

He pulled back to capture my gaze. "Then don't." He was serious and I swallowed hard. "Just think on it," he added. "We will do whatever you want."

"Okay," I said, the words barely audible from the lump in my throat.

"Are you hungry?" he asked, and I gave him an incredulous look. "Okay, dumb question. Joss made breakfast this morning and yours is in the microwave. She's a lousy cook, but it's hard to screw up biscuits from a can and gravy from a package. It's edible. Also, I knew you were probably getting low on clothes, so Joss threw yours in the washer and she left a couple of sundresses that she thought might fit you on the dryer. Help yourself to them. Later today, if you want to we can go by your house and pick up more clothes."

Wow. This man took such good care of me. "Thank you."

211

His eyes danced. "You're welcome baby. Now go eat and get all dolled up. There is somewhere special I want to take you today. It's one of my favorite places. My grandpa and I used to go there all the time. Plus, I have a surprise for you."

"Oh Cooper." I latched on to him tighter. "I love you."

"I love you too, my angel."

***

Bouncing back in the house with a huge grin plastered on my face, I hit the button on the microwave to reheat my breakfast and grabbed my phone. There were a couple of text messages that I would read in a minute, but first I dialed Megan. I knew she had had a rough couple of nights and I wanted to check on her, but I'd decided I wouldn't bring up Granny unless she did. I didn't want to cause her undo stress. She answered just as I was about to hang up, and she sounded like I had awakened her.

"Meg, are you okay?" I asked her.

She yawned. "Yes, I was just catching a nap. We had a long night last night."

I frowned. "I'm so sorry Megan. I should be there for you."

"For what? To listen to me bitch and moan? No, you are better with Cooper where you are at." She was fully awake now and back in mom mode. "Speaking of Cooper, how are things going with him?"

I giggled. "It's…. He's…well, everything is just perfect."

"I'm so glad to hear that Stacy. I told you the right guy would come along."

She was right as usual. "Yes, and I mean it's been crazy fast, but I think he's the one."

Megan's tone turned serious. "Just promise me you will take it slow."

It was too late for that, but I didn't tell her so. Instead I said, "Of course." The last thing I needed was her worrying about me. "And by the way, Cooper won't leave my side. His main priority is keeping me safe." And lucky for me his second priority was making me come. I didn't tell her that though.

"That's good to hear. Jack assured me that he trusts Cooper. That guy has got it bad for you. Oh, and thanks for taking Granny last night. I hope she wasn't too much trouble."

"No, of course not," I lied. "It's the least I can do with you on bed rest and all." I truly wished I could do more for her, but she was right. All I could do was sit and hang out with her. I couldn't cook, I didn't clean, and I didn't really have any skills when it came to managing pain or pushing a baby out.

"Okay, Stace, I'm going to get off here and try to finish my nap. Thanks for calling. I love you."

"I love you too, best friend," I said, meaning every word.

I was giddy with excitement and I knew today was going to be a fabulous day. Just Cooper and me...no Granny, no kidnappers, no stress. I was so full of love I felt like my heart was bursting at the seams. Finally the heavens had shined down upon me, and no matter what I was facing, I knew with Cooper by my side we could conquer anything.

I threw my clothes in the dryer, gathered my breakfast, coffee, and a glass of orange juice, and settled at the table. When I was about half way finished with my breakfast the doorbell rang and I froze. I didn't know if I should answer it or not. It was Cooper's house, so probably I should go get him. But what if it was a salesman or something? I didn't want to disrupt his workout for that. So I should just answer the door. Right? But it could also be the kidnappers. Maybe they had tracked me down. But I quickly nixed that idea. They wouldn't ring the doorbell. Would they? At a loss for what to do, I peeked out the peephole, hoping to see a Girl Scout selling cookies. I could sure use some cookies. Cooper ate very clean and didn't understand the importance of junk food. And believe me, I'd looked. There was not a Pop-Tart to be found.

I tried not to be disappointed when I found the person standing on the other side of the door wasn't a Girl Scout. She was a girl though, and a gorgeous girl at that. All I could see was her face, but she was flawless, with a long mane of blonde hair and amazing, sea green eyes. She was also an impatient girl, as while I was staring at her she continued to ring the doorbell. Although she looked like a Barbie doll, she didn't look like a kidnapper or a dangerous person, so I answered the door.

The peephole didn't do her justice. She was a few inches taller than me, and about thirty pounds lighter, and was wearing an itty bitty tank top that showed plenty of tanned, toned midriff, and impossibly short cut offs that showed acres of tanned legs. Her nails and toes were manicured, her eyes were smoky, her hair was curled, and she looked like she'd just stepped out of a Victoria's Secret catalog. She took in my appearance and smiled, showing off two rows of perfect, white teeth. She stuck her hand out and I automatically took it, smiling.

"You must be Josslyn," she said. "Cooper talks about you all the time. I'm Kayla."

My smile died on my lips and I began to channel my inner badass. I wanted to tell her who I really was and tell her where to go, but she didn't give me the opportunity. She pushed past me into the house and I stood there, stunned.

"Where's Coop?" she asked, and I decided then and there that I was going to fight for my man. Crazy Kayla was going down.

"Look...Kayla you said? Um, Cooper talks about you all the time too. As a matter of fact, we just talked about you yesterday. He has a girlfriend now, and he wants nothing to do with you, so if you could just run along it would be greatly appreciated." I held the door open for her, but she didn't move. Instead she laughed.

"Okay, sure, whatever." She laughed again like I was a freaking comedian. "Oh, that's funny. Coop has a girlfriend? Sugar, Cooper doesn't *do* girlfriends. He does friends with benefits. Now where is he? I have something to give him."

I wasn't sure what to do, but I knew I was going to stand my ground. "Well, he has a girlfriend now and she's a badass, so you need to leave. He's not even here anyway," I lied.

"Wow, look at you, all protective of your big brother. It's so cute." She began walking through the house. "But I know he's here. His truck is out front, and the Vette and Harley are in the garage. I looked. Now where's he at? I'll only be a minute."

This bitch had stamina, that was for damn sure. "What do you need to give him? Give it to me and I'll be sure he gets it." She poked her head in his bedroom and I looked for something to bang her in the head with. The thought of her in that bed with Cooper was just too much. I knew there were women in his life before me, but seeing her in his bedroom made it all hit home. She put her hands on her hips and pouted perfectly plump, red-lined lips.

"Sugar, I need to give it to him in person." She wiggled her eyebrows and did a little shimmy. "If you know what I mean."

My inner badass was building strength. "No, I don't know what you mean, and whatever you've got he doesn't want." I grabbed her by the hair and drug her outside. "He said you are a crazy, stalker chic, and if you don't leave now I'll kick your scrawny ass."

She held up her hands in front of her. "Okay, geez, take it easy. Can you just go tell him I that I have something for him? I tried giving it to him Wednesday, but by the time he got there I was running late for class and didn't have time. If he doesn't want to see me I'll leave, but I want to hear it from him."

My heart hit the floor as her words registered. "Wednesday? As in last week?"

"Yeah, I swung by his office, but by the time he showed up I had to get to class. I have some things that belong to him. Not to mention we have some unfinished business. He said he would get with me this week. I have a couple hours to spare, so here I am."

"So you saw Cooper last Wednesday." It wasn't a question. She bobbed her head up and down and popped her gum. She was still babbling about something, but I completely ignored her. Cooper lied to me. He said he hadn't seen her in weeks. Weeks! That was the word he used. And then he looked me dead in the eye and told me he would never lie to me. Boy, did I feel stupid now.

"You know what Kayla? Excuse me for a second, let me give him a call." I practically ran to Josslyn's room, grabbing my cell phone along the way. I was fighting back tears, and when the call connected I could barely choke the words out. I knew Megan would kill me, but I was desperate and I would deal with her later. I had been Granny's one phone call, and now she was mine.

We formulated a quick plan and I grabbed a grocery bag from the kitchen and shoved my clothes from the dryer into it, scribbled down a quick note to leave on the counter, and then went back to Kayla. "I found him. He's in the gym and he's all yours." As she was walking to the back door, I took off out the front at a dead run. My forever had lasted all of a week. I could handle kidnappers and any pain they could inflict on me, but I couldn't handle the pain of Cooper lying to me. He was just like all of the rest of them. I should've known better. Now I did.

***

I waited by the water tower in the field a couple of blocks from Cooper's for what seemed like forever. My face was tearstained and I couldn't calm my rapid heart rate. It was like I could literally feel the pieces of my heart breaking.

Granny finally showed up driving my car. She slammed on the brakes, parked the car, got out, and handed me an Almond Joy candy bar, which was my favorite. I tried to smile but my heart wasn't in it. This was way worse than anything chocolate could fix. She didn't say anything and I was thankful for that. I threw my bag of clothes in the back seat and got behind the wheel. I didn't know where I was going, I just knew it needed to be far from there. Far from Cooper.

The scumbag liar.

Who I was madly in love with.

Damn! I hit the steering wheel as a fresh batch of tears fell down my cheeks. I tried to suck it up and figure out what to do. I couldn't go to Meg's or any of the girls' houses because I would put them in danger. Mickey would be my best, but he lived with his grandma, and I didn't want to be responsible for anything happening to her. I didn't have any family except for my mom, and I was pretty sure my house was a bad idea too.

"Where are we going?" Granny asked.

"I don't know. Just away from here."

"Want to tell me what happened?" she asked, and God love her she didn't know what she was asking for. I spilled it and she looked at me, stunned. "That's it?" She patted my leg and I thought comforting words would come out of her mouth, and I desperately needed to hear them. But this was Granny I was dealing with. She dug around in her purse until she found her stun gun. She then grabbed the wheel and spun us off the road.

"What are you doing?" I screamed.

"We are going back to give that little tramp a talking to." I shook my head. "Don't worry, Granny's got your back. If she even lifts a finger towards you I'll pump her full of juice."

216

"No! I am not going back there." I pulled back onto the road. "I'm not even mad at her. I'm mad at Cooper. He's the one that lied to me."

"Probably you just misunderstood him."

"No, he said *weeks*. Plural. And I specifically asked him when he stopped seeing her. I don't know why he lied about it. There was no reason to."

Granny waved the stun gun around. "Men lie. It happens. Get over it. Now let's go zap that ho and fight for your man."

I took the stun gun away from her before she zapped herself. "We aren't zapping anybody, and Cooper isn't my man." Not anymore. The dam of tears broke again and I cursed myself for falling in love with him and for being such an idiot and thinking he loved me back.

"Are you on your period? You sure are crying a lot."

I opened the candy bar with my teeth and shoved half of it in my mouth. "I don't want to talk about it anymore," I said with my mouth full. "Now just drop it. I'm going to drop you back at Meg's and then I'm going home to eat ice cream and watch Lifetime."

***

Cooper was downing a Gatorade having just finished his workout. He couldn't wait to get inside and get his hands all over Stacy's luscious body. He had said no sex today because he wanted to give her a break, but he thought back to her in his baggy sweats and that faded t-shirt without a bra and he was rock hard. Something about seeing her wearing his clothes just set him off. He preferred her with no clothes, but if she had to wear clothes, he liked seeing his on her. Even with her hair piled on her head in a messy bun and not a touch of make-up, she was irresistibly sexy. And she was his. She was all his, and he still wondered how he got so damn lucky.

The door opened and he smiled, thinking she had to come to him because she missed him as much as he missed her. He turned toward the door and said "Hey ba…." But his mouth abruptly shut when he saw Kayla standing there. Panic roared inside him. "Where is she?" he shouted, barreling past Kayla back to the house. Kayla followed closely behind. Cooper threw the back door open and scanned the house. He looked in every room, yelling for her, but she was nowhere to be found. He found the note on the counter with the two haunting words that ripped his heart in two. "You lied," was all she'd written, but it was enough. He got the picture. She was gone.

He had to find her. He had to fix this.

He turned to Kayla, his rage barely controllable. "What did you say to her?"

"Geez Cooper, you and your sister are like really protective of each other." Kayla laughed, pulled a beer from the fridge, opened it, and held it out for Cooper. He didn't take it.

"My sister?" he asked, confused.

"Yeah, Josslyn. She told me you were in the gym, then she left." She took a pull on the beer.

"What was she wearing?" It had to have been Stacy. Joss would have kicked Kayla's ass.

"Cooper, you are freaking me out. What do you care what she was wearing?"

Cooper loomed over her. "What. The. Fuck. Was. She. Wearing?" His tone was low and serious, and Kayla took a step back, her eyes wide.

"Sweats, Cooper. She was wearing sweats and a ratty old t-shirt. I thought maybe she was going for a run or something. By the looks of her, a run wouldn't be a bad idea."

Cooper lost it and stared at Kayla, his eyes full of fury. "What the hell is that supposed to mean?"

Kayla took another step back. "Well, I mean she just looks a little...I dunno, fat or frumpy."

"She looks healthy, not all anorexic like you. She has curves."

She slapped him across the face. "You never complained about my 'anorexic body' when you were fucking me. What is your deal anyways? You are acting crazy weird. If I didn't know better, I'd think there was something going on between you and your sister. Gross." She turned to leave and Cooper grabbed her arm.

"She's not my sister, Kayla. She's my girlfriend, and I have to find her."

"Your girlfriend? You told me you don't do girlfriends." She was on tiptoe, inches from his face.

"I do now!" he snapped.

She shrugged her shoulders and popped her gum. "Well, I guess fat girls need love too."

"Do NOT talk about her like that!" He'd never hit a woman, but this one was testing his patience. He bore down on her. "Now what did you say to her? What upset her enough to leave?"

Josslyn arrived and led Gus to the back yard. After Gus was stowed, she came to Cooper's side. "Tell me Kayla! What the fuck did you do?" He was yelling and didn't care who heard. He had lost all patience with Kayla, and he had to get to Stacy. If she went home and they were still watching her house.... He shook the thought out of his head. He couldn't think about that.

Joss had had enough. "You better start talking skank, or I will beat it out of you." She backed Kayla up against the porch railing, and Kayla caved and started crying.

"I just told her I had something to give you. She asked what and I gave her a little shimmy and shake."

Cooper ran a hand over his face. "You told her you were here to sleep with me?"

She looked at her feet. "Well no...I mean, not in so many words, but the implication was there."

Cooper kicked the porch and Josslyn laughed. "Wow, an educated skank. Does your head hurt from using such big words?"

Kayla's eyes searched Cooper's. "Look, I'm sorry, okay? That wasn't even what pissed her off. When I told her that, she told me you had a girlfriend and told me to leave, then she dragged me out the door by my hair." That made Cooper smile. She must have used her badass skills. "That's when I got pissed!" She rubbed her head and tears spilled from her eyes. If she was looking for sympathy she was looking in the wrong place.

"Kayla, I'm going to ask you one more time, and if you don't tell me what the fuck you did, I'm washing my hands of it and letting Joss kick your ass." Josslyn tightened her grip on Kayla.

Kayla sniffled and wiped her nose on the back of her hand. "Okay, I just told her we had unfinished business from when I stopped by your office last week. She asked me what day and I told her Wednesday, and then she said, 'Wednesday of last week' and I said yes, and then she said she would call you. Then she told me you were in the gym and she left. That's all Coop. I swear!"

He was confused and racked his brain. He hadn't lied to Stacy about anything. Kayla did stop by the office, but that was before he met Stacy. He hadn't *been* with Kayla in over a month. He thought about the two words written in that note, and then like a ton of bricks it all fell into place. He'd told Stacy he hadn't seen Kayla in weeks. He'd meant seen as in dating, not seen as in stalking. Shit. He had to find her. He scanned the yard. She was on foot. She couldn't have gone too far.

"Can I still kick her ass Coop?" Joss asked with a twinkle in her eye.

"Later," Cooper said. "Right now we have to find her. Let me grab a shirt and my keys." He ran in the house and Josslyn led Little Miss Skank to her car.

"You're going with us so you can clear up all the bullshit you started. And then you are going to stay the fuck away from my brother, or I swear I will make you swallow your perfect teeth. Cooper is happy. Truly, completely happy, and I refuse to let you mess that up for him."

Kayla pulled her hand free. "You can't make me go. That's kidnapping."

Josslyn cracked her knuckles and removed her shoes. "Okay, I'll just knock your teeth out." She danced around Kayla. "Ain't nothing to it, but do it."

Kayla jumped out of Josslyn's reach. "Okay, geez, I'll go. Just don't hit me."

Josslyn put her shoes back on and led Kayla to her car. Cooper blew out of the house with his keys in one hand and cell phone in the other. Josslyn ran to him and gave him a hug.

"We'll find her Coop."

"She could be in real danger, Joss. I mean, she's the only one that saw that whole kidnapping thing go down. They've trashed her house looking for her. She's a threat to them. If they find her before I do...."

Joss knew Cooper was scared and it broke her heart. "They won't Coop. We'll find her. Let's go. The skank and I will follow you. You try calling her?"

He nodded. "Straight to voicemail." His voice dropped low. "I love her, Joss."

She held his face. "I know you do."

"I can't begin to think of what I'd do if I lost her."

"You won't Coop, but seriously, time's ticking. We need to get a move on."

***

Granny was being a pill as usual. We were sitting in the car in front of Megan's house engaged in a screaming match. Megan was at the doctor's and wasn't there to help me reason with Granny, and Jack was probably at work. Granny was insistent on staying with me to keep me safe. I wanted her at Megan's to keep her safe. We were at a stalemate.

Granny crossed her arms over her chest and set her jaw. "I'm not getting out of this car. I'm not leaving you alone."

"Granny, I'm worried about your safety. If the kidnappers come back I don't want you to get hurt."

Granny dug in her handbag. "Stacy, I'm armed to the teeth. Nobody's gonna hurt me. I'll shoot the shit out of them." I kind of wished Granny still had her gun. I didn't really know how to use a gun, but I'd sleep better knowing I had one.

"I thought you left your gun at the bingo hall."

"I did." She pulled out a large gun with a long barrel. "But I stole Jack's big gun." She held it up proudly and set it on the dash.

"Granny! Jack is going to kill you! What the hell were you thinking?"

She kept digging in her bag. "I didn't know what I was getting myself into when you called. I just knew you needed help. So I grabbed everything I could think of." She held out her stun gun.

"Granny, how many guns do you have in there?" I asked cautiously.

"Well let's see, we have Jack's big gun, my handy dandy stun gun, and my battery operated fun gun."

I cringed and she winked at me. "I stole this from the Kaboom Box."

"Granny—"

"No wait, there's more. I also have brass knuckles, soap in a pillowcase, bug spray, hairspray, and a lighter. Those kidnapping sons of bitches won't know what hit 'em. Let's roll!"

Reluctantly, I put the car in drive and drove to my house. We parked in the back and I found my hide a key and let us in the back door. As soon as the door opened a piercing shrill assaulted my ears. Somebody, probably Jack, had had an alarm system put in, and I didn't know the code. Hell, I didn't even know I had an alarm.

I froze, not sure what to do. I looked around and noticed my condo had been cleaned. Jack must have been busy. I felt so consumed with guilt that he was doing all of this when he should have been at Megan's side. Some friend I was.

I grabbed my phone charger and a couple of changes of clothes and we got the hell out of there. I couldn't stay. It wasn't safe, and any minute the cops would be there and I had no idea how to explain a stolen gun and a vibrator. It was just a conversation I preferred to avoid. We were in and out in a minute tops, and I knew there was only one other place I could go. I didn't want to go there, but I was out of options. At least we would be safe. Or I hoped so anyways.

***

Cooper drove like a bat out of hell to Stacy's, calling Jack as he drove. Jack answered curtly.

"Is Stacy with you?" Cooper asked, trying to keep the panic from his voice.

"No, I was just about to ask you the same question."

"Any idea where she would go?" His voice was desperate and he knew it, but he had to find her.

"Well, I just got a call from the alarm company, and someone set off the alarm I had installed at her house. Could have been her or the bad guys. I don't have any intel yet. I'm heading there now."

Cooper floored it. "Me too. I'm about five minutes out."

"What the hell happened, Cooper?" Jack demanded.

"Look, it's a long story. Let's just focus on finding her first." Cooper's voice was tight, and all he could think of was finding his girl.

"I'll see you there," Jack said and ended the call.

Cooper's mind was racing. What if he was too late? What if they already had her? Oh God, he couldn't lose her now. He'd waited thirty years for her to come along, and the thought of having her ripped away from him was more than he could bear.

He slammed on the brakes in her driveway as Jack pulled up behind him. Cooper pulled his gun from the console, and he took the front while Jack cleared the back. They met in the living room. The house was clear, no sign of Stacy or any bad guys. Cooper noticed the house had been cleaned and put back in to some semblance of order.

"I had a service come in and clean for her," Jack explained.

"What do we do now?" Cooper asked as the first police car screeched to a stop.

Jack's expression was grim. "I don't know, but we have to find her." Jack pointed out the fact that Stacy's car was gone.

The police came up to them, and Cooper let Jack handle it from there. He paced back and forth, racking his brain for what to do. He couldn't just stand there and do nothing. They could have already nabbed her. She could be dead right now for all he knew.

Josslyn ran to his side as the first teardrop slid down his cheek. He should have handled Kayla and gotten that restraining order, and none of this would have happened.

A black SUV screeched to a halt, and a very pregnant Megan got out and waddled to Jack. She was crying and hysterical.

"Jack, Granny is gone!" He held her in his arms and tried to calm her down. "I went to the doctor and then to the store to pick up a few things, and when I got home she was gone. I've been calling and calling, and all I get is her voicemail."

Cooper's heart went out to Jack. In addition to having to deal with Megan's pregnancy complications and Granny MIA, now he had to tell her about Stacy.

"Oh my God!" she shrieked after Jack told her what was going on.

A thought occurred to Cooper. Granny knew where he lived. What if Stacy had called Granny and had her pick her up somewhere by his house. "Hey, does Granny have a set of keys to Stacy's car?"

There was recognition in Jack's eyes. He was thinking the same thing Cooper was thinking. "No, but we have a spare set on our key holder. Stacy's been known to lock her keys in her car a time or two."

"So what if Granny got the keys and picked Stacy up? Where would they go?" Cooper asked.

Megan wiped her eyes but the tears just kept falling. "I don't know. The only family Stacy has is her mom, and they aren't on the best of terms; but I suppose if she didn't want to be found she could go there."

Cooper was revved. "Okay, let's go to her mom's then."

Megan frowned. "We can't. We don't know where she lives." She sniffled and Jack rubbed her back. "She's...well she's just different. She's a hippy that lives off the land and grows marijuana plants. She has an old RV that she used to move around a lot. Half the time Stacy couldn't even find her. She's been living somewhere south of town for a while, but I don't know where. She does have a cell phone though. Let me try to call her." Megan waddled away to get her cell phone, and Josslyn entered the conversation.

"So, we think Granny and Stacy are together?" she asked.

"Probably," Jack said. "Now we just have to figure out how to find them." Jack frowned. "Before it's too late."

Josslyn clapped her hands. "I've got it Coop." She held up three fingers and ticked them down one by one. "House arrest, bitches!"

***

I pulled up at my mom's and cringed. This truly was the last place I wanted to be, but I really didn't have any other options. I didn't want to be found and this one was the one place nobody would find me. Mom stayed pretty much off the radar and lived in the middle of nowhere. I may be miserable here, but I wouldn't be dead.

I climbed the steps to the RV, poked my head inside, and hollered for my mom. She didn't answer, and I knew I would probably find her in the greenhouse. I turned around and ran right into Granny. We both made our way to the greenhouse that was set up to the side of mom's RV.

As I opened the door, I heard CCR playing softly in the background. My mom was trimming plants and bobbing her head to the beat. She wore a flowing maxi dress, her long hair in two braids falling down past her breasts. I turned the music off and she glanced up, saw me, and then set her cutting shears down and came to me. She pulled me into a big hug, and as strained as our relationship could be, I was glad to be in her embrace. I did love my mom and I knew she loved me. I tried to keep it together, but I started bawling the minute my head hit her chest, and I couldn't stop.

"It's okay dear. I'm here. Everything is okay now." She rubbed my back and spoke comforting words in my ear.

I shook my head against her chest. "Mom, nothing is okay. It's not ever going to be okay." If the kidnappers didn't kill me I was sure I would die from a broken heart anyways. I was crying uncontrollably so Granny filled her in on everything. I suddenly realized I was wearing Cooper's clothes still and I smelled like him. I had to get him off me.

"Mom, can I use your shower?" I asked.

"Yes dear, you can use whatever you want." I told Granny to behave and headed to the RV to get Cooper's scent and clothes off me. In the shower, my tears fell like the water that ran down my body. I was so scared and so lost, and I just didn't know how I was going to get through this. My mind drifted to me and Cooper in the shower. How could he have held me the way he had and lied to me? I just didn't understand. He knew I was already broken. Why break me even more? He seemed so different, so genuine, but he was just like all the rest of them.

I stayed in the shower until the water turned cold and I was scrubbed clean. I toweled off and dressed in a pair of jeans and an old Guns and Roses t-shirt. I tossed Cooper's clothes in a plastic bag and tied it shut, then brushed my hair and pulled it back into a sleek ponytail. I caught my reflection in the mirror and noticed the sadness in my eyes. I felt it in my heart. Cooper's betrayal cut me deep. I could care less about some clumsy kidnappers. At least if they killed me I would be out of my misery.

I rejoined Mom and Granny in the greenhouse, and found Granny with a bong in one hand and a bag of cheese puffs in the other. She was alternating between smoking the bong and stuffing her face.

I gave my mom a pointed look. "Really, Mom? You got Granny stoned? Like I don't have enough to worry about."

"Honey, I did no such thing. She got herself stoned." Granny gave me a thumbs up and hit the bong. I took it out of her hands and set it on the table. "There's plenty more if you want some, dear. It might calm you down a bit. You are too stressed."

I rolled my eyes. "I don't smoke, Mom. And besides, you and Granny are both stoned. Someone needs to stay sober to keep us safe."

"Honey, nobody will find you out here," Mom said, and I hoped she was right. The last thing I wanted was to be found. I knew Cooper was probably looking for me right now, and as much as I wanted to be in his arms, I never wanted to see him again. All week he'd been playing me just like he did all this other "girl friends." I was nothing special. Just his little play toy until he got tired of me.

"Are you hungry dear?" my mother asked me, and I remembered I didn't get to finish my breakfast. I nodded and eyed the cheese puffs. Granny hugged the bag close to her in a death grip. "Well, let's go make you something to eat sweetheart." She held her hand out to me. "C'mon." I took my mother's hand and squeezed it. My mom may be a pot-smoking hippy, but she was still my mom and I knew I could always count on her to have my back. I hated to admit it, but being with my mom made me feel safe. I motioned for Granny to follow us, and Granny got up, grabbed the bong, and took my hand.

"Stacy," Granny whispered. "I can see voices." Great. Now Megan was really going to kill me. I'd not only put Granny in harm's way, but now I was responsible for getting her wasted.

The three of us walked out of the greenhouse and stopped dead in our tracks when we saw the dark van. My heart thudded in my chest as fear crippled me. I was only kidding about the kidnappers killing me. I didn't really want to die. And I sure didn't want to be the reason Mom and Granny died too.

We hurried back into the green house and my mom threw the deadbolt. The door was sturdy, but it wouldn't stop anybody if they really wanted in. I had to think fast. Granny was giggling and I shushed her, but that only made her laugh harder. My mom armed herself with a sawed off shotgun she pulled from the corner of the greenhouse. Geez, when had my mom acquired that? She pointed it at the door. What had happened to make peace, not war?

"Mom, put that down!"

She shook her head and tightened her grip. "Nope. Not going to happen dear. Nobody hurts my baby."

I was afraid she would wind up shooting me or herself in her foot.

"Hey, that's a great idea," Granny said, and retrieved Jack's big gun. Suddenly I couldn't figure out what I was more afraid of, some dumb kidnappers or a couple of stoned old ladies with guns.

Granny got out her stun gun with her other hand. "Bring it on bitches! Granny is ready to rock and roll!" she slurred. I took Jack's gun from Granny, but she wouldn't give up the stun gun. I gave up and sat Jack's gun down on the table that my mom used to process her pot. I pulled my cell phone from my pocket and powered it on. As I waited for it to come on I weighed my options. If I called 911, my mom would probably go to jail because of the pot. Granny would probably Taser a cop, and that was probably more punishable than bowling for trolls at the bingo hall.

So the cops were a no go. Jack was my best bet. Megan was going to be mighty pissed at me, but Jack was my only option. Of course, he probably wouldn't make it in time to save us. The kidnappers were already there, and it was a fifteen-minute drive from town.

My phone finally came up and I tried to call Jack, but I had no signal. Frustrated, I threw the phone across the room and asked Granny for her phone. She didn't have a signal either. "Fuck!" I blew out a breath I had been holding. I knew what I had to do. I didn't want to do it but I had no choice. I had to save Granny and my mom. After all, it was because of me that they were in harm's way.

***

Cooper flew through town, following closely behind Jack, who was following a cop car with lights and sirens blaring. Joss and Kayla were behind him. He'd tried to talk Joss into staying back with Megan, but she flatly refused. Jack had called Josie to go stay with Megan and try to keep her calm.

Jack had spoken to the police and confirmed that Granny did in fact have a tracking device on her ankle. It took all of two calls to find out where they were, which was just a few minutes away. Cooper had been frantically calling Stacy's phone, but all he ever got was voicemail. There was a good chance she was safe. Not many people knew where her mom lived, and unless the kidnappers were watching her house, saw her car leave, and followed it, they would have no way of finding her. He tried to take deep, calming breaths, but he knew until she was in his arms he wouldn't be able to relax.

He just wanted to find her, explain the whole Kayla thing, make everything right, and then get lost inside her. He needed her. He craved her. She made him whole and complete, and nothing would ever be okay again if he lost her.

The cops and Jack pulled over to the side of a dirt road and got out to talk. In the distance, Cooper could see an old RV set up a ways back from the road. Stacy's car was parked in front of it, and behind it was a dark van. Cooper's heart dropped. They'd found her. He didn't know how, but they had. He was too late.

The police radioed for back up and an ambulance just in case.

In case she was hurt.

Or worse.

Cooper couldn't stand there any longer. He had to get to her. She needed him. He'd already let her down once. He wouldn't let it happen again.

Jack snapped on a Kevlar vest and readied his weapon. He was going in with the cops, and they had instructed Cooper to stay back.

Fat chance of that happening. Stacy was in there. His Stacy! His heart pounded in his head and he saw red, and took off after Jack and the cops. Nothing was going to get in his way of getting to her. He just prayed to God they weren't too late.

***

"Where are you going, dear?" my mother asked, panic evident in her voice. I couldn't look her in the eyes because of the pain I saw there. I shouldn't have come here. Now my mom was in the middle of all this. I was terrified both for myself and for her, but I put on a brave face. Granny was uncharacteristically quiet, and I knew she was scared too.

The banging on the door got louder, and I knew it was only a matter of time before the door busted or the kidnappers gave up on the door and knocked out a window. I was running out of time.

"Mom, lock this door behind me!" I shouted, loud enough for her to hear over the banging.

My mother gasped. "Stacy, no!"

I put my hand on the doorknob. "Just lock it, okay? Promise me!" My mom was crying. "It will be okay Mom. I'm sure they just want to talk to me."

Granny came up behind me. "If you're going, I'm going too." She giggled and clicked the hammer back on Jack's big gun. Her stun gun was in her other hand. Mom came up behind Granny, still carrying the shotgun.

"Me too," Mom said. "We are in this together, Stacy."

Granny high fived her. "One for all and all for nothing." Okay, so that wasn't the way the saying went, but who cared. In a few minutes it probably wouldn't matter anyway. "We're like *Charlie's Angels*." Sure, except they were trained and knew how to fight and shoot guns and stuff. They were some bad asses. We were just asses.

I exhaled a deep breath and sent up a quick prayer. "I'm coming out," I shouted, and I slowly opened the door.

There were two thugs waiting for me. One was really big, and had a really big gun in his hand pointed right at my chest. The other one was short and scrawny, with long, dingy blond hair and yellow teeth. I didn't know which one it was, but one of them smelled like they hadn't showered in weeks. I didn't know if it was the smell or the fear, but it made my stomach roil.

Jerking forward, I threw up all over the big guy with the gun. He jumped back, trying to get out of the way, and my badass skills kicked in. I charged him while he was caught off guard, and landed a strong, sturdy kick to his nuts. He dropped the gun and I picked it up just as the short guy, or Stinky as I preferred to call him—since he was responsible for the stench—jumped on my back and tried to take me to the ground. The gun was waving around till I lost my grip on it and dropped it. Stinky threw me to the ground and picked up the gun. I then tried his tack and jumped on his back and tried to choke him, but we all froze when the first shot rang out. That's when all hell really broke loose.

***

Jack and the officers were trying to come up with a game plan, but as soon as they heard the gunshot all bets were off. Cooper took off at a dead run with Jack right behind him. He didn't have a weapon and wasn't wearing a vest, and the cops were trying to keep him back but they were fighting a losing battle. He was going in for Stacy, and they'd have to shoot him to stop him. He prayed as he ran for God to please let her be okay. Back up was on its way, too, as Cooper heard the faint sounds of sirens.

He reached the greenhouse in record time and took in the scene before him. An older lady with long braids stood with a shotgun on her hip, pointing it at some big guy. Granny held a large revolver on the smaller dude. Stacy lay on the ground, not moving. He rushed to her side and began inspecting her body for bullet holes or blood, or anything to indicate what had happened to her. He felt his world slowly slipping away from him and he felt empty, completely hollowed out. He checked her pulse and breathed a sigh of relief when it throbbed beneath the pad of his finger.

The big guy mouthed off and Jack pistol whipped him in the nose and shut him up. He was spitting blood and Cooper wished the cops weren't there. He wanted to kill these motherfuckers for what they had done to Stacy. Cooper pulled her limp body into his arms and caressed her face. Her body twitched and her eyelids fluttered. "That's right baby. Come back to me," he cooed as Jack flagged down a medic and they came immediately to Stacy.

Joss and Kayla had also come up, and Kayla's eyes were huge with fear. He wanted her out of there. The last thing Stacy needed to wake up to was Kayla. He told Joss to get rid of her and that he would call as soon as he knew something, but Joss refused to leave him. Instead, she threw her keys to Crazy Kayla and told her use her car to get to Cooper's to pick up her own car. Kayla didn't need to be told twice. She sprinted to Josslyn's car and burned rubber.

The officers had cuffed the bad guys and were leading them to their patrol cars as smoke billowed out of the greenhouse. The pungent smell of marijuana hung in the air. A fire truck was already en route, and Cooper cradled Stacy in his arms and carried her to the ambulance, where they were just rolling a stretcher out for her.

Jack found Granny in the greenhouse and dragged her outside and over to the ambulance. The paramedics put an oxygen mask on her and began checking her vitals. Stacy's mom seemed fine, just concerned for her daughter. She refused medical treatment. Cooper laid Stacy on the stretcher and climbed into the ambulance with her. He was not leaving her side, and this time he meant it.

Jack and the paramedics were getting the story from Granny and Abigail, Stacy's mom, when Stacy opened her eyes. She tried to sit up and took off her oxygen mask. Her eyes found Cooper's and they watered with tears. "Cooper. You came for me?"

Cooper's body relaxed as relief washed through him. "Of course I came for you, baby. I love you."

She ran her hand along his arm. "You lied to me."

He shook his head. "It was just a misunderstanding. I'll explain it all to you when this is over. I will fix this Stacy. I will fix us."

She nodded and closed her eyes. The medics went to work on her and told her to just relax and she would be fine. As it turned out, she hadn't been injured at all. When she was on the little, stinky guy's back, Granny had taken the opportunity to stun gun the dirt bag, but she missed and got Stacy in the ass instead. It was enough to distract the little guy while Abigail crunched the butt of her shotgun into his ribs. Abigail then held both of the bad guys at bay while Granny reentered the greenhouse and, using her can of hairspray and a lighter, torched it so the cops wouldn't find the pot...which would have been a good plan if not for the unmistakable smell filling the air. Everybody but the bad guys was smiling, and Cooper wondered how much of that had to do with all the secondhand smoke they were inhaling.

Jack entered the ambulance and spoke softly to Stacy. He took her hand and Cooper hated the jealousy that that simple touch provoked. "You okay kiddo?" Jack asked, and Stacy opened her eyes and nodded.

"How did they find me?" She asked Jack. "I thought we would be safe here."

"It's my fault, Stacy," Jack said, and Stacy's shook her head. He nodded. "I should have been more cautious, Stace. They put a tracking device on your car, probably at the same time they ransacked your house. I checked and double-checked everything making sure you would be safe, but I didn't even think about your car. I feel like a fucking idiot."

Stacy squeezed Jack's hand. "It's not your fault, Jack. They would have found me eventually. I couldn't hide out at Cooper's forever."

Jack turned his angry gaze to Cooper. "And what the fuck, man? I thought you were going to keep her safe?"

Cooper knew he deserved that one. He didn't respond.

Stacy's eyes met Cooper's. "Jack, it wasn't his fault. I'm the one that left. I needed to clear my head. A lot has happened in a week. I just needed a breath of fresh air."

Cooper had been fighting to keep his hands off her, but he couldn't resist anymore. He lovingly caressed her cheek. He knew she was mad at him, but the fact that she was alive and okay was all he needed. He could fix everything else.

The paramedics came into the ambulance and it was becoming mighty crowded. They asked Jack to step out, and before he did he turned to Stacy, silently questioning if she was okay with Cooper staying. She nodded.

"Okay, I have to find a cell phone that works out here. I have got to call Meg." He left the ambulance, looked back, and gave Stacy a thumbs up. She returned it.

Cooper took her hand and kissed her knuckles. "I was so scared, baby. I thought I had lost you." She squeezed his hand and his heart swelled with hope.

"Why Cooper?" She whispered.

"Because I love you."

"No, why did you lie to me?" The paramedics finished Stacy's vitals, nodded to Cooper, and got out of the ambulance to give them some privacy. Stacy removed her oxygen mask again and sat up, and Cooper pulled her into his arms. He tilted her head up and stared into her chocolate brown eyes.

"Stacy, I didn't lie to you. When I told you I hadn't seen Kayla in weeks, I meant I hadn't dated her in weeks. I told you she stalked me, and she did come to my office the other day trying to lure me back, but I told her to leave. I met you later that day. Kayla and I have been done for over a month. She just has had a hard time accepting that."

"It's true, Stacy," Josslyn said, and Cooper and Stacy both looked at her. They hadn't even seen her come in. "She admitted that she had embellished the truth and led you to believe her and Coop were still on. I almost knocked her lights out. Hell, I even kidnapped the bitch and made her come out here with me so she could tell you herself, but Coop sent her packing."

"You swear?" Stacy asked.

"Baby," Cooper said. "I told you, I will never lie to you."

"You promise?" she asked with tears in her eyes. "Because I've already been broken, Cooper."

"I promise." He said it with no hesitation, because he meant it with all of his heart.

"And you're sure you don't want Crazy Kayla? I mean, she's gorgeous and skinny and young." She was full on crying now, and Cooper held her closer. "I'm just average, Cooper. Nothing fancy, Nothing special."

"You are so wrong, Stacy." He nuzzled his nose in her ear. "You are so not average. You are off the charts sexy. I love your curves, and your curly hair, and the freckles that sprinkle your nose and cheeks. I love your sense of humor, and the way you blush beet red every time I touch you. I love the way you fit in my arms, and the sleepy little snoring sounds you make in my ear."

"Pretty much he just loves you!" Josslyn said, summing it up for him. "Now hurry up, kiss and make up already."

Cooper found her lips and she opened hers, allowing his tongue to dance with hers. The fact that she was kissing him back was a good sign. When she wrapped her arms around his neck and straddled him, Josslyn laughed.

"O-kay, and I'm out! You two have fun now." She exited the ambulance and shut the door, giving them total and complete privacy.

"You're sure you want me, Cooper?"

"I've never been more sure of anything in my life."

233

She cupped his face with her hands. "Because what you see is what you get Coop. I don't do fancy and flashy. I'm not flawless. I like things simple and pure, and on my best of days I'm a mess. I can't give you my all, and then you wake up someday and decide I'm not good enough. I can't go through that pain again."

He kissed her forehead. "Honey, I know Scott cheated on you, but I guarantee you it wasn't because you weren't good enough. You are —"

She laughed. "Well actually, it was." She smiled. "He left me for a guy. His name is Alex, and they have two four legged babies and live just down the street from me. We do dinner once a week."

Cooper didn't know what to say to that. "Well, you certainly don't have to worry about that, baby. And as far as you being good enough, honey, you are damn near perfect and far more than I could ever deserve. But I promise to spend the rest of my days trying to be worthy of your love and making you happy." He brushed away her tears. "Move in with me Stacy."

Did he actually just say that out loud? Never had he lived with a woman other than his mom and sisters. He was just fine with being a bachelor for life. But there was something about Stacy that changed all of that, and the thought of her not being in his bed tonight was unbearable. He stared into the pools of her gorgeous hazel eyes, waiting for her answer. If she said no, he didn't know what he would do.

"Can I think about it for a minute?" she asked, and he nodded.

"But if you say no, I'm taking up permanent residence on your couch." He laughed like he was joking, but he wasn't. He was dead serious. "I can't live without you, Wrecking Ball. I love you."

"I love you too, Cooper." She ravenously kissed his mouth. "I love you so, so much."

They were in each other's arms, oblivious to the rest of the world, when suddenly the ambulance started shaking. Mickey's voice was unmistakable as he chanted, "If the paddy wagon's rockin', don't come knockin'." Cooper opened the door and Mickey, Josslyn, and Josie stopped rocking the ambulance. Stacy stood to get out, and Megan launched herself into Stacy's arms.

Megan was crying, and that brought on a fresh set of tears for Stacy.

"When did you get here?" I asked the gang.

"We just pulled up," Megan answered. "We would have been here sooner, but we had hell finding the place. Jack's directions sucked and we got lost."

"Twice," Josie added, then pulled Stacy into a hug. Mickey and Cooper shook hands, and everyone was all smiles, riding the adrenaline high. Or probably it was the marijuana burning that was keeping everyone happy. Either way, it was good to see everyone smile.

Stacy took Cooper's hand and introduced him to her mother, who was talking to the cops. Jack had worked his magic and the marijuana was not going to be an issue. Stacy breathed a huge sigh of relief, and eventually the cops and firemen left.

Granny was passed out in a lawn chair with cheese puffs in her mouth. Mickey lifted her up and deposited her in his car. Jack put Megan in his truck, which was probably a good idea considering the amount of pollution in the air that the baby didn't need. Stacy hugged her mom and said goodbye as Cooper trudged across the field to get his truck. Josslyn could drive Stacy's car, because Cooper wasn't letting her out of his sight.

Once everyone was loaded up in their respective vehicles, they made a convoy to Stacy's house.

***

After the day I'd had, the last thing I needed was drama. So when we pulled into my driveway and I found Thad sitting on my porch, I knew this was not going to end well. Cooper spotted him about the same time I did and looked at me. I shrugged. I couldn't help that he was there, and I had no clue why he would be.

I faced Cooper. "Remember the asshole I told you about that dumped me on Valentine's Day via text?"

Cooper nodded.

"Well, that's him. Feel free to kick his ass."

"That I can do," Cooper said, and put the truck in park.

We got out and I checked the mail on my way to the porch. Thad stood, stumbled, and held onto the porch railing. I was clear across the porch and I could smell the alcohol radiating from him.

He stumbled forward, his arm outstretched for a hug. I dodged him and introduced him to Cooper. They shook hands, and Thad seemed to be confused when I used the word "boyfriend" to describe Cooper. Everyone would be there soon and I didn't need an audience.

I asked Cooper to please let me handle this situation, and promised that if I couldn't handle it I would let him know. He lounged in the doorway, looming large, dangerous, and sexy as hell. Even his menacing face was hot.

"What do you want, Thad?" I asked, my voice flat.

"I want you, Stace. It's always been you." He reached a hand out to touch me, and I slapped it away. "Please give me another chance."

"Thad." I couldn't help that I felt a little sorry for him. "We are done. I'm with Cooper now. You need to leave." I scanned the block for his truck and found his bike parked across the street.

He hit his knees and hugged my waist. "You don't understand, Stace. I fucked up. I know I did, but I swear to you I'll fix it. These four months have been hell. I need you back."

I peeled his hands off me. "Thad, you're drunk. You don't even know what you are saying." I helped him stand, then sat him in the porch swing. "Look, Mickey and Josie will be here in a few, and I'll have one of them take you home. You can come get your bike whenever. But after that, I don't want to see you again."

"But what about our date?" How freaking drunk was he?

"Thad we have no dates. We are done."

"That's not true," he slurred. "You're my date to Josie's wedding, remember?"

Shit. I had totally forgotten. "It's not a date, douche bag. I'm just going to link arms with you and walk down the aisle. That's it. My date to Josie's wedding is Cooper."

"All of her dates from now on are with me, buddy," Cooper said, and Thad tried to get up, but Cooper pushed him back down. "Just sit there and take it easy until your friends get here."

"Stacy, I love you! I know it's a little late, but I do. I can't be without you." His words were slurred and I stepped back, because with every word he said spit flew from his mouth.

There was a time when I had longed to hear those words from him. Now he was just annoying me and I was losing my patience. I knelt down so that I was eye level with him. "Thad, I don't love you. I love, Cooper. You need to move on like you told me I should do. I did, and I'm truly happy." He had tears in his eyes and I made my tone gentler. "There is a special girl out there just waiting for you. You just have to be patient."

My tender tone did nothing to calm him. He stood and steadied himself. "You're right, Stace. There is somebody out there for me. Somebody that won't mess with my head and beg me to take them back, and when I decide to they practically spit in my face."

"Thad, just shut up, okay? You aren't doing yourself any favors here. You're drunk and belligerent, and you're about to get your ass kicked if you aren't careful. I don't love you, Thad, and after Josie's wedding I don't want to see you again. Got it?"

"Yeah, I got it. And it's cool. All I really wanted today was a piece of ass anyways. I don't love you. I never did. You were just my personal little whore until I got tired of you."

Thad never saw Cooper's punch coming, but I'll bet he sure as hell felt it. Cooper knocked him clean out and he crumbled to the porch. I stepped over him and opened my door. Thank God the alarm didn't go off, because I'd had my share of cops for the day.

I surveyed my house. It was clean but nothing was where it belonged. It didn't feel like home anymore. And not just because of the break in, but because home was wherever Cooper was. With him was where I belonged. Cooper wrapped his arms around me from behind and nuzzled my ear, and I allowed myself to just melt into him. He was my home. He was my everything.

Everybody showed up and crowded around Thad where he lay on the porch. Mickey scooped him up and Granny repeatedly kicked him in the ass. She was a bad ass too. Mickey more or less carried him to his car and strapped him in. Jack rode his bike home for him so that I wouldn't have to deal with Thad again except for Josie's wedding. I was grateful for that.

Megan said she was starving, and Josie decided we should have a BBQ to celebrate her getting married, me getting laid, Granny getting stoned, and Megan and Jack having a baby. It sounded like a fabulous idea, except that I had no food in the house that we could BBQ, and I didn't even own a grill, so we settled for ordering pizza and hot wings. Granny was awake now and was eating Pop-Tarts and cereal straight out of the box. Apparently she had a bad case of the munchies. In fact, I think we all did.

Josslyn showed up with a case of beer. Jack and Mickey returned and the pizza came, and we all sat in the grass in the backyard and ate and talked and had a pleasant time. I had missed these guys, and I considered myself very blessed to have them in my life. Cooper and I had a hard time keeping our hands off each other, and by about nine o'clock everyone got the hint that we needed some alone time and started leaving. One by one I hugged each and every one of my dear friends, and they filed out until it was just me and Cooper. Josslyn stayed behind to help clean up. We gathered all the garbage and disposed of it, then I went inside, grabbed a blanket, and laid it out in the yard. Joss announced she was going to head home and I hugged her goodbye.

Cooper and I lay down on the blanket and gazed at the stars. He held me in his arms and we stayed like that in silence for a while, both of us lost in our own thoughts. After what seemed like an eternity, I rolled over on top of him and lightly kissed his lips. He deepened the kiss and I tugged his shirt up so that I could run my fingers across his bare chest. His breath caught as I took his nipple in my mouth and tugged on his nipple ring with my teeth. I could feel his growing erection poking me in the butt.

"I want you inside me, now," I said, and ditched my jeans while Cooper lost his. I sank down on him, my body slowly stretching to take all of him. He felt delicious, and as I rode him I stared into those blazing blue eyes, and there was no mistaking the love he felt for me. As I was getting close, Cooper buried his head in my chest, took my nipple into his mouth, and tugged gently with his teeth. I rolled my hips with each thrust to take him even deeper, and Cooper, sensing my release, grabbed me by my hips and slammed me harder and faster up and down his magnificent cock.

"Oh baby, you are so tight and you feel so fucking good."

I opened my eyes and looked directly into his hooded eyes filled with love.

"I love you, Cooper." I told him as the first wave of my orgasm over took me and my body began to shake. Cooper was right there with me, spilling his seed into me, filling me with his love. He pulled me down into his arms, his cock still inside me. I raised my head so I could see his face.

"Cooper?"

"Yes, baby."

"Take me home."

Cooper searched my eyes. "Are you saying what I think you're saying?"

"Yes," I kissed him lightly on the lips. "Now take me home."

***

She'd said yes. Holy shitballs! Cooper couldn't have been happier or more excited. He had been fully prepared to crash on her couch, or if he was lucky in her bed. But this? This was epic. His dream of having her in his bed every night had just come true, and he couldn't hide his joy. They folded up the blanket and he followed her inside to pack a few things. Taking a large suitcase from her closet, she began opening drawers and filling the case with enough to get her by until she could get everything packed and moved. Cooper just stood around with a silly grin on his lips.

"Oh shit!" Stacy said, covering her mouth with her hand. "What about Granny?"

"She left with Megan and Jack. I'm sure she's fine."

Stacy frowned. "I know that, but I mean, Granny is supposed to be staying here with me. Meg is on bed rest. She can't handle Granny right now."

As long as he got Stacy in his bed he didn't care what he had to do. "Granny can come too. I have three bedrooms."

"Yeah, but one of them is your office." Stacy worried her bottom lip, and Cooper couldn't help but touch her. He rubbed her cheek.

"So? I have an office at work. We will convert the home office into Granny's room. Joss can take the couch until we get it done. It's no big deal." Hell, he'd build Granny a guesthouse if that's what it took. He didn't care. Just as long as Stacy was with him.

Stacy thought about that for a minute. "Cooper, Granny is a handful. Are you sure you are up to this?"

He didn't hesitate. "Absolutely."

"And you are sure Joss won't mind?"

Cooper laughed. "Are you kidding me? Joss and Granny are new BFFs. Joss for sure won't mind. Hell, she will probably enjoy having Granny around."

She nodded and gave him a quick peck on the lips. "Thank you," she said, looked around her bedroom, then closed her suitcase and let Cooper carry it to his truck. She quickly packed another bag of her toiletries, and by the time Cooper came back in she was ready to go.

***

We were almost out the front door when I remembered something else. I ran to the kitchen and packed up the Pop-Tarts, cookies, and junk food. Living with Cooper and waking up in his arms everyday would be Heaven, but by God when my inner fat kid was awakened at two in the morning, I was going to have something to feed it. Cooper was going to have to live a little, and learn to eat a little recklessly every now and again.

***

Cooper was laughing and told her they had grocery stores for that kind of thing. She just handed him the first bag and she carried the second. Jack had explained the alarm to Cooper, and as they were leaving he set it and locked the door. Stacy was all smiles and Cooper's heart swelled. This was a big step they were taking, but he knew in his heart it was right. It was the right time and with the right woman. He knew life as he knew it was over and he looked forward to this new life with Stacy. As a matter of fact, he couldn't wait to get her home.

Home.

His home.

Their home.

***

I was bursting at the seams with excitement and couldn't wait to get to Megan's so I could tell her the good news. She was gonna flip, and hopefully in a good way. I could already hear her voice in my head scolding me for moving too fast. But she'd seen Cooper and me together, and she knew I was happy. She would support whatever decision I made.

I was sitting beside Cooper in his truck and his hand was on my thigh. I inhaled his scent and shivered as desire and excitement coursed through me, and I wondered if the butterflies in my tummy would ever fly away and whether Cooper had them too. Turning to look up at Cooper, I stared at his beautiful face and smiled when I realized that that was what I would be waking up to every day. Cooper caught me staring and smiled at me. I beamed back at him and linked my arm in his, bringing myself as close to him as I could get without climbing in his lap...which, once I thought about it, sounded like an amazing idea.

We pulled up to Megan and Jack's, and as I turned sideways to get out of Cooper's truck, he spread my knees and stood between them. His electric blue eyes shimmered, and he tilted his head and claimed my mouth passionately but gently. I wrapped my arms around his neck and scooted closer to him until I felt him thick and hard against me.

"God, baby, I can't wait to get you home," Cooper said, and I couldn't wait either. But we had to get Granny so Megan could rest. After all she and Jack had done for me, it was the least I could do. Meg really needed me right now and since I didn't have to hide out from kidnappers, I was going to be there for her in any capacity I could.

"I can't wait either, Cooper. Let's grab Granny and run." Cooper stepped aside and let me out. When my feet hit the ground, my bad ankle gave way. I had been really careful with it and babying it, but anytime I put too much weight on it, pain shot through my entire leg. I knew I should be wearing my boot and I sensed a lecture coming, but Cooper just gave me a pointed, knowing look and carried me to the door. I snuggled into him.

"You know, I like being in your arms like this. I may never wear that stupid boot again if you keep this up." I ran my finger down his jaw line.

"As much as I love having you in my arms, when we get home you are going to be a good girl and put that boot on and wear it until the doctor says otherwise."

I nipped at his ear. "What if I choose to be a bad girl?" I asked, my voice low and husky.

Cooper groaned and buried his nose in my hair. "Woman, you are going to be the death of me."

I laughed. "Maybe, but if so I'll make sure you die a happy man."

"I'm already happy, baby. I have you. You are my happiness."

I wrapped my arms around his neck. "I love you Cooper."

Before we even had a chance to knock, the door swung open and Granny stood before us, dressed head to toe in black leather. She had gone heavy on the eyeliner, and one of her fake eyelashes was crooked. She looked like a dominatrix Granny. Megan was behind her, trying to rein her back into the house.

"Granny, seriously, I so don't need this right now," Megan told Granny. "Just come inside. It's after nine already. People your age are in bed by now."

"People my age? Oh please. I'm in my prime, Meggie, and you only live once, so you just gotta live it up." She threw her handbag over her shoulder. "Besides, I had a real good nap earlier when I was stoned, so I'm good until midnight at least." She threw us the peace sign. "Later bitches."

Megan looked to me for help and I shrugged my shoulders. I had no clue how to deal with Granny.

"Where are you even going, Granny?" Megan asked.

Granny's eyes lit up. "I'm going to a rave with my new friend Cher. Well, his name is Todd, Cher is his stage name. Anyway, it's going to be a riot." Granny sat on the porch swing clutching her handbag. "You kids go on in. I'll just wait here on Cher. Don't wait up."

Cooper had let me down and I limped inside Megan's house. Megan looked…tired. She just seemed exhausted. I gave her a hug.

"Aren't you supposed to be in bed?" I asked, taking a seat on her couch.

She sighed. "Well, that's the plan, but you know how it is." She nodded towards the door, and I knew she was talking about Granny.

"That's why we are here," I said. "Well, it's not the only reason, but we will take care of Granny." Jack entered the living room, his cell phone to his ear. After he was finished with the call, he put the phone back in his pocket and plopped down on the loveseat beside his wife. His hand automatically went to her belly, and Megan covered his hand with hers. They were so happy and so in love, and I was truly happy for them. I hoped Cooper and I shared the same level of happiness.

"Granny is taken care of," Jack said. "I called Mickey, who called Matt, who called somebody else, who called 'Cher.' I told them I would shoot anyone that showed up and ask questions later." Megan rolled her eyes, but I had a feeling Jack actually meant it. Between the sleepless nights with Megan and having to rescue me, he was probably at the end of a very short fuse. I went to the front door to get Granny, but Megan waved me back to the couch.

"She'll be asleep in ten minutes. Jack will get her later." As I sat, she tapped the arm of the loveseat. "Okay sister, let's hear it."

I feigned dumb. "What are you talking about?"

Megan smirked. "I know you, Stace. I see that sparkle in your eye. Something's up."

She knew me too well. "Okay, so I...." I looked at Cooper. "We have some news." Cooper rubbed my knee and I couldn't wipe the sappy smile off my face. I fanned my face and Megan motioned for me to hurry up. "I'm moving in with Cooper," I said, and Megan looked at me, stunned.

"But, it's only been like a week...."

I was prepared for this. Why did I feel like I was confessing my first kiss to my mom? "I know, and trust me, I know it's fast, Meg, but this is real." Cooper snaked an arm around my waist. Josie had come into the living room picking at a salad. She sat beside Cooper and me. "I love him, Meg. And he loves me too. This is the real deal. And he even said Granny can come too."

Megan opened her mouth to speak, but stopped when Josie said. "Okay, rewind. What did I miss?"

I filled Josie in and she squealed with delight. "I told you he was your prince."

I eyed Cooper and I had to admit that he was in fact my prince. Josie watched us closely. "Does this mean you are ready for the Boom Boom Kaboom box?"

Jack cut Josie off. "We are still on for Wednesdays though, right?" Jack and I went to AA meetings on Wednesdays. Even though neither of us had touched a drink in quite some time, we still went and gave one another support.

"Of course," I told Jack.

"Okay, well, if you are happy, we are happy for you." Jack was too sweet. Megan was a lucky girl.

"Don't worry about Granny," Megan said. "We will figure something out with her."

"Meg, you are about to pop. You are supposed to be on bed rest. After all you and Jack have done for me, it's the least I can do." I hated to admit it, but I had actually enjoyed Granny the last couple of days. "And anyway, it's not like it's forever, right? I mean, your dad will cool off at some point. He always does."

Megan frowned. "He's really pissed this time, Stace. I had him talked into taking her back, but now she's paid for the damages to the bingo hall with his credit card, so we have to start the whole 'cooling off' period again."

"She's really no trouble, and my sister is crazy about her," Cooper said, giving my knee a squeeze. "She can stay as long as you need her to."

"Thank you." Megan smiled and started breathing shallow. Jack held her hand and breathed with her.

Josie looked at the stopwatch she was wearing around her neck. "Eight minutes," she announced, and Megan let out a deep breath.

I sat there in stunned silence. Don't get me wrong. I knew where babies came from and all that jazz. What I didn't know—and never wanted to know—was how they got out of there. I knew *how*...I did pay attention in health class...but the whole process just seemed barbaric to me. I would have to be drugged and knocked out to ever give birth. I was just not made for pain, and Megan looked like she was in a lot of it. She was still doing quick slow breaths. I eyed Jack. "Is she okay?"

He rubbed Megan's back. "Yes," he said, which didn't reassure me. "The doctor said this is Braxton Hicks labor. It's been going on all week."

Josie held up the stopwatch. "Jack breathes with her and I time everything." My heart ached. I should have been here helping or doing...something.

Megan rubbed her belly. "I'm totally fine, Stacy. Don't worry about me. You guys go have some fun."

I didn't want to leave her, but I couldn't wait to get to Cooper's. "Are you sure, Meg?"

She waved me off. "Yep. I'm sure. I'm not even in real labor yet. I still have three weeks to go." If this was just false labor, I never wanted to experience the real deal. I was such a wuss when it came to pain. And three weeks? Are you fucking kidding me? I couldn't take three seconds of it.

"And you will call me the minute anything changes?" I took her hand and squeezed it.

"Of course." She shooed me away and Jack helped her stand. "Now run along." Megan pulled me into a hug. "I love you Stacy, and I'm truly happy for you and Cooper. I think you found a keeper." Her eyes were filled with tears and I knew her hormones were probably haywire at that point in her pregnancy. She hugged Cooper and said she was going to get ready for bed. "This baby has just zapped all of my energy," she said, and although I knew the longer she carried the baby the better it was for the baby, I was worried about my friend. She looked miserable, and I knew it was selfish of me, but I just wanted that baby out of her already.

Jack walked us out and we found Granny passed out on the porch swing. "She can just stay here tonight, and we will figure something out with her tomorrow."

"Jack, are you sure?" I asked.

"Yeah, she's already out. There's no since in waking her. She's fine for the night."

Cooper helped Jack carry Granny inside and get her settled. I carried her handbag in, and Josie grabbed me and pulled me into the den. She was giddy with excitement and jumping up and down. "Okay, so tell me all about it," she said, and I shushed her so she would keep her voice down.

"He's amazing." I couldn't control the squeal in my voice.

"And the sex?"

As if my smile didn't say it all. "Off the charts!"

She gave me a knowing look. "I told you."

"Yes. You did. Now I know what all the fuss is about!"

She hugged me. "I'm so happy for you Stace." She winked and formed a gun with her thumb and index finger. As she shot it at me, she said "Kaboom." Then blew on her finger.

As I walked in the front door of Cooper's house—no, *our* house—I was filled to the brim with contentment and happiness. I couldn't believe how much had changed over the course of a week. I was actually excited to see what the future held. Although it had been a long, rough day, I felt better than I had in a long, long time. Maybe ever.

Cooper brought in my suitcases and stowed them in his room...oops, *our* room. Okay, this was going to get some getting used to. It was getting late and I was tired, but sleep was the last thing on my mind. I was too filled with excitement to sleep. I went about unpacking my snack food bags. I needed cookies...and milk, and maybe a moon pie or two. Cooper joined me in the kitchen and sat on a barstool, watching me.

"What?" I asked him innocently.

He shrugged. "Nothing. Just can't believe you are in *our* kitchen, and tonight you will be in *our* bed."

I leaned on the counter, giving him ample view of my cleavage. "Don't get used to seeing me in the kitchen. I don't spend much time in kitchens. Too many sharp objects and fire hazards."

"And what about bed?"

I twirled my hair. "Same problem. Seems every time I get in that sucker something pokes me or catches on fire." I leaned closer and licked his bottom lip. "Not that I'm complaining. I like to live a little on the dangerous side."

"Really? I hadn't noticed. I thought life with you was going to be simple and boring." He palmed the back of my head and brought his lips to mine in a teasing kiss.

Josslyn picked that moment to enter the kitchen. She had a towel around her neck and wore a sports bra and spandex, obviously fresh from a workout. She opened the fridge, took out a bottle of water, and gulped it down in two drinks. "Eew. Get a room!" she told us.

Cooper pinched his nose. "Get a shower!" he replied teasingly, and we all laughed. His tone turned serious as Josslyn was walking away after throwing him the finger. "Hey, before you hop in the shower, I need to talk to you."

She stopped and faced us with a knowing smirk. "What's up?"

"Stacy's moving in," Cooper told her, and her smirk turned to a grin.

"Sweet!"

"You're good with it?" Cooper asked. He and Josslyn were very close and she got protective over him at times, but her smile was genuine and she seemed truly happy for him. It obviously meant a lot to him that she approved.

"Absolutely!" She hugged first me and then Cooper. "I love you big brother, and all I've ever wanted for you is to be happy. And I see that you are, so I think it's a great idea."

"Okay, here's the other thing—" he started.

Josslyn jumped up and down. "I'm going to be an auntie!" she yelled, and Cooper and I both shouted "No" at the same time. I flashed back to Megan in "fake labor" and cringed. "No babies," I said.

Josslyn excitedly waited, so Cooper told her about Granny. "Granny is going to crash here for a while too, and I volunteered you to take the couch until I can convert the office into a bedroom for her."

"Okay, that's fine Coop. But I have some news too."

Cooper jumped up and down. "I'm going to be an uncle!" He thought it was hilarious, but neither of us laughed.

Josslyn rolled her eyes. "No babies." She shivered and I had a feeling that since she was a nurse she knew a hell of a lot more about how babies come out, and by the look on her face it was obviously something she didn't want to endure either. Josslyn and I bonded in that moment. "But, I have been offered a long term contract at the hospital here. It's in addiction and substance abuse, and that's kind of where I want my career to go, so I think I'm going to take it."

Cooper hugged his little sister. "That's awesome, Joss. I'm so proud of you. How long is your contract and when do you start?"

"I start in two weeks, and the contract is for six months. They wanted a year, but I negotiated down to six months. That way if I don't like it I'm not stuck, and if I do like it I can just re-up for another six months." She took another bottle of water out of the fridge and took a long pull on it.

"Well, I think that's a great way to go about it. Leaves your options open." Cooper wrapped his arms around both of us. "I can't believe I'm going to have my two favorite girls living with me."

"Um, Coop about that; I actually think I'm going to look for a place of my own," Josslyn said, and I hoped it wasn't on account of me.

"You aren't doing that because of me, are you?" I asked.

She dismissed it with a wave. "No, it's not that. Well, yeah, I think y'all need your privacy and all, but I had already decided it before you guys got here."

"Joss, you know you are welcome to stay," Cooper told her, and she nodded.

"I know Coop, but I think I want my own place for a little while. You know, see how the rest of the world lives. Mow my yard and take my trash out to the curb."

Cooper laughed. "You won't do either of those things."

"You're right. I'll call you to do it. That's what big brothers are for." She shrugged. "Anyways, I'm going to start looking tomorrow. I'll call the real estate offices and see what's available."

"Hey," I said suddenly as a genius idea occurred to me. "My condo is going to be empty. I have a lot of furniture and appliances there, so you wouldn't need to purchase those things. It was completely remodeled a couple of years ago, and it's very modern."

Cooper's hand found my ass. "Great patio for stargazing," he said, and I blushed, remembering making love to him in the grass. "It also has a brand new security system, so I won't have to worry about you being safe."

"Yeah, and you could move in whenever you want and move out whenever. No lease or anything like that," I added.

Josslyn shook her head. "I'm not going to live there for free. If I take it, I insist on paying rent."

"That's not necessary Josslyn; my condo is paid for. I don't need rent. Just pay the utilities." I wasn't going to budge on this one. I was moving into her house, and although she said that had no bearing on her decision, I didn't completely buy it. "The only way I will let you pay rent is if Cooper lets me pay rent."

Cooper drew his eyebrows together. "Not happening, baby."

I crossed my arms over my chest. "Well, I'm not budging. No rent."

"I have an idea that may work for everyone," Josslyn said. "What if I move in your condo and let Granny move in with me?" I was shaking my head, but she continued. "I mean, she's crazy cool, and I wouldn't mind the companionship. I've never lived alone before; I went from Mom and Dad's, to a dorm room, to here with Coop, so having a roommate would be cool for my first grown up experience."

I was still doubtful. "You don't know what you are saying, Joss. Granny is crazy. She's a handful, and although I love her dearly, she can be a pill. She goes clubbing in gay bars and dates drag queens."

She shrugged her shoulders. "So? It will just keep life interesting." I still was not convinced, so she continued. "And anyway, it's just for six months. That will give you and Coop some 'honeymoon' time, and give Megan and Jack time to settle in with the new baby. If I can't handle Granny, I know where you live."

Cooper was nodding. "I think it's a great idea. I'd feel better not having Joss be there alone."

Josslyn rolled her eyes. "Anyhow, we don't have to figure it all out tonight. I'll check out the condo tomorrow, and you can clear it with Megan and Jack and make sure Granny is onboard."

"Okay, so let's table it until tomorrow," Cooper suggested.

"Sounds good," Josslyn said. "Well, I'm off to shower and then bed. I'll leave you two lovebirds to it." Cooper pecked her on the cheek and I told her goodnight. It was so amazing how all of this was turning out. Everything was falling into place just like it was meant to be. I searched Cooper's eyes and I knew at that instant it *was* meant to be.

We were meant to be.

EPILOGUE

It had been two weeks since I said yes to Cooper and took the plunge and moved in with him. For the first time in those two weeks we were alone. We were lying in bed, wrapped in each other's arms after one of our magical marathon love making sessions. I didn't know how it was possible, but every time we made love it got better and better, and every day I fell deeper in love with Cooper. He was all I could have ever dreamed of and more. He made me insanely happy, and for the first time in a long time I was excited to see what the future held. As long as Cooper was in it, I didn't care what other craziness got thrown at me. And I knew there would be craziness. Between Granny and my little group of friends, crazy was a constant. And there had been no shortage of crazy in the last couple of weeks.

Josslyn had taken me up on my offer to move into the condo, and after extensive deliberations with Megan, we had in turn taken Joss up on her offer to roommate with Granny. Mr. Johnson wasn't budging on letting her come back, and Megan and Jack would be busy with the baby, and Cooper and I.... Well, we were just going to be busy, so it worked out for everyone. And Granny loved the idea. She and Josslyn had become fast friends, and Josslyn's social life was more Granny's speed than mine had been. Their evenings were filled with rock and roll, double dates, and drag queens. The party never stopped for those two.

Granny had given up rap for grunge and metal and was sporting a new goth style, complete with a lip piercing and a black leather wardrobe. She got her first tattoo and her hair was currently styled in a hot pink mohawk. She was staying busy booking gigs at the old folk's home for a Rolling Stones cover band that she was singing backup for. Also, oddly enough, she had taken up gardening, which was a perfect age appropriate activity for her except for the fact that all she was growing was pot. She had added that to her nightly medicine regimen, and claimed her arthritis had improved, which had helped her love life. She and Old Lady Gentry had rekindled their friendship once again, and were trying to launch a PBS show offering dating tips for those in advanced age. They called it "That '70s Ho" and while they had a growing Internet following, the networks had yet to call. I doubted that would deter Granny one bit. Granny was a free spirit and not easily deterred.

Josslyn had started her job at the hospital and was enjoying her new position. She had settled into my condo which, thanks to Jack and Cooper, had been cleaned, repaired, and refurnished. She had even planted a couple of rose bushes, and she and Cooper built a flower bed. I had introduced her to the rest of my crew, and she had quickly become one of the girls and joined in on our weekly lunches. She tended to date the inked up bad boys, and had a soft spot for rockers that were no good for her. She went through boys like Granny went through moonshine, and she always had some juicy story to tell, so the matchmaking had been focused on her lately. A part of me felt sorry for her, but in reality I was just glad the focus was off of me. Besides, Josslyn was a real badass. She could hold her own.

Speaking of being a badass, Crazy Kayla was no longer a problem. Josslyn had a "heart to heart" with the poor girl, and no restraining order was required. I was going to handle it, but Josslyn was on her period and was feeling bitchy and aggressive. And besides, I had just had highlights put in my hair and I didn't want any of them pulled out, because I had to look good for Josie's wedding.

And what a wedding that turned out to be. It was definitely one for the record books. It was all going great and according to plan until Granny and Mickey got stoned, called up a few friends, and turned the wedding aisle into a drag queen runway. Everyone showed up. Cher, Christina, Joan Rivers, Marilyn Monroe. It was pretty entertaining until Mr. Johnson, Megan's dad, finally reached his boiling point and reached in Granny's handbag, got Jack's big gun, and fired a shot in the air. The bullet ricocheted off a ceiling beam and hit the breaker box, which resulted in the power going off. Everybody got really quiet, and then there was madness and mayhem. In her haste to escape, Marilyn Monroe broke a heel, fell, and knocked Cher down. Before we knew it there were drag queens and glitter everywhere. Josie, ever prepared, pulled a flashlight out of her bra, lit up the runway, and insisted the wedding would proceed. Jack found a few candles to light and the church was dimly lit in a romantic glow. Since there was no power, the "Wedding March" couldn't be played, so Granny grabbed a mic. There was a collective sigh as we all braced ourselves, and Granny didn't disappoint. Since her conversion to rock, she had only learned a few songs, and somehow the Rolling Stones' "Satisfaction" and Ozzy's "Crazy Train," while completely fitting, didn't quite seem appropriate for a wedding. So she belted out AC DC's "You Shook Me All Night Long," which, given Josie's man eating past, *was* surprisingly appropriate. And Granny had some skills…she didn't sound half bad. Who knew?

Everything was back on track; Dr. Ross and Josie were holding hands, reciting their vows, when Megan suddenly let out a shriek and her water broke, soaking her silver matron of honor dress. Jack rushed to her side and helped her to a pew. The preacher stopped in mid-sentence and stared at Megan with panic all over his face, but Megan signaled for him to go on. The wedding would continue. Josie, ever prepared, dug in her bra, found her stopwatch, and in between reciting her vows she timed Megan's contractions, which were coming faster and harder. Probably an ambulance should have been called, but Megan refused. She was not leaving the wedding until Josie was Mrs. Dr. Jon Ross.

As soon as the preacher told Dr. Ross to kiss his bride, I rushed to Megan's side. Megan, breathing very short, shallow breaths, pulled me close to her and whispered in my ear. I pulled away in horror and shook my head, my eyes wide. There was no way I could do what she was asking me to. I just couldn't. Meg was my best friend and I would go to the ends of the earth for her, but I would faint if I did what she was asking me to do. The look in her eyes was pained and afraid, and I didn't know what to do. I froze.

"Meg, let's just call 911," I told her, but Jack was already on the phone.

"Stace, I don't think there's time. Just look!"

Okay, so Meg and I were close and I had seen her naked before. That didn't bother me. What I had never seen before, and never wanted to see ever, was a baby coming out of her hoohah. I was afraid I would never be able to get the image out of my head.

I shook my head and patted her belly. "The ambulance should be here soon, Meggie. Just breathe."

Jack disconnected his call and came to her side, held her hand, and breathed with her. Mr. Johnson was in shock beside his daughter, and Mrs. Johnson was clapping her hands and jumping for joy.

Megan's voice took on an anxious shrill. "I think I'm having this baby!"

"Yes, honey you are," Jack told her.

"I mean now!" she said.

Josie and Dr. Ross were presented to the church as husband and wife and took their traditional walk down the aisle together.

Mickey had suggested that he and Jack direct traffic and get vehicles moved to clear a path for the ambulance. Jack kissed his wife and told her he would be right back. I was sitting beside Megan in the pew, holding her hand. I was unsure what to do, but I knew I wasn't leaving her side. Cooper was in front of me, squatting by Megan, timing her contractions. I didn't know much about having babies, but I heard it took a while, so I was confident the ambulance would arrive in time. Megan, on the other hand, didn't think so.

"Stacy, I think I am having this baby right now! There's no time! Just look and see." I saw Dr. Ross making his way through the crowd of guests and I sighed with relief. He would know what to do.

"Megan, I don't even know what to look for!"

"Look for a baby, dammit!" Okay, well duh, I knew that. An old lady stopped Dr. Ross and was giving him a hug. Geez, hurry up! Megan was about to pop and I was going to have to deliver the freaking baby if he didn't get his ass over there.

I didn't get a chance to respond because before I knew it, Granny had knelt down in front of Megan and ducked her head under Megan's dress. Granny used to be a nurse and had probably delivered a baby or two during her career. I didn't know if Granny could still do it, but I was just glad that was not my head under there.

Jack rushed back in as Granny's head poked out from under the dress. Granny looked around the church and her eyes zeroed in on the baptismal. Dr. Ross finally made it to Megan. He began assessing the situation as Granny filled him in on her idea. He nodded his head, and he and Cooper pulled Megan into a standing position as Jack re-emerged. Most of the wedding guests had crowded around Megan, and Jack cleared a path as Cooper and Dr. Ross led her to the baptismal.

"Looks like we are having a water birth!" Granny announced, and Mrs. Johnson kissed her crucifix and crossed herself.

They got Megan to the baptismal and slowly lowered her in. Jack pulled the curtain shut to give her some privacy. I sat in the pew in shock until I heard Megan cry out for me, and Cooper came out and told me to go in. Although it was the last thing in the world I wanted to do, I wouldn't let Megan down. I would hold her hand and stare off into space. I didn't have to actually see the baby come out.

I slowly made my way behind the curtain as I heard Megan let out a muffled grunt.

Dr. Ross said, "One, two and...." As he said three there was unmistakable sound of a baby crying just as sirens were coming from outside.

"It's a boy!" Jack shouted with excitement. The crowd went wild, and there were hoots and hollers from the other side of the curtain.

When I had entered the baptismal, I entered from the wrong side and witnessed the miracle of Baby Westin's birth. I was pretty sure I would never be the same. I was scarred for life, but at the same time it was the most beautiful thing I'd ever seen. I made my way to Megan just as Dr. Ross placed the baby in her arms. Granny couldn't find a blanket, so Joan Rivers offered her scarf and Megan swaddled the baby with it. Baby Westin opened his eyes, looked around, and proceeded to scream his head off. I didn't blame him. If I had been born in a baptismal surrounded by crazy people, I would have screamed too. The EMTs took Mama and baby, and we all formed a convoy to the hospital.

Mama and baby were doing great, and two days later they were settling into their new routine at home. I had been spending my days at Megan's helping out the best I could, considering I couldn't cook, didn't really clean, and knew absolutely nothing about babies. I just held little Jack Jr. while Megan took short naps, and when the baby was asleep I helped Jack with laundry and dishes. Mrs. Johnson brought food over every day, and I mastered the microwave to warm it for lunch. Jack had taken a couple of weeks off work, and between the two of us, Megan was able to rest and relax and just enjoy the experience of motherhood.

And I must say, I was thoroughly enjoying my new role as auntie. I was over the moon in love with that precious baby boy. It almost made me want to have one of my own, but then the painful mental image of the little guy coming out would re-emerge, and I decided I'd just play auntie. I was not made for pain, and I liked my hoohah just the way it was.

Mickey hit it off with Marilyn Monroe, AKA Doug, and they had been inseparable ever since. He even brought him as his date at the first dinner party Cooper and I had. Scott and Alex showed up too, and informed me that they were going to get married and asked me to be the maid of honor. I agreed only after they agreed to let me pick out my own dress. Scott gave me a hug and told me he loved me, and was happy for me and Cooper. I really didn't need his blessing, but I was touched that he still cared, and I was glad that Cooper was okay with Scott and I remaining friends.

Thad had made a couple of lame attempts to get me back, but had finally given up after Cooper had a chat with him. In a way I felt sorry for Thad, but that faded quickly as I reminded myself that he'd brought it all upon himself. He was history, old news, and anything I thought I ever felt for him was gone, right along with him.

Josie and Dr. Ross were honeymooning in Fiji, no doubt enjoying paradise and each other. She had posted pictures of her and her new hubby on Facebook, and the look of love in their eyes made my heart swell. I was so happy for my friend. I never knew a love like that existed, and now that I too, had found it with Cooper, I couldn't imagine a day without it. And I didn't plan too. Cooper was mine and I was his, and as far as I was concerned, forever with him wouldn't be long enough to experience all the love I had for him, but I was going to give him all I had every day for the rest of our lives.

Amy Johnson

ABOUT THE AUTHOR

I live in New Mexico with my husband, children and 4 dogs. I am currently working on my next book which is a sequel to Meg's Moment. I enjoy writing, reading and crafting.

Author's photo taken by Leslie Bailey Photography.

www.ingramcontent.com/pod-product-compliance
Lightning Source LLC
Chambersburg PA
CBHW020551180626
46810CB00007B/2463